Sara,
you a[...]
your family. Enjoy Georgia's
Journey to Sedona.
God Bless,
Sherry

# THREE MOONS OVER SEDONA

**SHERRY HARTZLER**

*Sherry Hartzler*

*2010*

ROCK HOUSE PUBLISHING
LOGAN, OHIO

*Three Moons Over Sedona* is a work of fiction. All characters and names portrayed in this novel, or the depiction of locales, are either the product of the author's imagination or used fictitiously.

Any resemblance of any character or person in this novel, either living or dead, is purely coincidental. Business establishments and events in this novel are the product of the author's imagination and any resemblance is purely coincidental. Any references to specific names or products are mentioned only for the sake of providing a sense of reality to the story.

Library of Congress
Washington, D.C.
Copyright © 2009 Sherry Hartzler

ISBN #13: 978-0-9793822-1-5
ISBN #10: 0-9793822-1-1

Printed in the United States of America
Rock House Publishing

For information about this novel, contact the publisher:
Rock House Publishing at rockhousepublishing@ohiohills.com

FIRST EDITION
*Cover design by Suzanne L. Karshner*

For my loving husband, Thomas Keith Hartzler
I love you. Thank you for making this book possible.

Look for

# ISLAND PASSAGE

In March of 2010

# ACKNOWLEDGMENTS

First and foremost, thank you to my friend and critique partner, Barbara Whittington, who has always been there whenever I needed advice or encouragement.

Thank you to Glenn A. Karshner and Rock House Publishing for believing in this project and all the assistance you have given to make this book a reality.

Love and appreciation to my fabulous friends and grammar wizards: Cinda Barton, Jenny Beard, Marsha Clark, Nancy Green, Pam Gary, Barbara Whittington and Justine Wittich.

Much appreciation extended to my friend and cover artist, Suzanne L. Karshner.

Thank you to my now-grown children, Stephanie Savage and Eric Hartzler, who so patiently endured an overwhelming gambit of emotions while writing my stories. I love you dearly.

A big hug and kiss to my mother, Juanita Mae McCreary—the best cook this side of heaven.

A big round of applause for the Hocking Hills gals, primo artisans with a flair for gardening and passionate lovers of good food and wine: Jenny Beard, Bobbi Bishop, Nancy Green, Mary Holl, Suzanne L. Karshner, Shirley Landis, Donna McKnight, Bev Riggs, Debbie Thrush, and Donna Welch. You are all an inspiration to the soul. Thank you for reading and re-reading.

A special thanks to my former boss, Kathleen A. Hanley. Kathleen practiced law in Columbus, Ohio, before moving to Tucson, Arizona, to find her own dream. You go, girl!

Loving thanks to wonderful friend and work side-kick, Debbie Cole, who, for over twenty years, patiently listened to story ideas, plotting and character development.

Also, a loving thank you to my nieces, Josie McNamara-Brown, Paula Mae Mitchell, Colleen Parrish, and Laura Mae Cimini, the little girls, all grown up now, who constantly asked, "Aunt Sherry, when will you ever get a book published?" Well, sweethearts, here it is—Enjoy!

# CHAPTER ONE

Georgia Mae Brown wanted out of her life. No rush. She'd already waited fifty-three years. Before leaving the house that April morning, she paused at the mirror by the back door and smoothed down a few stubborn gray hairs, taking serious note of the fine lines around her eyes and mouth. She faked a smile at her reflection, satisfied that in the mellow light of the pantry she still looked more young than old.

She tucked Ed's white T-shirt into her jeans and grabbed her purse from a coat hook, forgetting all about the five thousand dollars she had earlier stashed at the bottom of her handbag. At the moment, money was the very least of Georgia's worries. She had plenty of that—enough for another whole lifetime. *Her lifetime.*

Outside the back door, she stumbled over fat Oscar curled up on the stoop, outfitted in an infant's dress complete with pink, lacy pantalets. The black cat quickly skittered out her way, meowing up at her. Oscar's owner, Mrs. Otis, lived next door and suffered from dementia. Over the past several months, the elderly woman had progressively slipped back in time to when her daughter was still a baby. Most afternoons, weather permitting, Mrs. Otis walked a baby stroller up and down the sidewalk with Oscar bundled and strapped inside. The cat suffered through these misguided maternal episodes with laid-back ears, a throaty growl, and a few

1

defiant whips of his tail. Nonetheless, in exchange for food, the noble alley prince seemed more than willing to tolerate his role as a four-legged cross-dresser.

*Meowwww.*

"Hold on, Oscar," Georgia said, kneeling down beside the cat. "I'll get you out of all this fluff, but I'm out of milk this morning."

*Meow.* The cat rolled over onto his side, stretching into a belly pose, ready to be undressed. She gave him a quick rub under the chin before unfastening the seed pearl buttons under the tiny collar and pulling off the dress. She then slipped the cat's backside and legs out of the pantalets, noticing with a smile the opening Mrs. Otis had cut into the fabric to accommodate Oscar's tail.

*Poor woman.*

Poor Oscar!

She patted his head. "Keep your chin up, ol' boy. At least you don't look bad in pink." The cat brushed against her calves, no doubt expecting his usual saucer of milk. Georgia generously stroked his back as Oscar purred into her hand. Georgia whispered, "We sure do make a lonely pair, don't we?"

She got up and left the clothing on the step to later deliver to Mrs. Otis after she returned from the grocery. Hurrying down the walk to the garage, she called over her shoulder at Oscar, "I bet you'd like to leave town, too. We could both start over again, couldn't we?" Oscar jumped up and trotted after her as if he might seriously consider her proposal. But a few feet shy of the garage, the cat dropped to the walk and stretched out, sniffing at the morning air, perhaps deciding he'd just wait there until she returned with the milk. It seemed that even Oscar knew she would never in a million years have the guts to really run away from home.

Hurrying on into the garage, Georgia bypassed her sensible Honda Civic and slid behind the wheel of Ed's 1976 Fleetwood Cadillac—red convertible with white leather interior. She had never driven Ed's car before. The engine turned over on the first try. No fuss at all. She firmly told the car, "Ed's dead."

Determined not to lose her nerve about driving the car, she threw it into reverse, backed out of the garage and careened over the edge of the driveway, devastating a bed of spring daffodils. The slaughter of blooms thumped like tiny heartbeats against the undercarriage of the car. Georgia kept on backing, ignoring their plight. At the curb, she smacked two garbage cans with her bumper and sent those rolling down the sidewalk. Finally, she brought the car to a halt in the middle of the street and took in a soft breath. "Easy does it, girl," she whispered into the console, the radio speakers blaring out the old sixties tune, *Come On Baby Light My Fire.*

She gathered her wits, firmly positioning her hands at ten and two on the steering wheel, then at a slow, steady speed drove to the end of her street and turned left onto Cleveland Avenue. No cars in sight, she slammed the accelerator to the floor, and the Fleetwood jetted forward in a blowout of gasoline fumes and oil. The engine whined in protest beneath the wide front hood, clearly perturbed at this harsh treatment. After all, the car, like Georgia, had never had but one lover—Ed.

Shaking her head, she mumbled into the windshield, "*Ed. Ed. Ed.*"

She passed the legal speed limit of forty-five, hitting fifty, then sixty miles an hour, fate giving her green lights all the way to the Polaris Parkway. The possibility of a cop waiting at the next corner never crossed Georgia's mind. She only thought about Ed and what a damn fool he'd been for leaving this stupid car to her. Too bad he died the way he did. For that, Georgia could almost hate him. Unfortunately... she didn't. The tears she had shed since Ed's death had long ago dried up, leaving the anger to chafe at her insides like fresh sandpaper. Hate Ed? No, never.

At the first red light on the parkway, Georgia finally slowed to a stop and readjusted the rear view mirror to suit her. She then searched for the seatbelt strap, taking comfort in the cool leather seat that still smelled of Ed's last application of leather protector. As she snapped the buckle, her foot kicked something on the floor under the seat. Reaching down she snagged Ed's spare set of car keys attached to a Niagara Falls key chain. She stared blankly at the memento for a good long second before giving the keys a dismissive toss onto the passenger seat. *Who needs bad memories?*

The light changed. Georgia glided through the intersection keeping the legal speed of forty-five, deciding she wasn't ready to die—at least, not yet. "Relax," she whispered into the dash, trying to refocus on why she had left the house that morning—to buy a gallon of milk at the nearby grocery and a pint of expensive ice cream—vanilla, the coupon tucked inside her purse. She'd once read a magazine article about vanilla being the most popular ice cream flavor and how this rather neutral dessert preference signified an inability to take a risk. Georgia could not for the life of her understand what risk had to do with liking vanilla ice cream. Pure nonsense. It seemed every magazine article, every talk show on television wanted to analyze the stupidest things nowadays.

One hand steadied the steering wheel, using the other to forage through her handbag for the coupon. At the bottom, she found the wad of money she'd stuffed inside her purse a few weeks ago. No coupon—only the money and her wallet, along with an old grocery list in her daughter's handwriting.

Her daughter, Susan, lived on Bonner Drive—three blocks over from Georgia—with her husband and two children. Georgia's son, David, had married three years ago and moved to Boston. At the thought of her children, she closed her eyes for only a second before passing right by the strip mall. Well, it didn't matter. She would simply turn around at the next light. Up ahead, she noticed the entrance ramp to the interstate, a sign pointing to Cincinnati. She felt a wicked smile spread across her lips as she slowed down and made the turn onto the freeway. For the first time in a very long time, she didn't give a twit about Ed, his death, or what her children thought she should or shouldn't do with the rest of her life.

Since the funeral six weeks ago, thinking about Ed had taken up most of Georgia's time. Not the old Ed—but the young, handsome Ed, the boy she fell in love with at seventeen. The football hero who drove a '65 Mustang convertible, the boy who could have had any girl he wanted, but had chosen the bookish Georgia who blushed every time a boy smiled at her.

In high school, Ed had brought her out of all that shyness, encouraging her to be more spontaneous, loosen up, and have more fun, which usually translated into breaking her curfew, getting in trouble with her parents, then having to hold up her tired head in class on Monday mornings. On weekends, they went to movies and hung out with friends at the local hamburger joint. After dark, Ed drove the old gravel road to Moody's Orchard, where the two of them slid into the backseat and a young, naïve Georgia opened her legs to the breathless boy who fumbled at the buttons on her blouse and one-handedly unhooked her bra.

Now, years later, sitting behind the wheel of Ed's car, she found the more miles put behind her on the interstate, the more she enjoyed the ride. Elbow resting on the open window, she noticed Ed's sunglasses still hooked on the visor, his last pack of chewing gum carelessly tossed on the dash as if he might suddenly reappear at any moment to claim it. *Poor Ed.* He probably thought he could take it with him.

The Fleetwood was the first car Ed ever bought new and drove right off the showroom floor. A bit of sadness pricked through the hard shell of Georgia's heart, thinking back over those early years and how they thought their lives would turn out so much grander than their parents' lives. However, in the last ten years or so of their marriage, Ed had seemed dissatisfied in ways Georgia never understood. Nothing excited him anymore, his only passion being the Fleetwood, which he often drove by himself, not even bothering to ask Georgia to come along for the ride. Never once did he ever consider selling or trading it in for a newer model. Now, it was Georgia who sat behind the steering wheel of Ed's beloved car, thinking how ironic that in the end she had gotten *everything*, even the painful secrets he had kept from her.

After the funeral, Georgia had found a stash of money while sorting through Ed's things in the garage. Twenty-dollar bills bound with a length of bale string in the bottom drawer of the tool chest, another five hundred tucked inside the pages of the garden tractor manual. The treasure hunt continued. Inside a wooden crate shoved under the workbench, Georgia discovered three thousand dollars! An old coffee can tucked in behind the garden rakes held another five hundred. Like an Easter egg hunt, she searched every nook and cranny of the garage and then the attic, making one big pile on the kitchen table where she counted and stretched a postal rubber band around the bundle before stuffing it inside her purse.

She popped a piece of Ed's gum into her mouth, relishing the cool, mint taste, enjoying the ride, driving nowhere in particular. Why hadn't she done this before? Not a cloud in sight, the blue sky shimmered like an upside-down ocean, even though the forecast on the radio called for light showers. Georgia squared her shoulders and took in a deep breath, determined not to think about the weather or about how far she'd already driven. She only wanted to enjoy the moment.

Thirty miles from Cincinnati, she veered off the interstate and turned into a gas station, pulling beneath the pump canopy directly behind a Volvo station wagon with Arizona tags. She turned off the engine, eyes focused on the back of the station wagon, wishing she had more of a destination than the miles she had already traveled and very shortly would have to re-travel.

She pumped gas into the car, unable to take her eyes off the Arizona plates—*Grand Canyon State*. She bit into her lower lip, considering. She had always wanted to see the Grand Canyon, but Ed never liked to travel too far from home. They owned a neighborhood hardware store that Ed was sure couldn't survive without them. Getting him to Niagara Falls on their twenty-fifth wedding anniversary had taken a lot of talking on Georgia's part, even going so far as to threaten to go alone. She out-and-out lied, telling Ed she'd already made reservations at a hotel with a lovely view of the falls. Ed finally relented, but not so willingly. He growled and grumbled for two weeks leading up to the trip, and then again growled and grumbled for two weeks after they'd come back home.

She had hoped the trip to Niagara would revive something lost in their marriage. For sure, great disappointment comes with great expectations. Niagara Falls churning in all its magnificence might as well have been water rushing down a city storm gutter for all the interest Ed showed during the trip.

Georgia finished filling the gas tank and tore off the credit card receipt. She needed to get back home. Thinking about the trip to Niagara had only depressed her even more than she already was. A young woman got out of the passenger side of the Volvo and stretched. She smiled at Georgia. "Hi."

"Hello," Georgia responded. The woman reminded Georgia of her own daughter, Susan. She pointed to the back of the Volvo and license plates. "Where do you live in Arizona?"

"Tucson." The woman brushed at the travel wrinkles in her skirt, glancing over at the next line of pumps where a good-looking teenager cleaned the windshield of his Jeep soft-top. The woman's lips formed a winsome smile as if the boy reminded her of someone from her past. She looked back at Georgia and shrugged. "It's a lot different than Ohio."

Georgia twisted on the fuel cap and finished up. "Do you like Arizona?"

"It's okay," she said with a heavy sigh. "I've lived there all my life." Her smile weakened as she tossed coffee from her stainless travel mug with an elaborate swish. "My husband grew up in Cleveland. We went there for a funeral. Now we're headed home." The woman cocked her head and focused on the Fleetwood. "Nice car. Is it vintage?"

"Huh? I don't think so." Georgia didn't consider the car to be all that old, at least not so old as to be called vintage. "My husband bought it new years ago. He never drives it much." How easy to talk about her husband as if he were still alive. She fought the urge to elaborate about Ed being dead and all, but feared if she started blubbering about her problems, she might not be able to stop.

The woman's husband impatiently tapped the hood of the car, and then slid back inside the Volvo, a clear signal to his wife that she had better hurry up and get in. *Let's go.* The woman shook out the last drops of coffee, saying to Georgia, "If you ever make it to Arizona, you must visit Sedona. The red rock is simply breathtaking."

Georgia got back into her own car, now ready to go home. She had had a grand morning on her short adventure, but enough fooling around, all this feeling sorry about how her life had turned out. Then, just as she was leaving the station, it started to rain, and that depressed her. She shivered and pulled her seashell-pink sweater around her shoulders, the same sweater she'd hastily pulled from the pantry hook that morning. Watching the Volvo disappear down the highway, she thought about the woman's offhand suggestion that she visit Arizona. As she approached the entrance to the freeway, a small quaking sensation moved from her abdomen and into her chest. On impulse, she turned right instead of left. Okay, she definitely wasn't ready to go home, at least not yet. Why not travel on to Cincinnati, maybe stop for lunch?

The man and woman from Tucson, Georgia surmised, were somewhere in their early thirties, most likely caught up in raising young children and already worrying about saving for college tuitions, not to mention gathering enough equity on their present house to gain a decent down payment on a bigger house in a nicer neighborhood. They were the puppy-yuppies, the *I-want-it-now, Let's-run-the-credit-card-to-the-max* generation. The vague possibility of one day needing long-term nursing home care and supplemental health insurance had not yet entered their minds. Growing old? Definitely, absolutely, not on their agenda.

Georgia's daughter, Susan, had majored in accounting in college. After graduation, Susan worked for a large insurance company where she met and fell in love with Louie. The night before their wedding, Susan informed Georgia that she'd had an abortion her sophomore year of college. After this confession, Susan had simply smiled and hugged Georgia, saying how much better she felt now that she'd finally told her mother the truth.

Well, Georgia didn't feel better. She felt as if something had suddenly died inside of her, and she could've easily slapped the premarital bliss right off her daughter's face. When Susan walked down the aisle the next afternoon in that eight hundred dollar pearl encrusted wedding gown, Georgia could only think about that little speck of a baby that might have been her grandchild and who had never had a chance to be born. Better off if Georgia had never known what she had lost.

In Cincinnati, Georgia never intended to cross over the Ohio River and into Kentucky, but the bad memory of how Susan had told her about the abortion on the night before the wedding made her angry all over again. This confession had come from a child who had once thrown a major tantrum after her brother, David, accidentally stepped on a robin's egg that had fallen from the limb of a tree and into the soft grass. Susan had raised such a commotion, sobbing that her brother had killed a baby bird inside the shell. David, who was eight at the time, had merely shrugged and shoved his hands deep into his coat pockets, eyeing Georgia for forgiveness.

\* \* \*

By early evening, a blitz of billboards for Nashville motels, gas stations and restaurants popped up along the highway. Bone-tired from traveling for so many hours, Georgia decided to stay at a motel and return to Columbus in the morning. The thought crossed her mind to give Ed a call so he wouldn't worry about her, but then she remembered that Ed was dead, buried under a pile of muddy spring dirt at Fairhaven Cemetery. She no longer had to worry about telling Ed anything.

Georgia pushed on toward Nashville. She would call Susan later, after settling into a motel room. Susan could then call David to let him know she wasn't at home, thinking if he tried calling her and didn't get an answer, he might worry. Not that David called home all that much, maybe once or twice every couple of months. David and his wife, Lori, were both lawyers in a big law firm in downtown Boston and equally wrapped up in their careers and east coast lifestyles. So far, no children, and Georgia didn't expect any in the near future. Lori wasn't exactly the warm and fuzzy type, and rebuffed any conversation geared toward babies and all the upheaval they brought into a young couple's life.

Not far from Nashville, Georgia found an outdated motor lodge a few miles off the interstate. A red neon arrow pointed into the parking lot, flickering as if it were gasping for one last breath before going out altogether. The inside of the office smelled of stale coffee and cigarette smoke that had long ago turned the walls a nasty yellow. An older woman stood behind the registration desk with a newspaper spread out in front of her. She glanced up at Georgia and adjusted her glasses. "Help you?"

Georgia fumbled at the catch on her purse, already regretting not pulling into a reputable chain hotel located a few miles closer to the city. She cleared her throat. "I need a room, please."

"You alone?" the woman said, shuffling the newspaper to one side and lifting a pen from a quart jar on the counter. Georgia thought of her own quart jars obediently lined up on her cellar shelves and filled with last year's tomatoes, green beans and pickled beets. Now, with Ed gone, how would she ever eat all that canned food? What a waste, growing all those vegetables in the garden plot behind the house, picking, cleaning and finally sealing everything in jars with no one to eat them. Why go to all that trouble when all a person had to do was pick up a can of beans or tomatoes from a grocery shelf, on sale, three cans for a dollar.

"Ma'am?"

"Hmm. Yes."

"One night?"

"Yes."

"Elvis?"

"Excuse me?"

The woman pulled off her glasses and attempted to clean the smudged lenses with a crumpled tissue from her shirt pocket. "Driving that old Cadillac out there, I thought you might be headed for the Hall of Fame. That's where most people seem to be headed when they stop here overnight."

"Uh, no." Georgia managed a weak smile. "Just passing through." She knew the woman was fishing for more information, but for once in her life Georgia didn't feel compelled to explain herself. Much easier that way.

The woman slipped her glasses back on her head, the lenses still smeared. "Some folks think he's still alive, you know." When Georgia made no comment, the woman cleared her throat and opened the registration book on the counter. "Sign here. My name's Edith. I run this place." She shoved the book under Georgia's nose. "If you haven't eaten, there's a truck stop about a mile down the road—ice and vending machines right outside the front door. Sorry, that's all I can offer."

Georgia handed Edith a credit card, wanting to pay cash, but figured Edith might get suspicious if she brought out a wad of money tied up with a rubber band. "I don't need anything. Thank you anyway."

From a nearby cabinet Edith brought out a set of bath towels complete with a miniature bar of soap with Twin Oaks Motel printed in faded gold letters on the outside wrapper. She placed them on the counter. "Enjoy."

Georgia parked the car in front of cabin 4. Inside, she found a double bed that fit into the room as snug as one square box fits into a slightly bigger square box. The bathroom could have served better as a closet, cramped with a sink, commode and a claw foot bathtub no more than half the size of her tub at home. Water dripped from the leaky tub spout onto a rust stain resembling the shape of California.

No telephone on the nightstand, Georgia reluctantly trudged back to the office to inquire about making a long distance call. Edith pointed to a pay phone at one corner of the cluttered office, her eyes never leaving the television set. Georgia hoped Edith might offer to leave the room, give her a little privacy. No such luck. Edith seemed glued to the worn corduroy recliner, a bag of potato chips propped in her lap, a red plastic deli cup on the floor beside her.

Dialing Susan's number, Georgia tucked her head deep into a corner of the makeshift booth. On the fourth ring Susan's voice mail picked up. Georgia let out a sigh of relief at the prospect of simply leaving a quick message and then hanging up. She barely said hello before Susan answered in a frantic state. "Mom? Thank God it's you."

Georgia almost hung up but decided it would be better to deal with her daughter now rather than later. "Susan," Georgia said, aware of a nervous twitch developing above one eye. "I'm—"

"Mom," her daughter interrupted. "I've been trying to reach you all day. Honestly, *Mother*, you should get a cell phone."

"Well, I suppose that's a good idea," she said sweetly.

"Mom, are you all right? You sound funny."

"I'm fine, dear."

"You promised to take care of Samantha this morning. Did you forget?"

"Oh, I did forget." Her heart sunk inside her chest. How could she have been so irresponsible? That was the reason for her hurried trip to the grocery that morning, to pick up milk to make waffles for her granddaughter's breakfast. Susan had promised Louie that she would work a few hours at the hardware store, and now, without a sitter, and because Samantha was ill with a strep throat, she would have no choice but to take the child to work with her. Brown Hardware had been in Ed's family since 1940. Louie took over as manager after Ed's death. Guilt washed over Georgia. "I'm sorry, Susan."

"There's something wrong. I know it. Where are you?"

"Nothing's wrong." Georgia whispered.

"Mom?" Susan's voice raised an octave. "Where-are-you?"

"Nashville," she blurted out at bit too loudly.

Her daughter gasped on the other end of the line. "Nashville! How on—"

"I drove here myself," Georgia interrupted. "In your father's car."

"You never drive Dad's old Cadillac. Why now? God, Mother, are you having a breakdown?"

"No, I don't think so, dear." She turned and threw a nervous smile in the direction of the recliner, hoping Edith wasn't listening, but knew it was already too late. Edith's head was cocked to one side, her hand on the remote, the volume lowering a few bars on the television, no doubt to better hear her conversation with Susan. In the background, the newscaster rambled on about another suicide bombing in the Middle East. A rational thought flickered through Georgia's head that she should be more concerned about the violence in the Middle East than with Susan's minor irritation at not having a babysitter.

"You're coming home tomorrow, right?"

Georgia bit down on her lower lip to keep *yes* from spilling out of her mouth. It seemed Georgia had spent the better part of her time being at the disposal of everyone else. Now, she wanted the right to be *irresponsible*. She needed time away from her normal life to think about the pain of losing her husband... and the deception. Why couldn't she just say that to Susan? When had she fallen into the habit of letting her children make decisions for her? She knew the answer. She had always been the one to give in to others. Ed always used to say, "Don't make waves, Georgia."

"Mom? Are you still there? Hey, if you're sick or something, Louie and I will come and get you."

"I'm not sick. I just wanted to be alone—"

"Well," Susan interrupted with parental authority. "It's decided. You're coming home tomorrow. You promised to watch Samantha and Benjamin Saturday night. Louie and I have that wedding in Cleveland. Remember?"

Georgia cleared her throat, aware that the twitching over her eye had worked itself into a blurry throb. She needed an aspirin. "No. I think I'll be a bit longer."

"Longer?"

Silence.

"What do you mean, *longer*?" Susan demanded.

Georgia shrugged into the receiver. "Dunno, for sure. It just felt good leaving this morning." Yes, that did feel better, just letting the truth roll off her tongue.

"Mom? Are you sure you're okay?"

Georgia tightened the receiver against her ear. For the first time since they had started talking, Susan sounded genuinely concerned. Afraid she'd lose her nerve, Georgia said, "Yes. I'm fine. I'll be home in a few days."

"Really, Mother. You can't—"

"Don't worry. I'll call tomorrow. Goodbye, Susan." Georgia hung up. On her way out the door she thanked Edith for letting her use the phone. The woman could only nod, because her mouth was stuffed with another handful of potato chips. Noticing the sprinkling of crumbs on the greasy carpet around the recliner, Georgia's stomach knotted up with a desperate kind of hunger.

Outside the office, she plunked three quarters into the vending machine and pushed the button under a chocolate bar. She hadn't felt hungry all day, but after talking to Susan, she needed something to quiet the panic filling her stomach. She tore off the candy wrapper, devouring it in four eager bites. The sugar rushed through her blood stream like heroin surging through an addict's veins.

Back inside her room, Georgia folded herself into the claw foot tub in the closet-sized bathroom. She pulled her legs into her chest as tears trickled down her cheeks. Holding her shins tight with her arms, she rocked back and forth, wondering just how and when she'd grown to be a fifty-three year old widow with grown children and grandchildren. Last she remembered, she was eighteen, almost beautiful, and Ed was the love of her life.

Ed had been the first boy to ever touch her—the one and only boy. A faint smile warmed her lips, remembering how it was between them, so sweet and innocent. Neither one of them really knew what making love was all about. Lathering the worn washrag with the Twin Oaks soap, her thoughts sifted back to the young Ed, in blue jeans and white T-shirt, a pack of cigarettes rolled up in one sleeve saying, "Georgia, baby, sweetheart, I love you." Oh, what powerful words those were to a girl who had felt unloved all her life.

Her senior prom, the night everything changed, Georgia felt like Cinderella in her spaghetti strap gown of rose satin, her hair done up in an elegant twist. "God, you look so beautiful," Ed whispered, handing her a florist box with an orchid wrist corsage. He dutifully posed with her in her parents' living room for family snapshots, one of which she still had somewhere in the attic.

It could have been the dreaminess of her last prom, or maybe the gown and dyed-to-match heels that made her feel so grownup. She didn't know for sure, but whatever the reason, Georgia had been easily persuaded by Ed to do *it*. At their regular parking spot at Moody's Orchard, his breath hot and damp against her ear, she allowed Ed to pull down her panties and enter her. The urgency of his body sweetly surrendering into hers empowered Georgia in a way she had never before thought possible. She had made Ed wait all of three months—an eternity in terms of necking and petting. Georgia felt no shame in losing her virginity on prom night. They were in love.

By graduation, six weeks later, Georgia was pregnant.

The bath water had long cooled to lukewarm, now on the verge of chilly. Georgia climbed out of the tub and wrapped herself in a towel. Standing nose-to-nose to the mirror, she whispered, "Where did you come from old woman?" She touched the ends of her salt and peppered hair hanging limp around her shoulders and took note of how her lips had thinned over the years. Only her blue eyes looked unchanged, staring back at her from beneath a creased, serious brow. She lightly touched the skin at the sides of her jaw, a little slack unless she forced a smile, which temporarily remedied the problem.

Georgia brushed through her wet hair, letting the towel drop to the floor, grateful the bathroom mirror measured no bigger than a cereal box. Before stopping at the motor court, she'd had the good sense to stop at a drug store and buy deodorant, toothpaste and a toothbrush. Having no clothing other than what she'd worn that day, she crawled naked under the cool sheets and closed her eyes. The bedding smelled a bit musty, the mattress lumpy, but Georgia felt too tired to care, more tired than after Ed's funeral when she had slept for three days.

In the middle of the night, Georgia sat upright in the bed and turned on the bedside lamp with its forest scene shade. Wide awake, she stared up at the ceiling of her small room and considered the cracks running like broken veins through the plaster above her head. When she moved her head a tad to the right and squinted, the Virgin Mary appeared. She imagined hundreds of people flocking to the Twin Oaks Motel to experience this miracle in a cracked ceiling. Maybe Edith could have this portion of ceiling removed and sell it on eBay? People were such suckers for stuff like this. Georgia yawned and turned over in the bed, snuggling into a more comfortable position.

She yawned as her eyes drifted shut. In the morning she would definitely return home. She'd left two library books on the dining room table—seven-day loaners—due back on Monday. And Oscar would be there on her back stoop waiting to be undressed and fed. The thought came to her that she should've brought Oscar with her. If she had, they might travel cross-country together and become good friends like Steinbeck and his dog, Charley. She yawned and turned off the lamp, sinking into the body warmth of the bed. In the dark, Georgia could be anyone she wanted to be.

# CHAPTER TWO

Georgia was up at six the next morning, dressed in the jeans and white T-shirt she had neatly folded the night before and left on the chair beside the bed. She threw her toiletries into the drugstore bag and glanced around the room to see if she had forgotten anything, then remembered she had nothing *to* forget. The realization of having only the clothes on her back gave her an odd, exhilarating sense of weightlessness.

Outside, the Fleetwood waited for her like a faithful red dog, and this morning the car seemed more Georgia's than Ed's. A good night's sleep had done wonders for her perspective. Going home didn't seem quite so urgent. Besides, what would it hurt to pretend she had a destination somewhere other than where she had come from? First thing after breakfast she would find the nearest AAA and ask for maps of Oklahoma, Texas, New Mexico and Arizona. *The world awaited her.* Bolstered by a good night's sleep and the fresh morning air, Georgia started the car with renewed purpose and moved it over by the office to turn in the cabin key.

Edith sat outside on the top step of the porch smoking a cigarette. She raised her coffee mug to Georgia. "Coffee?"

"Sounds good." Georgia handed the key to Edith.

"Sugar? Cream?"

"Black."

Edith stood up and straightened the front of her sweatshirt. "Right back," she said, disappearing inside and returning a minute later with a steaming mug for Georgia. "Here you go." Edith squinted into the morning sun. "Where you headed now?"

Up close, Edith's face looked tough as shoe leather. She wondered if the woman had a husband, and if so, was he dead or alive? Most likely dead, Georgia figured, or just plain shiftless, considering the state of disrepair the motel showed in the light of day. She took a sip of coffee and answered Edith's question. "Arizona."

"You don't say." Edith tugged again at her sausage casing of a sweatshirt. "How long you stayin'?"

"A week, maybe two." Georgia had no idea where that had come from, but decided a week or two sounded good.

Edith finished off the last of her coffee and placed the cup on the step beside her. "Well, when you drive back to Ohio, don't look for this place to still be here."

"Oh?" Georgia focused on Edith with new interest.

Edith's eyes crinkled, looking into the sun. "Sold it, all fifty acres. They're building a housing development here called Mystic Meadows. Next week a bulldozer's coming in and everything goes."

"Are you all right with that?" Feeling sorry for the woman, Georgia leaned an elbow on one knee, listening intently to Edith go on about selling the motel and property. Fact was, it felt good listening to someone else talk about their grief for a while instead of nursing her own.

"Oh sure," Edith said, waving a dismissive hand in the air. "Since my Lloyd died three years ago, I can't keep up on the maintenance. The whole place needs a couple of coats of paint, another year a new roof. I can't take care of it without hiring someone and putting out a bundle of money. My daughter's been after me about moving to Seattle so I can be close to the grandkids." She shrugged. "Might as well."

Georgia finished off her coffee, which tasted surprisingly good. She handed the empty mug back to Edith and thanked her. "I hope you'll be happy in Seattle."

"Any place is better than here."

Georgia already had her hand on the door when she suddenly turned to face Edith. "Why?" The answer to her question felt intensely important.

Edith put her hands on her wide hips and looked up at the sky as if considering her answer. She sighed. "Don't you ever get tired of staying in the same place?"

Georgia shrugged. "Sometimes," she lied. Until yesterday morning, Georgia, never in a million years, would have ever considered traveling by herself to an unknown place.

"It gets to be a bore, don't you think?"

"Hmmm. I never thought about it before." This time, the lie slipped easily from her lips.

Edith shook her head. "All those years of living and hoping for something better. Then, one day, your ordinary life ends and there's nothing more to get all excited about. Maybe after I get settled in Seattle I'll take one of those bus tours. I've heard people talk about how nice they are, going all over the country, even Alaska."

"I'm going to Sedona," Georgia said out loud, in the open, like a real, honest-to-goodness destination, as if she were really going to go there.

Edith gave her a wide smile. "That sounds real nice. And you've got a fine car to travel in. I hope I didn't insult you with the Elvis comment yesterday. Most people who stop here for the night seem to be looking for something in their past. Say, maybe I'll buy myself a nice big car and drive to Seattle." With a great amount of effort, Edith pulled herself up from the step and lit another cigarette. She laughed and coughed a smoker's deep cough. "My daughter would have a fit, me driving all that way by myself." Edith narrowed her eyes at Georgia. "You have family worried about you?"

"Yes," Georgia sighed. She sat down on the step beside Edith and gazed out over the vacant field behind the motel, imagining row after row of neat vinyl-sided houses with brick or faux stone fronts sprouting up as fast as last year's corn crop. "My husband died six weeks ago. Yesterday I woke up, got into the car and just kept driving. The more miles I traveled, the less guilty I felt."

Edith's eyes widened. "Well, now, it doesn't look as if it hurt you any." She blew out an exaggerated puff of smoke. "I say keep on driving, girl."

"Do you really think I should?"

"Sure." Edith snuffed out the cigarette in the gravel at her feet. "When I move to Seattle, my daughter's going to make me quit smoking. In six months or so I'll be seeing more of my grandchildren than I probably want to. More than likely I'll gain ten to twenty pounds because chocolate cake fills up something sad inside me. I'll start sneaking cigarettes out in the garage and get caught by my daughter who'll make me feel like a naughty ten-year-old."

Georgia laughed.

"Don't laugh," Edith said with a weary smile. "I'm serious. It's amazing how you spend all those years raising kids, and suddenly, one day they turn on you, laughing at your clothes, your face, your life, every little thing you've become because you've sacrificed all the best stuff just so they could have it better."

"Oh." There was an element of truth in what Edith said. Georgia's grandchildren still enjoyed baking cookies and coloring pictures at the kitchen table, but one day they'd grow bored with homemade cookies and refrigerator art, and move on to cruising the malls with friends and walking twenty steps behind you just to avoid the embarrassment of being seen with someone *older*.

Edith kept talking. "Before long, you're nothing more than a babysitter for the kids. Then, you start resenting it. You end up sitting on the couch and fighting with the grandkids over the cartoon channel, while you want to watch the Lifetime channel or CNN."

"Why move to Seattle?" Georgia asked. "Why not go on that bus tour and buy a condo instead of moving in with your daughter? It's not too late to change your mind."

Edith's eyes misted over. "I could, but I won't. Right now I miss 'em, you know, my daughter, the grandkids. They're all I have left in the world." As if remembering her smoking days were numbered, Edith pulled out another cigarette. "Later," she said around her first puff. "I can do for myself, later."

Georgia wanted to object, but realized it was fruitless to do so. Edith had already made up her mind. *Later?* Waiting on *later* was like waiting on your next heartbeat, done and gone before you knew it.

* * *

Georgia reached Memphis by early afternoon and still couldn't get Edith off her mind. She wanted to turn the car around and tell Edith one more time that it might not be such a good idea moving to Seattle and living with her daughter. She wanted to convince Edith to hop on the next bus to Alaska.

Not until somewhere around midnight did Georgia pull into a busy rest stop, thinking it silly to pay for a motel room in the middle of the night. She had driven twelve hours, minus restaurant and gas refill stops. She could barely hold her eyes open. Locking the doors, she crawled into the backseat and fell into a deep sleep. The thought never once entered her mind that she should call Susan and Louie.

The next morning, Georgia groaned at her reflection in a long mirror over four sink basins in the chilly restroom. Her hair stood out in every direction, one side of her face imprinted with the seam of the leather seat. She splashed cold water on her puffy face, brushed her teeth and tried to smooth down her hair with a dab of water.

In the next town, Georgia located a discount store and bought new panties, a fresh T-shirt and a pair of jeans for the sake of slipping into something clean. No sense spending good money on new clothes in an expensive shop when she already had a full closet at home. In a fast-food restroom, she cut off the tags with fingernail clippers and slipped into her clean outfit. Standing on tiptoes to get a better view in the mirror she combed through the ends of her hair with her fingers. At the bottom of her purse she pulled out a pink elastic band that belonged to her granddaughter, Samantha, and gathered her hair back into a messy ponytail.

Fast food containers littered the inside of the car from two days of travel. Ignoring the clutter she tossed the plastic bag with her dirty clothes on the passenger seat and backed out of the parking slot. This time Georgia didn't think twice about heading west.

* * *

In Oklahoma City, she passed a strip mall and noticed a beauty salon called the Cutesy Curl, a handwritten sign in the window saying, *Walk-Ins Welcome.*

"Oh dear Lord," Georgia said two hours later after the stylist finally twirled her around to face the mirror. The young woman had suggested to Georgia that she cut her hair and let her weave in a few golden highlights to cover the streaks of gray. Georgia blinked in surprise at the stranger in the mirror who simultaneously blinked back, apparently amazed at the change, too.

"Gorgeous," Lou Ann whispered from behind her beautician chair. "Ma'am, if you don't mind me saying so, you look ten years younger." Lou Ann, nine months pregnant, could barely contain her excitement at having taken a dowdy middle-aged woman and making her second-glance worthy.

Lou Ann's hair fell to her shoulders, equally divided into pink and green, the shorter crown hair spiked with mousse, creating a sort of punk version of the Statue of Liberty. She chewed gum with an unrestrained gusto, definitely grape. The artificial flavor floated in the air like the sugary scent of cotton candy. Lou Ann blew a bubble and snapped it, deftly sucking the gum back inside her mouth. "Mrs. Brown, I've gotta' say I really outdid myself today."

Lou Ann appeared to be no more than eighteen, a wisp of a girl with a micro mini molded over her tiny hips, a red knit jersey maternity top with a smocked bodice revealing a basketball-sized bump in the middle. Gold hoop earrings dangled from each lobe. Bizarre style and all, Lou Ann's personality still managed to emit a sweet undercoating of vulnerability.

In the mirror Georgia smiled her approval at Lou Ann. The girl certainly knew her stuff. She did look younger. Incredible what a good haircut and a little touch of hair color did for the morale. Ed would never have approved of such a drastic change in her appearance. He'd say, "I like you natural, Georgia. Why try and make yourself something you're not?"

"See, I told you so," Lou Ann gushed. Her eyes then sparked with a new idea. With a quick snap of the fingers Lou Ann turned on the heels of her sneakers. "Whoa, I have the most fan-tas-tic idea. You just sit real quiet, now. I'll be back in a sec. Sweetie, you need a brand new face to go with that amazing hairstyle."

The young woman disappeared into a back room, coming out a few minutes later with blue plastic basket filled with every cosmetic goodie Georgia could ever imagine. "Close your eyes," Lou Ann ordered. Georgia obeyed. How could she protest? Lou Ann seemed to be having so much fun creating a whole new person out of her.

Lou Ann set about working on Georgia's face, fluffing, brushing and rubbing on an assortment of creams and powders. After gliding a subtle shade of coral lipstick over Georgia's lips, Lou Ann said, "Now open your eyes."

Georgia gave out a little gasp of surprise, barely recognizing the woman who had been hiding under her skin the whole time. Lou Ann took a few steps back, a wide smile stretched across her small face, pleased as punch.

Lou Ann rubbed in a bit of powder over the tip of Georgia's nose. "If you use cooler shades, you don't look all made up. I put on just enough to bring out the natural beauty of your face."

Lou Ann told Georgia her boyfriend promised to marry her before the baby's arrival. By the size of her belly, Georgia guessed she didn't have much time left. Lou Ann examined a chip of polish on her fingernail. "Joey's buying me a diamond ring for my birthday next week." Georgia averted her eyes from Lou Ann's tender display of trust and prayed this Joey person wouldn't let her down. Before leaving the shop, Georgia secretly peeled a crisp fifty-dollar bill from the bundle stashed in her purse and slipped it under Lou Ann's large roller brush.

At the cash register Georgia paid for the services and Lou Ann proudly handed her a pink business card with scarlet lettering. "Now, if you have any questions at all, give me a call. The company pays for these cards, you know. We're very professional here."

Georgia again thanked Lou Ann for the splendid job she had done on her hair and makeup. She also bought all the makeup, every pretty bottle and tube that Lou Ann had used on her face. Lou Ann slid all her purchases into an attractive pink bag and tied it with a frilly ribbon. Such a silly thought, she knew, but Georgia had the same good feeling about buying the makeup as she did whenever Ed had put four new tires on her car. How pathetic was that? With new determination, she carried the pink bag out the door and smiled approvingly at her reflection in the shop window.

Later that same day, she pulled into a gas station, filled up, and removed the fast food trash from the car. Most definitely, the car was now hers, not Ed's. And it hadn't been so bad traveling alone. All the time in the world to think about nothing in particular or turn on the radio and sing along to an old sixties tune that made her feel young again. In all her life, she never would've guessed just how much fun she could have with only herself as company.

Before Ed died, she had been afraid to travel any farther than the next town by herself. The ego works that way, making you afraid to take that risk, a risk that could very well change your whole way of thinking. She thought of the daffodils in her yard, the ones she had clobbered while backing out of the driveway, but at the same time still rooted to that small patch of ground for all eternity.

Georgia's biggest fear about traveling alone was having a flat tire, or the engine overheating, or, her biggest dread, a stranger asking for a ride to the next town. Now, after two days, she didn't think so much about the hazards. For the first time in a very long time, Georgia felt alive, her insides vibrating with an energetic balance that wavered between paranoiac wariness and the innocent curiosity of a child. Like a roller coaster ride, she was on-board for the thrill and excitement of the moment.

The Fleetwood had a brand new set of tires. Ed had replaced the battery six months ago. All in all, the car was travel-worthy. She patted the nape of her neck, peeking at herself in the rearview mirror for about the hundredth time since leaving the beauty shop.

Mid-afternoon, she stopped at a diner and ordered a chef's salad, spreading a Texas map across the Formica tabletop. She thought if only Ed had been a bit more adventuresome, they might not have grown so far apart in their relationship. Perhaps she hadn't really known her husband all that well, after all. Only the outside of him, like how he hated creamed corn, loved a juicy New York strip, or couldn't tolerate overly emotional people who cried at the drop of a hat. As for the inside of Ed, she could only think of something vague and undefined, like a room filled with furniture but nothing you could comfortably sit on.

Georgia gripped the steering wheel of the car, now more than ever determined to make it to Sedona. Whatever awaited her, she was ready to embrace it. Tears sprouted from the corners of her eyes and slid down her cheeks. Her nose started to run. She fumbled on the dash for a tissue. "Ed. Ed. Ed." she moaned, wiping at her nose.

Ed had made a good living at the hardware store that his father opened on Market Street in 1940. Their children, Susan and David, grew up in the house on Stilson Avenue before going off to college. No problem, except for when the kids were grown, graduated and off on their own, Ed still pinched pennies. In the end, all those years of miserly rainy-day squirreling of money meant nothing: Ed couldn't take it with him. Now Georgia had both the time and Ed's money to do whatever she wanted to do. Until Ed died, she'd envisioned the second part of their lives to be a time of rediscovery, a time for falling in love again, thus, the uneventful trip to Niagara Falls. Now, it just didn't matter anymore.

Georgia stopped at an ice cream shop and ordered a hot fudge sundae. Georgia's downfall: hot fudge, peanuts and soft vanilla ice cream. The middle-aged manager gave her a flirtatious wink. A hot blush burned her cheeks; a girlish giggle erupted from her throat.

"I gave you extra hot fudge," he said with another wink. "No charge."

Georgia all but dropped the ice cream down the front of her T-shirt. Her ears heated with embarrassment. She politely thanked the man as she backed out the door.

Ed had liked her hair shoulder-length. After thirty years of marriage she hadn't thought much about cutting it other than the regular six-week trim. After spending the morning in Lou Ann's beautician chair, Georgia felt as light as a feather, not a care in the world. To be honest, Georgia's stomach alternately soared with glorious, razzle-dazzle anticipation or plummeted into God-will-get-you-for-being-so-happy dread. Glorious, razzle-dazzle finally won out. She felt like a kid again, only this kid had enough money to buy a brand-new life.

On the outskirts of Oklahoma City, she bought a durable suitcase, another pair of jeans, three blouses, a light jacket, two bras and a package of Fruit of the Loom hi-cut panties. She found a decent motel and settled into the room with her new purchases. At nine that evening, she called Susan.

"Mom?" Susan said, choking with relief. "Hold on a minute." Susan turned away from the receiver saying, "Not now, Benjamin. Let Mommy talk to Grandma." Then, more composed she said, "Mom, where are you? This escapade of yours has gone far enough. I need you to come home."

"You need?" A streak of anger like hot liquid poured down Georgia's back. She was in no mood to talk about what Susan *needed*.

"I miss you, Mom," Susan said, much softer. "And I depend on you when I—"

"Need a babysitter," Georgia finished for her.

"Well, you've always said I could depend on you."

Guilt curled around Georgia's toes like a tough grapevine, moving over her feet, roping her ankles, threatening to pull her back to where she belonged. A week ago, she would have given up and given in to what everyone expected of her. *Not this time.*

"Mom, where are you?"

"Oklahoma City," she said, sounding as irritated as she felt.

"JESUS! Oklahoma! Have you lost your mind?"

Georgia sat down on the edge of the bed and stared at the veneered desktop with its free pen and postcards organized at one side. While listening to her daughter rant and rave about all the dangers of traveling alone, Georgia opened the top drawer and found a Gideon Bible. Even here, in a strange place, she knew it would be there—something real and tangible, not to be criticized or compromised, something constant that she could count on finding in most motel rooms in the country. Whoever these Gideon were, Georgia silently thanked them. "Susan, I don't know when I'm coming back."

"Mom, don't hang up! Where are you staying? I'm going to call David and give him the number. Maybe he can talk some sense into you. Obviously, you've had some kind of breakdown."

Georgia could hear Susan banging drawers at the other end of the line in search of a pen and notepad. "Susan just because I leave home doesn't make me crazy. I'm sorry I can't be there whenever you need me to baby-sit or run an errand."

Silence.

Georgia recognized her daughter's abrupt silence for what it was, merely a ploy to deflate her newfound sense of independence. She wasn't about to let her daughter treat her like a child. She spoke up. "And don't you dare call your brother and get him upset. Your brother's got enough on his mind already." When Susan didn't respond, she added, "I'll call you later." Georgia hung up, imagining Susan standing in her kitchen holding the dead receiver in her hand.

She busied herself getting ready for bed, but ended up tossing and turning on the annoyingly crisp sheets, unable to sleep. Tiptoeing down the hallway, she filled a bucket with ice and returned to her room. After a second shower and with the bathroom still steamy, Georgia dumped the ice into the sink, and then turned on the faucet. With cupped hands, she gathered cold water and ice and drenched her face until everything felt numb.

Every pore instantly froze in place. She had once read that a movie star did this every day and that's why he still looked so young. When she pat-dried her face with a fluffy towel, she gazed into the mirror and decided her skin did look a smidgen younger.

She then crawled back into bed and fell into a deep sleep. In the morning she left the motel at the crack of dawn anxious to move on through the panhandle of Texas. Reaching Amarillo, she slipped into a clothing shop at an upscale mall. Georgia bought a colorful ankle-length broomstick skirt and gauzy blouse with a drawstring neckline. At another shop she purchased a pair of espadrilles and a straw shoulder bag.

Georgia went from shop to shop, brandishing money from the stash at the bottom of her purse as if suddenly drunk on the power of knowing she had plenty of it. At the cosmetic counter of an expensive department store, she dabbed on a sample of cologne costing seventy-five dollars an ounce. She had never before treated herself to something so extravagant, probably because Ed never thought to buy such a personal gift for her, not for her birthday, their anniversary, or even Christmas.

As she put the bottle back on the counter, Georgia recalled the receipt from the fancy department store she had found in the glove compartment of Ed's pickup truck not long after his funeral. Somewhere around Valentine's Day stingy Ed had purchased a two-ounce bottle of cologne costing one hundred fifty dollars. Not for her—for someone else. On that same Valentine's Day Ed had given Georgia a two-pound box of cheap chocolates—creams, no less. She hated creams. She'd told him that a thousand times before, but he never listened. Tears burned behind her eyes as she touched the bottle of cologne, remembering the hurt as plain as the saleslady standing in front of her who was enticing her with the bonus cosmetic bag with the gold trim.

She told the clerk that she wanted the largest bottle of the cologne they had. "And I'll take the large bottle of moisturizer." Under her breath Georgia whispered, "This one's on you, Ed."

# CHAPTER THREE

Georgia met Luke Perry at a café bus stop in Amarillo. Not Luke Perry, the television star, just a regular Luke Perry who had missed his bus and needed a ride to the university in Flagstaff. Overhearing Georgia tell the waitress about her trip to Sedona, he boldly walked up, introduced himself and without the slightest hesitation, asked Georgia for a ride.

Wearing a snug black T-shirt and cargo pants, the young man had an incredibly sweet face, a face any mother would love. Yet, Georgia took serious note of his ponytail and the gold loop hanging from one earlobe.

"Name's Luke Perry," the boy said, digging into his side pocket and producing his driver's license and student identification. He handed both to Georgia as if seeing them would make her less suspicious about giving him a ride. "Look, Ma'am, I really need to be back in Flagstaff by tomorrow morning. I'll even drive your car for you. The past two summers I've driven package delivery trucks. I've won company awards for safe driving. Tonight, you can sleep like a baby and wake up in Flagstaff, like, thirty miles from Sedona. Don't turn me down, okay?"

Georgia felt her mouth open and close but nothing came out. All her life, she had been warned about picking up hitchhikers along the highway, the horrible things that can happen to a defenseless woman. This is exactly what she'd feared all along. She might end up a missing person and the worst possible photograph ever taken in her life plastered all over the evening news. Georgia imagined Susan's tearful face on the local news saying, "I knew something like this would happen. I warned my mother not to travel alone. She wouldn't listen." Georgia fumbled with the catch on her handbag. "I don't think—"

"Wait," Luke interrupted, holding up five fingers and pulling a cell phone from the side pocket of one trouser leg. "If I call my mom and she convinces you I'm on the level, would you at least consider giving me a ride?"

*His mother?* Up close, Luke had a tiny shrimp-shaped scar on his chin. Her son, David, had a scar in almost the same exact spot, where, at the age of eight, he'd fallen off his bike and smacked the curb with his chin. Georgia remembered pressing a kitchen dishtowel tight against his jaw while Ed drove like a maniac to the emergency room of River Lake Hospital. Eight tiny stitches later, David was back riding his bike as if nothing had happened.

Georgia tried to politely disengage herself from the conversation by giving Luke a little wave of her hand. "Sorry," I can't possibly do that." She closed her eyes and shook her head, but he had already punched in the number.

"Mom? Hey, I missed my bus in Amarillo. I know, Mom. Now listen to me and don't go ballistic. Some lady's offered me a lift to Flagstaff." Georgia opened her mouth to object, but Luke winked and went right on talking. "Mom, don't worry about me. Let me explain, okay? I went down the street to a bookstore and lost track of time. When I got back, the bus had already left. No, Mom, she's a really nice lady. She reminds me of you." Luke laughed, and his face lit up like a little boy's, knowing, for sure, he's made it through the yelling part and now sees the sunnier side of all the trouble he's caused. Lovable and mischievous, Luke knew exactly how to play his hand. Calling his mama in front of another mama and asking for sympathy on both ends. Georgia couldn't help but like him.

Luke held out the phone to Georgia. "Mom wants to talk to you." He leaned in close and whispered, "She wants to make sure you're not some nutcase who's escaped from prison or an asylum."

"Heavens, no." Georgia pressed the cell phone tight to her ear. "Hello?"

His mother started right in. "I swear that boy's going to be the death of me." She sounded out of breath. In a down-to-earth, deep southern voice, she said, "Goodness gracious, forgive me. I don't mean to sound irritated, but that's exactly what I am. What *is* your name, dear?"

"Georgia. Georgia Mae Brown."

"Well, Mrs. Brown, I'm grateful you offered my son a ride to Flagstaff. You're traveling on to Sedona? Is that right?"

"Yes." Although she'd never once offered Luke a ride, the more she talked to his mother, the more Georgia felt obliged to do it. She tugged at her earlobe, listening to Luke's mother, her resistance dissolving faster than a sandcastle at high tide.

"My name's Constance. And don't you worry. My Luke's a good boy, raised right. His father's been dead now for ten years. Luke's going to college on a scholarship, did he tell you that? Only one more year, and then he graduates. He's intelligent, but forgetful—always late for something—like missing that bus today."

Luke hiked his backpack over one shoulder, watching Georgia's face and grinning like a Cheshire cat, knowing his ride to Flagstaff was in the bag.

After hanging up with his mom and seeing the Fleetwood, Luke begged to drive. Georgia politely refused, not wanting to hand the keys over to someone she had known for only forty-five minutes. From the moment she pulled away from the bus stop, bad thoughts started going through her head. The woman on the other end of the Luke's phone could've been anyone. Georgia could end up being murdered along some dark, desolate road, her body thrown into the weeds and not found for weeks, or months!

The humiliation of her body being found by someone picking up aluminum cans alongside the road made her mouth go dry and her hands tremble. Then, the police would come, sirens blaring, the news media in white vans with those rug-beater looking antennae on top. The police would stand outside their cruisers drinking coffee and shaking their heads at the stupidity of the woman left dead in the ditch.

Never in a million years would the authorities ever suspect sweet-faced Luke to be capable of murder. No suspects found, Susan and David would call Nancy Grace on CNN and Georgia's fatal error in judgment would be broadcast all over the world.

"Your top," Luke said, "Let's take it down."

"Excuse me?" Georgia said with a start, at the same time searching beside her for her purse just in case she had to hit him over the head with it. She had driven only twenty miles with Luke in the car and already something dreadful was going to happen.

Luke pointed to the roof of the car. "The top. Let's take it down, okay?"

A hot blush warmed her cheeks. "I don't know how."

"Easy as pie. There's a rest stop a few miles ahead. Pull over there."

In a matter of minutes, Luke had the convertible top folded back and they were on the road again. Georgia relaxed behind the wheel, the wind blowing in her hair. She even managed a smile at her passenger. Luke unhooked Ed's sunglasses from the visor and slipped them over Georgia's eyes. Too big for her face, they slid down her nose. Luke laughed. "Lookin' good, Mrs. B."

It wasn't until after their dinner stop that Georgia let Luke take over the driving. By then, she found herself feeling more grateful than suspicious about giving him a lift to Flagstaff. Over a meal of hamburgers and fries, Luke spoke about growing up on a small ranch in Oklahoma, and how after his dad died, his mom had to sell out and move to the city where she got a secretarial job at a big insurance company.

After his meal, Luke did a quick check for cell phone messages, raised an eyebrow, and then shut the phone. "My family didn't much take to an apartment after living on a six hundred acre spread out in the middle of nowhere. We didn't have a whole lot of extra money, but Mom always made do for us kids."

"She sounds like a fine lady."

Luke settled into the corner of the booth, a toothpick hanging from one corner of his mouth. He patted his stomach. "She's a good cook, too. Not like this hamburger and fries stuff. My mother knows her way around a kitchen."

"The kitchen's my favorite place to be, too." She smiled at Luke, grateful she had taken the chance and let him come along with her. He was funny and polite. Luke's company felt like a breath of fresh air. Georgia couldn't remember the last time she'd laughed so hard.

"Say, Mrs. B., what're you doing driving all this way from Ohio by yourself?"

Her stomach immediately twisted into a tight knot at the mention of home. For a few blessed hours, she had been able to forget about her own problems, listening to Luke ramble on about his family and admiring his obvious love for them. She pulled a fresh napkin from the holder and fussed at a dab of ketchup on the table. "My husband died six weeks ago."

"Oh, man, I'm sorry." He sat upright and slapped one hand against his forehead. "Ah, forget the question. Sometimes I have this weird knack of saying the wrong things." He held up both hands. "Don't even answer."

"It's okay," she assured him. "There's not much to tell. My husband died suddenly. I decided to take a little trip and get myself together. That's all." Georgia then told Luke about Susan getting upset because she'd refused to sit with the grandkids on Saturday, while Susan and Louie attended a wedding in Cleveland.

Over a second cup of coffee, Luke called his roommate, Steve, and Georgia, sitting right across from him, felt uncomfortable listening in. "I'm on my way back to Flagstaff," he said. Georgia pushed the last fry across her plate and into a puddle of ketchup. The low, whispered words spoken to his roommate were definitely intimate, and Georgia felt her cheeks burn with embarrassment. It had never occurred to Georgia that Luke might be gay. She excused herself and found the way to the ladies' room.

At the restroom sink, she patted cold water on her face, surprised she didn't really care one twit about Luke being gay, not really. Georgia ran a brush through her hair and whispered to her reflection, "Just breathe. By this time tomorrow, you'll be in Sedona." What she would do after she finally got there, she had no idea. But, for once in her life, Georgia refused to fear the unknown. She zipped the brush back inside her purse, squaring her shoulders. One line of graffiti written with a red marker stood out on the white cement block wall: *IF YOU'RE READING THIS, YOU NEED A FUCKING LIFE*. Georgia exhaled sharply, whispering to herself, "Amen to that."

\* \* \*

With Luke now driving the car, Georgia closed her eyes and fell asleep. She dreamed about Ed, mowing the back lawn, his forehead furrowed in aggravation, upset he couldn't stop the approaching thunderstorm coming in from the west. The wind kicked up, rattling the tin roof on the garden shed; an earthy scent filled Georgia's nostrils. Lightening forked across the coal-black sky, followed by a deafening crack of thunder. Round and round Ed mowed, getting closer to the center of the yard.

In her dream, Georgia stood on the back patio, yelling at Ed to get inside the house before he got struck by lightening. The fool wouldn't quit, and Georgia knew why. He planned on taking the boat out on the reservoir that afternoon after the weather cleared. She then felt a few heavy drops of rain, the kind of rain you see and hear in an animated movie, *plop plop plop*. Ed pushed the mower into the last round, almost finished. Except... he ran out of gas.

Georgia woke up with a start, the dream stopped just when Ed started cursing at the lawnmower for running out of gas. She came out of the foggy sleep, shifting in the seat as someone opened the passenger side door. Instantly, she raised her head and blinked up at Luke. His smile reminded Georgia of her son, David.

"We're here!" he said with a wide smile.

"Oh?" She looked around at the parking lot of an apartment complex set back in a tall grove of ponderosa pine. "Already?" She rubbed the sleep from her eyes.

Luke helped her out of the car. "You slept like a baby, Mrs. B. You were dog-tired."

Georgia stretched her legs while Luke opened the trunk to retrieve his backpack. A tall, willowy blonde with the face of a cover girl appeared from out of nowhere and held out her hand to Georgia. "Mrs. Brown? Hi, I'm Stephanie Barton. Thanks so much for giving Luke a ride."

"Yeah, Mrs. B.," Luke said, coming up beside the girl and looping an arm around her shoulders, giving her a quick kiss on the lips. "Meet Stevie, my roommate." He held a finger to his lips and whispered, "Just don't tell Mom."

Georgia gave out a small gasp. "*This* is Steve?"

Stephanie smiled apologetically, and Georgia realized Luke had most likely played this silly joke before. With her elbow, Stephanie gave Luke a playful jab in the ribs. She said to Georgia, "Why don't you come up to the apartment. I'll fix you a cup of coffee or tea."

Georgia shook her head. "I should be going, but thank you, anyway." She turned to Luke. "And thank you for getting me here safely." Luke bypassed Georgia's outstretched hand and wrapped her in a suffocating bear hug.

"Mrs. B. I loved every minute. You know where I live now, so don't be a stranger." He laughed and hitched his backpack over one shoulder. Stephanie waved goodbye as they walked toward the apartment building, arms looped around each other's waists, undoubtedly happy to be in each other's company.

Georgia sighed and opened the car door, thinking how nice to be so young and in love with their whole lives ahead of them. She got back into the car, ready to finish the last miles of her journey. An old saying popped into Georgia's head, something like if you knew then what you know now—would you live your life differently? Georgia tightened her grip on the steering wheel, warning herself not to sink into the OCD misery of past regrets. She said out loud, "Don't *even* go there, girl."

# CHAPTER FOUR

A spring thunderstorm rumbled throughout the canyon, vibrating like surround-sound in a movie theater. Georgia slowed the car and turned on the wipers as she maneuvered the winding Route 89 through Oak Creek Canyon, now only a few miles from her final destination. She could hardly contain her excitement at the sight of majestic red rock formations rising high above the highway on one side, and then falling into deep, crooked gorges on the other side.

Reaching the Sedona city limits, Georgia lowered the volume on the radio. Tourists with opened umbrellas bustled along the narrow sidewalks in front of artisan shops or ducked beneath low, frontier-type storefronts with awnings to keep from getting soaked by the downpour.

Pulling into a parking slot, Georgia shut off the engine, her heart pounding like an old washing machine inside her chest. "Oh Lord, now what?" Her hands shook as she opened her purse and dug out the tube of lipstick purchased from Lou Ann. She twisted the rear view mirror and smoothed the tenseness from between her eyebrows before applying the lipstick.

She took in a deep breath and got out of the car, deciding a hot cup of coffee and some breakfast might do her good. Rounding the first corner, she discovered a stone café with red gingham curtains in the front window. Lowering her umbrella, she went inside and slid into the booth closest to the door. The aroma of fresh-brewed coffee filled the dining room, calming her nerves. A few booths back, a man sat alone reading a newspaper, the only other person in the café. He glanced up as she sat down and said, "Good morning," then returned to his newspaper, spreading it out flat on the table to turn the page.

"Good Morning," Georgia said back, sliding her gaze to the counter with its neat row of stools, anxious for a waitress to appear and take her order. The man raised the newspaper in front of his face again. Georgia fumbled with the catch on her purse, feeling almost girlishly awkward in the man's presence, as if she had met him somewhere before but couldn't quite place when or where.

Growing more impatient, she glanced at her watch and decided she might skip breakfast and get a coffee *to go* instead of sitting here alone. She wondered with vague curiosity, what with the steady rain outside, why the quaint café wasn't busier? And where was the waitress?

The man dropped the newspaper again and studied her over half-glasses. "She's in the kitchen," he said, as if reading her mind. "Short of help today."

"I'm in no hurry." She turned away and caught her blurry, fish-eyed reflection in the stainless steel napkin holder. She pressed a hand firmly against her forehead, feeling all at once let down, like a kid after opening all the Christmas presents in one flurry of excitement, then wondering, *Is that all there is?*

All the anticipation and inspiration of the past few days was sinking fast into a thick quagmire of guilt. What in the hell had she done—traveling two thousand miles to a place she'd never even heard of before, and all because some silly woman at a gas station near Cincinnati suggested it. *Nuts.* No wonder Susan was so upset with her. Georgia shook her head, thinking she would just have to find a way to make it up to her, maybe a few gifts before starting home.

In the past few days, Georgia had changed her hair and clothing, foolishly expecting some cockeyed miracle to happen when she got to Sedona. What did she expect—a brass band playing in the middle of the street, cheering her arrival? Panic gripped her limbs, a judgmental voice inside her head telling her what a stupid fool she'd been for believing something special might be waiting here for her. *Nothing.*

Georgia fiddled with the napkin holder, turning it away from her so she couldn't see her bloated reflection. She should be home, in her garden, or what soon would be a garden after the sun warmed the earth enough for planting. The daffodils she'd flattened in her haste to leave the house that morning, were undoubtedly ruined, at least until next spring when new green sprouts would again pop up through the thawed soil. Things like that, Georgia could count on being there. *Here?* Everything here was unknown, unfamiliar, totally out of her realm of being.

For the first time since leaving Ohio, Georgia thought about how Susan had probably come to the house that morning and discovered the bed of flattened daffodils, and then peeking inside the garage, found the Fleetwood gone—a car Georgia had never before driven—and her own car still parked in its regular spot. Then, Georgia imagined Susan going from room to room inside the house, growing more frantic and wondering where her mother could've gone so early in the morning, without leaving so much as a note on the kitchen counter. In Georgia's defense, she had only planned on going as far as the grocery store, no farther.

Now, after arriving in Sedona with nothing more than a new hairstyle, makeup and the one extravagant outfit purchased at the upscale mall in Amarillo—an outfit Susan most likely would laugh herself silly over, saying, "Really, Mom, give it up, the sixties are, like, way over."

Georgia ripped out a napkin from the holder and held it to her trembling lips, figuring she greatly deserved the grand disappointment of finally getting to Sedona and finding the same ol' Georgia Mae Brown at the other end of her rainbow. She moved the napkin to the back of her neck, feeling the heat rush down her back and into her limbs. Hot tears prickled behind her eyes threatening to explode at any second. No doubt, Susan had been right all along about having suffered some sort of nervous breakdown. And now, two thousand miles from home, she would have no choice but to swallow her pride, call Susan and Louie, and ask them to come get her.

She risked a glance at the gentleman in the other booth, still engrossed in his newspaper, but, at the same time, Georgia knew he was watching her. He turned a page, adjusted his reading glasses, and then looked straight at her, or so she thought. Georgia quickly averted her eyes. Okay, maybe she was being a bit paranoid—he could've been looking past her and out the window behind her, most likely checking to see if the rain had stopped. It had.

The waitress still hadn't appeared to take her order. Putting her feet under her, she decided to leave and find another restaurant. Gathering her purse, she started to slide out of the booth. At that moment, a young woman pushed through the swinging door from the kitchen carrying two plates. "Be right with you," she called out, placing an order of scrambled eggs and toast in front of the gentleman in the booth.

Georgia suddenly felt trapped, unable to breathe. The backs of her eyes bulged with an intense pressure that numbed her cheeks. She grabbed a menu from its holder and held it in front of her face. Closing her eyes, she took in a deep breath, but jumped like a scared rabbit when a hand pressed into her shoulder.

The waitress looked down at her with sympathetic eyes, handing her a cloth napkin that she'd pulled from her apron pocket. "Ma'am, you sit still now and take it easy."

Georgia let the menu fall against her forehead, dabbing at her tears with the napkin that smelled freshly laundered. She longed to bury her face in its softness, wanting to disappear completely. She kept her head low, behind the menu, thinking for sure the man eating his eggs and toast wished he'd gone somewhere else for breakfast. Who needed all this drama so early in the day, anyway? It was all so hopeless. Tears streamed down her cheeks, her lips trembled.

The waitress returned with a pot of coffee and a cheery smile. "Feeling better?"

Obviously not, but still Georgia managed to let go of the menu long enough to swipe the crumpled napkin under her nose and mumble, "Yes, thank you." Try as she might, Georgia couldn't even manage a weak smile.

The waitress looked to be about the same age as Georgia's daughter, a pretty young woman with an oval face framed with dark hair pulled into one thick braid that snaked down her back. Her dark eyes narrowed at Georgia with genuine concern, which only made it harder to stop the water works going on inside her head. Her vocal cords struggled to relax enough to reassure the waitress that she was all right, but the only thing that came out was, "Argh."

The waitress leaned in close, whispering, "Say, honey, if you're sick, I'll get Doc." She nodded in the direction of the gentleman eating his scrambled eggs in the back booth. The man immediately glanced up at them. The waitress said real gentle, "You want me to get him?"

Georgia let the menu drop to the table and managed to squeak out, "Heaven's no!"

"You sure?" she asked, clearly worried. "Doc's mostly retired now, but he'd sure help you, if you want." She turned to him. "Right?"

Doc removed his glasses, folded his newspaper, and then started to get up. Georgia adamantly shook her head. She mustered a smile, saying, "I'm fine, really." *Please don't think I'm crazy.*

Doc sat back down, taking a sip of coffee, but kept a wary eye on her just the same. A decisive nod told her he'd be obliged to help, if she changed her mind. Georgia's face heated with embarrassment, willing her insides to calm down enough to at least collect her purse and umbrella and get out of here before they called 911. She'd already made a big enough spectacle of herself for one day. And it was still early in the morning.

"Thank you. No need to fuss over me. I'm definitely better." Georgia gestured to the carafe the woman still held in her hand. "I'd like a cup of coffee, maybe a glass of water?"

"Sure thing. Oh, my name's Trish and welcome to the Soft Rock Café." She poured coffee into a heavy white mug, and then slid it under Georgia's nose. Georgia's hand shook as she added cream before taking a sip. It tasted good. The muscles at the back of her neck began to relax. She dragged the napkin into her lap and clasped her hands together as if the pressure might stop her knees from shaking under the table.

"There now, you're looking much better," Trish cooed. "Say," she said, pointing a finger at Georgia. "I know what you need to turn your day around." With that, Trish bounced off in the general direction of the kitchen, leaving Georgia to sit in an awkward silence with the handsome retired doctor who'd only been partially introduced to her.

As if sensing her discomfort, Doc got up from his booth and walked to the sideboard and refilled his coffee, turning to her, "More?"

Georgia managed an appreciative smile. "Yes. Thank you."

He refilled her cup, returning the carafe to the warmer. "Trish means well," he said with a tolerant grin. "I've known her most of her life, but I've got to warn you about her."

"Excuse me?" Georgia looked up at him, a bit confused.

With a subtle tap of fingers to his lips, Doc's eyes slid to the kitchen door. "She's fixing you something to eat." He tugged thoughtfully at one ear. "You see, Trish is like one of those people who sings in the shower and thinks she's a star. In reality, she stinks. Do you get my meaning?"

"You mean the food isn't good?"

"Ah, Trish makes a better waitress than a cook. Today, the regular cook's not here, so that means Trish has taken over kitchen duty." He held up a hand in a kind gesture. "She tries hard to make things right." He shook his head. "I guess with Trish, recipes and ingredients kind of get lost in translation." Doc smiled down at her. "How're you feeling now, Missy?"

A hot blush stole across Georgia's cheeks. No one had ever

before in her life called her Missy. "Better. I'm sorry for making a scene." She fussed with the napkin in her lap.

He stood over her in a doctor's pose, arms crossed, nodding in agreement. "Panic attacks aren't fun. How long have you been having them?"

"Panic attacks?" Georgia's voice went up an octave. She had no intention of getting into a discussion about her problems with a stranger who had turned out to be a doctor and who might see her for the coward she really was—a runaway fifty-something-year-old woman with no life. She shrugged. "Oh, it's nothing. The last few months I suppose."

Doc placed a firm hand on her shoulder. "You don't have to explain anything to me." He gave her a kind smile that crinkled the edges of his sapphire-blue eyes. He said, "I own a small ranch outside of Cottonwood. That's where I spend most of my time now, except for an occasional trail ride through parts of Colorado or Wyoming."

"Trail ride?" Georgia arched an eyebrow, grateful that he'd politely changed the subject.

"I'm hired on as camp doctor for those city fellas who come out west for a little excitement. They get bellyaches from eating too many cowboy beans or fall off horses and break arms and legs."

His intense blue eyes complimented his steady, reassuring voice, as comforting as spring rain against a tin roof. Georgia liked him and wanted to ask if he would sit with her, finish his coffee and talk about nothing in particular. Also, there was something familiar about Doc that Georgia couldn't quite figure out. Then, it came to her. Doc's silver hair and the way it parted naturally to the right with a slight wave, reminded her so much of Ed.

While not unusual for most men to steadily grow bald with age, Ed's hair had not only remained fully intact, but, over the years, had turned an enviable shade of silver, making him even more handsome than when he was a young man.

Both Georgia and Doc jumped when Trish burst back through the swinging door between the dining room and kitchen. Doc leaned over and hastily whispered, "If you come back for lunch, I'm warning you, don't order the meatloaf. Keep it simple, something like peanut butter and jelly."

Georgia gave him a teasing smile. "But you ate your breakfast here. No complaints?"

"Nothing much to eggs—break 'em and fry 'em up." He turned to Trish with a full smile. "What's the lunch special today, Trish?"

"Meatloaf," she said, checking the level of the coffee on the burners as she passed them.

"Ahhh," Doc said, throwing a knowing glance at Georgia. "Are *you* making the meatloaf, Trish?"

"No." Trish rolled her eyes at Georgia. "Mary Jo's making the meatloaf."

Doc gave a hearty laugh. "My granddaughter's never made a meatloaf in her life." He gave Trish a hug, and then grabbed his cowboy hat from the bank of hooks beside the front door. "Have a good one," he said to both of them. He paused after opening the door and turned to Georgia. "Nice meeting you, Ma'am."

"Nice meeting you, too," Georgia said, her cheeks growing hot. Doc left the café, pulling on his cowboy hat outside the door, tugging the brim low over his brow. Georgia watched him with interest until he disappeared around the corner. A smile crept to her lips.

"Nice man," Georgia said.

"The best," Trish wholeheartedly agreed. She slid an unsavory looking cinnamon bun on a chipped blue plate in front of Georgia. "I thought something sweet might make you feel better." Trish then slipped into the booth on the opposite side with her own cup of coffee. "You mind?"

"Not at all." Georgia shrugged, throwing an anxious glance at the swinging door into the kitchen. "Won't you get into trouble? You know, with Mary Jo, your boss?"

Trish's lips formed a teasing smile as she leaned across the table. "I am the boss. I own this place."

Georgia felt both eyebrows go up. "You do?" Her eyes took in the dining room, thinking how nice to be so young and have such a fine place of business. "It's very nice." She meant every word.

"How's your sweet roll?"

"Tasty," Georgia lied. The bread was downright tough, the icing as gritty and abrasive as sand. By comparison, Georgia's own homemade cinnamon rolls were pure ecstasy to the palate. Of course, she would never tell this to Trish. After all, it was the thought that counted, Trish bringing her this food, and then taking the time to sit and talk with her. Georgia swallowed more coffee to moisten the last bite of sweet roll. "Did you bake these?"

Trish hunched up her shoulders, as if she'd been picked out of a criminal lineup. "Yes," she confessed. "But you don't have to lie and tell me they're good. Doc teases me all the time about what a bad cook I am. This morning I couldn't get the yeast to work right. I think I killed it. And then I left the rolls in the oven too long."

"Do you usually do the baking here?"

Trish burst out laughing. "Are you kidding? Cook's in Phoenix for a few days. No one touches the kitchen when she's around. But her daughter had a baby a few days ago. She'll be back on Monday. I hope. *God,* I hope."

Georgia poured more cream into her coffee, enjoying Trish's company and listening as she prattled on about her inability to cook. Trish's outpouring of bad luck when it came to keeping good employees had a surprisingly calming effect on Georgia's nerves. When Trish finally said she had to get back to work, Georgia said, "Thank you for taking the time to sit with me. I apologize for—"

"Forget it." Trish waved away the apology. "Actually, you did me a favor." She whispered across the table, "I bribed Mary Jo into making the meatloaf, and it's downright ugly in the kitchen. Without Cook, we're like the blind leading the blind around here. Especially since Mary Jo's a vegan."

"A what?"

Trish scrunched up her eyebrows. "Huh? You never heard of a vegan."

"I have no idea what that is."

"Vegans eat nothing but salads and wear, like, plastic shoes and throw raw eggs at people wearing fur coats and Italian leather shoes. To Mary Jo, putting her hands into raw ground beef is as disgusting as us shoving our hands into a bowl of cow guts."

Georgia shivered at the thought but smiled at the mirth in Trish's eyes. "I don't understand. If you can't cook, why did you buy a restaurant?"

"Stupidity, I suppose." She scooted into the far corner of the booth, getting comfortable. "I grew up in Tucson. A couple of years ago, I'm driving through Sedona after visiting Doc and Mary Jo in Cottonwood, because I've known them forever. Well, I notice this café's for sale. The realtor gives me a real spiel about it being a good investment. I planned on hiring a manager to run the restaurant." Trish let out a heavy sigh. "It's been two years now. I've been through three cooks, five waitresses and a new roof. No manager. You'd think by now I'd at least know how to make a decent toasted cheese sandwich. Truth is I'm an absolute klutz when it comes to cooking."

"I doubt you're all that bad."

"You are too kind." Trish put her hand over her heart, feigning gratitude. "Well, if you don't believe me, ask one of the other customers. Oh, yeah, guess you've noticed. I don't have any." Trish clapped her hands. "Hey there, I got you to smile, didn't I? That's nice. Say, what's your name?"

"Georgia Brown."

"Where're you from?"

"Ohio."

"Let me guess. Cleveland?"

"Columbus."

"You have a husband wandering around Sedona while you're out shopping?"

"I'm alone."

Trish bit into her lower lip, waiting for an explanation.

"My husband died," Georgia explained. "I had a tough time handling his death." The rest of her flight-from-life story flowed easily out of her. She told Trish about how she'd left Columbus in the Fleetwood and about how on the first night she stayed at Edith's rundown motel outside of Nashville. She talked on about sweet, pregnant Lou Ann in Oklahoma City who had cut and colored her hair and had not only given her a new face but the courage to go on with her journey. She laughed, recalling her hookup with Luke Perry in Amarillo and how he'd driven the car all night to get to Flagstaff so he wouldn't miss his class at the university.

Elbows propped on the table, chin in hands, Trish listened intently. She acted as if Georgia were telling the most fascinating story she had ever heard. "My goodness, you've had quite the trip, haven't you?"

With little encouragement, Georgia rambled on, giving Trish the short-but-sweet version of her life, glossing over the bad stuff. Her words gained momentum, gushing out of her mouth like water through an open flood gate. She finally let out a long breath, saying, "My goodness, I've told you my whole life story. And you, sitting here so polite, listening to me ramble on about my boring life."

"I've enjoyed hearing your story, Georgia Brown," Trish said, smiling. "People interest me."

"Yes, I can tell." Georgia fumbled around inside her purse looking for her wallet. "Can you recommend a place to stay tonight?"

"Sure. There's a hotel down the street called Red Canyon Suites. Not fancy, but it's clean and the beds are comfortable." Trish paused, as if considering something, and then said, "Maybe by tomorrow you'll decide to stay a few days longer, take in some tourist sights."

Georgia noticed Trish's smooth, porcelain complexion and the unbelievable length of her dark eyelashes. Trish's kind of beauty rarely jumped out at first glance, but grew on you the more you took notice. "Well, I can't say for sure I'll do that, but right now I could use some help finding a nice gift shop."

Trish gathered the money and bill, smiling as if she held a

secret. "In Sedona, there's about a million of those to choose from. But the Moon Tide's right next door. Zoe's got the best selection of gifts in town. Here, wait, you've got change coming."

"No, you keep it ... for listening." Georgia opened the door.

"Georgia?"

"Yes?"

"You forgot something." Trish held up the clunky Niagara Falls key chain, jiggling it a little before handing it over. "Niagara Falls, huh. Special occasion?" ·

Georgia tucked the keys into her purse. "Twenty-fifth wedding anniversary. Ten years ago."

"Wow," Trish said, totally impressed. "Not everyone nowadays can say they've been married over ten years, let alone thirty-five."

"I suppose you're right," Georgia said with no enthusiasm, thinking that in the end, Ed had turned their marriage into an embarrassing joke.

Outside, the rain had stopped. Tourists again crowded the sidewalks. Georgia sat down on a dry bench under the gift shop awning. She wanted to catch her breath after having talked practically nonstop for over an hour to the sweet waitress at the café, something Georgia didn't ordinarily do. Granted, it seemed almost as if the young woman had been purposely pulling personal information from her. Just being nice, she supposed.

The shop that Trish had recommended for gifts was right in front of her. Georgia wished she could put a bit more enthusiasm into finding mementos for family members or had another destination that promised a new round of hope. Right now, her only destination was to find a hotel later in the afternoon and check in for the night.

First thing tomorrow morning, she would inquire around town about used car lots. She would then sell the Fleetwood to highest bidder, and then purchase a ticket on the next bus headed east. After having driven two thousand miles alone, Georgia certainly felt capable of finding her way back home in one piece. *Maybe.*

# CHAPTER FIVE

Soft flute music greeted Georgia as she stepped over the threshold and through a beaded curtain into the Moon Tide Gift Shop. The showroom was surprisingly spacious with a bank of floor-to-ceiling windows that framed a magnificent view high above Oak Creek. Something sweet and earthy permeated the air inside the Moon Tide, and Georgia could not explain the strange familiarity she instantly felt in this new-age, offbeat environment of beads, crystals and artisan jewelry.

Georgia crossed the shiny hardwood floor to a display case filled with a dazzling assortment of southwestern jewelry. Her eyes fell on an oval turquoise slider, perfect for Susan. As for Louie, the silver money clip at the far end of the case. She rested her hands on the edge of the glass, soaking up the laid-back atmosphere of the shop's interior. Two other customers browsed the book display at the far corner of the shop while another middle-aged couple conversed with a saleswoman near a wall of shelves, filled with bins of rocks and crystals.

Georgia moved closer, beside a rack of less-expensive beaded necklaces, her eyes settling on the exotic saleswoman with dark hair that curled softly to the middle of her back. She eavesdropped on their conversation, listening to the saleswoman talk about yoga and meditation. Georgia was fascinated by the bird-like fluidity of the woman's hands as she talked to her customers.

49

The saleswoman closed her eyes, saying to the couple, "Don't use the abdomen to breathe." She demonstrated, holding her hands lightly to her diaphragm. "Learn to deepen the lungs and charge the body with oxygen." The man intently watched the in and out movement of the saleswoman's chest until his wife gently elbowed him in the ribs.

"It's all about controlling the breath," the saleswoman explained. "Rid the body of stress. Eliminate what makes you desperate."

*Desperate?* Georgia's ears perked at the word, because that's exactly how she'd been feeling since Ed's death. She knew then, at that precise moment, that she wanted out—but out of what? Yearning tugged impatiently at her insides. Georgia knew then that the answer was very close, if only she would open her mind to it. She edged further into the conversation, totally captivated by the woman's voice.

"What is your name, dear," the older woman asked the saleswoman rather condescendingly, at the same time giving her husband a curt nod, as if to say, "I'll show you this woman's nothing but a big fake and talking a bunch of hooey."

"My name is Zoe," she answered, sending Georgia a friendly smile to let her know she would be with her momentarily.

Embarrassed for having been caught eavesdropping, Georgia stepped back to the jewelry case. From the corner of her eye, Georgia watched Zoe place two crystals into the palm of the man's hand, closing his fingers around them. She said, "Live your life with faith and hope, not as the ego demands. The ego dies, our spirits soar." She took a step back from the couple and pressed the palms of her hands together, bowing her head. She whispered, "*Namaste.*"

*Namaste?* Georgia had no idea what the word meant, but it sounded so peaceful, as if she were listening to the pleasant sound of water bubbling over rocks in a shallow stream. A sweet calmness enveloped her body as she took in a deep breath through her nose, eyes brazenly studying the woman for any clue as to what she should do next.

When Zoe reached out and softly touched the man's hands, his wife's face went from a pasty white to a bright crimson within a matter of seconds. Crossing her arms, she sarcastically said, "O-kay."

Zoe simply smiled at the woman and with a swish of her skirt deliberately turned her attention back to the woman's husband. Georgia noticed how her own skirt resembled Zoe's vibrant broomstick skirt cinched at the waist with a purple fringed belt. Georgia only wished she looked half as beautiful and stunning in the garment.

The jealous wife did not appreciate being ignored by a woman who a majority of men will trip over their own feet looking back at on the street. She glared at Zoe, rolling her eyes to the ceiling and mumbling, "I've had enough of these shenanigans."

Zoe pointedly ignored the woman's rude remark and continued talking to the husband. "Place the crystals beside your bed each night. Let the energy flow into your spirit and bring comfort and peace."

Totally mesmerized by Zoe's exotic beauty, the man ignored his wife's body language, saying, "I'll take them all." He coughed when his wife roughly tugged at his arm. He gently pulled away and told Zoe, "I like them. They're pretty."

"You've chosen—"

"Do they come with a gift box?" the lady rudely interrupted, fussing with an over-processed curl that had escaped her lacquered helmet of hair. Eyebrows twitching, she visibly showed her displeasure at her husband's flirtatious teasing, possessively hooking onto his elbow. She might have lost the war, but she wasn't about to shrink into the background and let this beautiful woman persuade her husband to buy up half the shop's merchandise.

"Of course." Zoe produced a gift box from beneath the counter, and then finished up their purchase. The couple started for the door, the husband carrying the gift bag already tucked inside a bigger bag with *I Shopped Red Rock Sedona* written on the outside.

With a weary smile, Zoe turned to Georgia, looking as if they both shared the same exasperation in having to deal with sometimes rude tourists and their predatory hunt for the ultimate gift. "May I help you?" Zoe said, pausing at the counter to straighten pamphlets before giving her full attention to Georgia.

The woman's complexion was incredibly flawless, dark coffee swirled with a generous dab of heavy cream, her full lips covered in a lush plum lipstick. Zoe's beaded earrings quivered as she cocked her head to one side, waiting for Georgia to find her tongue again. Most likely, Zoe was used to people going dumbstruck in her presence, and she didn't appear the least bit uppity about her goddess status. In fact, if anything, she seemed almost apologetic about it.

Zoe smiled, still waiting.

Georgia pointed at the top of the jewelry case, forcing her words. "I'd like to see the turquoise slider and the money clip, the one beside that sliver bracelet."

Zoe slid back the glass door of the case. "Ah, good choices." She brought out the pieces and placed them on a display mirror in front of Georgia. "And this, too?" Zoe scooped up a silver chain with a beautiful dark crystal, the one Georgia had been admiring for herself.

"How did you—?"

Zoe's dark eyes sparkled with amusement. "A good guess."

Georgia caught a glimpse of a sign hanging behind the counter. *Readings.*

"You tell fortunes?"

"Hmmm. Fortunes? That's for gypsies. I'd rather think of myself as something, ah, a bit more mysterious. Have you ever had a reading?"

"Me? Never."

"It's your aura," Zoe said, lining up the pieces of jewelry on the mirror. "I've never seen one so vibrant and clear as yours."

"My what?" Heat radiated from Georgia's cheeks.

"Your aura, energy field."

"Oh? Like halos on angels?"

Zoe's smile seemed indulgent. "Hmmm. I guess you could call it that. I'd love to do a reading for you." The thin silver bracelets on Zoe's wrist rattled enticingly. Georgia glanced over one shoulder, uncertain. A woman earlier perusing the book section left the store, passing two more women coming inside and hurrying over to the jewelry showcase. "You're busy. I—"

"Nonsense." Zoe left the counter and went to the back of the store, calling up the stairway to the loft, "Rosie?" A woman around Georgia's age hurried downstairs to assist the customers.

"There, now that's settled. Are you still interested?"

*Interested?* "Oh, I don't know." Georgia wished she could think of a polite way to say no, but didn't want to hurt this nice woman's feelings. She hated being pressured into things she didn't feel comfortable doing.

Zoe persisted. "You look as if you might like a piece of good news."

"Good news?" Georgia reconsidered, thinking perhaps something positive might be just the tonic she needed. She nodded her head and said, "Why not?" Besides, it felt rather nice to have someone as beautiful as Zoe—who so obviously didn't need anyone's attention—take the time to talk to her.

Over the years, Georgia had somehow misplaced the art of girly chit-chat and gossipy cliques. How could she have not missed the joy of being with old friends? At parties and other social get-togethers, Georgia usually drifted in the general direction of the kitchen to help with food preparation or refreshments, giving out recipes for her lemon glazed pound cake and collecting dirty dishes for cleanup. In the kitchen, she had a voice and everyone listened, even her husband and children.

Since high school, what with being caught up in raising a family, working part-time at the hardware store and taking care of her home, Georgia had lost track of the majority of her girlhood friends. In truth, Georgia had never felt any great loss, thinking the time had long passed for giggly gossip sessions or beauty tips, considering them to be a relative waste of time. However, new friendships didn't come easily to Georgia, and being so busy with her own family, she saw no need to fill all the empty spaces inside herself. There would be plenty of time to concentrate on what she needed after the children grew up, after Ed retired from the hardware store, and after she'd finally figured out what she truly wanted from her life. So far, she had been little more than an accessory in other people's lives and now wanted no more of that. She wanted her own life, her own thoughts—the right to dress in something artsy and kind of off-the-wall without others looking at her as if she'd lost her *fricken* mind.

"Come with me." Zoe motioned for Georgia to follow her to the rear of the shop. Once there, she held back a curtain, revealing a small room only big enough to hold a table and two chairs. The walls were draped in generous folds of dark blue velvet. Georgia shivered. The heavy curtains reminded her of the soft, pleated interior of Ed's coffin. Georgia bit into her lower lip, debating whether or not she should turn around and make a run for the front door. Curiosity won out. Choosing the chair closest to the door, she sat down and kept a tight hold on her purse. "Like I said before, I've never done this."

"Don't be nervous. It's painless." Zoe sat opposite her at the table and brought out a large deck of funny-looking cards.

Georgia tucked her purse in her lap, fearing a trap door might be in the floor, ready to swallow her up. Even though Zoe looked genuinely harmless, it sure didn't hurt to be cautious. After all, if someone were to take her purse, where would she be? No money, no credit cards, no driver's license!

"Shuffle the cards," Zoe instructed.

Georgia wedged her purse into the tight space between her lap and the table, collecting the clumsy cards in both hands. Twice the size of an ordinary deck, they kept slipping from her fingers. These cards were different from anything she'd ever seen, bearing strange pictures of people in long biblical robes marked at the top with words like Justice and Death. Georgia's toes began to twitch, as if begging to take flight from the room. What in the world had she gotten herself into?

"Now, cut the deck."

Georgia did as told.

Zoe fanned the first pile out on the table. "Select a card."

Georgia obeyed, handing the one she'd picked to Zoe. "Clarity," Zoe said, eyebrows raised. "You have some psychic ability yourself."

"I do?"

"Yes."

"Well, imagine that." Georgia leaned into the table, now giving Zoe her full attention.

"Never second-guess yourself." Zoe again shuffled the deck, the flicking sound adding to the mystery of what the cards might reveal. "You have a great love and devotion to family."

Georgia thought of Susan and Louie and the grandchildren, tears stinging the backs of her eyes. "Yes," she said, thinking this woman was only telling her what she wanted to hear, at the same time fishing for more information.

Zoe held the cards in front of her. "Pick another."

Georgia sniffed back the tears and pulled another card from those laid out on the table. Relax, she told herself. Enjoy this new experience. After all, this was really no different than sliding a quarter into the weight machine at the mall arcade and getting some innocuous fortune like, *Great wealth awaits you.*

"You're a traveler," Zoe said, sounding surprised.

Georgia pursed her lips, trying not to laugh, because, more than likely, ninety-five percent of the people walking the streets of Sedona were tourists. Georgia shrugged, keeping her eyes on the cards. So far, this fortune reading seemed pretty much like general stuff that could be applied to anyone willing to suck it in and make it their own.

Zoe gathered the cards and handed them to Georgia. "Shuffle again and divide the cards into three piles. These next cards represent what you want in life, what you don't want, and what you'll get."

Georgia's ears perked. Now, this was something she definitely wanted to know. She did as instructed, shuffling and separating the cards into three piles, picking one from each pile, and then sliding them over to Zoe, who turned the cards face-up on the table.

Zoe pressed a finger into the first card. "What you *want* is to be grounded." She then placed her entire hand over the second card. "What you *don't want* is stress. Stress fragmentizes your thinking." Zoe paused before turning over the third card. "What you'll *get* is balance, but only if you follow the path you're on now." Zoe looked directly at Georgia. "Very good, indeed."

Actually, Georgia had been hoping for something a bit more specific. "My future? What else do you see there?"

Again, Zoe shuffled the cards, saying, "The next seven years will be fantastic. Whatever you want to do in life, give yourself permission to do it."

"Oh? That sounds nice."

Zoe's crinkled up her nose and sniffed. Her eyes locked on Georgia. "Do you smell gasoline?"

"What?" Georgia sniffed the air, too, but could only make out the soothing scent of eucalyptus.

Zoe closed her eyes. "A man is pouring gasoline into a lawnmower—the kind you ride on." She shook her head, confused, as if some psychic wire inside her head had suddenly short-fused. "That's weird. Does that make sense to you?"

Georgia shrugged, not sure if Zoe had made a connection or

not. Ed loved that stupid riding lawnmower, but she wasn't about
to give away any specifics about her life. She'd practically talked
that young woman's head off at the café next door about her
personal life, and she didn't have the strength to go into all that
heartache again, especially not with a woman who claimed to see
into her future.

"His name was Ned?"

The hairs on Georgia's arms stood straight up. Georgia leaned
into the table, definitely intrigued, knowing she had purposely not
revealed Ed's name to Trish at the café. Names like Ned and Ed
were close enough. "Ed," Georgia corrected.

"He's here with us," Zoe whispered.

Georgia hunched her shoulders, her eyes darting around the
closet-sized room, ready to make a quick exit if things suddenly
got too weird.

"He loved you very much. He wants you to know he's sorry."

"Sorry?"

Zoe tilted her head to one side as if someone were whispering
into her ear. "On your birthday, he wished he'd taken more time
picking out a card for you, instead of grabbing the first one off the
rack."

The four walls closed in around Georgia, making her feel as
if she might suffocate in the velvet-lined room. She clasped her
hands in her lap, interlocking her fingers and squeezed tight, firmly
telling herself that Ed couldn't possibly be in this room whispering
information into this woman's ear.

"He's sorry about what happened," Zoe said. "He says you
know what about."

Hearing this, Georgia almost choked on the breath mint she'd
earlier popped into her mouth. She unlocked her fingers and
gripped the edge of the table. "I want to go now."

"He's distraught."

Georgia's eyes stung with fresh tears. "Distraught? Well, he
should be."

Zoe grimaced. "He knows how much he hurt you."

Tears sprouted from the corners of Georgia's eyes, hot and remorseful. Her lower lip quivered. "I miss him. No one seems to understand how much I miss him. My daughter... my son, they go on with their lives. Nothing makes sense anymore."

Zoe plucked a tissue from the box at one side of the table. "Here."

"Thank you," Georgia mumbled, wiping at her nose. She sniffed loudly. "I'm sorry. It seems anymore I cry for no reason at all."

"Don't be embarrassed." Zoe then slid the entire box of tissues under Georgia's nose.

"You stay here for a few minutes and rest. Take all the time you need. Ned's death happened so suddenly. It takes time to heal."

"Ed," Georgia again corrected around blowing her nose. "My husband's name was Ed."

"Yes." Zoe came round the table and patted her shoulder. "You're exhausted. Rest your head on the table." From out of nowhere Zoe produced a pillow that matched the blue velvet curtains and left her alone in the room.

Not having the strength to argue, Georgia allowed her head to drop into the pillow, thinking she would only shut her eyes for a few minutes. Only a few minutes.

When Georgia finally opened her eyes, for one disoriented moment, she thought she'd somehow fallen inside Ed's coffin. Then, she remembered coming into the Moon Tide to buy a few gifts and how Zoe had talked her into having a reading done. She sat up straight and glanced at her watch. She gasped, realizing she had been asleep for almost an hour.

Zoe poked her head through an opening in the curtains. "Oh, good, you're awake. I kept checking on you, but you looked so peaceful, I decided not to wake you."

Georgia blinked at the sudden light flooding in from the showroom. She rubbed at her sleep-swollen eyes. "Oh dear." Her legs felt numb from sitting too long in one position and it hurt to move them. "I'm so sorry." She stood up and willed the blood to flow down into her legs again.

"No problem," Zoe said in a sweet voice.

Georgia shook off the fuzziness that had settled into her feet, wanting to leave here as soon as possible and find a motel room. She looked forward to crawling into bed for the night and watching the late news. Her first and only day in Sedona had left much to be desired, but, she supposed, all journeys—good or bad—must come to an end at some point in time. No doubt, this time next week, she'd be home and in her own bed with all the memories of her Arizona trip safely tucked inside her head. Her life would then go back to normal.

As if reading Georgia's mind, Zoe asked, "Are you staying in town overnight?"

Georgia groped around under the table for her purse that must have fallen off her lap while she napped. "Yes. A nice woman at the café next door recommended a motel."

"Trish? Oh yes, she came looking for you about twenty minutes ago."

Georgia laughed. "Does Trish follow all her customers around town?"

"No, only the people she takes a special interest in. Trish is kind of like a soft-hearted kid who drags home puppies and injured birds." Zoe walked Georgia to the front door. "Oh, here, I almost forgot. I have a present for you." She took hold of Georgia's hand. In her open palm Zoe placed a small silver ring.

Confused, Georgia asked, "What's this?"

"Toe ring."

Georgia suppressed a giggle. "Toe ring? For me? Well, imagine that."

Zoe grinned. "Yes, imagine that."

\*\*\*

After settling into her motel room, Georgia called Susan. Her daughter picked up on the second ring.

"Mom?"

Georgia took in a deep breath, fully anticipating her daughter's anger and knowing she deserved every hot word. Instead, Susan's voice sounded small and frantic, like the time when she was three and had gotten lost in a department store. Georgia had found Susan at the information desk, face smeared with tears, her small body trembling with fear. Georgia had hugged her tight, whispering, "Don't cry, sweetie. Mommy's here. You're not lost anymore."

"Mom?"

"I'm here, Susan."

"Where?"

"Sedona. I always wanted to see Arizona. So, here I am."

"Oh." Susan replied softly.

"How are Samantha and Ben?"

"They're fine. Yesterday, Louie's mother took them on a picnic. They're staying with her over the weekend."

"Hmmm." Something like nettles prickled at her insides. "That's nice." Georgia removed her espadrilles and tried on Zoe's gift. She held out her foot and admired the toe ring. "I called to give you the telephone number of the motel." A long silence followed, and for once Georgia did not feel obliged to fill up the emptiness with words.

"Mom?"

"Yes."

"You sound different."

Georgia glanced at her reflection in the mirror over the dresser and silently agreed with her daughter. She said, "Well, I am different."

"Are you having a good time?"

"I'm having a wonderful time. Thank you for asking."

Another long pause.

"Are you coming home soon?" Susan asked cautiously.

Georgia sighed into the receiver. "I don't know." And she really didn't know. She decided to change the subject. No sense opening that can of worms. "How's Oscar? I'm worried he isn't getting enough to eat."

"Oscar's fine. Samantha and I go over to the house every morning and make sure he's fed."

"Is Mrs. Otis still dressing him at night?"

"Mom, Mrs. Otis fell and broke her hip. Thank God Beverly arrived for a visit yesterday morning. She found her mother on the kitchen floor. I talked to Beverly after the emergency squad left. She said she's putting her mother into a nursing home after her release from the hospital."

"That's sad."

"Beverly's moving into Mrs. Otis's house."

"Oh? I suppose that doesn't surprise me. Beverly's always loved her mother's house."

Susan yawned. "I think Beverly's been waiting for the chance to move back in and sell off her mother's antiques. She told me she plans to remodel the kitchen first thing."

"What about Oscar?"

"Beverly said the cat can stay as long as he's not too much trouble."

"How thoughtful of Beverly," Georgia said sarcastically, feeling as if she had somehow betrayed Oscar by leaving him behind on the stoop four days ago. Well, nothing could be done about that now. Georgia remembered Beverly as being a no-nonsense child with a dull personality. At least now Oscar wouldn't have to suffer the indignity of having to cruise the alley at night in a pink layette.

\*\*\*

The next day, Georgia shopped every T-shirt and gift shop in Sedona. Exhausted and bored with the main streets, she took to exploring the side streets, discovering an outdoor store where she purchased a pair of khaki shorts, several safari-like shirts and one good pair of sturdy boots. The clerk gave her hiking maps of the area and told her the best guides to contact. And then, Georgia spent the next several days hiking the narrow paths along Oak Creek. In her fancy outdoor gear, she felt as chic and adventuresome as Meryl Streep in *Out Of Africa*. One tourist—after stopping into the Moon Tide to thank Zoe once more for the toe ring—even asked how much she charged for hiking tours. Zoe, having caught part of the conversation, covered her mouth to keep from laughing out loud.

The third day after her arrival in Sedona, Georgia took a helicopter flight over the Grand Canyon. After landing again, she could only think if she died tomorrow, she would consider her life complete. And with each passing day, Georgia grew more in love with the independence and empowerment Ed's money provided. She answered to no one and did as she pleased.

The Soft Rock Café became Georgia's regular hangout to eat her meals. Turned out, Trish's cook never returned from Phoenix, and the food ordered from the menu was barely palatable. It really didn't matter, though. Georgia enjoyed her daily conversations with Trish and Mary Jo, who was still in college and only worked in the café part-time and during the summer months. In the days after her arrival in Sedona, Georgia also kept a watchful eye out for Doc, the gentleman she had met her first day in Sedona, but never saw him again.

Several times, Georgia almost asked Mary Jo about her grandfather, but thought better of it, fearing any personal questions about his whereabouts might be misconstrued as something other than polite curiosity. Georgia couldn't help but notice how both girls were keen on teasing each other with little mercy until one of them finally gave in and walked away. It occurred to Georgia that if the two women devoted themselves to the art of cooking as diligently as they did to annoying one another, the food might be more edible and the café fuller with customers.

In the past week, Georgia had gotten to be quite friendly with

Trish and Mary Jo, especially Trish who had taken to bringing an order of whole wheat toast and a rubbery poached egg to her table as soon as she walked in the door each morning. Trish always came at her with the same surprised greeting. "Say, Georgia, you're still here!"

Each afternoon, after a long hike, Georgia would stop into the Moon Tide and have a cup of tea with Zoe. At the end of her first week in Sedona, Georgia noticed an ad for summer employment on the bulletin board: *Bright, Friendly Person Needed.*

The very next day Georgia arrived at the Moon Tide, hoping she wasn't too late to apply for the job. She caught Zoe as she unlocked the shop and breathlessly asked, "Is the summer job still open?"

"Yes. Do you know someone?" Zoe flipped the sign on the door to Open.

"I've decided to stay in Sedona for the summer. I'd like the job."

Zoe paused and lowered her head, fussing with the end of a loose curl, considering Georgia's proposal. "You've worked retail before?"

"Yes." Georgia tugged at the zipper on her purse, digging out pen and identification, ready to fill out employment information. "I helped Ed at our hardware store. I managed everything in the office, including inventory." Georgia knew she sounded a tad eager but didn't care. She wanted the job. "I know lots about small appliances."

Zoe's lips spread into an amused smile. "Can you start today?"

\* \* \*

Georgia didn't mind first day jitters. Except for getting used to the new-age merchandise, which was a bit different from selling mixers and toasters at the hardware store, clerking at the Moon Tide was relatively easy. Georgia handled the cash register just fine. Math had been her best subject in high school, making her quick and efficient with the customers' change.

The shop grew busier around the lunch hour. A woman in a tie-dyed shirt came up to the register. "Vortexes," the woman said, expectantly.

"Excuse me?" Georgia had no idea what the woman was talking about.

"Do you have any books on the Sedona vortexes?"

Zoe quickly came to her rescue. "Are you interested in alien encounters?"

The woman gasped. "Heaven's no! I don't believe in all that nonsense. I only want a book on the vortexes and maps telling me where they are. They are real, you know."

A pleasant half-smile traced Zoe's lips. She slipped on half-glasses hanging from a beaded chain around her neck, glasses so obviously a fashion statement and totally unnecessary. Perfect women like Zoe seldom suffered ordinary inconveniences such as bad eyes.

She turned to Georgia and explained, "Vortexes are like energy reservoirs. Every crystal sold at the Moon Tide has been exposed to an energy field in this area. The crystals then become like little storage containers. People from all over the world come to Sedona to experience vortex phenomenon."

Zoe turned back to the customer in the tie-dyed shirt. "We have an excellent selection on the subject. Come with me."

Georgia followed them to a corner in the store where Zoe pulled out several books from a long shelf and handed them to the tie-dyed lady. She smiled sweetly. "Feel free to relax in our Comfort Zone and look over the books. Enjoy. If you'd like, Georgia will bring you something to drink. Tea, perhaps?"

The Comfort Zone consisted of two overstuffed chairs with matching hassocks. Miss Tie-dyed, wearing a shiny new pair of hiking boots and carrying a backpack purse that easily cost three hundred dollars, didn't have to be asked twice to settle into one of the chairs like a nesting bird. She asked Georgia to bring her a cup of tea. Earl Grey, if you please.

Georgia hurried into the kitchen at the rear of the shop next to Zoe's living quarters. Vortexes? Aliens? She dragged a mug from the top shelf and ripped open an Earl Grey. For heaven's sake, what had she gotten herself into? She poured hot water into the mug, adding a teabag.

Zoe stuck her head around the doorway of the kitchen. "You're doing great, Georgia. Keep it up." She disappeared, but then popped around the corner again, saying, "Remember, all the customer really wants is to believe in *something*. Without belief, you have no faith."

Georgia's zest for selling gained momentum throughout the afternoon. By four o'clock, she'd already sold ten silver necklaces, five Navajo rings, two Hopi bracelets and over a dozen rock crystals energized at the Bell Rock—or so Georgia told them. What Zoe had told her was, indeed, true: People only wanted to believe in *something*. What possible harm was there in doing that?

Zoe locked the door after the last customer left the store at six o'clock. She turned to Georgia, her face beaming. "Sweetie, you're a natural for new-age retail." Georgia felt herself blush as she went about balancing out the register, pleased her first day of work had gone so well. When finished, Georgia reached for her blue sweater just as Zoe presented her with a small white box tied up in a red bow. "A gift for you. Call it a thank you for a fabulous first day."

"Another gift?" Georgia eagerly accepted. She removed the lid on the box and discovered a pair of silver hoop earrings tucked into a fold of black satin.

Zoe touched one of Georgia's pearl earrings. "Working here, I thought you might want to wear something besides these Barbara Bush relics."

"Oh?" Georgia touched the cultured pearls Susan and Louie had given to her last Christmas. She had always had the tendency to leave in earrings, sometimes for weeks at a time. This was a habit she attributed to not really caring all that much about jewelry. Her major piece was a diamond necklace Ed bought ten years ago, a Christmas special kind of thing that every other woman in America was wearing at the time.

Zoe burst out laughing. "I'm kidding. The earrings are just my way of saying you're definitely hired!"

The very next day, Georgia moved out of the motel room and into an apartment above the Soft Rock Café. After making her decision to stay for at least the summer, everything fell into place as easily as the last few pieces of a complicated puzzle. Trish led her up the back stairway to the apartment, saying, "I moved to a house on the outskirts of town, along Oak Creek. So, if you like the apartment, you can move in today."

She followed Trish through the living room with a stone fireplace, a much smaller version of the one downstairs in the dining room. There was also a kitchenette, bedroom and a black and white tiled bathroom, complete with shower. Georgia thought it couldn't be more perfect. The furniture left behind by Trish was a bit frayed at the edges but definitely suitable for Georgia's needs. She would paint the small kitchen a bright yellow and polish the worn wooden floors until they gleamed with new life.

Trish opened cupboards. "Everything in the apartment stays. I bought all new stuff for my own place, figuring I'd rent this as furnished." She turned to Georgia. "The rent is definitely negotiable."

"It's perfect." Georgia waltzed through the apartment, visualizing new curtains, bright area rugs, anything to cozy up the place and make it her home, at least for the next few months. "I love it." She gave Trish an enthusiastic hug.

Trish, a bit embarrassed at Georgia's sudden burst of exuberance, handed her two sets of keys to the apartment, grinning from ear to ear. "Make yourself at home." She started to leave, but then hesitated. "Say, if you're only working a few hours for

Zoe in the afternoons, why not work at the café in the mornings?" Georgia could barely make her mouth work to say, "Yes!"

\* \* \*

So began a routine that greatly suited Georgia, helping Trish with the breakfast and lunch shifts at the café, and then working afternoons at the Moon Tide. Two weeks later, Trish finally gave up on Cook ever returning from Phoenix and asked Georgia if she might consider being chief cook and baker for the hours she worked. Georgia didn't have to think twice about accepting Trish's proposal.

Georgia loved the café kitchen with its stainless steel gas stove and huge refrigerator. The length of shelving above the chopping block displayed glass jars filled with flour, sugar and salt. One open cupboard revealed an assortment of mismatched crock bowls and ice-blue spice jars. Even though Georgia enjoyed her job at the gift shop, Trish's kitchen became her real home away from home.

Trish must have understood the longing in Georgia's eyes to take complete charge of the kitchen, because one afternoon she threw up both hands and said to Georgia, "You do what you want with the place. I won't interfere."

"You mean it?"

"Sure, be my guest. What's your poison?"

Georgia smiled. "Cinnamon rolls. I make the best ever."

"Okay, tomorrow morning, three dozen, right here in the case. We'll see if anyone notices the difference." Trish broke out laughing and leaned against the chopping block, sizing Georgia up and down. "You really are a godsend, Georgia."

Georgia snapped a clean white baker's apron from the bin and tied it around her waist, "Day after tomorrow, you'll need six dozen."

# CHAPTER SIX

An iridescent snake slithered through a crack in Georgia's nightmare, curling itself around her feet. Although good sense told her this was only a dream, the snake nonetheless looked real enough. Surprisingly, Georgia felt no fear. The reptile did not seem all that threatening, perhaps only weary, as if it wanted only to rest at Georgia's feet before slipping off into someone else's nightmare. Georgia's eyelids fluttered open into the real world, just as she kicked the snake aside, shooing it away. "Go on. Get! And don't come back."

Fully awake now, Georgia sat up in bed and hugged both her knees, hoping to relieve the tightness inside her chest. Moonlight bathed the room in a shimmering light, so that when she held out her hands, they appeared soft and delicate, like a child's. She vaguely recalled the nightmare with the snake's brilliant, jewel-like colors and wondered what it could mean? Well, whatever it represented, Georgia knew she was no longer afraid to face it.

She had been in Sedona for nearly three months now and felt her journey was a sort of backhanded blessing, a journey she still couldn't imagine ever ending, at least not too soon. Since moving into the apartment above the Soft Rock Café, Georgia had woken up a few times in the middle of the night, disoriented, but then realized she was in her own apartment, sleeping in a bed borrowed from Trish.

Gathering sheet and blanket around her chin, Georgia thought about Ed and how they had once lived what she had considered to be a normal, ordinary life. They had raised two children with all the usual calamities, but nothing like raising kids today. Kids today seemed angry and unhappy, given too much stuff and still wanting more, like overdosing on chocolate, leaving you sick and empty after the sugar high is gone.

Georgia slipped out of bed and lit a vanilla-scented candle from the Moon Tide. From a dresser drawer, she pulled out the embroidered red silk shawl purchased at the boutique across from the café and carefully laid it out at the end of the bed. She then slipped out of her new white cotton nightgown with the embroidered bodice and draped the silk shawl around her bare shoulders and breasts. The memory of nursing her babies tugged pleasingly at her body, the completeness she had felt with their tiny bow mouths clamped against her nipple.

As Zoe taught in her weekly yoga class, Georgia sat in the center of the bed, legs crossed, palms pressed together, her mind attempting to seal out the distractions and daily irritations that cause internal distress. She took in a deep breath, exhaling through her nose, the anxiety finally loosening its hold, uncoiling like a boa constrictor from around her chest.

Her son had called the night before and told her it was time to wind up her little road trip and return home. David had said, "We all understand why you did it, Mom, but *enough's enough*."

Georgia's eyes had prickled with tears at David's sharp words. With Susan, yes, she never would have been so sensitive—Susan always came off a bit edgy—but not David. She'd always thought he understood her best.

"Meaning what, David?" she had said, struggling with the need to speak her mind but not wanting to alienate her son.

"Mom, don't get defensive," he'd said, his voice raised. He then abruptly cleared his throat, no doubt embarrassed that he had spoken to his mother with such disrespect. "We're worried about you," he countered. "Susan calls every day asking me what to do about you."

"What to do *about* me?" Blood had pounded behind her eyes, threatening a headache. Her children had no right to treat her as if she were a child who needed an ultimatum, or some kind of threat that implied an "or else." *Or else what?* After moving into this apartment for the summer, Georgia had subconsciously drawn an emotional line in the sand, knowing she would never again let anyone cross it without her permission. She had hoped her children would eventually come to understand and accept her flight from reality, but now David—by far the easiest to please— had grown weary of having to deal with his sister's daily long-distance complaints.

"Look, Mom. You're old enough to know you just can't take off on a joy ride without worrying people. You have responsibilities— the hardware store, the house. You're being selfish leaving everything at loose ends, expecting Susan to take up the slack."

Georgia finally found her voice. "Louie's running the hardware store. Your father should've had something in place for him years ago, but he didn't want to give control to Louie. And you call me selfish? Come to think of it, I'll give Louie and Susan control of the hardware store. As for the house, I'll deal with it later."

"Mom, *what* are you talking about?"

"What?" Georgia threw the question back in his face, fed up with this discussion about what she should or shouldn't do. Did she pry into the lives of her children? Absolutely not. Did she tell Susan how to clean her house, treat her husband, or raise her children? Did she ever once tell David that he married the wrong woman? Not once.

"Are you thinking about moving out there?" David had said this as if horrified, as if she were considering a move to Bora Bora.

"Well..."

David lowered his voice. "Mom, I don't blame you for running away for a few weeks. You needed to get a new perspective on things. Now, it's time to come home. And I don't like the idea of you driving back alone. Sell that old car of Dad's. Buy a ticket and fly home. I'll fly in, too, and meet you there, myself. We can talk." He sounded so pleased, having come up with such an irrefutable solution to a rather pesky problem. One she couldn't possibly refuse. Well, he'd better get a grip, because she wasn't going anywhere, not unless she wanted to go.

"No, David."

"No?"

"I'm staying at least until the end of summer. I'm happy here." No response. "David, did you hear me?"

He had then sighed into the phone, clearly exasperated. "There's nothing more I can say to change your mind?"

"Nope. I'm fifty-three years old. I don't need you or Susan organizing my life." She started to say goodbye, but David stopped her.

"Mom, I'm sorry about what happened."

"Happened?"

"Mom, you know, about Dad."

"I don't want to talk about it."

"At the funeral, all those people staring at you and knowing the truth. It was humiliating for all of us."

"David, stop it. I'm hanging up now. Say hello to Lori for me."

"Lori's in New York." His tone had shifted from authoritative to evasive. "She's visiting her mother for a few weeks."

"Is her mother ill?" Georgia had asked, concerned.

"No. Lori's interviewing with a law firm there."

"Oh? You're relocating to New York?"

He hesitated. "Not exactly."

"David?"

"Yes."

"Did Lori leave you?"

"Yes."

"I'm sorry, sweetie."

"Don't be. It's mutual. Lori doesn't want children. I do. This has been an issue with us for years. You've known that."

"Well... yes," she admitted. "I did know, but I always thought she'd change her mind. You're both still young."

"She won't budge on the subject. And I won't either."

"Honey, is there anything I can do?"

He let out a sarcastic laugh. "No. Like you, I don't want to talk about it. Okay?"

"Okay."

"Mom?"

"Yes?"

"She broke my heart."

Georgia adjusted the shawl around her shoulders and straightened her spine, still sitting in the middle of the bed, aware that every muscle in her body had stiffened up again. The idea of David's getting his heart broken by a woman who, in Georgia's opinion, had the emotional level of concrete, upset her greatly. She attempted to relax, concentrating on the present moment, thinking how happy she'd been since taking over as manager of the Soft Rock Café, an eatery that had primarily survived on the loyalty of friends and naïve tourists. Trish had once said that she suspected the shopkeepers forewarned tourists that if they valued their GI tracts, to avoid the Soft Rock, at all costs.

And there had been other changes for the better in Georgia's life—simple changes, but, nonetheless, important changes that made her feel alive again. Like placing clay pots of robust flowers on deep windowsills and rearranging the tables to make the atmosphere more home-style and inviting to the customers. Her first week as manager, she'd taken down the faded gingham curtains in the dining room and replaced them with crisp, white valances to let in more natural light. She then added plantation blinds, easily shut to block out the afternoon glare of the sun.

After changing the curtains, she then decided to paint the dining room walls a soft buttery yellow, the molding and door frames a deep forest green. She hired a professional to inspect the creek-stone fireplace and remove a dozen years or so of debris from the chimney. On chilly mornings, a warm mesquite fire greeted the locals. They ordered breakfast, caught up on town gossip while nursing that second cup of coffee before having to open their own shops and specialty stores.

Trish seemed to relish every improvement in the café and was quick to encourage Georgia to do as she pleased. The influx of new customers found them either rushing around the café to keep up with the food orders, or Georgia, with hammer and a small bag of nails, hanging a collection of prints on loan from a nearby art gallery.

The only tense moment came when Zoe confronted Trish about *trying to steal* Georgia away from the Moon Tide to work full-time at the café. Georgia had been quick to intercede. She calmed them down, agreeing to work out a schedule that would accommodate both businesses. Although a stand-off between the girls had caused a minor disruption for those around them, Georgia never fretted. If she had learned anything about Trish and Zoe in the short time she'd known them, it was that they constantly bickered back and forth. When the smoke cleared, the girls always made up. Even with the ten year difference in their ages, Zoe and Trish had an almost twin-sisterly devotion to one another. It seemed the only thing they both agreed on was that Georgia had a knack for knowing what people wanted, and it would be best to give her a free rein when it came to both businesses.

From the storage barn behind the café, Georgia rescued a wide plank table and cleaned off decades of dust that had dulled the wood. Young men from neighboring businesses helped to carry it into the dining room, where Georgia then applied a fresh coat of wax. She didn't bother to repair or hide any of the scratches and indentations left by prior owners, feeling these marks on the table had been well-earned. Trish, not so convinced of its timeless beauty, remarked, "It's old and ugly." Georgia only ran her hand over the worn surface, saying, "She may be old, but she's sturdy and has more character than all the laminated tables made in China."

Georgia then found ten mismatched chairs—each painted a different bright color— and shoved them under the table. Georgia reserved this section of the dining room for the early-bird locals, free to sit together and enjoy that first cup of morning coffee, talk over the weather and local gossip, before having to deal with the rest of the day.

Much to Georgia's delight, some customers arrived before the light of day, just to get first-dibs on the first batch of cinnamon rolls pulled from the oven and iced. It wasn't long before she hired two more waitresses to help out in the dining room, while Georgia bustled around the kitchen with cups of flour and bowls of batter, never missing a beat. Mary Jo even pitched in, swallowing her vegan pride to work the griddle, not only frying up eggs and pancakes, but also grilling side orders of ham, bacon and sausages without audibly complaining about animals dying violently and lectures on the chemicals used to preserve meat.

Eventually, even Zoe had softened to Georgia working both places, often coming into the café before opening her own shop. She sat with the others at the big table, drinking green tea and nibbling on a piece of dry wheat toast. No amount of coaxing could convince Zoe to taste one of Georgia's sweet rolls, always saying, "Thanks, but no thanks. Too much sugar."

Georgia suspected that Zoe came in most mornings just to make sure Trish didn't dissuade her from working those few hours at the Moon Tide in the afternoons. Georgia never hid her feelings about how she loved the café kitchen best, but she continued working for Zoe out of loyalty, she supposed. After all, Zoe was the one who had taken a chance and hired her without even knowing her. Georgia had since then proved herself, organizing menus at the café and putting together recipes that could be refrigerated until the next day before hurrying next door to the Moon Tide. In the evenings, Georgia returned to her cozy upstairs apartment and dropped contentedly into bed. She had never slept better in her life.

It was heavenly to live over the warm kitchen of the café with its gleaming pots and pans, clean towels and aprons neatly folded in the bin, all ready for the morning hustle and bustle of getting the dough working for the rolls and bread. Her apartment, with its front room view of downtown Sedona and a backdrop of red rock and sky, was a retreat from the outside world.

When Georgia had first told Susan about her two part-time jobs, her daughter had blurted out, "A cook in some tacky café and selling goofy crystals to tourists? Have you lost your mind?"

Georgia had merely rolled her eyes to the pressed tin ceiling of her new apartment, saying, "You have no right to judge me, Susan." Then, as if to reinforce her newfound sense of strength, Georgia had glanced down at her feet and wriggled her toes, admiring her toe ring against the pink nail polish she had bought from the drug store. Yep, she had definitely come too far to give up and go back now.

"I put flowers on Dad's grave yesterday," Susan had said during another grilling phone call. "I don't care what he did—he's still my father." Susan's words had come out harsh and defensive. Guilt oozed over the telephone line, pouring into Georgia's ear like heavy cream. "Carnations," Susan added with an air of smugness. "Dad's favorite."

"How thoughtful, dear." Georgia had responded, struggling to keep her voice calm. She hadn't wanted to talk about Ed. There had been several days at a time now when she never thought about Ed at all—a kind of short vacation from her grief and anger.

"Thoughtful?"

"The flowers, Susan," Georgia had snapped back. "Your father would've appreciated the gesture." If she thought anymore about Ed, she would have to think about the house from which she had fled, like, an eternity ago—the empty house with no junk drawers, a bedroom closet lined with shoes according to season and hangers filled with dresses, skirts and blouses. The upper closet shelves piled with winter sweaters stored in the plastic zipper bags she had purchased on sale in January, buy one—get one free. Once more, Susan had hung up in a huff.

Georgia hated these exasperating conversations with her daughter, phone calls that made her think about her pantry cupboard filled with cans of chicken noodle soup, spaghetti sauce, bags of brown sugar and chocolate chips. In the refrigerator a carton of sour cream and cottage cheese, the expiration dates ticking away like fungal time bombs, although, most likely, Susan had already rid the refrigerator of perishables many weeks ago.

Georgia yawned, sliding the red shawl from around her shoulders, knowing she had to get some sleep before the alarm went off at five. She slipped back into her nightgown. No more stupid dreams about jeweled snakes crawling around her feet. Blowing out the vanilla scented candle, she crawled under the warm quilt and plumped the pillows, tucking one between her legs to relieve the emptiness that stays for a lifetime after carrying a child in your belly.

Lifting arms over her head, she gripped two of the brass bed rails, wondering how many women had given birth or even died in this old bed. Georgia had found the bed shoved behind a pile of lumber in the barn. No telling how many years it had been hidden away there.

Trish had helped Georgia dust off the cobwebs, and with a little soap, water and polish, the brass shone with new life. After moving the frame upstairs, Georgia drove to Flagstaff and bought a new mattress, sheets and a down comforter. Inside a quaint antique shop at the edge of town, she had found a handmade wedding ring quilt and pillowcases with crocheted edges. How glorious it had felt to spend an entire afternoon buying hundreds of dollars worth of bedding just to make sleep more pleasant.

Georgia debated whether or not she should buy the brass bed from Trish and keep it for the rest of her life. Then, the thought came to her that she might never make love again, that no one might ever hold her again, and this beautiful, soft bed was made for lovemaking. What a sad conclusion to her life that would be, to die one day in this bed without ever having been loved again.

The full moon shimmered outside her window; a small breeze tugged at the lace curtains. This was her third full moon since coming to Sedona, and those three moons over Sedona had breathed new life into an otherwise empty soul. She was a new being, but aware that within, she still carried the old regrets and yearnings from her past. How was that possible to have such passion for the present moment and yet grieve so earnestly for the past? If she were young again, she would give birth to her babies and know how to be a better mother to them. And Ed. What about Ed? If she were young again she might know how to be a better wife to him. But how foolish was that, wishing for a second chance to make Ed comfortable in a marriage that most likely would never have happened if she hadn't gotten pregnant in the first place? *Foolish indeed.* Georgia pressed the pillow tight between her knees and sighed into the moonlit darkness. Most of all, and most importantly, she wished she had learned to love herself better.

# CHAPTER SEVEN

Georgia lifted the last of four lemon meringue pies from the oven, the tangy, sweet aroma wafting through the café kitchen and into the dining room. The pie recipe had come from Georgia's mother—but not so willingly. When her mother died fifteen years ago, Georgia found the recipe tucked inside a dresser drawer, hidden beneath a pair of black dress gloves and a younger photograph of her father. For years, Georgia had begged for the family pie recipe. "There is no recipe," her mother always replied, tapping the side of her head. "It's all up here." Exasperated, Georgia often pleaded, "Mom, write it down?" And her mother always promised she would—*someday.*

Finding the recipe in the drawer after her mother's death, Georgia realized it had been there all along, that her mother had simply chosen not to give it to her, most likely because she had never forgiven Georgia for getting pregnant in high school and forfeiting the scholarship to the university.

Pure spite motivated Georgia to run off thirty copies of the recipe, tacking every one to the community bulletin board at the library. Two ladies Georgia recognized from her mother's church, noticed the new posting right away and cried out in unison, "Good heavens, that's Evelyn's lemon pie recipe." They both snatched up several copies, one of them saying excitedly, "I knew it. Evelyn used rum in that recipe." She told all this to Trish while working in the kitchen, wishing she could have the same easy conversation with her own daughter. Susan would only tell her to get over it, that Grandma Evelyn was a mean, vindictive woman who had sucked the life out of anyone who loved her.

Period.

No discussion.

Four magnificent pies cooled on the granite counter of the café, lovely peaks of toasted meringue begging to be cut into, eaten and licked from the lips. Georgia hadn't baked a lemon meringue pie in years, not since David's birthday five years ago when he and Lori had come home for a visit shortly after they were married.

Lori had no qualms about voicing her opinion of the Buckeye state—she didn't like it. Lori pronounced Ohio *O-HI-O* with disdain, as if it were a cornball punch line in some redneck joke. She thought of Columbus as being totally unsophisticated and as boring as white rice on a white plate. Two days into their visit, Georgia overheard Lori tell David that she was going back to Boston, with or without him, that she was sick to death of cornfields, silos and farm tractors.

Georgia tossed the potholders on the counter beside the pies and peeked at her watch to check the time. She had promised to drive Zoe to Scottsdale to visit her mother who resided in a nursing home there. Exactly why Zoe didn't own a car of her own was a mystery, but Georgia had never asked. She only knew that twice a month Zoe borrowed Trish's Jeep to make the drive to the ritzy suburb of Phoenix. Today, however, Trish's car was still at the auto shop getting a brake job.

Georgia finished cutting and slicing vegetables for the lunch salads when Zoe breezed into the café kitchen, asking Georgia if she were sure she didn't mind driving her to Scottsdale. "No problem," Georgia said, sliding a mug of green tea in front of her. Zoe wore an exquisite cream linen suit and white silk blouse. Around her throat a rope of pearls glistened against her dark skin like tiny bits of moonlight. With her long hair drawn back from her face, the effect was dramatic, emphasizing high cheekbones and full lips. Zoe was absolutely stunning.

"I don't want to be any trouble," Zoe insisted. "I'll drive your car, if Trish needs you here at the cafe. I have plenty of insurance, just no car." Zoe opened her handbag and sifted through the contents until finding a lace handkerchief to blot at the tiny beads of perspiration on her nose.

Georgia wrung out the dishcloth and gave it a toss over the drying rack. "I've already checked with Trish. No trouble at all. I want to go into Scottsdale and do some shopping." Georgia sighed as she tugged on the bow at the back of her apron. "It's David's birthday today."

"You don't say," Trish said, as she passed through the kitchen on her way to refill the coffeepot. "How old?" Georgia slapped at a smudge of flour on the front of her red cook's apron in an effort to hide the tears welling up behind her eyes. Thinking about David made her as close to homesick as she had ever felt since arriving in Sedona three months ago. Of course, that didn't really make any sense, because David, for the past five years, had lived in Boston. Georgia rarely saw her son more than twice a year, anyway.

"He's thirty-four." Georgia shook her head and laughed. "Can you believe that?" Her mind wandered off to the last conversation she'd had with David about his separation from Lori and their disagreement about having children. Not only did Lori not like children, she didn't seem to care for anything David cared about. From the very beginning of their relationship, Georgia had felt that Lori wasn't a good match for her son, but, of course, had kept that to herself, hoping, for the sake of her son's happiness, that she was wrong.

Zoe pushed back her cup of tea. "There's a mall not far from the nursing home. Of course, you won't find anything better than what you'll find right here in Sedona."

Georgia laughed. "Spoken like a true Sedona business woman."

"I usually visit with Mother for a few hours," Zoe said. "I hope you won't get too bored wandering around Scottsdale." Zoe took her cup to the sink. "Mother expects me at noon. The woman has Alzheimer's, but she still manages to know when I'm five minutes late."

"Oh, that's sad," Georgia said. "About her having Alzheimer's, I mean." Georgia checked the small bathroom off the kitchen to make sure it had plenty of paper towels and toilet paper.

Zoe waved a newly manicured hand in Georgia's direction, minus her usual collection of silver rings and bracelets. "Yes, it's sad, but she still has her moments." Zoe played with the small pearl ring on her left hand. "Mostly, she's quiet and agreeable."

"Are you feeling all right?" Trish asked Georgia. "You don't look so good this morning. Going with Zoe today will cheer you up. Her mother's quite the character."

"Shhh," Zoe held a finger to her lips. "Don't scare off my ride."

Trish ignored Zoe. "And don't worry about the café. I've got plenty of help around here today."

Georgia gave Trish a quick nod as she sorted through the last of the clean silverware from the wash room, dropping spoons, forks and knives into separate holders. "I'm looking forward to seeing Scottsdale." She tossed Trish a smile, thinking how pretty she looked in a simple denim skirt and white T-shirt. Dark hair braided and pulled back from her face, she nearly glowed with perpetual happiness. Georgia couldn't help but wish her son had married someone more like Trish, as beautiful on the inside as she was on the outside. So unlike Lori, who possessed a freeze-dried smile and haughty sophistication that warned: Look all you want but don't touch. Now, that woman was making her son hurt like he had never hurt before.

Maybe after they returned from Scottsdale later in the afternoon, she would call David and wish him a happy birthday, tell him about the lemon meringue pies she'd baked that morning, all because she'd been thinking about him. And, mostly, let him know how much she loved and missed him.

Trish pulled out a stool from the worktable and patted the cushion, saying to Georgia, "Sit down. You make me dizzy with all the work you do. You don't have to leave right this minute."

Georgia poured a cup of coffee and sat down at the table,

thinking about last minute details to be done before she left, such as Trish retrieving the pans of meatloaf from refrigerator to oven in time to make the daily special menu. She pulled a writing tablet from the center of the table and started making a list for Trish.

"You never talk much about your family," Trish said. "I make it a policy not to butt into a person's personal life, but you and I have become pretty good friends. So it's okay. Friends can do that, right?"

What Trish said was true; they had become good friends, and a generation gap or two didn't make much of a difference. She finished up the list, ripped off the page and gave it to Trish. "How old are you, Trish? The truth." For the last few months, whenever Georgia asked Trish her age, she got answers anywhere from twenty-one to thirty-five. Trish could easily pass for any of these and relished teasing Georgia about what her age really was, as well as any other information about her personal life.

Trish's mouth twisted into a lopsided grin. "Hey, I thought I was asking all the questions here." She laughed and added a shrug. "Thirty-one, next month."

"A mere youngster," Georgia teased, suspecting that this time, Trish had told the truth. Although she loved Trish's light-hearted nature, she knew the girl kept more than a few secrets tucked like pieces of stolen candy beneath her otherwise cool exterior. Trish only gave out as much information as she wanted others to believe.

"Why don't you call David this evening?" Trish suggested, sliding clean plates onto the shelf above the worktable. "Wish him a happy birthday."

Georgia's vision blurred with tears. She grabbed a tissue from the box on the ledge beside the telephone and blew her nose. "I might do that."

Swallowing the last of her tea, Zoe got up. "Trish is right, you know. Call your son tonight. Tell him that you love him and say happy birthday." Zoe wrapped Georgia in a warm hug. "Trish isn't the only friend you have here in Sedona. I'm attached to you, too."

Zoe's gesture of friendship caught Georgia off-guard. She sniffled, "I often wonder what I would've done if I hadn't met the two of you my first day in Sedona." She held the used tissues under her nose and sniffed.

Gently taking hold of Georgia's shoulder, Trish turned her toward the granite counter. "Look at those magnificent pies you baked this morning. The whole town is lucky you landed here."

Zoe quipped, "Before you came to Sedona, Trish couldn't melt ice without creating an environmental catastrophe."

Trish huffed and rolled her eyes to the ceiling. "We all can't be as perfect as you." Then, she turned to Georgia, saying, "You're just jealous because Georgia loves me best."

Never in her life had Georgia felt so loved and accepted, having these two friends practically fighting over her affection. "I love both of you."

Trish's expression turned reflective. She bit into her lower lip. "Georgia, maybe your mother didn't really mean any harm holding back that pie recipe for, like, years and years. Maybe she was, you know, scared. Everyone holds back little things in relationships, because they're afraid if they give everything away, they won't be needed anymore."

"Oh?" Georgia said, eyebrows raised and marveling at Trish's insight. "Well, I never thought about it that way." Then, it occurred to Georgia that her mother had left the recipe in a place where it would easily be found. What Trish said made perfect sense, that her mother hadn't meant to be spiteful, but only wanted to be needed. Don't we all?

Zoe patted Georgia's back, "Speaking of mothers, it's time we headed for Phoenix. And, if what Trish said is true, I'm wondering what delicious secret my mother is holding back from me. Definitely not a pie recipe," she said with a sarcastic smile. "You see, Georgia, my mother's fixation leans more toward collecting rocks—the kind measured in a large number of carats."

# CHAPTER EIGHT

The Heavenly Mesa Nursing Home in Scottsdale appeared to be more on the level of a first-class resort rather than the last-resort for the elderly and infirm. Georgia easily surmised by the ritzy entrance that any resident of this place had to have lots of deep, plush pockets.

Georgia drove the car up a palm-lined drive that circled beneath a wide portico. If a uniformed bellhop pulling a brass luggage rack suddenly dashed out from behind the automatic glass doors, Georgia would not have been the least bit surprised.

She turned to Zoe, awestruck. "This is a nursing home? Unbelievable." Georgia whistled, staring in disbelief at the gorgeous Santa Fe structure, complete with massive carved wood doors that opened into a lush green courtyard with a natural rock fountain.

Zoe gathered her red leather clutch and a small bouquet of daisies purchased from a nearby florist. "I know, it's a bit quaint," Zoe joked, laughing as she opened the car door. She turned to Georgia. "Two hours. If I'm not waiting outside, come to Room 135. South wing." She then got out, walked through the courtyard and disappeared through the soft swoosh of the automatic doors.

Two hours and four shopping bags later, Georgia returned to the deserted entrance of the Heavenly Mesa. She had enjoyed a fine afternoon alone, reminiscent of the three days spent traveling to Sedona. Although the upscale shops were a bit pricey, she'd managed to find a few bargains with enough change left over to buy a vanilla latte in a coffee shop, where she sat and watched the people pass by the front window.

No sign of Zoe outside the main entrance, Georgia smiled, pleased for the opportunity to satisfy her curiosity as to the interior of this palace. Georgia's own mother had spent the last few years of her life in a nice nursing home but nothing as opulent as this. After parking in the visitor's lot, she checked her lipstick in the rear-view mirror before getting out and hurrying to the front entrance.

The reception area was pure southwestern with its terra cotta floors, Navajo rugs and adobe fireplace, reaffirming to visitors that they were definitely not leaving their parents or grandparents in a place where they had to feel the least bit guilty. Here, assisted-living residences were more cause for envy than guilt. Who wouldn't want to be pampered twenty-four hours, seven days a week for the rest of their life?

The far end of the lobby opened into a dining room laid out with white tablecloths, china and gleaming silverware. Soft classical music floated in the air, and Georgia could easily believe a maitre d' might suddenly appear to ask if she had decided to stay for dinner?

Georgia walked to the front desk and asked the receptionist, "I need directions to the south wing?"

From out of nowhere, a security guard suddenly appeared at her elbow. "Who are you visiting, Ma'am?"

Georgia stammered, trying to think of something to say. Zoe had never mentioned her mother's name. "Well, actually, she's my friend's mother. I'm kind of embarrassed because I don't know her name, but she told me to go to room 135, if she wasn't waiting out front."

"Are you Ms. Brown?" The man's blue eyes rested steadily on hers.

Georgia nodded. "I am."

"We've been expecting you. Please follow me." He exchanged an amused smile with the receptionist before turning his attention back to Georgia, as if they had shared some private joke. "This way, please."

Georgia followed him down a wide, plush carpeted corridor to a room flanked by two potted palms. The guard tapped on the door, then told her to go on inside. Georgia tentatively poked her head around the edge of the door and found Zoe sitting in a wing chair beside a massive four-poster bed. The only light in the room came from a single lamp beside the bed, heavy draperies covering the windows and blocking out any natural light. The air in the room reeked of a deadly sweetness, like that of a funeral parlor, the kind of air you'd rather not breathe in.

"Zoe?" Georgia whispered as she softly shut the door behind her. Her eyes darted to the walls, where every square inch seemed to be covered with dozens of framed photographs of people who looked eerily three-dimensional in the dark shadows of the room. Her eyes moved back to the bed and now took in the slight form of a woman buried beneath a white satin comforter.

Georgia's eyes widened with shock as she moved closer, seeing the woman's small head tucked into a pillow, her skeletal face covered in a thick layer of theatrical makeup, complete with two bright pink circles on her cheekbones. Lipstick, red as blood, ran amok across her jaw and cheeks, much like a child's aimless scribbling on a cracked wall.

The old woman suddenly opened her eyes and narrowed them at Georgia. "Are you the angel of death?"

Georgia's eyes shifted again to the walls and the photographs covering them, now identifying the people as being famous movie stars—some long dead—but all taken with a much younger version of the woman now lying in the bed. "My God, its—"

"Gloria Atwater," Zoe finished with a weak smile. "She's my mother."

"For heaven's sake," Georgia gasped. "Why didn't you tell me?"

"Are you the angel?" the woman said, clearly aggravated. She groped at the edges of satin comforter, tugging and pulling at it.

"No, Ma'am. I'm just a regular person."

Zoe patted the cushion of the chair beside her. "Come and sit. Mama's having a good day. Do you mind if we stay a while longer?"

Georgia shook her head, unable to pull her eyes away from the bed. "I don't believe it. Gloria Atwater."

"Just a person," Gloria grumbled, shifting her eyes to Zoe. "Who is she? Why is she in my room?" The woman's body stirred beneath the comforter, clearly agitated.

"Mama, this is my friend, Georgia. Remember, I told you about her. She works with Trish at the café."

Gloria wrinkled up her nose as if she had just smelled something dead. "Georgia? What kind of a name is that?" A withered hand came out from under the bedding. A bony finger pointed at Georgia. "I know you. You can't fool me. You're here to take my last breath." Gloria raised her head from the pillow as if ready for a good fight. "These damn people around here think I'm nuts. Well, I'm not. I know what day it is. It's Sunday, right? And the president is Ike." She pulled indignantly at the end of her chin. "I'm having dinner at the White House on Thursday. Florry's handling all the arrangements." Her eyes sparked with defiance, as she sank back into the stack of pillows supporting her head.

Even with the heavy makeup, Georgia still recognized Gloria's classic bone structure and piercing blue eyes. "Miss Atwater, I'm so honored to meet you. When I was a little girl, I used to walk around in my mother's high-heeled shoes, pretending I was you."

Gloria slipped a hand out from under the covers and snapped her fingers at Zoe. "You there, do we have a signed photograph for this lovely girl? Go fetch Florry. She knows where I keep them." She then flailed her arms at Zoe. "Tell Florry the script from the studio is pure shit." Gloria pointed a bossy finger at Georgia. "Do you know Florry?"

"Florry was my mother's assistant," Zoe explained. "The best friend she ever had. She died five years ago."

"How sad," Georgia said, clearly seeing the pain behind Zoe's eyes and watching as she quickly looked away, rubbing at her eyes with the back of her hand.

Gloria struggled to sit up, her fingers reaching for a robe at the foot of the bed. With one gnarled hand, she motioned for Georgia to come closer. The woman's eyes sparked with new energy. "I have a beautiful vagina."

Georgia's eyes darted to Zoe.

Zoe's lips tightened, struggling not to laugh. "Oh, Mama. You're confused."

"It's pink," Gloria insisted, clutching at the edges of the robe.

"It's a *velour* bathrobe, Mama, not a vagina. Your *velour* bathrobe is pink," she gently corrected.

Gloria's mouth puckered into a childish pout. She pressed the pink bathrobe into her sunken chest and sighed. "You're right. I know you're right." She turned away, sad-faced, a tear trickling down one cheek. "I'm getting worse, yes?"

"Yes." Zoe took a wipe from the bedside table and dabbed at her mother's cheek, working it along the crescent-shaped smear of lipstick on her chin. "Mama, why don't you let the attendant help you apply your makeup?"

"They empty bedpans," Gloria hissed, her expression sour. She slapped Zoe's hand away. "Do you think I want them applying my makeup? For God's sake, don't you know who I am?"

Georgia handed her another wipe, watching as Zoe removed the eye shadow from Gloria's eyelids and the black line from an eyebrow pencil that wandered across her mother's forehead like a crooked country road.

A blue-veined hand reached out and caught hold of Zoe's wrist. "Where's Florry?"

"Florry's dead, Mama."

"Dead?" Gloria eyes widened. "When?"

"Five years ago. We took her home to New Orleans. You gave her a funeral wake that threatened to raise the dead."

"Oh my." Gloria settled into the pillows. "I think I do, but things get so jumbled up inside my head." She glanced around the room like a cat seeing ghosts in every corner, eyes darting from one photograph to the other.

Georgia followed Gloria's eyes to the photographs, recognizing in one her co-star who danced cheek to cheek with Gloria Atwater in an old movie, both smiling into the camera, not a clue that one day they'd wake up and find themselves old.

Zoe threw the used wipes into the trash container. She opened Gloria's makeup case and picked out a soft, beige face powder.

"How about we touch you up a bit?" Zoe winked at Georgia. "You never know who might drop by."

"I miss Florry," Gloria said, raising her chin and closing her eyes.

"I'm sure you do." Zoe opened the compact and blew loose powder off the mirror. "She was your best friend and your assistant." Zoe patted fresh powder around Gloria's eyes, cheeks and jaw line, applying a small amount of blush, a thin line of eyebrow pencil, and, finally, a soft touch of lipstick.

Gloria pulled back a bit, saying, "She was colored, you know, but she was my best friend."

Zoe finished packing away the cosmetics, her jaw muscles tight, as if someone had slapped her. She gave Georgia a faint smile. "The last time I visited, she thought I was Florry." She turned back to her mother. "Florry never minded you being white," she joked with her mother. "She took good care of you. You took good care of her."

"Florry was my best friend," Gloria said, fussing with the glittery buttons running down the front of her nightgown.

Zoe poured a glass of water for her mother. "Here, the nurses left these pills for you." Zoe slid the bedside table over to her mother with the pills laid out on top.

One by one, Gloria pinched a pill and put it into her mouth, followed by a tiny sip of water. "The other one," she said between gulps, "the green quilted satin robe you gave me for Christmas last year." She swallowed the last pill. "I wear that one, too."

A tissue in hand, Georgia dabbed at a dribble of water on Gloria's chin. "You were always a classy dresser, Miss Atwater."

Gloria's eyes softened. "Thank you, Florry."

Georgia, like most of middle-aged America, knew Gloria's life story almost as well as their own. Once, a great star, her photograph regularly featured on popular magazine covers, articles praising her adoption of an orphan from Jamaica, and how she was accepting more mature characters roles on television, just so she would have more quality time in which to raise her daughter.

A mischievous grin softened Gloria's face. She handed the glass to Zoe. "Not at the same time, right?"

"What?" Zoe asked, clearly lost in her own thoughts.

"I'm talking about the bathrobes. I can't wear them at the same time. I know that." She smiled and cocked her head in a teasing pose, revealing a glimpse of the young and beautiful Gloria Atwater.

"Georgia's right, Mama. You were always a class act." Zoe settled a hand on her mother's forehead, her eyes filled with tears. A deep quiet filled the room. Gloria closed her eyes as if Zoe's gentle touch had brought relief to her restless body.

When Georgia started to move the bedside table away from the bed, Gloria's eyes suddenly popped open. Her hand slipped out from under the comforter and caught hold of Georgia's wrist. The old woman's grip was surprisingly strong.

"Thank you, Florry."

"You're welcome, Miss Atwater." Georgia said, turning to Zoe, who gave her an appreciative smile.

Gloria then violently shook her head as if trying to clear her senses. "I'm getting worse." She released her death grip on

Georgia's wrist and allowed Zoe to tuck the comforter snug around her frail body. Zoe then lightly kissed her cheek.

Georgia recognized the fear in Gloria's eyes. After watching her own mother's descent into the horrible illness, she knew it wouldn't be long before Gloria would deny knowing everyone she knew and loved, right down to her own reflection in the mirror.

Gloria rolled her head back and forth on the pillow, groaning softly. "Zoe, you've been a good daughter. I'm sorry." Tears welled up in the old woman's eyes.

Leaning close to her mother's face, Zoe gently untwisted a tangled strap of her mother's nightgown. Her daughter's touch seemed to quiet Gloria. Remembering a nice settee in the hallway, Georgia collected her purse and whispered, "I'll just wait outside."

At the sound of Georgia's voice, the intimate mother-daughter moment was over. Gloria pulled her head back in the pillow and narrowed her eyes at Zoe. "Who are you?"

* * *

Passing through the lobby on their way out, Georgia wanted badly to reach out and give Zoe a hug, but knew her friend was in no mood for sappy sentiment. Instead, Georgia said, "I'm so sorry."

Zoe shrugged. "Don't be. She's probably already forgotten us being there."

"Sad." Georgia adjusted her purse under her arm. "You could've warned me who your mother was before I came into the room."

Zoe sighed, sounding exhausted. "Sorry. Sometimes it's easier not telling anyone."

"How long has she been ill?"

They were inside the car now, fastening seatbelts. Zoe shrugged. "Four years now. In the beginning it was only a little memory loss. She didn't think it was serious, you know, getting older and all that. But then it got so she'd drive somewhere and couldn't remember where she was going or how to get home."

"How terrible."

"For a year or two she managed to keep up appearances without too much trouble. She did this even after going to the doctor and getting the diagnosis. Eventually, the forgetfulness got so bad she couldn't leave the house at all. Her agent finally announced her retirement from public life and her move to Arizona. She bought a house in Phoenix. For a while that worked out fine, but then it got so I couldn't leave her alone because she insisted on smoking cigarettes and leaving them lit all over the house. I hired nurses, but they all quit because she treated them like crap. Eventually, she came here, to Heavenly Mesa. Her decision. Not mine." Zoe laughed. "The staff adores her, letting her tap a hundred nail holes in the walls to hang those blasted movie photographs."

"I used to watch your mother on the movie channel."

"Uh huh. You and a million other people on the planet." Zoe let out long-winded sigh and readjusted the knot in her silk scarf, a clear signal she was done with the conversation.

Georgia turned the car onto Ventura Boulevard to catch I-17 to Sedona. Zoe looked exhausted, digging around in her purse and finally pulling out an aspirin bottle. She undid the cap and popped two into her mouth, followed by a quick sip of water from the bottle tucked between the seats. "Thank you for coming with me today. I didn't mean to sound ungrateful, you know, being short with you. I know you're curious about my mother. Everyone is. Don't take it personally. There are certain issues I can't talk about with anyone, not even you, Georgia."

Georgia blended into the freeway traffic. "You don't have to explain. I understand."

"You've been a godsend, Georgia. You and Trish are the best friends I've ever had in this world." These last words came out choked. She turned her head to look out the passenger side window.

Georgia reached over and patted Zoe's hand. "You miss your mother, I mean the way she used to be."

Zoe turned and stared at her for a long moment. Then, without warning, Zoe threw back her head and let out a big whoop of laughter. "Miss her? Oh, God, Georgia, you are just too sweet for this mean ol' world."

# CHAPTER NINE

They were within twenty miles of Sedona when it began to rain. The wipers groaned in an effort to keep up with the deluge going on outside the car. Inside, Georgia could barely make out the lines on the road through the windshield.

"I'm hungry," Zoe said from out of the blue. These were her first spoken words since leaving the nursing home in Scottsdale. Georgia's forehead creased with confusion. If Zoe had said she wanted to spend the afternoon skiing down Mount Everest, yes, Georgia could almost believe that more than her insisting they stop in the middle of nowhere and eat. No way.

"Hungry?" she repeated with disbelief. Zoe was never hungry. Not like three-meals-a-day hungry. She rarely ate more than a handful of raw vegetables at one sitting or maybe a grainy slice of bread, the kind that sprinkles healthy seeds everywhere after biting into it.

"There's a truck stop not far from here." Zoe cracked the window and leaned her head into the rain as if she might help Georgia see the road better. Instead of helping, the damp air steamed up the windshield, making it even more difficult to stay on the road.

"Close the window."

Zoe gave her a hurt look. "Don't be angry, Georgia. By the time we're done eating, the storm will be over."

"Zoe, we're almost home. It's bound to let up soon. I'll just drive slowly. When we get back, I'll fix you something at the café. Besides, I promised Trish and Mary Jo I'd help with the dinner shift."

"I'd rather eat now," Zoe insisted.

After a full day of driving, shopping, and then meeting a real movie star face-to-face who turned out to be Zoe's mother, Georgia had little strength left to argue. Zoe pointed out where to pull off the road. The wipers flapped uselessly back and forth as she turned into a sandy parking lot. Only then was Georgia able to make out what looked like a barn with a rickety front porch. The faded sign under the eaves read, Frontier Cafe.

She pulled the car close to the porch steps, and then shut off the engine. "You want to eat *here*?" Georgia's eyes swept over the weathered tin-roofed structure that appeared abandoned except for a dab of buttery light oozing from the two front windows.

"Sure. And don't be so judgmental." She playfully slapped Georgia's hand.

Georgia shrugged, giving up. "Well, let's be quick about it. I promised Trish I'd close up the café tonight."

***

Once settled in one of the six worn leather booths with scarred tabletops, Zoe ordered a cheeseburger deluxe, fries and diet soft drink from a waitress wearing tight jeans and a T-shirt plastered with about every item from the menu. Hearing Zoe's order, Georgia couldn't believe her ears. Zoe never ate meat. *Never.*

Georgia ordered coffee, determined to keep her mouth shut, while Zoe ate her meal. Hopefully, the storm would pass quickly, and she could take Zoe home to pout about her mother all by herself.

"Pass the ketchup," Zoe said not all too kindly, after the waitress delivered the cheeseburger platter. Thunder rattled the fragile walls of the Frontier Café. It sounded and felt as if the entire building just might collapse around their ears. The lights flickered several times, but somehow the electric managed to stay on in spite of the ruckus going on outside.

Georgia raised a suspicious eyebrow as she pulled the ketchup from the holder and slid it across the table. Whatever Zoe was trying to prove by eating a plateful of food that could clog the arteries of an elephant, Georgia decided she'd let it pass until tomorrow after she'd gotten a good night's sleep.

When they'd left the nursing home, Zoe had unpinned her hair, letting it fall around her shoulders in a dark fluff of wild curls. Since then, the bow of her silk blouse had also come undone, the ties now dangling dangerously close to the greasy plate of food. Georgia opened her mouth to warn her, but then thought again. It was very much apparent that Zoe could've cared less about the blouse.

Zoe made a puddle of ketchup beside the fries. Then, with a flick of her fingers, she tossed the ties of the blouse over each shoulder, out of harm's way. "You know, Georgia, you're driving me nuts."

Georgia shrugged and took a cautious sip of coffee that had all the appearance and tasted as if it had spent the day simmering on the burner. "You're the one who wanted to stop and eat, not me. I'm not hungry."

"Oh, pa-lease," Zoe said around a mouthful of ketchup-soaked fries. "Look outside. It's storming. You can't drive if you can't see the road. Besides, I couldn't stand you giving me the silent treatment."

Georgia's head jerked up. "Me?"

"You haven't said a word since we left Scottsdale. You don't fool me. I know what you're thinking. You think I'm a cold-hearted bitch for leaving my mother in a nursing home three hours away."

"That's not true. And I'm not Trish, so don't think you'll going to start an argument with me just so you can let off steam."

Irritated, she poured a generous dab of cream into her coffee to kill the strong taste. "You're being paranoid. I'm the last person to judge anyone for what they've done or haven't done. I had a terrible relationship with my own mother."

Zoe glanced up from her plate. "You did?"

"Sure. My mother and I never got along. What a martyr she was. I'm surprised the Pope hasn't canonized her."

Zoe snickered. "Why, Georgia, you really do have a sense of humor, don't you?"

"Remember me telling you about the pie recipe this morning?" Georgia worried a pack of sugar between her fingers. "And like your mother, my mother had Alzheimer's. So, I know what you're going through. Sometimes, it comes down to survival. You've got to learn to let go of all the guilt and pain and find a new path for yourself."

The rain clattered noisily against the tin roof of the diner. A flash of lightning supercharged the parking lot outside the window, followed by a jarring crack of thunder. It didn't matter. They were safe inside the café. She hated to admit it, but Zoe had been right, insisting they stop and wait until the storm passed. Georgia recalled how lovingly Zoe had straightened the strap of her mother's nightgown. Then, it suddenly occurred to Georgia that Zoe had very badly wanted something from her mother, but most certainly whatever Zoe had wanted, she wasn't able to ask for, herself. Assuredly, Zoe's sullen mood was most likely connected to some horrible disappointment rooted deep inside an unhappy childhood. At this point, Georgia only wanted to go home and recoup from the day's events. Watching Zoe's anger rise like a volcano spewing hot lava was not pleasant, and she wished the rain would finally stop so they could get out of this deplorable café with the polyester curtains and scuffed floors that looked as if they hadn't seen a mop in several weeks.

Zoe piled a side of mayonnaise on top the burger. She rearranged the lettuce, tomato and onion and finished it off with two slices of pickle to make the burger super-deluxe. "Gloria Atwater was not, I repeat, NOT a good mother." She threw the red tasseled toothpick to the side of the plate and sawed through the towering cheeseburger with a dull table knife.

"Zoe, if talking about your mother upsets you, we can move on to something else, okay?"

"Maybe I don't want to talk about something else."

"Do you want me to get angry at you, is that what you want? Go ahead, Zoe, scream your head off, if that would make you feel better."

Zoe slammed the fork to the table. "God, I don't know what I want. It was a hell of a lot easier dealing with Mama when she wasn't sick. I could just hate her then, plain and simple." She turned her attention back to her plate. "I need more ketchup."

Georgia tapped the side of the ketchup bottle already under Zoe's nose, shifting one hip off an exposed spring in the lumpy booth cushion. She watched Zoe squirt more ketchup on the plate, thinking how freakishly odd to be sitting in this five-star dump of a truck stop, watching Zoe manhandle a cheeseburger and dripping ketchup from one end of the table to the other.

"You don't hate your mother, Zoe. You're only angry at what the disease is doing to her." Georgia caught a glimpse of the waitress watching them from behind the lemonade dispenser, no doubt trying to decide whether or not the two crazy women who had drifted in from the storm were merely crazy or outright dangerous.

Licking a dribble of mayonnaise from one finger, Zoe gave Georgia a devilish grin. "Oh, dear sweet Georgia, you have no idea what that woman was really like."

Georgia again shifted her weight in the seat, her left buttock detecting yet another exposed spring. "Zoe, you're upset. Let's talk about this tomorrow when you're in a better mood."

Zoe wiped at her mouth with a paper napkin, shaking her head as if Georgia just wasn't getting the point. "I hardly knew Mama. To her, I was nothing more than a publicity prop."

"I thought you were a vegetarian?" Georgia joked, hoping a little humor might lighten Zoe's dark mood.

Zoe picked up the cheeseburger and took a hearty bite. "I am vegetarian." She chewed until her eyes watered, and then she gagged. Georgia scrambled to hold out a napkin for Zoe to spit the food into. One fat tear slid down Zoe's cheek, as she shoved the platter to the center of the table. "My God, I haven't eaten meat in two years." She crushed the napkin to her nose and blew hard. "I promise I'll calm down. Okay?"

"Okay." Georgia agreed. "If you do, I promise to listen."

Arms folded on the table, Zoe lowered her voice to a whisper. "On my thirteenth birthday *Life* magazine approached my mother about a second photo spread, a sort of follow-up to the one they did after she adopted me. By then, Mama's career had pretty much slid into the toilet, but she was still determined to play the twenty-something beauty queen. She only played those bit TV parts, because the movie offers stopped coming her way."

The waitress came over and cleared the table, keeping a wary eye on them. Georgia ordered hot tea for both of them, thinking hot water and a tea bag would be a safe bet in this place. Again, the lights flickered, and the rain continued to pound against the tin roof.

Zoe sniffed and pushed several curls away from her face. "My mother invited fifty kids to the party, all younger than me. I only knew one of them. She was the daughter of another movie star who I shall not name because I still can't stand her. The spoiled little bitch told me that her mother had given her a one-hundred-dollar bill for coming to my birthday party. To make the day even more hideous, Mama hired a small circus, complete with tent, clown and an elephant that had two bowel movements on her precious lawn." She had the party professionally catered, complete with a three-tiered pink cake. God, to this day, I can't tolerate anything pink."

The tea came. Zoe stopped talking long enough to tear open

the teabag and dip it into the silver pot of hot water. Georgia poured a packet of sugar into her tea, waiting.

Dark circles bruised the soft skin beneath Zoe's sad eyes. Georgia wondered if perhaps she should suggest they leave right now, before Zoe suffered a complete breakdown in this godforsaken place. As if reading Georgia's mind, Zoe shook her head that she wasn't going anywhere until she was finished with what she wanted to say.

"When the photographer came to our home, my mother kept pinching the underside of my arm, saying, 'Smile, baby. Smile for the camera.' In my head, I still see her in that red and white sundress she'd bought on Rodeo Drive. She'd dressed me in a blue satin dress borrowed from wardrobe at the studio. I was Shirley Temple, all pleats and frilly bows, a hemline up to my ass. I looked hideous." Zoe crumpled the napkin in her hand. "Mama was furious that my dress was too tight. Florry could barely get the back zipped up. What did Mama expect? I already had boobs and legs as long as a newborn colt's. Ridiculous."

Georgia stirred her tea, listening, recalling in great detail that particular issue of *Life*. She had placed the magazine on a coffee table she'd purchased on credit from a local department store, along with her other favorite monthly magazines.

At twenty-two, Georgia had already been married five years. At the time, Susan was only a toddler, grabbing at anything within reach, especially magazines. She took a keen liking to the woman in the red and white striped sundress on the cover, carrying it around the house until the front page pulled away from its binding. Presenting the wrinkled cover to her mother, Susan said, "Pretty cake." Susan then pointed to the little girl at the head of the table. "Me," she'd exclaimed in the broken vocabulary of a two-year-old. Georgia had laughed. "You want a birthday party?" Susan gleefully clapped her hands. "Birph-day." Georgia had laughed, throwing the ripped cover into the trash, but not without taking one last look at the picture of Gloria Atwater presiding over a long table of smiling children and handing out the first slice of cake to her daughter.

"I don't remember the cover photo as being anything horrible," Georgia said, truthfully.

Zoe laughed. "Right before that cover shot, I spilled red punch down the front of that wretched dress. On purpose, hoping she'd let me change into one of my own dresses. Mama threw a fit when she saw the stain, but she made me wear the dress, anyway. She jerked me down on the chair behind the cake so the stain wouldn't show in the photograph. But the studio made her pay for the dress, I think because she'd taken it from wardrobe without permission." Zoe picked up a leftover fry and dipped it into the ketchup. Instead of putting it in her mouth, she wrote in the Formica table top *Bad Girl*. "The birthday party publicity backfired. The studio dropped her for good. No more leading lady, just bit parts, secondary characters." Zoe shrugged, meticulously folding her napkin and then crushing it inside her fist. "No one wanted her."

Georgia changed position in the booth, stretching her numb legs. The waitress asked if they wanted anything else. No, they were ready for the bill. Georgia stacked the dirty dishes and slid everything to the edge of the table. She said to Zoe, "I don't know what so say."

Zoe lips trembled with emotion. "None of it matters anymore."

Georgia drained the last of her lukewarm tea, waiting for the bill. She glanced at the clock over the lunch counter, knowing she'd never make it back to Sedona in time to help Mary Jo and Trish. She was beyond trying to rush Zoe out of the Frontier Café, even if the rain suddenly stopped. "What happened after the party?" Georgia asked.

"The next morning, Florry told me Mama got sick and had to go to a special place to get well again. She'd given Florry permission to take me to New Orleans to live with her brother and his wife."

"You must've been terribly lonely, being separated from

your mother and living in a strange city with a family you barely knew."

Zoe shook her head. "Not so. Living in New Orleans was like coming home. Florry's brother, Gabe, played the horn, pure jazz soul. His wife, Mary, took me to watch him perform in clubs along Bourbon Street." Zoe sighed. "School was easier there, too. No one knew me. I liked being anonymous. Even after Mama got better, I asked to stay in New Orleans with Gabe and Mary. By then, I think Mama had finally given up trying to fit me into her life. She gave her consent. After graduation I went on to college and made New Orleans my permanent home. After graduation, I opened a bookstore and tearoom on Royal Street. By then, Mama kind of slipped into the background of my life. I barely knew her anymore."

"What happened to Florry?"

Zoe opened her handbag, pulling out a compact and lipstick. She didn't answer until she'd smoothed the deep plum shade over her lips. She closed the compact and dropped it back into her handbag. "After Mama's breakdown, Florry rented a house near the sanitarium in Boulder. She'd fly to New Orleans every couple of months and stay for a week, check on me, and then go back to be with Mama. I never understood the relationship between them. Florry waited on her hand and foot as if she were a baby. When Florry was diagnosed with colon cancer, Mama hired a nurse, paying for everything until the day she died. She had Florry's body flown to New Orleans where Mama gave her the biggest wake in the city's history." Zoe shook her head. "Turned out, Mama really did love her." Zoe shrugged. "At least she loved someone."

"Sad story," Georgia said.

"Yeah. Almost ironic. Not long after Florry died, Mama found out about her own illness. That's when she called and asked me to stay with her until the end." Zoe yawned. "Like any good daughter, I told her yes." She laughed. "We hardly knew each other."

"Do you love your mother?" Georgia asked.

"Of course I do." She sniffed. "I just don't like her much."

"Because...?"

Zoe fidgeted with the pearl ring on her finger. "Because I wanted her to love me, and she never could. Today, she almost said it, but didn't." Zoe's eyes filled with tears. "Why?"

"I don't know, Zoe. I suspect some people, for reasons they only know, have trouble expressing love. It doesn't mean they don't care, it only means they're sad and lonely on the inside."

Zoe quickly retied the bow on her silk blouse. Combing back her hair with her fingers, she secured the loose ends with a silver comb retrieved from her purse. She pointed outside. "The storm's passed. Enough of all your amateur psychology, okay? I'm sorry for crying on your shoulder."

"I didn't mind at all."

Zoe then got up, straightened her shoulders and walked out of the Frontier Café leaving Georgia behind to pay the bill. Georgia gave the waitress a twenty and told her to keep the change. For the first time since they'd come inside, the waitress actually smiled. "Gee, thanks."

Outside, Zoe stood on the porch, waiting. Without looking at Georgia, she said, "I'm sorry."

"For what? I'm your friend, Zoe. Friends listen to friends when they're hurting inside."

Zoe pulled sunglasses from her purse and slid them over her eyes. "I feel like an idiot for being so emotional."

Rain dripped from the edge of the roof and onto the ground. Georgia wanted to say something to make her feel better but knew there were times when silence was far more soothing than any amount of spoken words.

The last of the afternoon sun suddenly broke through the clouds. In the parking lot sat the Fleetwood, all shiny and clean after the storm.

# CHAPTER TEN

G eorgia stepped along the steep trail hugging Oak Creek, working her way back to her apartment above the cafe. After spending the day with Zoe, and then offering to close up the café for the night, Georgia was exhausted. She had gotten a late start on her evening walk and had ventured much farther than planned. Now she questioned her sanity for having chosen the slippery creek path instead of taking the sidewalks, illuminated by street lamps.

Arriving at the last bend in the creek, Georgia heaved a sigh of relief at the sight of the light from her porch. At least, she had had the good sense to turn it on before starting out on her walk.

Georgia took in a deep breath, enjoying the combined scent of foliage and damp earth along the creek. Content, she gazed up at the spots of lights coming from inside houses high above the creek and dark windows of the closed shops, thinking herself to be a very lucky woman, indeed.

She passed beneath the high balcony of the Moon Tide and heard the door open above her head. Thinking Zoe must have seen her coming along the path Georgia opened her mouth to call out, but froze in place when she heard a man's voice float down through the floorboards.

"Zoe, come out here," he said. "The fresh air will do you good."

Georgia halted mid-step, knowing if she so much as moved a muscle, the man—whoever he was—standing above her, would know someone or something was under the deck. Not wanting to go into some lame explanation, Georgia decided to stay-put, hoping the man would simply go back inside and give her time to hurry on to her apartment. No such luck. Zoe stepped out on the balcony, too.

Georgia clamped her jaw shut, trying to ignore the tiny spasm developing in her right knee. If she didn't find a way to sit down soon, she'd topple over into the creek bed.

Zoe's voice came down through the cracks in the wood floor. "I'll fix you a drink. Scotch?"

"Sounds good." The man sat down heavily in one of the two outdoor chairs above her head. Georgia had placed the chairs there herself not more than a week ago, thinking Zoe might enjoy coming out on the balcony in the evenings to relax with a glass of wine.

"Ice?"

"No ice," he said. "I need it warm and potent. It's been one of those days. How's your mother?"

"Losing it. Back in a minute."

Georgia swallowed hard, thankful for the large rock positioned right behind her. She eased her backside down on it and slowly stretched out her legs. No telling how long she would have to stay-put. She had waited too long. If they found her out now, she would never be able to give a plausible explanation as to how she had ended up under the balcony. Zoe's bare feet padded softly above Georgia's head. She then heard the dull clink of a heavy highball glass being set on the small table between the two chairs.

Zoe said, "Now relax and tell me what you're in a huff about."

The man said nothing. The weight shifted in a chair above Georgia's head. She didn't need eyes to tell her that the man had pulled Zoe into his lap and was kissing her. Zoe's soft moan brought a warm smile to Georgia's lips. Having spent the day with Zoe, she'd found out more about her in the last twelve hours than in the last three months. One thing for certain, the man sitting on the balcony with Zoe was definitely more than just a close friend.

Georgia rested her head in her hands, elbows on knees, taking in slow, deliberate breaths, and listening to the conversation filtering down from the floorboards of the balcony.

"Zoe, you are the most beautiful woman I've ever known."

"Don't start, Jake. You know that irritates me."

"What?" the man teased.

"Beautiful. A goddamn empty word, that's what it is."

"Zoe, you're the only woman I know who considers it an insult to be called beautiful."

Georgia held her breath as the conversation turned more personal. She considered covering her ears, but didn't, and her cheeks burned with embarrassment. For the umpteenth time, she wished they would go inside, and then she could go on to her apartment. Her legs were getting cramped from sitting in a crouched position for so long.

The boards trembled slightly when Zoe slipped from the man's lap and walked to the edge of the balcony and rested her elbows on the railing. Georgia could see her fingers dangling over the side. If Zoe were to lean out just a few more inches, Georgia would be within plain sight, sitting on the rock at the edge of the creek. Georgia squeezed her eyes shut and waited to be found out. When the automatic lights at the bottom of Georgia's steps snapped on, she nearly jumped out of her skin. Her hand flew to her mouth to muffle a small gasp. She thought for sure Zoe had heard her. When nothing happened, Georgia relaxed and allowed herself to breathe again. At this point, if she were found out, there would be no plausible explanation for hiding beneath the dark balcony, eavesdropping. Still standing at the railing, Zoe asked, "If I weren't beautiful, you wouldn't give me a second glance, would you? Stop grinning. I'm serious."

"Well... that depends."

"On what?"

"I'm a politician, Zoe. I always tell the truth." He laughed, a very genuine laugh, Georgia couldn't help but smile.

Zoe responded with a seductive chuckle. "Honest politician, huh? In that case, give me the truth, nothing less."

Georgia heard someone or something coming along the creek path. She looked up, and to her horror watched the neighbor's black lab sniffing his way along the stone bank. Georgia didn't move a muscle, hoping Petey didn't catch sight of her. As if hearing Georgia's thoughts, the dog raised his head and sniffed the air until he spotted her. Wagging his tail, he trotted along the creek toward her, one paw kicking up a small rock that rolled down the bank and splashed into the water.

Silence.

Above her, Zoe sang out, "Well, hello down there."

Georgia sucked in a breath, holding it tight inside her chest, realizing she'd been caught.

"What?" the man asked.

Georgia stiffened when he, too, got up from his chair and moved to the railing above Georgia's head. Georgia's eyes locked on the dog, not even daring to blink. The dog jerked his head upward, wagging his tail in greeting.

Zoe cooed, "No scraps, tonight, Petey. Go home now before you get into trouble."

The dog whimpered as if to say, "Ah shucks."

"Go," Zoe said more sternly.

Petey whined again, this time sounding like, "Yes, Ma'am." He then turned and trotted back in the direction of the art gallery where he lived with his owner. Georgia puckered her lips and let out a sigh of relief. Zoe was amazing with both dogs and people. Everyone wanted to please her. Everyone, that is, except her own mother.

The man above Georgia's head cleared his throat. "Don't you think it's a bit risky standing out here in the open with me? Your friend next door might see us."

"Georgia's not home."

"Are you quite sure?"

"Positive. She takes a walk every evening and always turns on the outside light before she leaves. If we see her come around the corner, we'll just sit here quietly in the dark until she goes inside."

"Unless..."

"You wouldn't dare make a sound. If you do, I'll never speak to you again."

"Liar."

"It's for your own good, Jake."

"Not true," he objected.

"Sweetie, I know what's best for you." Zoe's voice turned solicitous. "Let's go inside. I'll show you how to relax."

"Zoe, I want you to marry me. Now. I don't want to wait until after the election."

Georgia pressed her hands against her mouth to stifle the squeal that threatened to escape. *Marriage?*

Zoe's voice suddenly turned serious. "No, Jake. I'm not marrying anyone, especially you."

"Zoe, I know you love me."

"Yes, and that's exactly why I won't marry you."

The man's shoes shuffled against the floorboards. "That doesn't make good sense." His voice was gruff, exasperated, sounding as if the subject of marriage was nothing new between them.

"Jake, the press would eat you alive if they ever dug into my background. You know as well as I do that if you really want to win the senatorial race, you can't marry me."

"You're being paranoid, my dear."

Zoe grunted. "That's the second time today someone's called me paranoid. You, most of all, know I'm not. My biological mother dumped me in a trash barrel and left me there to die. How would the voters feel about that? Gloria Atwater adopted me to give her image a shot in the arm. My whole life's been a lie, Jake."

"Zoe, you're wrong. I don't give a damn what's in your background. I love *you*. That's all that matters."

"You say that now. What about five years from now? You'll still be dealing with rude remarks people make about your wife.

And they will. You know they will. It's human nature to take down whoever's famous and powerful. I'll be almost fifty then, not as young, not so beautiful. I couldn't stand to see the resentment in your eyes when you finally realize I'm right about this."

The man moved close to Zoe, his voice low and irritated. "I should've known better coming here tonight. You're always like this after visiting your mother. I'd hoped your friend going with you might have made it easier on you."

"This is our problem, not Georgia's."

"I'm only saying you've gotten close to her, maybe even closer in some ways than you are to Trish. From what you've told me, she's a good friend to you. She makes you smile, Zoe. What's wrong in saying that?"

"Nothing. I like Georgia. She's... thoughtful and kind and *ohmygod* she thinks my mother is actually a nice person. Look at these chairs. Georgia mended the wicker seats for me. She's brilliant. A domestic goddess. I admire her and the normal life she's lived." Zoe sighed.

"Where's Georgia from?" Georgia heard the click of a lighter and then the smell of an expensive cigar floating down in the evening air. With the creek bubbling in the background and the night air setting in, Georgia felt as if she might doze off.

"Ohio."

"Hmmm."

Zoe let out a girlish giggle. "I have an idea. Georgia would make the perfect political wife—sweet and totally willing to stand by her man. Beneath that little apron of hers, she's intelligent and insightful. I doubt the woman's ever had so much as a traffic ticket in her whole life. And she's about your age, Jake. Maybe, you ought to seriously consider proposing to Georgia."

A glass slammed against the table top above Georgia's head. "Stop it," he growled. "Don't make a joke about my love for you, Zoe."

Zoe's voice turned spiteful. "I told you from the beginning I wasn't interested in a cottage with a picket fence. That fantasy doesn't exist. Tell you what. Why don't you go into Scottsdale and find yourself a beautiful white woman with teeth like fucking piano keys, a degree in political science and then marry her. That would guarantee you winning the election."

"Zoe—"

"Did you honestly think I'd consider opening myself up to people asking stupid questions like 'Excuse me, Mrs. Senator, exactly what are you? Black? Indian? French? Italian? Oh, you have no idea? So it's true your biological mother dumped you in the trash after giving birth to you? Oh, by the way, we hear you read palms, been abducted by aliens and talk to the dead. Is all this true?"

"Stop it, Zoe."

"And," Zoe added. "There's the little issue about the murder. Oh, yes, it's been a big secret, but not for long."

"Zoe, you know that never happened. Your mother put that all in your head."

A glass tumbled to the floor and rolled off the edge of the balcony, shattering against the rocks. "Now look what you've made me do. Well, I'd better finish my own drink before you spoil that, too."

Georgia couldn't believe how quickly their conversation had turned ugly. She suspected Zoe had gulped down her scotch and imagined how it had burned her throat. Zoe never drank other than socially. "I don't want to talk about this any more. If you do, I'll ask you to leave."

"Zoe, my darling, I'm so tired I can barely hold my eyes open. I don't want to fight with you."

"No. Don't touch me. Not now."

"Do you really want me to leave?"

"God no," she said in a choked breath. "I'm sorry. Forgive me."

"I always do, don't I?"

Zoe sniffled. "I promise to be good, but first I have to tell you something, Mr. Senator." The teasing had come back into her voice.

"What?"

"You need a haircut."

"I'm not a senator yet, darling."

"You will be. Charming men always get what they want in life."

"I want you, Zoe."

"Tonight, you'll have me. Come on. Let's go inside. I'll make it easy on you. No demands."

Georgia waited until the lock clicked on the door. She then stood up, but too quickly. A pain shot through her right knee from being hunkered down on the rock for so long. She climbed up close to the building so she couldn't be seen from any of the windows, walking in the shadows until coming to her stairway. It was late. It felt as if a thousand years had passed since they had left for Scottsdale that morning.

Georgia turned the key in the door and flipped off the outside light. She quickly undressed and slipped into bed, but couldn't sleep. A full moon poured through the open window, keeping Georgia wide awake and wondering about the man on Zoe's balcony. Georgia rolled over and closed her eyes to shut out the moonlight, too lazy to get up and close the shade.

Who was this Jake person, anyway? Georgia had to admit she liked the man's voice, soft and sincere, but had no face to put with it. Her imagination conjured up a tall, handsome gentleman with kind, gentle eyes and a thick shock of hair, not to mention intelligent. What she couldn't understand was why Zoe seemed so adamant about keeping their relationship a secret? Georgia snuggled into the covers and yawned. Tomorrow she'd toss out a few questions in Zoe's direction, hopefully to ferret out information about this mystery man.

Georgia groaned as she pulled the comforter up under her chin, knowing full well that sometimes a person is better off not knowing every answer to every question. As her mother always used to say, "Ignorance is bliss, child."

# CHAPTER ELEVEN

Georgia broke three eggs into a crock bowl and whisked the devil out of them. Good therapy for a sour mood. Just half past ten o'clock, she had already snapped several times at the breakfast shift workers, and then promptly apologized for her sharp tongue. She brushed a stray hair away from her face with an elbow and paused long enough to take in a deep breath. Since opening her eyes that morning, she had felt out of sorts for no particular reason other than wondering about Zoe and her admirer. Adding a half cup of milk and a dash of salt, she gave the eggs another good whisking before pouring the slimy mess into a hot skillet. Georgia shut her eyes to stop the tears. No time for feeling sorry for herself. Nothing ever comes of that. She worked the eggs into a fluffy scramble before sliding them onto a stoneware plate, finishing off the order with three slices of crisp bacon and wheat toast. She handed the plate to Mary Jo who was on her way to the dining room.

Georgia wiped her hands on her apron and glanced up at the clock. Zoe still hadn't come into the café for her morning cup of tea and biscuit slathered with a teaspoon of honey. Earlier in the morning, Mary Jo had come into the café saying how strange that the closed sign was still hanging on the front door of the Moon Tide. Mary Jo said that she had even knocked on the outer door, but no one answered.

Trish didn't seem all that concerned. All morning long, Georgia had fought the urge to fish information out of Trish about the mysterious man in Zoe's life. Then, just when she had worked up enough courage, the café became crowded with customers and Georgia busied herself at the stove, too involved to think about Zoe and her admirer.

Georgia had already started the morning cleanup when Trish came through the swinging door with a full tray of dirty dishes. "I think we're clear until lunch."

On Trish's heels came Zoe, all smiles, her hair hanging loose around the shoulders in a soft tangle of curls. She went directly to the shelf for a mug, and then to the teakettle on the stove.

"Well, good morning Miss Zoe," Georgia said. "Or, should I say, good afternoon."

Trish shivered, shedding her morning apron and replacing it with a fresh one for the afternoon. "Watch out, Zoe," she warned. "Georgia's in a snit this morning."

Zoe lifted the glass dome covering the last cinnamon roll of the day. She gave Georgia a bright smile as she placed the sticky bun on a plate.

Georgia glanced at Trish, eyebrows raised. Trish cleared her throat and went back to helping Mary Jo put away the clean dishes from the roll-cart from the dishwashing room. "Well, I declare." Georgia folded a dishtowel and tossed it on the counter, suddenly feeling a little dizzy. She took in a deep breath and continued her cleanup.

Zoe sat down at the kitchen table and sipped her tea. She then broke off a piece of the roll and took a bite. "Oh, these *are* good."

Georgia said, "I thought you didn't eat sweets or meat?"

Trish gathered a bag of fresh leaf lettuce and put it into the sink for rinsing. "Better cool it, Zoe. Georgia's mighty touchy this morning."

Georgia only grunted as she shoved an oversized pot onto a high shelf. Zoe's love life was none of her business, and if she chose not to share her secret romance, that was more than fine with her. But she couldn't deny that something felt very different this morning, like old men's aching bones that predict a sudden change in the weather.

Last night after returning from her walk, Susan had called. For the first time since Georgia had left home, her conversation with Susan was enjoyable. They talked about the kids and Louie and how everything at home was going well. Louie had put up some new displays at the hardware store and business was good. After hanging up the phone, Georgia sat staring into the darkness missing her family. She had tried to call David earlier but didn't get an answer. Although worried about him, she knew he was old enough to take care of himself.

Zoe got up from the table and opened the refrigerator in search of a lemon wedge for her tea. She said to Georgia, "Thanks again for taking me to Scottsdale yesterday."

Georgia wiped her hands on the dishtowel. "I owe you much more than a car trip. Without you and Trish, who knows where I might've ended up when I first came here." Tears suddenly poured down Georgia's cheeks. She wiped at them with the dishtowel, embarrassed. "My goodness, I don't know what's gotten into me."

Rushing to Georgia's side, Trish pulled out a chair. "Sit down," she said, patting Georgia's shoulder. "Today, we take care of you, Georgia Mae Brown. Right, Zoe?"

Zoe struggled to answer around a bite of cinnamon roll. "Come with me to Flagstaff this afternoon. We'll shop for new dishes for the café." Zoe picked up her mug and inspected a small chip around the rim.

Trish's eyebrows rose in mock indignation. She picked up the morning edition of the Phoenix newspaper and laid it out flat on the table. "Maybe, Georgia wants to take it easy, maybe read the newspaper."

Zoe's smile froze in place. Georgia looked down at the front page of the newspaper at two photographs, one of an older man with thinning hair, the other a paradox, a roguishly handsome man with a killer smile. The headline read: *Senate Race Heats Up*. Georgia's heart nearly stopped, realizing Zoe's horrified reaction meant the photograph was the same man she'd heard the night before from beneath the balcony of the Moon Tide.

"Who is this?" she asked, looking up at them.

Zoe shot Trish a deadly look.

Trish let out a nervous laugh. "Georgia, don't you recognize him?" She put a finger on the photo. "Jake Rizzo."

"Jake Rizzo," Georgia repeated, trying to place where had she heard that name before, but not recently.

"The astronaut," Trish gleefully provided.

"Yes, of course." Georgia adjusted her bifocals and pulled the paper closer. She had never paid much attention to the space program after the Challenger blew up. After that catastrophe, everyone seemed to have lost interest in the space travel.

Georgia sensed the tenseness between Trish and Zoe, as she stared at Jake Rizzo's photograph. She had no stomach for their arguing today and was about to tell them so when Zoe snatched the paper from under Georgia's nose. She folded Jake Rizzo's face in half and tucked it under her arm. Trish's smug expression melted into anxiety, knowing she had pushed Zoe too far this time.

The back of Georgia's neck heated in anger. "Okay, you two, what's up?"

Trish shrugged and said innocently, "Nothing."

Zoe likewise followed up with, "Nothing."

"Okay, that's enough. I'm not going to sit here and play games." She glanced up at the clock, 11:30. Another fifteen minutes and the café would be jammed with hungry tourists. She scooted Trish out of the way. "Let's get back to work."

Trish caught hold of Georgia's hand. "We're sorry, Georgia. We kind of got carried away." She turned to Zoe. "Sorry. Jake Rizzo is your business, not mine."

Zoe slapped the flat of her hand on the table. "Dammit, Trish, you started all this. What's with you today?"

Trish planted both hands on her hips. "What's wrong with me? What about *you*?"

"All right," Georgia said, stepping between them. "No more talk about Jake Rizzo." She retied the back of her apron, said under her breath, "I think it's time for me to go home."

Zoe and Trish looked up at the same time. Trish let out an audible gasp. Zoe said to Trish, "Now look what we've done."

Trish moaned, "She doesn't really mean it." She turned to Georgia. "Zoe and I always bicker. You know that."

Georgia shook her head. "My decision has nothing to do with either of you. It's me. Three months ago, I ran away from home. Now it's time to go back and face the music."

"Oh no," Trish whined. She slumped into the nearest chair and stared in earnest at Georgia. "We need you Georgia."

Suddenly Georgia saw the irony in what she had done by leaving her house on Stilson Avenue, wanting to escape Susan's constant hovering. In Sedona, she had inadvertently created a parallel world, complete with the obligation to sort out the problems of the two women who had befriended her. To find the truth about herself, she simply had no choice but to return home and face her fears. If she didn't do that, she would spend the rest of her life wondering if she had merely been a coward for running away in the first place.

When Georgia said no more about leaving Sedona, Trish raised her voice, "Well, Zoe, you might've hired Georgia first but she loves the café best. You don't believe me? Ask her." They both turned to Georgia, waiting for an answer. Fed up, Georgia threw a dishtowel over one shoulder, about to tell them both to grow up, when the bell on the café door sounded. Georgia shifted her attention to the dining room.

Looking through the serving window, Georgia noticed a silver-haired gentlemen slide into the first booth, his back to her.

He pulled off a cowboy hat and tossed it on the seat beside him. Georgia's breath caught in the middle of her throat. The silver hair and the tilt of the gentleman's head as he opened the menu reminded her so much of Ed.

Tears flooded Georgia's eyes as she backed away, bumping into Zoe and Trish, who had stopped their bickering and moved up behind her.

The room swirled around her, as if she were on a merry-go-round, and then everything turned black, like a fade-out at the end of a movie. Her knees folded beneath her, soft as butter, and yet she didn't fall. Someone caught her and sat her firmly in a chair. She heard Zoe whisper, "Let's get your head down, sweetie." A firm hand pressed against her forehead. She heard Trish through a haze, "Here's a cold cloth for her head." Georgia heard the sharp squeak of the swinging door between the kitchen and dining room and Mary Jo's excited voice, "My God, what happened? I'll get Doc."

She woke up in her bed above the café, Ed's silver hair floating in a fuzzy pattern in front of her face. A deep groan escaped her throat. How long had she been out? She heard herself say, "Ed? Is that you? Am I dead?"

The silver-haired cowboy from the café hovered over her. He looked familiar—not like Ed at all. "Little lady, you gave us quite a scare." Zoe and Trish stood on either side of the bed, their faces drawn with worry. She tried to speak but couldn't. The inside of her mouth felt thick and dry. She managed to nod at the glass of water Zoe held in her hand. Doc helped her sit up. She took a grateful sip of the water. "Slowly," he warned her.

Zoe and Trish sighed in unison. "She's all right?" Trish asked.

The man smiled down at her.

She remembered now. Doc. Mary Jo's grandfather, the kind man who'd helped her that first day in the café.

"I think she's fine." He gave Georgia's arm a gentle pat. Georgia nearly swooned again at his touch. "She's tired. Let her rest a bit."

Strength surged back into her body, and she edged her legs to the side of the bed, wanting to get up. She said to Doc, "I know you, don't I?"

Trish piped in, "You met him the first day you came to Sedona. Remember? Mary Jo's grandfather. You weren't feeling good that day either."

Georgia lightly touched her forehead. "Yes, I remember." She gave Doc a little smile. "We talked about Trish's meatloaf."

Doc nodded as he helped her to stand up. "Sure did."

"I want to sit in that chair over there," Georgia said.

Trish and Zoe stood back, watching as Doc walked Georgia to the flowered chair with the matching hassock beside the window. He fluffed one of the couch pillows and cushioned it against her back. "There," he said. "Feeling better?" Georgia nodded.

Trish said with a dose of cuteness. "My, don't they make a sweet couple?"

"For once, Trish, I agree with you." Zoe crossed her arms and cocked her head to one side, studying Georgia and Doc.

"Okay, girls, don't tease the patient," Doc said. "Stop the chattering and let Georgia get some rest."

Mary Jo appeared in the doorway with his cowboy hat. "Is she okay?"

"Fine as rain, sweetie." He put his arm around his granddaughter. "Rest will be the best medicine for Georgia right now." And then, they were gone.

Zoe and Trish sat together on the couch, staring at Georgia.

Georgia said, "The two of you have businesses to take care of."

"We'll go in a minute," Trish said, getting up and tossing a light blanket over Georgia. "Zoe and I agree that it might be a good thing for you to go back and visit your family. You schedule the flight. We'll make sure you get to the airport. No way are you driving two thousand miles all by yourself."

Georgia relaxed, knowing the girls would not give her any

more trouble about returning to Ohio. She hated leaving Sedona and her new friends, but, for now at least, she knew she had to go home. She gratefully accepted their suggestion. "Okay, I'll leave the car." She held up a finger in warning. "You have to promise me that the two of you won't fight over who gets to drive it while I'm gone."

# CHAPTER TWELVE

"They won't lose my luggage, will they?" Georgia fumbled through her purse for identification, every tragic air travel scenario going through her head, making her even more nervous than she already was.

"Probably," Trish casually replied, attaching address labels to Georgia's two suitcases before moving them in the direction of the check-in desk.

Georgia bit into her lower lip, debating whether or not Trish really meant what she'd said. After all, handing luggage over to total strangers at the curb before going into the terminal somehow seemed a bit risky to Georgia. You couldn't trust anyone these days.

With the bags finally checked, Georgia rushed through the automatic doors of the main terminal, yelling, "Trish, slow down!"

Trish turned around and waited for her to catch up. "Maybe you shouldn't go today. You look too pale, as if you're sick or something."

For about the zillionth time this morning, Georgia regretted letting Trish drive her to Flagstaff to catch her flight. She could have easily hopped a motel shuttle service to the airport, but Trish had insisted on delivering her as far as the security gate. No doubt Trish had an ulterior motive, perhaps thinking Georgia, at the very last minute, might change her mind about getting on the plane and leaving Arizona.

They were almost to the gate when Trish pulled back on Georgia's arm with an apologetic smile. "Sorry for being so short with you. I know you're nervous about flying. I'm just upset, about you leaving, I mean..." Trish closed her mouth, unable to go on.

Georgia tucked her sweater under one arm along with her new cookbook, the one she planned to read during the four-hour-flight. "I know you don't want me to go, Trish." Just then, a man barreling toward her from behind accidentally caught her shoulder. The cookbook went flying from her arm and landed with a loud thud on the tiled floor.

The otherwise harried crush of people fast-walking the terminal suddenly stopped in their tracks and glanced nervously around. One elderly lady carrying an old-fashioned leather carry-on, clutched at her throat, saying, "Good Lord, I thought it was a gunshot."

Georgia quickly retrieved the book from the floor. Her face burned with embarrassment as she apologized to everyone within earshot. Trish crossed her arms and tapped her foot in mock impatience. "Must you always be the center of attention?"

Cookbook once again cradled in her arm, she moved along in line with itinerary, tickets and identification clutched in one fist. In her head, she went over the information for about the hundredth time. *No layovers to Columbus, not until the return flight four weeks from now in Chicago, that is, if she decided to make the return flight.* If not, Georgia would send Zoe a check for the ticket and apologize for her decision not to return to Sedona.

Georgia hoisted her purse strap on her shoulder and shoved her hair back from her forehead, exhausted by all the airport hustle-bustle. "What you said about me being afraid to fly, I'm not. I just haven't flown much."

Trish's eyes filled with fresh tears. "I wish you were my mother." Her lower lip quivered. "I love you, Georgia."

Thrown off-guard by Trish's emotional farewell, Georgia wrapped her in a tight hug. "I love you, too."

Trish gulped, clinging to the cuff of Georgia's blouse. "I'll miss you. Please come back."

Georgia gave her another hug, knowing that once she boarded the plane, she might never return to Sedona. She had to go now. One more word from Trish, and they would be back in the car in a nanosecond, headed to Sedona. She said to Trish, "I can't promise anything."

"Sure." Trish hiccupped. "I understand."

Georgia slipped off her shoes. "Do me a favor. Don't talk anymore."

Trish wiped her face with the back of one hand, smearing tears across her reddened cheeks. The announcement came over the system for first class boarding on Georgia's flight. Trish gently nudged Georgia. "That's you."

Georgia handed her ticket to security. "Zoe shouldn't have bought these first class tickets. Coach would've been fine."

"So talk to her when you get back." Trish tossed Georgia's handbag into the tub with her shoes. You will come back, won't you? And don't fret about the tickets. Zoe seldom pays full price for anything. The woman knows too many people in the right places." She gave Georgia one last hug. "I'll see you in a month."

Breaking away from Trish, she boarded the plane, which proved to be much more difficult than Georgia had imagined. She settled her purse under the forward seat and secured the sweater around her shoulders. A chant played over and over inside her head, *It's not too late. It's not too late. Get off the plane.* The chant abruptly went silent when the forward door thumped shut and the plane started backing away from the terminal. On the runway, the engine began its hyper-revving, gaining speed, finally lifting into the air. Georgia squeezed her eyes shut. All ten fingers gripped the armrests, as if she were in danger of falling off the edge of earth.

Perhaps she was.

* * *

Georgia fell asleep somewhere over Kansas and didn't wake up until the plane's descent into Port Columbus. There would be no one meeting her in baggage claim. She had purposely not told Susan, hoping to forego any fuss about her return. She quickly collected her bags, hailed a taxi, and then gave the driver her home address.

The trees along the highway were still summer green, showing only the slightest hint of color change in the cool, afternoon air. The leaves would soon drop by the thousands, rustling to the ground like dried paper before flattening into a dull brown with the next hard rain.

When the cabbie turned onto Stilson Avenue, Georgia's throat constricted with a strange emotion that was neither sad nor happy. At the first glimpse of her house, she felt a powerful sense of not belonging, like having to throw away a favorite dress and knowing you'll never wear it again.

\* \* \*

Georgia turned the key in the lock. Her hands full, she pushed open the door with one foot and heard the familiar squeak of the hinges. Her nostrils indignantly sniffed the stale air trapped inside the house. Georgia held her breath until she'd opened a few windows and let some fresh air invade the house.

Inspecting the plants on the kitchen window sill, she found them all healthy and getting on quite nicely without her. She turned on the teakettle to fix a cup of tea. Opening the dishwasher, she found it empty and looked for any telltale sign that someone might have at least had a cup of coffee in her absence. Nothing. The inside of the refrigerator had been scrubbed clean, emptied of perishables, leaving only an unopened can of Parmesan cheese and a jar of baby dills.

The electric rooster clock on the wall in the breakfast alcove hummed with self-importance, as if it alone had been responsible for keeping the world on time since the day she'd left. Through the bay window, she noted that Susan and Louie had kept up nicely with the yard work, the flower beds free of weeds.

Opening the back door, Georgia stepped outside, glancing next door, half-expecting Oscar to scamper through the hedge to greet her. When he failed to appear, she thought maybe tomorrow morning she would find him waiting on the back steps to welcome her home.

She closed the door and thought about calling Susan, but quickly put that crazy notion out of her mind. No sense jumping into hot water all at once. For sure, her daughter would be indignant for not being asked to pick her up at the airport. She could hear her now. "Really, mother. I can't believe you came home in a cab instead of calling me."

Tonight, Georgia wanted to be alone, time to readjust without all the weary drama of her daughter's onslaught of questions and what an inconvenience it had been keeping up with the hardware store and the kids without her help for the summer months. Undoubtedly, they would end up in an argument leaving them both hurt and angry.

The weary air travel that day suddenly caught up with Georgia. She wanted to go to bed, to drop her head on a pillow and fall into a deep, undisturbed sleep. Fixing her tea, she carried it into the bedroom and shut the door behind her. Not yet completely dark outside, Georgia thought twice about turning on a lamp. She knew any light shining from the windows would signal neighbors of her return and would start a chain reaction of phone calls that, in a matter of minutes, would travel three blocks over to Susan.

Georgia folded back the familiar blue and white bedspread, but then suddenly changed her mind, whipping the spread back in place. She had no intention of sleeping in this bed with all the memories crowding these four walls. She recalled the old photographs suffocating the walls of Gloria's room at the nursing home and wondered how the old woman could possibly stand all the ghosts from her past staring down at her. Ed seemed too real in this room, and it hurt, from the inside out, to think about him. There were certain things between them, even after his death, that needed to be dealt with. No more running away. With new determination, she ripped open the closet door and began tearing Ed's shirts, trousers and jackets from their hangers, letting them fall in a messy heap at her feet. She yanked so hard at the clothing that buttons popped off shirts and scattered around her bare feet like tiny seeds. She knew she might regret it tomorrow, but right now, the satisfaction of purging Ed's clothing gave her such relief, she couldn't stop herself.

Not until after she'd emptied the closet, did Georgia move to Susan's childhood bedroom and lie down on the bed. Her head no sooner hit the pillow than the phone rang. Georgia automatically rolled over and picked up the pink receiver of Susan's old phone.

"Georgia?"

Georgia sat up on the bed, now wide awake. "Trish?"

"Yes, it's me. I wanted to let you know that Susan called a few minutes ago. I told her you were there. Is that okay?"

"That's fine, Trish. I was going to call her, anyway." Georgia rubbed at her tired eyes, glancing at the bedside clock. Ten o'clock.

"How are you?"

Georgia sat up and pulled the covers around her. "About the same as when I left you this morning. I'm fine, Trish."

"Oh," Trish replied, sounding a bit hurt.

"And how are you?"

Trish let out a long sigh. "You don't really want to know, but since you asked, I'll tell you. Mary Jo's crying in the bathroom. She tried to make an apple pie like yours. But she sliced the apples too thick, and then accidentally used salt instead of sugar. She put the pie in the oven and forgot to set the timer. Now, the café smells like burnt apples."

"Poor Mary Jo," Georgia sympathized.

"And you'll be happy to know I followed your recipe for

meatloaf. Doc tried it and told me my cooking should be tested by the Food and Drug Administration."

"Oh, Trish, that's terrible." Georgia's heart fluttered at the mention of Doc.

"Then, Zoe told me the café smelled like some cheap burger joint when she came in for lunch today."

"Well, Zoe hates anything that smells like meat."

"Oh yeah? With my own eyes, I saw her eating a hamburger with a huge plate of fries at the Ponderosa Café down the street."

"You don't say." Georgia heard a car door slam out in front of the house. She peaked through the curtain and recognized Susan's van. "Gotta go, Trish. I've got a hurricane about to blow through my front door."

\* \* \*

"Mom, why didn't you tell me you were coming home? I would've picked you up at the airport. Promise me you won't ever disappear like that again." Susan immediately turned on the living room lights. "Why is it so dark in here?"

Georgia stood barefoot in the hallway, speechless, her red silk shawl wrapped around the shoulders of her white, cotton nightgown. Two thousand miles away, Georgia had learned to simply hang up the telephone when she didn't like how their conversation was going, but now, even standing in her own living room, Georgia felt intimidated in Susan's presence, totally back to *square one*.

"Susan?" Georgia whispered, tiptoeing into the living room, as if there were others sleeping in the back bedrooms. "Sweetheart, I'm sorry for not calling, but I wanted to be alone here for a while."

"Alone?" Susan said with sarcasm. "Isn't that what you've been for the past few months? And for heaven's sake what are you wearing?" Susan took hold of the fringe that edged the shawl around Georgia's shoulders and gave it an indifferent tug.

Georgia shrugged. No use trying to explain to Susan what the shawl meant to her. To make things easier, she pulled it off her shoulders and carefully folded it over one arm of the couch.

"My goodness, that garish thing certainly isn't you."

Georgia sighed. "No, I suppose it isn't me, not really...at least not here."

She wanted to tell Susan she had worn it shopping one afternoon in Sedona and received many compliments. Now, standing with Susan and back inside her old life again, Georgia second-guessed the sincerity of those compliments. Perhaps they were only being kind.

Susan raised an eyebrow. "Maybe you could give it to Samantha. She likes to play dress up."

Georgia noted her daughter's jeans with the legs severely creased, the crisp white collar of her blouse peeking out from beneath a theme cardigan with cappuccino cups embroidered across the front. The thought crossed Georgia's mind that someone as opinionated as Susan should consider shucking all the themes in her life and find her own definitive style. Loosen up a little, especially with Louie and the kids.

Susan straightened the magazines on the coffee table. "I almost brought Samantha and Benny over with me, but thought you might be tired. You can see them tomorrow. Besides, they were already in bed when I talked to that Trish person."

The hairs on the back of Georgia's neck stood up on end. She didn't like Susan talking about Trish so dismissively. Georgia deliberately thumbed through and then messed up the magazines Susan had just put back in order. "Susan, you don't know Trish."

Susan's eyes fell on the bags Georgia had left beside the couch. "New luggage?"

"Yes. Is there something wrong with that?"

Susan huffed, staring her mother down. "No. Is there something wrong in asking?"

Determined not to let Susan ruin her homecoming, she offered to fix her a cup of tea. Not waiting for an answer, Georgia started for the kitchen. When she passed Susan, her daughter reached out and touched her earrings.

"These new, too?"

"I bought them in Sedona. Turquoise."

Susan followed her mother into the kitchen. "I know what they are, Mo-ther. I've always thought turquoise was kind of tacky."

Georgia set the teakettle on the burner. "Oh, really? She pointedly looked down at Susan's theme sweater. "Well, I like the earrings."

Susan shrugged. "It's okay on you, though."

The water heating for the tea, Georgia searched through one of her bags, at the same time digesting her daughter's backhanded insult. "Here, these are for you." She all but shoved a small blue box into her daughter's hands. "Turquoise earrings. They're Navajo, but if you don't like them, I'll give them to someone else."

"Oh?" Susan's impudence instantly turned to curiosity. "Oh, let me see." She opened the box, and her eyes brightened. "Oh, mom, I really like them." She gave her mother a weak smile. "I didn't mean what I said. I've just missed you so much and couldn't understand why you left without telling me."

Georgia helped Susan with the earrings. "I'm glad you like the gift. And I'm sorry I left without telling you."

"Are you happy now?"

"Happy?" Georgia pulled back a length of Susan's hair and felt its softness, as soft as when she was a little girl. "I'm happy now, here with you. That's most important, don't you think?"

Susan nodded, as she struggled to find her voice. She suddenly wrapped her mother in a hug. "Mom, I'm so glad you're home. I missed you. The kids missed you. Louie missed you." Tears rolled down her daughter's cheeks. Georgia took the cuff of her nightgown and gently wiped them away.

"Stop your tears, Susan. I'm home."

# CHAPTER THIRTEEN

"Uh oh," Georgia said under her breath. She gently nudged her granddaughter along the walkway of the Great Ape exhibit at the zoo; hopefully, before Samantha could ask something she wasn't prepared to answer.

"Grandma?"

Too late. They stood at the railing surrounding the outdoor wilderness area where a mama gorilla sat under a tree casually tugging at her nipples. Georgia cleared her throat and gave the child another little nudge to hurry her along.

"Grandma?"

"Oh, look there." She pointed at a baby gorilla turning summersaults in the grass beneath a tree, several feet from its mother.

"Are baby gorillas like people babies?" Samantha asked.

The baby gorilla stopped doing summersaults and sat staring at the blue sky, as if wondering if there were more to the world than this pretend jungle environment. "I think when they're babies, they're close." She glanced back at the mama who stared back at her with dark, scary eyes, as if to say, *Please get me outta here!*

Just then, she heard Benny shout, "You're it!"

Georgia searched through a nearby crowd for her grandson who had run off to play a game of tag with another boy he recognized from his school. His friend in a striped pullover dodged his mother's hand as she reached out to grab his collar. She missed. The boys then charged between an elderly man and woman who had stopped to smile at them. Georgia held her breath. If they accidentally bumped the couple and knocked them down, their fragile hips would be toast. Georgia shouted for Ben to be careful, shaking her head and wondering if taking them to the zoo had been such a bright idea after all.

Georgia had picked up the kids that morning, packing a picnic lunch since the beautiful fall day was sunny and still warm enough to be comfortable with a sweater. Later in the afternoon, she and the children would meet Susan and Louie at a restaurant near the mall for a family dinner.

In the reptile house a zookeeper fed a fat rat to a boa constrictor. This caught Ben's interest. He hung over the railing watching for at least ten minutes. At first, Georgia hesitated, thinking it might not be such a good idea for Ben to watch the snake swallow the rat, but decided it was a lesson in nature that had to be learned.

Moving into the aquarium, Samantha and Ben followed the railing along enormous tanks of shimmering water, reflecting like a thousand diamonds on the blue walls. Fish swam lazily from one end of the tank to the other as if sensing only a measly fifty feet or so of water lay before them instead of a thousand miles of ocean.

"Grandma, look! That flat thing with a tail like a dog. What's that?"

"A stingray," Georgia answered, smoothing back Samantha's braids, thinking how much they felt like Susan's when she was a little girl.

At noon Georgia spread out their lunch on a picnic table. Ben made a yucky face at the carrot sticks. "Don't like carrots." He pointed to the hamburger stand a few feet away. "I want a hot dog."

Samantha, content with her peanut butter sandwich up until now, piped in, "I want a hot dog, too." Georgia gave up on the nutritious lunch she'd packed and reached for her purse. After all, today was their day to do as they pleased. She handed out money to Ben and Sam, and then tore up the peanut butter sandwiches to throw to the birds.

Samantha gingerly licked ketchup from her fingers as she worked her mouth around the dog on a bun. "Grandma, are you crazy?"

Georgia gathered the food wrappers to later throw in the nearest trash container. "What? Who told you that?"

"Mommy did. She said you ran away from home because you went crazy."

"Is that so." Georgia crumpled a brown lunch bag and threw it in the wicker lunch basket she'd carried from home.

"Mommy said everything can get back to normal now. Does that mean you're not crazy anymore?"

"Hmmm." It hurt hearing her daughter's gossipy words repeated from the lips of her granddaughter. Samantha, on the other hand, looked enormously pleased that she had relayed so much grownup information, the impact, no doubt, evident on Georgia's face. Benny saved the day when he spilled his lemonade across the table. They all jumped up at once, the lemonade soaking into what remained of the food.

* * *

No sooner had they all ordered dinner that evening than Susan started preaching. "Mom, if you want to move somewhere, why not Florida? There's Sarasota, Fort Meyers, even Key West. You could buy a condo. We could visit you." Susan turned to her children, as if wanting them to join in on her enthusiasm. "Sounds like fun, doesn't it?" Ben let out a loud belch, and then giggled. Samantha was quick to agree with her mother. Georgia got the impression that this Florida thing had been carefully rehearsed with her children—Ben not so ready to obey his mother's wishes.

Georgia cut into her roasted breast of chicken, perturbed. "Did it ever occur to you that I might not like Florida?" Georgia took a bite of chicken and found it to be superbly moist with just the right amount of seasoning. She thought this would be a nice addition to the Soft Rock menu.

"Well, no," Susan said with hesitation. "What's wrong with Florida?"

"Nothing. I don't want to live there."

"Really, Mother." She glanced at her children, clearly aggravated. "Could we please discuss this some other time? Not in front of the children."

"You brought up the subject, Susan. I didn't." Georgia gave Louie an apologetic look. "I'm sorry, Louie, but I've got to say this." She turned back to Susan. "You didn't mind telling the children I was crazy when I went to Sedona, did you?"

"Well, I..." Susan stopped mid-sentence and nervously wiped at her mouth.

Louie cleared his throat as he slipped his chair back a few inches from the table. "Susan, that's enough. Your mother doesn't need anyone directing her life."

*God bless Louie.* Georgia had always loved him, but now she could've jumped up and given him a kiss. "Thank you, Louie."

"Well, I want you to be happy, Mom," she said with an injured expression. "Is that a crime?"

"No, it's not." Georgia gave her daughter an appreciative smile. "Right now, I need time and space of my own to think things through."

Susan's eyes narrowed, her mouth puckered into the spoiled pout of a little girl who can't get her way. "Space? You're going back to Arizona, aren't you? Oh, Mom, I thought you'd gotten all that café and artsy stuff out of your head. You're not an ordinary cook or clerk, Mom."

"Susan, I've cooked and cleaned for my family for over thirty years with little or no thanks at all. I get more respect from strangers than I do from my own family." Her face heated with anger, and she took a long sip of ice water to keep from saying something she might later regret. Samantha and Benjamin sat stick straight in their chairs, mouths open—eyes darting from mother to grandmother, acutely aware they were witnessing no ordinary argument.

Georgia thought back to that morning at the zoo and how the mama gorilla had looked so bored with her life within that cage. Or, at the aquarium house, how the fish continually swam for miles and miles, going absolutely nowhere.

Lifting the cloth napkin from her lap, Georgia got up and left the restaurant without saying goodbye to anyone. At the next block she called a cab with her new cell phone, vowing that she would never again allow anyone to put her inside a cage.

The next day, Georgia contacted a realtor and put her house on the market. Whether or not she stayed in Columbus or moved to Sedona, the house on Stilson Avenue had to go. All the important memories were inside her head. She didn't need four walls to make them any more real than they already were.

A few days after the realtor stuck a *For Sale* sign in the front yard, she met Susan for lunch at a tearoom. Georgia expected yet another confrontation, this time about selling the house. They ordered broccoli quiche served with tiny warm loaves of bread. The lunch quickly went downhill from there.

Susan vigorously peppered her quiche. "You're selling the house?" *As if she didn't already know.* "Where will you live?"

"I'll rent a furnished room for a few weeks until I decide what I'm doing." Georgia shrugged. "I'm not worried about it."

"You're doing this out of spite because of Daddy." Susan's eyes misted with tears.

"Your father's gone. David's coming home for a few days to help sort through the house. I want the two of you to take what you want. What's left, I've arranged to donate to charity." Susan opened her mouth to object, but Georgia held up a warning finger. "Susan, don't start anything with your brother."

"What are you talking about?" Susan chided.

"David agrees with my decision to sell the house. He's already in enough pain about the divorce. It's final next week."

Susan stopped her sniffling, her forehead furrowing with consternation. "My brother hasn't called me once about the divorce."

"This isn't about you, Susan." Georgia pushed her plate away, already having lost her appetite. Not that she had expected the lunch to go smoothly, but she hadn't meant to hurt Susan. Her daughter could be stubborn and difficult, but she wasn't a mean person. Maybe a bit controlling and insecure, but never mean.

Marrying Louie had been the best choice her daughter ever could've made. He ignored all the little aggravating flaws in Susan's personality, flaws that would have driven any normal man insane. It seemed that Louie saw only the good in Susan, and there was certainly a lot of that after scratching through several layers of toughness. Louie was capable of bringing out the best in Susan, and, deep down, Georgia suspected her daughter knew just how lucky she was to have him. As far as Georgia was concerned, Louie was next door to being a saint.

Susan shoved her plate to the center of the table and gave her mother a quirky smile. "Lori never deserved David."

Georgia smiled. "On that, we both agree."

Later that evening, Zoe called in a panic. "It's my mother, Georgia. She's had a stroke."

"Oh, no." She asked the next question carefully, fearing the worst. "How is she?"

"She's stable, but the left side of her face is paralyzed. I'm staying in Phoenix in a hotel near the hospital. Her mind's gone back thirty years. She thinks I'm ten. Georgia, I don't think I can stand much more of this." She paused. "She's in bad shape. This might be the end."

"Do you want me there? I'll come. You know I will."

"No. I... needed to hear your voice. I'm better now."

"Zoe, I mean it. If you need me, I'll be on the next flight out there." A part of Georgia wanted her to say *Yes*.

Zoe choked back tears on the other end of the line, but then managed to chuckle. "Trish would give anything to hear you say that. She hired a cook but the woman's inhuman. Her name's Helga. She orders Trish around like a waitress. Mary Jo calls her *Helga the Hun* behind her back, but she jumps like a scared rabbit whenever the Hun comes into the dining room."

"Dear, sweet Mary Jo. She doesn't deserve having to cope with both Trish and Helga."

"At least Mary Jo can leave at the end of her shift. It's Trish who's about to flip out, because she's there all day."

"Well, Trish deserves a little of what she gets from Helga."

They both laughed, lessening the tension about Gloria's stroke. Georgia half-expected Zoe to ask whether or not she'd made any decision about returning to Sedona. She didn't, and for the moment, Georgia was relieved she hadn't brought up the subject. However, she was surprised when Zoe, in saying her goodbye, told Georgia, "I love you."

The next morning Georgia walked the five blocks to the hardware store. The air smelled crisp and clean, autumn leaves showering around her shoulders. She had walked this route to the store many times over the years. This morning would be her last time. She had a plan that might be good for everyone concerned, especially Susan.

Georgia had kept her distance from the store since Ed's death. Louie, thank God, had taken over the management and had done a wonderful job in Georgia's absence. Ed had always planned on Louie taking over the store when he retired, but had never gotten around to going to an attorney and making everything legal.

She stood in the doorway by the small appliance display, pleased by all the improvements Louie had made inside the store— the aisles neat and orderly, updated overhead lighting brightened the showroom, and a fresh coat of paint covered the walls.

Amos greeted her at the front door. He had worked at Brown Hardware since he was sixteen. "Well, look who's here!"

"Hello, Amos. How's your wife and family?"

Amos gave her a vigorous hug. "The family's great. You look great, too, Georgia. I guess your little trip agreed with you."

"It did, Amos. It surely did."

"Louie's in his office." He gave her a sidelong glance, knowing the real reason she was here this morning. She had called Amos first to let him know her plans for the hardware store, wanting his approval. He couldn't have been happier.

She handed Amos a baker's box filled with warm chocolate chip cookies to take home with him. This had always been a tradition between them, bringing Amos a treat to take home to the kids, even though she knew Amos's children were grown and on their own now. She knew the gesture was appreciated. Amos had been a good friend to her and Ed.

His face broke into a big grin as he made a fuss of sniffing at the edge of box. "Mmm. Chocolate chip?"

"I didn't forget."

Amos tucked his head into his chest. "I'm sorry about what happened. I knew it was wrong and told Ed. He just wouldn't listen."

Georgia patted his shoulder. "Ed never did know how to listen, did he?"

\* \* \*

"Louie?" Georgia knocked on the open door of the cramped office at the back of the store.

Louie glanced up from the computer screen. "Georgia!" He quickly came round the desk and kissed her cheek. "What a nice surprise. Is something wrong? You look upset."

Georgia shook her head. "I wanted to talk to you—without Susan."

Louie let out a long sigh, "Georgia, if it's about the other night at dinner and the grief Susan's been giving you about the house, let me tell you she feels awful about the arguments. You know she doesn't mean to be so overbearing."

She patted Louie's hand. "I know she doesn't. Deep down, Susan's soft-hearted. She can't help it, I suppose, wanting to control everyone around her. Ed was the same way."

Louie chuckled. "I admit, she's pushy, but Susan would give her last dime to anyone who asked for it."

Georgia folded her hands on the big envelope she'd brought with her, resting it in her lap. "Louie, I've been to the accountant's office. He's told me the store is making a good profit. I appreciate everything you've done."

Louie sat on the edge of the desk, his arms crossed against his chest. "Thank you. And honestly, I'm glad you've stopped in today because there's something between us that needs to be dealt with."

She felt the muscles at the back of her neck tighten. She knew coming here this morning wouldn't be easy, but no matter how painful, she was determined to get through it and be done with it. "I appreciate your honesty, Louie. Whatever it is, I can take it."

"Ed was a good man." Louie moved behind his desk and sat down, nervously drumming his fingers on the worn leather arms of the chair. "I know the pain he put you through. And I understand why you left last April." He hesitated. "But... although I didn't approve of Ed's deceit, even knowing what I did, it never changed my opinion of him. I loved him like a father."

Georgia gave him an understanding smile and thought how much Louie's comment would have meant to Ed. "Louie, I'm not here to complain about Ed. The past is past. I'm here to talk about the future."

Louie drew in a deep breath and settled back into the desk chair that squeaked with every movement. "This sounds serious."

"It is." She scooted closer to the desk. From the oversized envelope in her lap she pulled out several documents and spread ·

them over the desktop. "The last few days I've been working with the attorney and accountant to draw up papers to make things all legal. I'm signing the store over to you and Susan. You'll find the price more than reasonable."

Louie's eyes widened as he read over the documents. "You don't mean it?"

Georgia smiled. "Yes, if you're interested." She slid the top document under his nose. "This is a Buy-Sell Agreement. I'm hoping you'll keep the store and property in the family for at least another generation. You've got a good business head on your shoulders, and I'd like for Ben to maybe take over some day."

"Thank you, Georgia."

"You're welcome." She started to get up, but sat down again. "Oh, I do have one request."

"What's that?"

"That you move into Ed's office upstairs."

"Well…" he hesitated. "I didn't feel right about going through his desk, not until you came back. I figured when you were ready—"

"I'm ready."

"Are you sure? Would you rather Susan or I go through it first? There might be something…" His voice trailed off to an inaudible whisper.

"All I need is a box of garbage bags. It shouldn't take more than five minutes."

One hour later, Georgia still sat behind Ed's mahogany desk, eyes swollen from crying. In her lap a stack of pink envelopes, all addressed to Ed. Shortly after Louie had unlocked the upstairs office, Georgia opened a drawer and discovered bank statements for an account she had never known existed. In the top drawer, a set of keys she didn't recognize. In the bottom drawer, the stack of pink letters with hearts drawn on the outside, like high school love letters.

Her stomach immediately twisted into a tight knot, the taste of bile stinging its way up her throat. Seeing all these unfamiliar items in her husband's desk made her feel as if her heart were breaking all over again.

"Mom?"

"David!" Seeing her son in the doorway, Georgia scrambled from the chair to greet him. He had arrived a day earlier than expected. The pink envelopes slipped from her lap and scattered around her feet. David caught her in a tight hug. She didn't want to cry, but couldn't help it. She hadn't seen him since the funeral, and he looked wonderful.

When she finally pulled away, she wiped at her face with both hands. Seeing the envelopes on the floor, she stooped down to gather them up before David could ask what they were. David knelt beside her, the weight of his arm on her shoulder. He knew. She was sure he knew. Oh, you'd have to be stupid not to know what the pink envelopes with all the silly hearts on them were. They gathered them all up in their hands and threw everything into the trash bag.

He said, disgusted. "I'm glad you're getting rid of all this trash."

Just having him here beside her, made Georgia feel much stronger. She had always considered David to be her greatest ally. "I thought you were coming tomorrow?"

"I caught an earlier flight." He slipped out of his jacket and gave it a quick toss over the back of the leather couch. "How're you doing, Mom?"

"I've been better." She raked her fingers through her short hair. "I've got a few more drawers to go through."

"Sure. How can I help?"

She shoved a stack of papers on the desk in his direction. "Help me sort through these, okay?"

They worked silently for the next hour. Now, Georgia sat behind the desk with a bundle of bank statements she'd found in the bottom drawer. David finished tying up the last trash bag. "I'll call the shredder service to take care of all these bags. You can't be too careful these days."

She gave the handful of bank statements to David. He quickly shuffled through them, his face going pale. He shook his head. "This makes me sick. I'm sorry, Mom. I should've gone through Dad's office right after the funeral so you didn't have to see this."

"I would've had to deal with it eventually. I'll live." At the moment, though, she felt as if she were losing Ed all over again, wondering if, maybe, he had never loved her at all.

David shook his head. "I know how much it must hurt you."

"David?"

"Yeah?"

"All this money your father saved. Do you think he planned to leave me? Do you think he would've married that woman? My God, she's younger than Susan."

David sat down on the couch, shaking his head. "We'll probably never know what his intentions were. For all we know, the woman was pushing him to do something he didn't' really want to do."

"I don't hate your father. Whatever he's done, I'll still remember him as being a good husband and father."

"Ah, Mom." He picked up a pillow from the couch and threw it at the family photograph taken more than twenty years ago, hitting the frame square, knocking it off the desk and onto the floor. "What a lying bastard, having a fucking heart attack in the middle of the reservoir on that stupid boat of his. And that trashy blonde freaking out because she couldn't get the motor started, calling 911 and ending up on the six o'clock news. I don't know how you held yourself together during the funeral, all those people knowing about what he did."

As sick as she remembered feeling about that day, what bothered her most at the moment was how Ed's indiscretion was affecting her son. Since her husband's death, she had learned to separate the intense emotions of anger and grief, both slapping at her insides like twenty foot ocean waves. She wanted to reassure David that while his father's betrayal had hurt, it had nothing to do with the love she still felt for him. "I was numb at first," she said. "Nothing short of an earthquake could've gotten a response out of me until after the funeral. I suppose that was a blessing." She reached out and took his hand and brought it to one side of her cheek. "I'm absolutely better, one hundred percent. We've got to think of the good times we all had together. Not the bad."

"I should've taken time off after the funeral to be with you— made sure you were all right. I guess we were all in shock about Dad dying and, you know, the other."

Georgia bundled up the bank statements and secured them with a rubber band. "You did the right thing going home with Lori. I had to figure out my own way to deal with your father's death." A small smile crept across her lips. "Besides, Susan was here and she had no problem telling me what I should or shouldn't be doing." This comment brought a grin to her son's face.

"Susan doesn't have a problem telling anyone what to do. She keeps wanting to talk about Lori and the divorce and just doesn't get it that I don't want to talk about it right now. She gets this hurt little expression on her face like when we were kids." David laughed. "She means well." He shook his head, his face shining with a new appreciation for his mother, the kind of look that says, Gee, I'm glad you're my mom. "Hey, look at you!" he said, placing his thumbs together to frame her face. "You look like a million bucks. Your hair looks great."

"Your sister thinks I've lost my mind."

"Susan thinks anyone with a different opinion from hers has lost their mind."

"You really don't mind that I'm selling the house?"

"Nope."

"Your sister thought I'd be happier living in Florida. I told her no."

"Where do you want to live, Mom?"

Georgia shrugged. "I don't know. But I know I'm not ready to join the trike crowd in the sunshine state."

"Take your time. You have the rest of your life to decide."

Georgia handed David a few more pink envelopes she had dropped on the floor and missed to shove into the bag with the others. "I only read a few of the letters before you arrived."

"Like I said before, they're trash, Mom."

Closing the bottom desk drawer, she said, "I don't understand how all this could've been going on behind my back. I never suspected a thing. How could I have *not* known?" She looked up at her son as if he might have the answer.

David tied up the last of the bags. He gave her a reassuring smile. "Don't kick yourself too much, Mom. I only found out yesterday that Lori's been having an affair with another attorney in New York for over six months, now. I never suspected a thing."

"Lori's a damn fool. And, for once, Susan agrees with me."

David slipped an arm into his jacket. "Susan's a lucky woman. Louie's a good guy. He's strong enough to protect Susan from herself."

Georgia smiled. "I doubt she'd agree with you on that point. Susan considers herself to be the main gear in that family."

David zipped up his jacket. "Since when did Susan ever agree with anyone?" He laughed. "Come on, Mom. Let's go. You're finished here. I'll take you to lunch so you can tell me all about your trip to Sedona."

Draping her sweater over her shoulders, Georgia followed David out of the office and down the steps into the showroom. They waved at Louie, who was busy at the counter with a customer. Georgia caught Amos as he came out of the stockroom. She placed the key to Ed's desk in his hand. "Tell Louie I'm through. The office is all his."

# CHAPTER FOURTEEN

Georgia watched Samantha scoop out the last of the dough and smash it in a lopsided mess on the cookie sheet. Georgia resisted the urge to make the dough pleasingly round like the others. *Some things aren't meant to be perfect.*

Sliding the last tray of chocolate chip cookies into the oven, Georgia turned to Samantha, and said, "Well, Sam, that's that." She clapped her hands and gave her granddaughter a quick buss on the cheek, thinking most likely this would be the last of anything she would ever bake in this kitchen.

The house had sold at the first open house and at a price Georgia thought she would never get. Now, she had thirty days to clean out the rooms and decide where to move. Susan and David were both upstairs, going through everything and deciding what they would keep for themselves.

She couldn't remember the last time David and Susan had been alone together in this house. Georgia heard them now in the upstairs hallway, alternately laughing and yelling at each other like old times. Their voices echoed throughout the house, sounding like music to Georgia's ears.

When Susan arrived at the house that morning, she lost no time claiming the dining room table and chairs, plus the twelve place settings of china that had originally belonged to Georgia's mother. As far as Georgia was concerned, Susan could have anything she wanted, so long as David agreed to his sister's taking more than her fair share. She knew that David could care less about the things in this house. Items not claimed by her children would be hauled away to an auction house or boxed up and given to charity. By next week, the house would be empty and ready to greet the new family, beginning a whole new cycle of life within these walls.

"Grandma?"

"Yes, sweetie." Georgia gathered up the messy bowls and utensils, reminding herself to start making a list of what she needed to do before closing on the house, like canceling the homeowner's insurance and calling for final readings on the utilities.

"Grandma," Samantha said, licking the last of the cookie dough off her fingers. "Are you going back to see Donna?"

"Who?"

Samantha put her hands on her hips and hunched her shoulders. "You know, Grandma. That person you stayed with when you ran away. The one who makes you go crazy."

"Oh," she said, now understanding. "Sweetie, Sedona's not a person, it's a place." She slipped everything into a sink filled with hot, sudsy water.

"Are you going there again?"

"I don't know, yet. Maybe."

Samantha's face scrunched with concern. "Oh, boy, that means Mom will probably start crying again."

"I hope not, but it's my decision."

Ben charged through the kitchen and grabbed up another cookie. "One more?"

"One more," Georgia said, handing him two. "The extra's for Uncle David."

Samantha sat down at the table with a glass of milk. "Mommy said Indians are moving into this house." She took her time swallowing the milk, looking at Georgia over the rim of the glass.

"They're from India. Do you know where India is?"

The girl shook her head. Then, very seriously, said, "I think it's somewhere down south like Florida."

Georgia couldn't help but laugh. "Well, it's across the ocean, thousands of miles away. They came to the United States because Rupin's going to medical school here at the university."

She finished cleaning the counter and sat down across from Samantha, gathering cookie crumbs into a pile with the side of her hand. "Rupin and Sunita are excited about moving into the house. They have a little girl named Sara, your age."

"Will she go to my school?"

"Probably."

"Is she nice?"

"Oh, yes. Maybe a little shy."

"Is she homesick?"

"I'm sure she is."

Samantha shrugged. "But why did the mom and dad leave India, if it makes their child sad?"

"Because any new thing can be sad in the beginning, but given a little time, Sara will make new friends, someone like you, and then it will seem more like home."

Samantha brushed her hand across the table, accidentally spilling what remained of her milk. The glass rolled off the edge of table and shattered against the tile floor. "Uh oh," Samantha said, jumping up from her chair.

"Don't move, Sam. You'll cut your foot on the broken glass." Georgia sprinted for the broom from the hall closet, sweeping the pieces into the dustpan. Grabbing a handful of paper towels, Georgia cleaned up the milk on the table.

"I'm sorry, Grandma." Tears welled up in Samantha's eyes.

"That's okay, sweetie pie. One less glass I'll have to pack."

"I don't want you to move," she sobbed.

"I know, honey. But things never stay the same."

"But why?" Her granddaughter searched her face for an answer. An answer Georgia didn't have. How could she explain time to a six-year-old?

"Let's go one day at a time, okay? Just remember, everything works out in the end."

Susan hurried into the kitchen, excited, a shoebox in her hands. "Look, what David found at the bottom of that old trunk in the attic." She placed the box on the table. "They're love letters to you, Mom, from Daddy." She looked at her mother and then to her daughter, seeing the tears. "What's wrong?"

Georgia's heart sickened at the sight of the shoebox. "Nothing's wrong. We spilled some milk." A prickling sensation pulled at the back of her scalp, as if the box on the table might hold a snake, ready to jump at her when she opened the lid. She'd forgotten all about Ed's letters. The last time she had sat down and read through them was not long after they'd moved into this house. She had almost thrown the letters away then, but instead shoved them into the trunk in the attic and forgot about them.

Removing the lid, Georgia recognized the program from her high school graduation and recalled how that night she and Ed had run away to get married. Beneath the program was a dried rose corsage with a pink ribbon. She found Ed's letters at the bottom, neatly stacked in groups of six and tied with blue ribbons. Georgia leaned close and sniffed for any lingering scent of the sachet she always wore that might have survived the mustiness of the attic.

Susan gave Georgia the sweetest smile. "I know they're private, Mom."

"Yes, they are. Thank you for bringing them to me."

Susan crinkled her nose. "What's that smell?"

"Oh," Georgia said, remembering the last tray of cookies. She'd forgotten to set the timer. Pulling on an oven mitt, she pulled out the blackened cookies and slid them into the trash. *Some things can't be saved and should be thrown away.*

David's return flight to Boston was scheduled for early the next morning. Susan and Louie were taking him out to dinner that evening. Georgia had begged off the invitation, saying she was too tired, but she suspected David and Susan both knew the real reason, she wanted to be alone. She waited until everyone left, when the only sound in the house was the sleepy *tick-tock* of the grandfather clock in the hallway, which Susan had also earlier claimed as her own.

Georgia fixed herself a bourbon and water, and then carefully spread Ed's letters out on the dining room table. In chronological order, she read each letter, alternately drinking and weeping over Ed's tender words scratched out on three-ring notebook paper, and then folded in a tight square to be passed in the hallway at school.

> *Hey Babe,*                    *December 13th*
> *I have to work at the hardware store Friday night. My old man told me I had to start learning the business. I guess I should if I want to make you a good husband some day. HA! Six more months and we can make our own decisions about our lives. Freedom! P.S. Have you heard anything yet about that scholarship? I know you want to go to college but some part of me hopes you get turned down. Sorry. I just love you too much, Babe.*
> *Future Husband, Ed*

> *Hi Hon,*                         *April 12th*
> *Hey don't worry about Trudy Wright. She only wanted to borrow a book for her seventh period class. Your (Ed always did have trouble with this particular contraction) still my best girl, Georgia. Your prom dress sounds beautiful! My girl will look like a million bucks!!!*
> *Love, Ed*

> *Hey Babe,*                       *May 23rd*
> *Don't worry about being pregnant. I don't care what your parents say, or mine either. I love you and want to take care of you for the rest of my life. You are the*

*most beautiful girl in the world. I can't imagine living
without you. I'll make you happy, Georgia, and even
if you can't go to college, I promise you won't regret
it. We won't end up miserable like our parents. And
Georgia most of all I want you to be exactly who you
are. Please don't ever change.*
*All My Love, Ed*

Georgia wiped at her eyes with the backs of her hands, a sweet
sadness filling her insides. They had both been so young, so naïve
about the grownup world. When had the two of them become
what they had promised each other they wouldn't become? They
were two starry-eyed teenagers beginning a marriage with nothing
more than their pooled graduation money and a tiny bit of a baby
growing inside her.

Georgia carefully tied up the letters and put them back inside
the box. Eleven o'clock that evening, she slipped into her housecoat
and pulled on her tennis shoes. She stepped outside the back door
with the shoebox in hand, and, to her utter astonishment, Oscar
came prancing up the sidewalk as if he had never been missing at
all. He meowed up at her as if to say, Okay, I'm home, hand over
the midnight treat. He brushed affectionately against legs.

"Well, look at you," Georgia said, sitting down on the bottom
step and letting him climb into her lap. "Where have you been?"
He purred contentedly, pushing his head into her hand as she
petted him.

The back porch light came on at Mrs. Otis's house, and
Georgia heard the storm door open. Beverly stuck her head out.
"Georgia?"

"It's me, Beverly. I came out for a breath of air."

She had run into Beverly only a few times since her return
home, asking about Mrs. Otis and wanting to see Oscar. Beverly
had told her that Oscar had disappeared. "Probably for the best,"
she'd said. "I'm not a cat lover."

Beverly made her way across the short distance of yard and joined her. When she saw Oscar, she said, "Well, I declare. He came back."

Oscar dug his front paws deep into Georgia's legs, as if claiming her for his own. "I guess he wanted to say hello to an old friend," Georgia said, lifting him to cradle him in her arms.

Clutching the throat of her chenille robe around her throat, Beverly shivered in the night air. "Looks as if you're getting ready to move soon, huh?" Beverly eyed the shoebox on the step beside Georgia.

"I'm sorting through odds and ends, letting the kids take what they want before getting rid of the rest of the stuff."

"I saw Susan and David here earlier. Nice having the family together again, I suppose."

"It was nice." With Beverly there wasn't much substance to a conversation, only stiff-necked politeness. Georgia longed to be back in Sedona where she could sit in the café kitchen and talk with Zoe and Trish about whatever was going on in their lives, nothing in particular, but somehow so much more interesting than Beverly talking about *blah blah blah.*

Beverly finally got her attention when she said, "Well, the cat looks as if he's found a home with you. Do you want him?"

Georgia stammered, "You don't mind?"

"Are you kidding? If he hadn't disappeared, I probably would've taken him to the animal shelter by now. Cat hair, you know. Makes my eyes itch."

Georgia hugged Oscar tight against her chest. *Animal shelter, indeed.* "I'll take him."

Saying goodnight, Beverly made her way back to her side of the yard. Georgia waited until she heard the door shut and lock before getting up from the step. With Oscar trotting along at her heels, she followed the stone path to the back of the house and the barbeque pit Ed had built in an era of neighborhood block parties. Without ceremony, Georgia dumped the letters into the pit and struck a match. She held the flame to one of the letters until it took hold, and then stood back and watched the fire greedily consume every letter in the pile.

Oscar watched from the edge of patio, his eyes reflecting the soft glow of the fire, tail twitching back and forth, waiting until she was finished. It seemed to Georgia that the cat knew exactly what she was doing and why she was doing it.

Last thing, Georgia threw the shoebox on the fire and watched as the flames leaped up and devoured it within seconds. Turning back toward the house, Georgia lightly lifted the hem of her bathrobe and said to Oscar, "Let's go home."

# CHAPTER FIFTEEN

"You're Jake Rizzo!" Georgia instantly recognized her seatmate on her connecting flight out of O'Hare. She recalled the newspaper photograph Trish had flaunted in front of Zoe on the morning she had made the decision to return to Ohio.

"That I am." He greeted her with a gorgeous smile as he stood up and obligingly held Georgia's pet carrier while she moved to the window seat and sat down. Returning the carrier, he sat back down, loosening the tie of his dress shirt. "Who's your friend?"

Georgia smiled, stowing her purse under the seat but letting the pet carrier rest in her lap. "This is Oscar. He's a bit groggy. The vet gave him something to keep him calm during the flight."

A pretty flight attendant came over and offered Jake a drink, maybe a pillow, perhaps her *phone number*? Jake shook his head that he didn't need anything at the moment. The attendant seemed disappointed for all her grand efforts to make her celebrity passenger more comfortable and to take notice of her.

Georgia couldn't exactly blame her. Jake was handsome, no doubt about it. Add being a retired astronaut from the space program plus running for political office, well, any woman would be crazy not to be attracted to a package like that.

Jake Rizzo was Arizona's favorite son. Georgia, after meeting him, could easily believe the U.S. Senate seat would be his for the taking. The possibility that he might one day run for President was not all that unbelievable. And, more than ever, she understood what Zoe was going through, loving a man who would once again put her into the media spotlight where she would be scrutinized to within an inch of her life.

Coach passengers boarded the plane, inching their way to the rear and causing the usual backup as they found their seats and stowed carryon luggage. Georgia silently thanked Zoe for the first class tickets and roomy seat, thus avoiding the forward-to-rear hassle of boarding.

She was anxious to see Zoe again. When she'd talked with her this morning, Zoe had insisted on meeting Georgia in baggage claim after the plane's arrival in Phoenix, saying she would be in the city, anyway, visiting her mother that morning. Georgia couldn't wait to see the expression on Zoe's face when she found out Jake was on the plane. Coincidence? Not likely. It occurred to her that Zoe had made both flight reservations, planned the seating arrangement with Jake.

Georgia fastened her seatbelt, and then pulled the cookbook from her bag, propping it on top of the carrier. She peeked in on Oscar, sleeping like a newborn kitten. Opening the cookbook, she thumbed through the pages. Two photographs fell out, fluttering into Mr. Rizzo's lap. He picked them up and handed them to her. "Cute kids."

Georgia smiled. "My grandchildren. They must've put them in the cookbook as a surprise."

"Gum?" He held out a packet.

"Thank you."

The flight attendant came forward, slamming overhead compartments. As she passed their seats, the attendant lightly touched Jake's shoulder. He seemed oblivious to the beautiful thirty-something girl who was desperately flirting with him. She looked disappointed and perhaps a bit irritated he didn't so much as look up and acknowledge her perfect smile.

After revving down the runway, the plane lifted into the air, and then leveled out into flight. The seatbelt sign went out. That's when Georgia turned to Jake with every intention of confessing that she was friends with Zoe. She opened her mouth to speak just as the flight attendant reappeared and leaned close to Jake, whispering something into his ear. He responded with a gracious smile, shaking his head. "No, I'm fine right here, but I appreciate the offer."

The attendant tilted her head, as if confused, as if he might have misunderstood her. She said softly, "I thought you might like more privacy over here." She then pointed to two empty seats on the other side of the plane.

Georgia turned the page in the cookbook, feigning interest, as if the recipe for pumpkin bread on page 35 was too good to be true. Her ears, however, were burning with curiosity.

"Actually, Georgia and I are traveling together."

*What?* She kept her eyes glued to the book, shocked by what he'd said, even more shocked when he lifted her hand from the cookbook and gave it a squeeze. "We're old friends."

"Oh?" The attendant's eyes widened, no doubt stunned. Then, she shot Georgia an appreciative glance, as if seeing her in an entirely new light. "I wasn't aware." Georgia shrugged and mouthed, that's okay, thinking there would be no more *touchy feely* pats for Jake Rizzo during the flight.

Georgia closed the cookbook. "Why, Mr. Rizzo, you knew who I was all along, didn't you?"

He laughed and gave her hand another squeeze before letting go. "Call me Jake. And yes, Zoe scheduled the flights. She asked me to take good care of you."

"Oh? I hope you don't mind."

"Mind? It was my idea. I invite Zoe to come with me on these business trips, but, she always turns me down. So, I thought I'd enjoy your company and Zoe agreed." Jake settled back in his seat, seemingly content to sit and chat with her for the next few hours. Although obviously confident and outgoing, Jake Rizzo lacked the arrogance that usually comes with being handsome, smart and totally accepted by ninety-nine percent of the people in your life.

Georgia asked, "Have you talked to Zoe this morning?"

"Yes. She's excited about seeing you again."

"How's Gloria? Any improvement?"

His jaw tensed. "I think the damage from the stroke is permanent. She's comfortable at the moment, but it won't last long. Zoe's having a rough time dealing with it all." Jake sighed. "I know this sounds callous, but I hope Gloria doesn't hang on for months or years. It's too hard on Zoe."

"I wish I could do something to help." The attendant brought their drinks and for the next few minutes they sat in silence.

Jake spoke up. "So far, Zoe's putting up a brave front. I only—" At that moment, a boy somewhere around the age of eight rushed past their row of seats. The attendant firmly told the boy to please use the facilities at the rear of the plane so as to not bother the first-class passengers. Georgia fumed on the inside, beginning to develop a genuine dislike for the attendant. If the young woman was a mother, she'd know that when a child's got to go, he's got to go, no matter if the *facilities* are in the front or the back of the plane. Georgia caught Jake studying her. "What?"

"You're a nice lady, Georgia. I can see why Zoe loves you. She doesn't get close to many people. She thinks emotional attachment is too risky."

Georgia felt her face grow hot. She liked Jake, felt as comfortable with him as she did with Zoe. "You mean, like Zoe falling in love with you, right?"

Jake took a slow sip of his coffee, adding another packet of cream. "I'm afraid Zoe's the only one who can answer that question. Not me." Another sip of coffee. "My sweet Zoe lacks a sense of security that only a good, nurturing mother could have provided.

Georgia loved his *My sweet Zoe* endearment. "How long have you known Zoe?"

"Almost two years. My sister introduced us at a family party.

I thought she was the most beautiful creature in the world. Until then, I never could've believed I'd fall in love again... not like the first time."

"First time?"

Jake's smile faded, his eyes dulling with an old grief. "My wife died five years ago. An accident." He swallowed hard. "A drunk driver went left of center. My ten-year-old son was in the car, too."

Georgia's chest tightened. "I'm so sorry." Somewhere in the back of Georgia's mind, she recalled the tragedy being on the news and in the newspapers but had forgotten over the years. No way could she even begin to comprehend the loss of a child.

"After the accident, I left the space program and moved back to Tucson. I pulled away from the outside world, that is, until I met Zoe. She's an extraordinary woman."

"I know," Georgia heartily agreed.

"A few years back, I did some political campaigning for some friends of mine. They thought my name on a few posters might draw a decent crowd. Then, last year the party bosses talked me into running for the Senate. Actually, I think I could do a good job for the people of Arizona."

"And Zoe? How does she fit into all this?"

"As my wife, I hope. She promised she'd give me a straight answer after the election. I'm afraid she won't accept."

"What do you want?"

"I say we get married now. What possible difference could it make? I'm afraid if we wait, she'll only come up with another excuse for us not to be together." He handed his coffee cup to the attendant and folded the nuisance of a tray back into the seat.

"Well, Zoe's stubborn, but I don't think she wants to lose you, either."

"I hope not." He sighed and reached up and adjusted the air flow. "What about you, Georgia? Did you find what you were looking for back in Ohio?"

Georgia smiled. "Oh, yes."

The attendant passed their seats again and for some unknown reason said, "Congratulations." Georgia gave her a brief smile, confused, not sure if the attendant was talking to her or the people in the row ahead of her. She turned her attention back to Jake who looked annoyed at the attendant's constant hovering. Georgia couldn't resist whispering, "Haven't you noticed? That young woman's got a major crush on you."

"Not my type," he said. "Tell me about your trip to Ohio."

"There's not much to tell. I settled an old account of the heart and had a nice visit with my family. I sold my house and worked out a deal with my daughter and son-in-law to buy the family hardware store. Then, this morning, I kissed my grandchildren goodbye and hopped on the plane. Who knows, maybe next year I'll change my mind, but right now, this is what I want."

"I'm glad you've decided on Sedona."

"Tell me more about Zoe," Georgia said, taking a peek out the window and seeing the flat terrain of Kansas below them. "What happened between Zoe and her mother?"

"If you were anyone else, I wouldn't say a word out of respect for Zoe. You, Georgia, deserve to know the truth about the woman we both love and care about."

"Thank you," she said.

He closed his eyes and took in a breath, letting it out slowly. "Gloria Atwater was a lush. Sober, the woman could be difficult, drunk, she was downright cruel. As a kid, Zoe learned to become invisible. Gloria's drinking binges might go on for days or even weeks, depending on her state of mind. The older Gloria got, the more she drank."

"How sad," she said.

"Yes," he agreed, "Can you imagine living in a household where happiness depended on the mood of one person? Zoe spent her childhood trying to figure why she was so unlovable to her mother. Later, she moved to New Orleans to live with Florry's brother and his wife."

"What about Florry? Was she any help?"

"Well, that's the curious part. Florry had no problem standing up to Gloria when it came to Zoe. And, I shouldn't tell you this, but Zoe always had it in her head that Florry was her biological mother."

Georgia felt her jaw drop. She whispered, "Is that true?"

Jake shrugged. "Maybe. Florry died of an overdose of morphine. Zoe believes Gloria did it to keep the truth from Zoe."

"Murder?" Georgia whispered, barely able to breathe.

Jake sighed. "Nothing much ever came of it. The woman was in so much pain and so near death, I wouldn't doubt Florry asked Gloria to overdose her. If anything, it was a blessing she died."

"What about Florry's brother in New Orleans? Would Florry have told him the truth about Zoe?"

"Gabe Lee died ten years ago. Heart attack. His wife eventually remarried and moved somewhere up the east coast."

The attendant made her final stroll down the aisle checking seatbelts before the descent into Sky Harbor. Georgia couldn't believe that she and Jake had been talking the entire flight to Phoenix. She took a quick peek out the window and watched the houses and streets as they became larger and more life-sized. She stuffed the cookbook into her bag and shoved it under the forward seat, anxious to see Zoe.

Jake said, "How's your buddy doing?" He tilted his head to indicate the pet carrier.

"Still dozing. Whatever the vet gave him, I think I could use a dose of it now and then."

In the past few hours, Georgia had grown quite comfortable with Jake and thought him to be perfect for Zoe. Politics or no politics, Georgia would give Zoe a good piece of her mind, telling her how lucky she was to have found a man who loved her so deeply. If only Gloria Atwater would let go of the truth about Zoe's birth mother before she died. Maybe then Zoe could make peace with her past.

"Zoe's meeting us in baggage claim," Jake said, taking Oscar's pet carrier from her and lightly touching her back as he directed her through the terminal crush. Jake's arm slid around her shoulder as they hurried toward the escalators.

From out of nowhere, a thin young man in a T-shirt and jeans leaped from the crowd and snapped their picture once, twice, three times. "Thanks a bunch, Mr. Rizzo." The man disappeared into the flow of people as quickly as he had first appeared.

"Who was that?" Georgia asked, still seeing dots from the flash.

"A reporter." Jake tightened his grip on her shoulder as if he meant to protect her from some unseen danger. "The election's getting closer. The polls say I'm in the lead, and it looks as if my opponent is trying to find something in my personal life to use against me. I hope you don't mind getting your photograph taken with me?"

She laughed. "They must be desperate taking a photograph of me."

Jake's brow furrowed with anger. "You'd be surprised how they can twist things."

They found Zoe waiting in the lower level. She looked gorgeous in jeans and a short white jacket, her dark hair loose around her shoulders. Seeing Georgia, she jumped up and hurried toward them. They exchanged hugs. "Oh, Georgia, it's so good seeing you back here. The minute you told us, Trish gave Mrs. Hitler the boot. Mary Jo's acting like a little girl set free on the playground." Zoe gave Jake a sidelong smile and leaned close enough to whisper, "Later."

He nodded, and then gave both women a gentlemanly bow. "Ladies, if you'll excuse me, I've got some campaigning to do before the election." He turned to Zoe. "Say hi to Sis for me?" And with that said, Jake handed Oscar back to Georgia and disappeared into the crowd waiting at baggage claim.

Zoe took note of the carrier and took a peek through the mesh. "A cat! You brought home a *cat*?"

"His name's Oscar."

"Trish will love him."

Georgia turned to Zoe. "Is Jake's sister coming to Sedona? I'd love to meet her."

Zoe's face took on a blank expression, as if confused. Then, she started to laugh. "Oh dear Lord, Georgia. You really don't know, do you?"

"What?"

"Trish is Jake's sister."

"No way! You never told me that."

"Must've slipped my mind." Zoe checked her watch. "Let's get going before rush hour hits Phoenix."

Georgia spotted her black suitcase that looked identical to every other one except for the red bow Susan had tied on it before leaving that morning. "Why would it slip your mind?"

Zoe shrugged. "Well, you've never met Jake before today, so why did you need to know Trish was his sister?" She pulled Georgia's bag off the conveyer belt. "Remember that morning you came into the café and Jake's picture was on the front page of the newspaper?"

"Sure I do."

"I was going to say something then, but you fainted. After that, you decided to go back to Ohio, so it really didn't matter about Jake being Trish's stepbrother."

"Stepbrother?"

"Trish's mother married Jake's father because she was a young widow with very expensive tastes. She needed an older man with lots of money."

They walked into the parking garage, Zoe rolling the suitcase and Georgia holding onto Oscar's carrier. "I hope you're not still mad at me."

"Why should I be mad at you?"

"Well, you know. That fight Trish and I were having right before you fainted. I should've told you earlier about Jake, but I didn't want to take the chance of anyone finding out about us. After the election, we'll see." Tears clouded Zoe's eyes. They arrived in the parking garage. Zoe pointed to where she had parked the car.

Georgia said, "Does the election outcome really matter? Do you want to lose him?"

Zoe kept walking. "Is that so terribly selfish?"

"Yes, if it's all about you." She walked faster to keep up with Zoe.

Zoe defiantly tilted her pretty chin into the air. "Well, then I'm selfish. Oh, Georgia, let's don't fight on your first day home. Okay?"

"Jake Rizzo loves you, Zoe. Don't mess this up."

With a toss of her hair, Zoe said, "My business, Georgia."

"You're not getting off that easy. I'll drop the subject for now, but I'm not going to see you ruin your life because your mother was mean to you."

Zoe made an abrupt halt and turned on Georgia. "Don't go there, Georgia. That's private. You know that."

"Sometimes the truth hurts, Zoe."

"Oh, God, Georgia, I'm sorry. I know you care about me, and I appreciate your concern. Please, let me figure this out on my own. Agreed?"

"Agreed," Georgia said, but not without adding, "For the moment."

They walked to Row C on level three and found the Fleetwood parked like a fat, old woman wedged between two skinny, more compact models. To Georgia, the car was the most beautiful sight in the world.

# CHAPTER SIXTEEN

Sedona!

Home at last!

Georgia no sooner stepped from the car outside the Soft Rock Café when Trish appeared from out of nowhere and wrapped her in a great, smothering hug. "Oh, thank God, Georgia, you're back." Trish looked adorable in a pleated skirt and soft yellow knit sweater with her hair pulled back into a neat twist.

Georgia stood back and eyed Trish up and down, still holding onto her hands. "Say, what's with the petite-sophisticate look?" Trish's usual wardrobe consisted of jeans and a T-shirt with some catchy environmental slogan emblazoned across the front.

Trish smiled and curtsied. "Like it? I've been volunteering at the Tourist Center."

"Where?" Georgia couldn't believe her ears.

"At the Tourist Center," Trish repeated. "You know, refilling pamphlet slots and talking to tourists about where to go and what to see here in Sedona."

"You're kidding?"

"No, I'm serious. I love it."

"Well, you look..." Georgia struggled to find the right word. "Very neat."

Trish looped an arm through Georgia's. "I've grown up, Georgia. You being gone for the past two months made me do a lot of thinking."

163

"Thinking? Do tell." Zoe pulled out the handle on Georgia's bag, a teasing smile pasted on her face.

Trish gave Zoe a hard look. "Don't start on me."

"What?" Zoe said, innocent. "I'm just curious about all this growth you're talking about. Volunteering was nothing more than an excuse to get out of the café whenever Helga was working the kitchen."

Trish's bottom lip puffed out. "That's not true."

"It is true." Zoe turned to Georgia. "I'll get someone to help with the luggage. I thought you might want to go inside the café and take a look around."

"Where is she now?" Georgia asked.

"Who?" Trish and Zoe asked simultaneously.

"Helga." Georgia said, exasperated, thinking Moe and Curly had nothing on these two. A real comedy team.

"I got rid of her," Trish said, crossing her arms and giving Georgia a smug nod of the head.

"Uh hum." Zoe countered.

"Well?" Georgia asked.

"Actually," Zoe said, glancing down at her watch, "Helga's on a flight to Vancouver as we speak. She's got an interview at a restaurant owned by a friend of mine." Zoe held up one hand and delicately blew on her fingernails. "What a coincidence. They needed a chef with a hard-edge to handle the kitchen staff—and we had Helga."

"Well, I suppose I should thank you," Trish said. "But I could've fired her myself."

"Oh? Helga scared the pee out of you."

"That's not true."

"What?" Zoe chided. "Georgia's back now. I bet in another week, you'll stop volunteering."

"That's not true," Trish objected.

"Sure it is."

"Stop bickering," Georgia ordered. She was tired and wanted

to go upstairs and get Oscar settled into the apartment. Tomorrow would be her first day back at the café, and she didn't want to start out tired. "And if the two of you can stop fighting for two consecutive seconds, I'd love to invite you upstairs. We'll open a bottle of wine. Besides, I want to catch up on all the gossip around town."

"Say, what's that?" Trish said, eyeing the red carrier.

"Oscar," Zoe said.

"What's an Oscar?" She looked at Georgia.

"My cat." Georgia unzipped the carrier and pulled out a drowsy Oscar and folded him into Trish's arms.

"Oh, Georgia, he's beautiful. I love cats." Oscar looked up at her with big, dopey eyes.

"God, what's he on?"

"A tranquilizer. Don't worry. He's coming out of it now."

She squeezed Oscar against her chest. "I'd love to have a cat."

"He's mine," Georgia joked. "All mine."

Upstairs, Georgia started a fire in the fireplace and sank into the sofa. How good to be in her apartment again, back inside the life she had come to love and had missed terribly these last two months. And having the two best friends in the world here with her now completed her welcome home.

"You look content," Zoe said, handing her a glass of wine.

Georgia pulled her red shawl over her shoulders. "I am."

Trish placed another log on the fire, and then dropped into the overstuffed chair across from Georgia. "This is nice. Together again."

Georgia winked at Zoe, pleading for her not to heckle Trish. Oscar, now fully recovered from his drugs, was quickly adapting to the cozy apartment. He finally stopped nosing around and crawled into her lap, tail twitching as he watched these two strange women talking to his mistress. Zoe said to Trish, "I'm sorry for kidding you about Helga."

Trish sipped her wine, eyes focused on the fire. "The devil's spawn," she whispered with all the drama of a 1930's movie. "When I first hired her, Helga seemed nice, kind of motherly. But a little each day, she took over everything and started bossing everyone around. It got so bad Doc wouldn't even come into the café for a cup of coffee. Helga told him he needed a wife. I think that put the fear of God into him."

Georgia and Zoe howled with laughter. Trish said, indignantly. "Well it might be funny now but it wasn't then. Doc thought Helga smelled like formaldehyde, you know, like something dead."

At the mention of Doc's name, her stomach twisted into a tight knot. In the past few weeks, the man kept popping into her thoughts, once even in a dream where they were dancing in the moonlight under Zoe's balcony. Georgia shivered, remembering another dream where Doc had kissed her tenderly on the lips. She had awakened with her heart racing like a teenager in love for the first time.

Zoe poured a second glass of wine. "Well, now, Georgia, why so quiet all of a sudden? You're blushing. Can it be Doc you're thinking about?" She cocked an eyebrow at Trish.

Trish said, "Now that you mention it, Doc has asked about you every day, wanting to know if you were coming back."

Zoe closed her eyes, grinning. "I think Doc's quite smitten with you, Georgia. Is the feeling mutual?"

"Don't start matchmaking me with Doc. I barely know the man." Georgia hiccupped. They all laughed.

Georgia changed the subject, fearing if they kept talking about Doc, she might say something she'd regret. Suddenly, she remembered Trish was Jake's stepsister. She blurted out, "Jake's your stepbrother!"

Trish pulled her legs up under her and gave Georgia a benign smile. "More like my real brother." She looked over a Zoe. "She's changing the subject on us."

Georgia sipped her wine. "What's it like, having a famous brother?"

Trish's eyelashes fluttered, teasing, but then the comedic façade faded into a reminiscent smile. "I was only three when my mother married Jake's father. Jake was in college, like twenty years old. From the beginning, I loved him. Some weekends, he'd come home and we'd go out for breakfast Saturday mornings—just the two of us. Our parents traveled a lot, so I stayed with nannies most of the time. Then, they sent me to boarding school. Jake felt sorry for me. My stepfather indulged my mother like a spoiled child. Of course, being thirty years younger, he probably felt he had to. I guess he really loved her. Unfortunately, she didn't love him."

Georgia said, "You poor, lonely kid."

Trish wiped her eyes on the sleeve of her soft yellow sweater. "My stepfather died when I was twelve. My mother inherited a fortune. If Jake ever felt slighted because Mom took more than her fair share, he never once showed it. A real brother, he was." She laughed. "After my stepfather died, my mother seemed to forget I existed. I felt so unwanted." She turned to Zoe. "I guess that's why we became good friends, huh?"

Zoe gave Trish's hand a tight squeeze. Georgia felt her heart go out to these two women drawn to one another through the misfortune of having mothers who did not know how to love their daughters. With all their teasing and bickering, Zoe and Trish loved one another like true sisters.

Tears spilled down Trish's cheeks. She said, "After Mom died, Jake took me in and gave me a home." Trish closed her eyes and stubbornly wiped at her tears with her fists. "Enough about me. I want to hear about Georgia's trip."

Georgia's lips felt numb from the wine, her speech coming out slow and drowsy. "No regrets. I sold the house and made peace with my family."

"Was Susan angry about your decision to come back to Sedona?"

Georgia covered her mouth and giggled. "She tried to send me to Florida."

Zoe bolted upright. "No! Only old people go to Florida."

"I told her no."

Zoe and Trish clapped their hands, cheering Georgia on. Another glass of wine and all three women abandoned the furniture and settled for the floor, propping themselves up with pillows pulled from the sofa. Almost midnight and emotionally charged from the wine and the giddiness of their being reunited, no one seemed ready to abandon the magical warmth of Georgia's apartment.

Georgia moved a pillow under her head and yawned, barely able to keep her eyes open. If she didn't get some sleep, she'd never wake up in time to start the cinnamon rolls. "My family's coming to Sedona for Thanksgiving," she said with another yawn. "I'm going to prepare one big dinner right here at the café for all of us."

Trish jumped up from the floor. "Georgia, that's wonderful! Mary Jo and Doc, too?"

Georgia laughed. "Of course." She turned to Zoe. "Jake's invited, along with your mother."

Zoe choked on her sip of wine. She pressed her right hand over her heart. "Good Lord, Georgia, you're drunk. Wait until morning. We'll talk then about having your family Thanksgiving." She said this with sarcasm.

"I think Jake would enjoy it." Georgia shot back.

"I'm talking about my mother, not Jake. Of course, I'll bring Jake. The election will be so over by Thanksgiving. No need to keep my distance from him after that."

Georgia sat up, ready to end the homecoming party and go to bed. "Well, of course, it's your decision. I can't make you bring your mother, but she's invited just the same. Besides, how much trouble could an old woman confined to a wheelchair cause?"

Zoe let out a long exasperated sigh. "Plenty."

\* \* \*

Early the next morning, Georgia tiptoed downstairs and entered the café through the back entrance. Switching on the light in the kitchen, her eyes sought out the damage. Like Mama Bear in the fairytale, she knew someone had been cooking in her kitchen. Plants were missing from the window sill over her desk, no doubt thrown out by the infamous Helga. All the beautiful drawings Ben and Sam had mailed to Georgia during the summer months had been banished from the bulletin board, replaced with ugly state regulatory posters normally hidden from sight in the pantry. Georgia opened a cupboard. Pots, pans and cookie sheets had all been moved. But where to?

Trish pushed through the swinging door, busily tying on her morning apron. "Helga didn't make cookies or cinnamon rolls," she was quick to tattle.

"Where are they?"

"The cookie sheets?"

"Yes, Trish." She sounded irritated, but couldn't help it. Before starting rolls, Georgia would have to first find everything and put it back where it belonged.

Trish pointed at the pantry. "In there. Top shelf."

Georgia opened the door and turned on the light. "Why on earth would she put them in here?" She pulled the cookie sheets down and returned them to the cupboard.

Georgia then stood in the middle of the kitchen, hands on hips, trying to place what else was missing. Suddenly, looking up, she hurried back into the pantry and slid the stepstool over to another shelf, finding the copper pots shoved to the back. With Trish's help, she brought them down and hung them on the beams in the kitchen.

Trish looked triumphant. "Helga didn't like copper pots hanging on the beams."

"Hmmm," Georgia said, opening drawers and cupboards, seeking out every misplaced item and returning it to where it had originally been before Helga.

"My potholders," Georgia said, patting the long countertop where she usually threw them when not in use. "Where are they?" Georgia loved those old potholders. Admittedly, they weren't much to look at, but they were old and soft and, well, they felt familiar in her hands.

"Helga threw them in the trash. She couldn't get all the stains out. Helga didn't like the plants or anything else personal in the kitchen. She thought it was unprofessional."

"Stop! I'm sick to death of hearing what Helga *did* and what Helga *thought*." She looked at Trish with all the determination of a military commander about to go into battle. "As of this moment everything in this kitchen goes back to the way I had it two months ago. Understood?"

Trish's mouth broke into a wide grin. "Oh, Georgia, you don't know how good it is to have you back. The locals were so scared of Helga, they hardly set foot inside the café." Trish shivered. "When she left town, I never felt so good in my life."

Georgia finished hanging the last copper pot on the beam hook. "There, that's better. Now, we'll start the first batch of rolls. In a few hours, this place will smell so good the whole town will be crowding in here." And with that, Georgia set about measuring flour and warming the yeast. Her hands busy, she settled into the rhythm of her work, feeling, at last, that she was finally home.

Georgia very much anticipated Doc coming into the café for a cup of coffee, so when she heard the front door open as she pulled out the first pan of rolls, Georgia wiped her hands on her apron, ready to greet him. Instead of Doc, Zoe flew through the swinging door and into the kitchen flagging a tabloid in the air. Her face was a firestorm as she slammed the paper flat on the table. "You won't believe this." She slapped the paper as if it were trying to make a slippery getaway off the table. "Those liars, those idiots! They'd do anything to sell crap!"

Mary Jo had followed Zoe in from the dining room. "What's wrong?" Mary Jo asked. She tugged the newspaper out from under Zoe's hand and scanned the front page.

Mary Jo gasped, "Oh, my God." She looked at Georgia. "Oh, no."

Georgia peeked over Mary Jo's shoulder. It took several seconds for her eyes to fully register the prominent photograph of Jake Rizzo and Georgia that dominated the front page, the one taken yesterday as they had made their way down to the baggage claim. "That little worm," Georgia uttered with distaste.

"Who," Trish asked.

"That photographer at the airport. He jumped out of nowhere and took our picture."

Trish read the caption beneath the photograph. "*ARIZONA'S FAVORITE SON GETTING MARRIED?*"

Georgia shrieked, "What!"

All three crowded close to the table, reading over Mary Jo's shoulder as she read the article aloud. "An undisclosed source revealed today that Jake Rizzo proposed to this mystery woman while traveling together on a flight from Chicago to Phoenix. The source also said the woman accepted his proposal."

Georgia let out another gasp. She pulled out a chair and sat down. "Oh, this is too much. I can't believe it." She knew now what the flight attendant had meant when she congratulated her. No doubt, the woman had practically broken her neck getting on her cell and reporting to that weasel of a reporter already waiting in the terminal.

With an air of importance, Trish cleared her throat and finished. "The future Mrs. Rizzo? Maybe. Either way, I'll wager we'll be seeing a lot more of her in the future, especially if Jake Rizzo wins the senatorial seat in Washington."

Georgia jerked the paper out of Trish's hands and flung it to the floor. "Why in the world would they ever print a lie like this?"

Georgia felt Zoe grip her shoulder. "I'm really sorry about this, Georgia. If I hadn't arranged for the two of you to come back on the flight together, none of this would've happened. I should have known better."

Mary Jo picked up the scattered newspaper and studied the photograph. "Wow, you know what? Actually, the two of you make a great looking couple."

Zoe snatched the paper away from Mary Jo. "I think you'd better get back to the dining room. Your public awaits you." Mary Jo shrugged and did as she was told. Zoe studied the photograph. "You know, she's right. You do look really gorgeous in this photograph."

Georgia felt herself blush from the top of her head down to the tip of her toes. "Zoe, this is no joking matter. What's to be done about this?"

Zoe shrugged. "Mary Jo's right. You do look every inch the political wife. As for handling the situation? We do absolutely nothing. Tomorrow someone somewhere in the state of Arizona will be lining the bottom of a parakeet cage with this newspaper." She sniffed. "Don't worry about it."

"They had no right."

Zoe sat down beside her. "*They* don't care. I only hope this won't dredge up the death of Jake's wife and child all over again. No telling what that would do to him so close to the election." She sighed. "I guess if he loses, that wouldn't be so bad, either."

"That depends," Georgia said, glancing over at Trish who was busy at the stove scrambling eggs for a customer.

"On what?" Zoe asked, intrigued.

The phone suddenly rang, one, two, three times. Mary Jo didn't pick up in the dining room. "It depends on what Jake really wants. If he loses the election, he'll only run again in the future." The phone was still ringing. Georgia was about to jump up and get it when Trish picked up. Tucking the receiver under her chin, she continued working at the stove.

Zoe closed her eyes and pursed her lips together. "You're right, Georgia. So right, that a part of me wishes the photograph were true. Because if it were true, you'd be standing beside Jake, giving him the support he needs to win this election. I can't do that."

"Jake's a fine man. He loves you. And I know you love him. In my book, that's all it takes to build a life together. Or, maybe, that's too easy for you."

Zoe narrowed her eyes at Georgia. "What do you mean, too easy?"

Georgia stood up and carried the newspaper to the trash container. "Risk losing all the pain you've been carrying around like some favorite stuffed toy to make you feel safe and secure. Somehow, I think it gives you the illusion of control. You've taught yourself that no one will ever love you for just you. And you're willing to sacrifice your happiness with Jake just for the sake of keeping your heart safe."

"Happiness?" Zoe let out a sarcastic laugh. "Oh, Georgia, you're being too philosophical. Besides, who would ever *choose* to make themselves unhappy?"

Georgia shivered at Zoe's cold tone, but wasn't about to back down now. "It's comfortable, keeping all that misery close to you. Take a chance, Zoe. Build a life with Jake. He's definitely worth the risk."

Trish was still on the phone, scooping scrambled eggs onto a plate, laughing so hard the plate slipped off the counter. She caught the plate before it hit the floor. "Oops! Just a minute." She handed the phone to Georgia. "It's your son, David."

"Oh?" Georgia pressed the receiver tight against her ear. "David?"

"Hey Mom. I flew into New York last night on business, and this morning when I stopped at a newsstand to buy a paper, well, the funniest thing happened."

"David, I—"

"The Phoenix newspaper was right out front, and golly gee, Mom, you'll never guess who was on the front page."

"David, I can ex—"

"Mom? I can't believe you know Jake Rizzo! When I was a kid, I idolized the man."

"You did?" She had never known that about her son. He sounded so excited, as if he were nine years old again.

"Sure. Don't you remember *The Right Stuff*? God, I loved that book. And I must've seen *Apollo 13* at least twenty times. Say, will he be there on Thanksgiving?"

"Jake? Yes, I think so."

"Wow!"

Although she'd been interrupted twice, Georgia still felt compelled to explain about the photograph in the paper. "It was all a mistake."

"I know Mom. Trish told me what happened. Say, what's she look like?"

"Who?"

"Trish."

"Oh?" Georgia glanced over her shoulder to make sure Trish was busy elsewhere and not listening in on her conversation. "She's cute. No, actually, she's pretty. And petite, not tall like..." She let the rest of the sentence drift away. The last thing David needed to hear was Lori's name.

"Married?"

"No."

"Engaged?"

"Nope."

"Trish will be there on Thanksgiving, too?"

"Hope so. I'll need all the help in the kitchen I can get. David? Did I mention that Trish is Jake Rizzo's stepsister?"

"You don't say?"

"David?"

"Yes, Mom."

"Did I mention she loves kids."

# CHAPTER SEVENTEEN

It was the day before Thanksgiving and Georgia was literally tied in a knot. Although she loved yoga, it didn't always love her. She liked to stay hidden at the back of the class Zoe taught once a week at the Moon Tide before opening for the day.

"Triangle pose," Zoe said over a background of soft flute music.

Georgia obediently extended her legs and raised her arms to the side, feeling her pelvis open and relax into a comfortable balance. She slowly leaned to the side, one arm extending into the air, the other touching the floor outside the ankle. Usually, Georgia could firmly hold the position with the other students, but today, she found it difficult to concentrate.

"Mountain pose." Zoe's voice seemed to float within music.

Georgia stood up and straightened her spine, palms pressed together in front of the heart. She took in a deep, cleansing breath.

"You okay?" Trish asked from a neighboring mat. Dressed in black coolie pants for fluid movement and a red tank top, Trish looked delectably tiny.

"I'm all right, why?"

"I heard you grunt."

"I did not grunt." Georgia tugged at the hem of her white T-shirt, in no mood for Trish's sarcasm. Before leaving the apartment

175

that morning, Georgia did nothing more than towel-dry her hair
and finger-comb a dab of mousse into it to keep everything in
place. Even Oscar had given her a look of disapproval as she hastily
dumped food into his bowl and slipped on a jacket.

Now, her hair stuck out around her ears, stiff as straw.
However cute this funky, I-just-rolled-out-of-bed style looked on
younger women, it did nothing for Georgia.

She did not like standing next to Trish during yoga class, but
Trish always sought her out. With seemingly little effort Trish
could pretzel her body into a lotus and sink into her third eye
before you could count to ten. Georgia envied Trish's agility and
her ability to focus, while Georgia constantly struggled with her
tired bones and muscles, forced to move in directions they hadn't
moved in years.

When Zoe first invited her at the beginning of summer to join
her class at the Moon Tide, Zoe had warned her that it would take
time and persistence to win back the body's trust and move with
the poses instead of against them.

"You did so grunt. You're not supposed to force the position,
Georgia."

"Shhh!" Zoe reprimanded them from the front of the room.
There were ten in the class that morning—eight women, two men.
Most of the pupils Georgia knew from the shops and cafés around
Sedona and had gotten quite friendly with them over the past
eight months.

"Modified cobra," Zoe said, easing herself to the mat.

Georgia dropped to the floor on her stomach and with her
hands slowly pushed up, inverting her spine. It felt as if someone
had cut off her breathing, like a water hose with a major kink in it.
Nothing seemed to be working right this morning.

Her thoughts jumped track to the Thanksgiving dinner
tomorrow when her family and friends would be gathered
altogether in one place. And, yes, there lingered a small
germinating seed of hope in Georgia's mind that maybe David and

Trish would meet and the two might fall in love. A silly notion, bound to disappoint.

"Ridiculous romance stuff." Zoe had quickly nipped Georgia's silly notion in the bud when she had confided in her the day before. Georgia had rushed over to help Zoe close up the Moon Tide for the evening and over a glass of wine, she had made the mistake of speaking her thoughts aloud. Georgia had been a little hurt when Zoe said, "Trish? Falling in love? I don't see it happening."

"I'm not saying it'll happen, Zoe. But it is possible."

"You're setting yourself up for disappointment, Georgia."

"I'm not expecting anything."

"Yes, you are."

"Don't you believe in fate?"

Zoe had given her a dismissive shrug. "Anything meant to be, doesn't have to be manipulated to make it happen."

Georgia had wanted to argue more but knew Zoe was right, although she could've said it a bit more tactfully.

Since Jake had won the senatorial election by an overwhelming majority two weeks before, there was no talking to her friend. No doubt, the reality of Jake's move to Washington at the first of the year was becoming too real for Zoe. In the last few days, Georgia had seen Zoe grow silent and moody, and in her own way, turning down Jake's proposal of marriage.

Now, with Thanksgiving tomorrow, Georgia couldn't be certain if Jake still planned on coming to the dinner. Zoe refused to give her a yes or no answer whenever she asked.

On her back, feet flat on the floor, Georgia lifted her pelvis and inverted her spine into bridge pose. Arms straight and hands clasped behind her back, she fought to keep her neck soft and pliant. It hurt. A sharp pain shot through the back of her neck and her thighs burned like crazy. Determined to hold the pose with the other students, Georgia ignored the pain. *Focus, damn it.*

Her thoughts went back to Trish, wondering why the girl seemed so determined to sabotage any chance of a relationship with any man she dated. Trish loved children and had even expressed to Georgia the desire to one day have several before she turned forty. But there seemed to be some inaudible alarm inside Trish's head cuing her to stop herself before getting too emotionally attached, which generally took two or three dates with an unfortunate suitor. Not that all of them gave up that easily. A few rejected suitors— ones not so easily put off by Trish's cooling off—had wandered into the café, either presenting her with two pound boxes of expensive chocolates or their arms cradling long-stemmed roses. One by one, she would thank them, and then politely show them the door.

Georgia opened her eyes and found Zoe standing over her, arms crossed and shaking her head.

"What?" Georgia said, embarrassed.

"Don't force the position." Zoe bent down and lightly touched the back of Georgia's neck, whispering, "Relax! If you don't ease up, you'll pull something major out of whack."

She gave up, lowering her behind to the mat. While the pain in her neck disappeared, her bad mood definitely did not.

Zoe patted her shoulder. "You'd better begin your relaxation. *Now.*" Zoe returned to her own mat at the front of the room. "Modified boat pose," she said to the rest of the class.

Trish whispered to Georgia. "Wow, you sure got into trouble."

"Quiet," Georgia growled through clenched teeth.

Trish mimicked Georgia's scowl. "God, you're so uptight today."

"Corpse pose."

Georgia obeyed Zoe, stretching out on her back, legs and arms relaxed, telling herself that at least this was one pose she couldn't possibly screw up. Closing her eyes, she must have dozed off, because the next time she opened her eyes, everyone had left.

Georgia got up from the floor, and then rolled up her mat. Zoe came in from the kitchen carrying two bottles of water. "Here, drink this," she said sitting down cross-legged on the floor. "Are you feeling better?"

Georgia took a sip of water. "Yes. I'm sorry about talking during class. It's so difficult sitting next to Trish. I can't concentrate. She makes everything look so easy."

Zoe sighed. "You're not supposed to compare yourself to others. Yoga is about how *you* are on the inside." With legs still crossed, she leaned back on her hands. "Sometimes I worry about you, Georgia. All stressed out about nothing. Even when you have nothing at all to worry about, you'll find a crisis to get all worked up about."

Georgia couldn't answer. She knew Zoe was right, but didn't want to admit it.

Zoe went on. "I know you're worried about tomorrow, having your family here. And fretting about David and his bad marriage breakup won't help. Most of all, and don't get mad at me, you're worried about how your family will see your new life here in Sedona. Up until now, it's all been kind of pretend, like playing house—not real—but lots of fun if you don't have to accept the responsibility of what you've left behind."

Georgia was steaming. She got up from the floor and tucked her mat in a corner by the kitchen door so she wouldn't forget it. "Well, you're certainly one to talk." She slumped into one of the big-cushioned chairs in the book corner. "Seems to me I'm not the only one having trouble with a past life. What about Jake? And your mother? Are you going to bring your mother to dinner at the café, or not? Do you resent her that much?" Georgia locked eyes with Zoe. "Be truthful."

"My relationship with Jake Rizzo is none of your goddamn business, and as for my mother, well..." She paused to catch her breath. "I'm not a coward. I'll bring her. Your whole damn family can sit and stare holes right through that mean old woman who'll probably insult every member of your family without batting an eye." Zoe waved both hands in surrender. "Be forewarned, there's no telling what will come out of Mama's mouth."

"The truth is—"

"The truth, Georgia, is you're having second thoughts about having your family here. In theory, it was a Norman Rockwell-moment-of-an-idea, but in reality, you're scared they won't like the café. And maybe, they won't like your new friends, either."

"That's ridiculous." A hot blush blossomed on both her cheeks. She turned to Zoe. "I suppose you're right. I am scared."

Zoe gave a lighthearted laugh. "Well, not entirely right, the part about not liking us? What's not to like? I just want you to realize how silly you are for worrying about nothing. Nothing at all."

Georgia took in a deep breath and let it out slowly. She studied Zoe for a moment, wondering how she could explain maternal love to a woman who had no children. "I can't stop being a mother. I love my children. When they hurt, I hurt. It's only natural that I look at Trish and think what a nice match she would be for David. Is that so crazy?"

"Definitely crazy. You can't make things happen, Georgia. Especially love."

The thin skin over Georgia's spine tightened. For the second time today Zoe had hurt her feelings. "Well, I don't think it's entirely impossible." Even as the words left her mouth, she knew that writing the screenplay for David and Trish like some movie-of-the-week romance would never work out. "Oh, I know you're right."

"Take my advice, Georgia. Don't get involved." Zoe let out a heavy sigh. "You don't really understand Trish. She's... complicated, more so than she lets on."

"Oh? How so?" Georgia felt a tiny pinch of jealousy squeeze a nerve at the base of her skull. After all, she worked closely with Trish on a daily basis. If she was hiding some secret about herself, Georgia would have certainly suspected something by now.

"Yeah, well Trish talks a lot about settling down, wanting the total cottage and picket fence thing, but she doesn't really mean it. It's like a dream for her, the perfect family she never had, but living it? No way. I can't imagine Trish falling hard for any man."

"Are you talking about Trish, or yourself? Maybe you're confusing your own fears and insecurities with Trish's."

Zoe's eyebrows furrowed with self-doubt. "Maybe." Her mouth twisted into a tight smile. "I hope you're right."

"Do you know something about Trish I should know?"

Zoe raised an eyebrow and sagely said, "We all keep secrets hidden on the inside of us, don't we?" Her expression turned pleading. "Oh, Georgia, let's get off this subject, okay?"

Georgia didn't want to get off the subject. If Zoe knew something about Trish, she wanted to find out what it was before pinning any hopes on a romance developing with her son. She followed Zoe into the kitchen, past the dream catcher hanging in the doorway.

"You're doing it again," Zoe said, rattling the lid on the sugar bowl to get Georgia's attention. Zoe had fixed a pot of tea. She pushed the sugar bowl toward Georgia. "Like I said before, Trish talks a lot about settling down, but marriage would only make her miserable. Take my word for it, Georgia, don't meddle."

"You're wrong. Why would anyone pass up the opportunity to fall in love with the right person?" Zoe gave Georgia a sympathetic look. "Okay, Georgia, I won't stomp on your perfect world dream. It's a long-shot, but you could be right about Trish and David."

Georgia didn't like Zoe patronizing her. "Zoe, please, if there's something I should know about Trish, tell me."

She shrugged. "Maybe."

"Well?"

Zoe shook her head. "I can't tell. I promised."

"Did Jake confide something to you about Trish?"

"Could be."

"Hmmm." Georgia got up, reaching for her hand-knit sweater, the one she had purchased in the Irish shop on Creek Street. She draped it over her shoulders. "I'm going to Flagstaff this afternoon to pick up an order for the café, then to the store to buy a fat turkey. Wanna come?"

Zoe's eyes filled with relief, as if knowing that even though the argument had not been resolved, it was over at least for the moment. She said, "I wouldn't miss that for all the green tea in China." She picked up Georgia's empty cup and studied the soggy leaves at the bottom. "Oh-my-gosh," Zoe said joking. "You're going to fall in love with the man of your dreams."

"Your tea leaf readings are as hokey as your card readings. Give it up, Zoe, before someone takes you serious and sues you. Frivolous lawsuits in America are rampant."

Zoe shot her a magnanimous expression. "Or, maybe, just maybe, the tea leaves tell the truth, that there's a handsome stranger in your future."

"Oh, sure. I'm not in the least bit interested in getting married again, not ever again in my life. I'm quite happy right where I am, thank you."

Zoe's grin widened as if she'd just been handed a small gift. "Imagine that. Trish once told me the very same thing."

Georgia's eyes narrowed sharply. "Are you telling me Trish has been married before?"

"I didn't say that." Zoe quickly turned and shoved the cups into the sink.

"You certainly implied it."

"Did not."

"Did so."

Outside the Moon Tide, Georgia gathered her sweater tight around her shoulders, wondering if she would ever find out the complete truths about the two women she now called friends. For now, she had enough to worry about, getting to the grocery to buy enough food to feed a small army. Tomorrow would either be a day to remember or one she would beg to forget.

# CHAPTER EIGHTEEN

Waiting for Zoe in the long checkout line at the supermarket, Georgia heard someone call out, "Mrs. B!" No one else except Luke Perry had ever called her Mrs. B. She glanced over her shoulder, but didn't see anyone she recognized. Zoe had gone off in search of the bread crumbs Georgia had forgotten to put on the grocery list. That had been almost ten minutes ago. Now the line had pushed her almost to the front where the checkout girl looked holiday-stressed.

"Hey, Mrs. B!"

"Luke?"

This time, Georgia turned and caught sight of Luke and his girlfriend, Stephanie, at the back of the line. It seemed like a million years since Luke had talked her into giving him a ride from Amarillo to Flagstaff.

A wide grin spread across Luke's face, excusing his way up the grocery line and leaving Stephanie to hold their place. "Hey there, I thought that was you. Can you believe this?" He excitedly opened his arms to her. "Wow! It's a small world, isn't it?"

"Luke, I—"

Luke cut her off, grabbing Georgia in a bone-crushing hug, his leather jacket scrunching against her ear as he rocked her back and forth as if she were a long-lost relative. When he finally let go, she tipped back on the heels of her Nikes to catch her breath. "Luke,

I never thought I'd see you again." She turned and waved hello to Stephanie who smiled sweetly as she politely jockeyed her heaped cart around a heavyset woman in a motorized cart. Georgia took note that the rude woman in the cart never uttered so much as an "Excuse me" or "Thank you."

"Mrs. B, you look like a million bucks! You decided to stay in Sedona, huh? That's fantastic!" Luke was chewing a piece of gum. Georgia could smell the cool, spearmint flavor, combined with the scent of his sporty cologne.

Georgia pushed her cart forward to stay in line with the others. "Yes. I'm working at the Soft Rock Café in Sedona."

Luke stuffed his hands in his bomber jacket. "Cool." He sounded impressed. His smile widened. "Hey, guess what? Mom's coming to Flagstaff. Me and Stevie, here, we're cookin' a turkey and making mashed potatoes, cranberry sauce, man, the whole works."

"How nice," she said, genuinely pleased that Luke had invited his mother. "That means your mother will find out you're living with Stephanie, right?"

"Mrs. B, you won't believe this, we're engaged." He turned and shouted back at Stephanie, "Hey, Stevie! Hold up your hand." Every person in the checkout line turned to stare at the beautiful blonde in the tight jeans and lambs wool jacket as she shyly held up her left hand. A long, drawn out *Ahhh* floated up from the line of people behind them.

Zoe reappeared with the package of breadcrumbs, her expression questioning why the entire checkout line had all at once erupted into smiles and friendly chatter. She looked at Georgia, who was talking to a handsome young man who had his hand on her shoulder.

"Well, it seems I can't leave you alone for two minutes without you making a new friend."

"Zoe, meet Luke Perry. He's the boy from the bus stop. Remember? I gave him a lift to Flagstaff when I first drove out to

Sedona?" She pointed to Stephanie. "His fiancé." Stephanie held up her hand. Again, everyone in line let out an Ahhh.

"How sweet," Zoe cooed, turning to Luke and giving him her full attention. "I hope you'll both be very happy."

Georgia's lips tightened, watching Luke blush, caught under the spell of Zoe's extraordinary beauty, definitely not the typical woman who shopped at a supermarket. "Knock it off, Zoe."

"Whatever do you mean, Georgia?"

"Luke, don't pay her any mind. My friend here hasn't got a romantic bone in her body."

"Not true, Georgia. I adore young love. It's all so innocent and hopeful."

Luke's bedazzled expression turned quizzical. "Say, you look familiar. Are you somebody famous?"

"Sure, sweetheart. You know what they say about everyone looking like somebody."

Finally, their turn to checkout, Georgia again congratulated Luke as she started to unload her cart.

"Let me help you." Luke hoisted two twenty pound turkeys onto the counter. "Mrs. B, you've made my day."

They finished emptying the cart. Luke gave Georgia another crushing hug, and then startled Zoe by doing the same to her, almost knocking her off-balance.

"Nice kids." Zoe shifted five loaves of bread to the back so they wouldn't get crushed. "It's nice to see marriage isn't out of—Shit!"

Georgia looked up, alarmed. "What's wrong?"

"Nothing," Zoe snapped back. She snatched a tabloid from the wire rack beside the counter and tucked it under the loaves of bread.

Georgia glanced back at the rack of tabloids, but Zoe shoved her forward with the cart before she could get a good look-see.

"Let's get out of here."

Walking back to the car, Zoe offered, "Your friends are nice. I hope they stay in love."

"Hmmm, you sound so optimistic."

"Sure."

Not about to give up her good mood after running into Luke, Georgia ignored Zoe's sudden foul mood, thinking how sweet of Luke to invite his mom to Flagstaff for a traditional holiday dinner. The boy certainly made no bones about saying how much he loved his mother. No doubt, he and Stephanie would have a good marriage and raise beautiful children.

Admittedly, running into Luke and Stephanie had only proved Zoe right when earlier she had told Georgia to leave people and their tally of problems to follow a natural course. Georgia knew she worried way too much about the personal lives of her children, the main reason she had left home in the first place. David was a grown man. He didn't need his mother's help in the romance department. Attempting to arrange a love match between Trish and David so soon after his divorce would certainly be courting disaster. But secretly, Georgia couldn't help but hope the spark between David and Trish would be there.

Zoe opened the trunk, and Georgia helped load the heavy bags. Once again, Georgia tried to lighten Zoe's bad mood. "It was nice seeing Luke again," she said, reflectively. "Now, it doesn't seem so scary having my family here for the week. Sedona's my home, and they'll love it, too. I know they will. You were absolutely right, Zoe. Some things are better left to fate."

Zoe stuffed the last bag inside the trunk without comment.

It started to snow—big, doily-like flakes that landed in their hair and on their coat sleeves.

Georgia took this to be a good sign. "Looks like Christmas, don't you think?"

Zoe grunted and slammed the trunk. "I never got all that worked up about Christmas."

"Oh?"

Zoe shrugged. "Memories."

They got into the car. Zoe turned the key in the ignition. She lowered the heater fan until the engine warmed up. They sat in silence for several minutes, Georgia noticing a tear slide down Zoe's cheek as she stared out at the falling snow. She opened her handbag and rummaged around for a tissue, handing it to Zoe. "Do you want me to drive?" she offered.

Zoe blew her nose, sniffing loudly. "If we sit here a minute, I'll be okay." She switched the heater fan to high and turned the radio volume down. "It's the memories that get to me—like the years I lived with Gabe and Mary in New Orleans. On Christmas Eve we'd go to midnight mass and the church seemed transformed into something magnificent, filled with candles. The stained glass windows were all so lifelike. It made me feel as if God was real, after all." Zoe blew her nose again and laughed. "Speaking of church, I have a confession."

"Confession?"

"At fourteen, I decided to become a nun. At the time, I couldn't imagine living anywhere more peaceful and safe than in a church. Don't look at me that way, Georgia. It's true."

Georgia knew her jaw had dropped open. Imagining Zoe dressed in drab, course clothing, without her silver and turquoise jewelry, not to mention having to cut off her beautiful hair to hide her head beneath a nun's cap would have been ludicrous.

Zoe shook her head. "I went to Sister Julie, excited to tell her what I'd decided." She wasn't pleased. "She told me it was a sin to mock the sanctity of a religious order."

"Oh, Zoe."

"I just wouldn't give up. Somehow I had to convince her I was on the level about the nun thing. So, I lied."

"Lied?"

Zoe sniffed. "I told her that God had sent the Angel Gabriel in a dream to tell me my life's calling was to be a nun. I figured if it worked for Mary, it ought to work for me."

Georgia swallowed a giggle. "What did she say?"

"She slapped me."

"She didn't?" Georgia gasped, touching the cuff of Zoe's cashmere coat.

Zoe sniffed again. "I really didn't want to be a nun. I just wanted Sister Julie to like me, like all the other girls in my class, the ones with normal families who had lots of love to share."

"My God, Zoe, that's horrible."

"Sister Julie called my mother a drunken whore and that her sins could never be washed away, no matter how hard I prayed. She said I was no different than my mother."

"What a nasty thing to say to a child."

Zoe put the car in reverse and backed slowly out of the parking space. "It hurt, I won't deny it. I went home that afternoon and locked myself in my bedroom. I took off my clothes and stood in front of the mirror to see if I could see the sin written on my skin like Sister said it was." Zoe shrugged, "In retrospect, I suppose she did me a favor." Zoe emitted a cynical laugh. "Can you see it? Me? A nun?"

"Well... I can't believe a nun would treat a child that way. Aren't nuns supposed to be, you know—"

"Compassionate? Encouraging?" Zoe buckled her seatbelt. "I suppose there'll always be the bad mixed in with the good."

"I'm sorry, Zoe."

"For what?"

"When you talk about your childhood, you sound so lonely."

"I was lonely. But I had Gabe and Mary. That made it better. Hey, there's a coffee shop. Let's drive through and get some to go. Okay?"

By now, Georgia had gotten used to Zoe ending discussions about herself by jumping tracks and mentioning something else, such as now wanting a cup of coffee.

* * *

The snowfall turned heavier as Zoe maneuvered through late afternoon traffic. Georgia sipped her coffee and watched the swirling flakes outside her window, thinking how much her life had changed in a matter of months. It was all so surreal, the thought of fixing a grand Thanksgiving dinner for all her family and new friends.

Last year, she had gathered her family for a big dinner on Stilson Avenue with Ed watching football in his recliner in the den and Louie perched on the edge of the sofa, as if he were ready and able if the coach called him into the game.

Samantha and Ben played a board game on the living room rug, bickering over whose turn it was. Susan helped out in the kitchen where she took this private moment with her mother as an opportunity to complain about the latest crisis in her life—seems a woman on her volunteer committee at the hospital got credit for a program that had been Susan's idea.

Georgia wrapped potholders around the handles of the heavy roaster holding the turkey, nodding as if really listening to her daughter's rambling on about how unfair it was for this woman to have received recognition for something she didn't do.

Georgia kept quiet, vowing to herself that Susan's latest problem would not affect her plans for a wonderful dinner with her family gathered around the dining room table decked out with her mother's precious china and crystal. She placed the relish plate in the center of the table and asked Susan to go tell the others that dinner was ready.

Then, it happened.

In a matter of seconds, her Norman Rockwell holiday was shot to bits as Lori burst through the front door with David close on her heels, arguing—as usual. Georgia knew instantly that her vision of a family dinner where everyone would sit down and enjoy each other's company was never going to happen. Undaunted by the intrusion, she transferred the browned turkey to the traditional platter. Georgia heard the door slam to the small bathroom off the hallway. "Dammit," Georgia muttered under her breath.

The day before when David and Lori had arrived from Boston,

Georgia had offered them David's old bedroom to stay in, but Lori had insisted on registering at a motel close to the airport. More than likely, Lori anticipated a quick getaway.

The family dinner was a bust with Lori and David barely speaking to each other or anyone else, for that matter. Susan, usually alert to the smallest speck of animosity between her brother and Lori, ignored their silence and chattered obsessively about her volunteer crisis to anyone who would listen. Ed and Louie talked about the next football game coming on that afternoon. Samantha and Ben bickered over what DVD they were going to watch later on the smaller television in the bedroom.

Georgia had all but given up, wishing she owned a big, rambunctious dog that would charge into the dining room and drag the tortured turkey off the table—anything to end the disaster that was playing out before her eyes. Even more disappointing was that no one seemed to care or even be aware of the dysfunction going on around them. First lesson in life: Don't ever wish for anything, it might come true. The leaping dog she had wished for came in the form of utter chaos, ignited by her own family.

In what seemed like slow motion, Samantha reached for a carrot stick and accidentally tipped over her glass of milk. The milk spilled across the table and ran off the edge on the other side. Ben—never one to miss an opportunity for attention—started crying over a week-old scratch on his arm to get out of eating his lima beans.

Then, like a boulder rolling down a mountain and building speed, Lori let out a blood curdling scream. Georgia watched helplessly as Samantha's milk dribbled into Lori's lap. Lori's face twisted into something ugly. "You little brat," she directed at Samantha. "Do you know how much this dress cost?" She then turned on Ben who was picking at the lima beans with his fork. "For God's sake, stop that insufferable whining." Throwing her napkin over her plate of food, she stood up and angrily inspected the wet spot on her dress.

David's face turned crimson, the exact shade of the cranberry sauce. Ed and Louie stopped talking football mid-sentence, Ed's fork midway to his mouth. In an instant, Louie shoved back from the table and protectively snatched Ben from his chair. Susan faced Lori across the table looking as if she might at any moment climb over it with all the ferociousness of a mama bear.

Lori's face went as white as the spilt milk. Her face grimaced, no doubt realizing what a huge mistake she had made by creating a scene with no possible good ending. David pulled the napkin off his wife's food. "Sit down," he ordered.

Lori turned on him. For a moment Georgia thought she might dump the plate of food over David's head. "I didn't want to come here anyway. I'm sick of you trying to mold me into your mother or sister."

Georgia got up from her chair and touched Lori's elbow. "Let's go into the kitchen, dear. A little cold water on your dress will help until you get it to the cleaners." She turned to everyone at the table and said, "We'll be back in a moment." She nodded for everyone to calm down and continue eating their meal, or at least try to eat.

In the kitchen, Lori dissolved into tears. "He wants a baby!" she wailed despairingly at Georgia.

"Who?" Georgia asked, as if she didn't already know. Lori's tears gained momentum. She sobbed, "David!"

Lori grabbed the dishtowel from Georgia's hand and flung it into the sink. "I don't want children. He can't make me want children."

"No, dear, he can't," Georgia whispered. "And if you don't want children, don't have them." This, Georgia said rather coldly. Not that she cared if Lori wanted children or not, but because David, for sure, wanted them. And Georgia knew then that her son's marriage to Lori was doomed.

No sooner had they returned to the dining room, than David apologized to the family for having to leave early, making the lame excuse about their having to get back to hotel, because they had an early flight the next morning. No one objected. Not even Georgia, who saw the folly of begging them to stay with the afternoon already in shambles.

"Careful, Zoe!" Georgia gasped as the car slid on the snowy road. Hot coffee slopped over the edge of Georgia's cup.

"Sorry, the road's icy. But don't worry. I've got it under control."

"Sure, you do. The snow's getting heavier."

"I hit a slick spot," Zoe said, her eyes focused on the road.

"I hope the weather doesn't get any worse with the kids coming in tomorrow. And don't forget to remind Jake to pick up your mother at the nursing home."

Zoe let out an exasperated sigh. "How can I forget? You remind me every five minutes."

"Okay, I'll stop obsessing."

Zoe pursed her lips. "Promise me you won't be disappointed if things don't work out the way you want them to."

Georgia smiled, "I promise, but only if you promise to at least try to have a better attitude about your mother." They rode a few minutes in silence. Zoe maneuvered the winding roadway into Oak Creek Canyon. Georgia yawned. "Were your holidays really that bad as a kid?"

"Is dirt dirty?" Zoe said in a flat tone. She slowed down as they came up behind a snowplow stopped in the roadway with its emergency lights flashing. "You're curious about my past life?"

Georgia shrugged. "I can't help but be."

"Most people are."

"What was it like when you were younger and still living with your mother?"

Zoe slowed to a stop behind the plow. "I never saw her much. When she wanted me around, that usually meant she needed something from me. At Christmas, Mama threw big, elaborate parties lasting from Friday night to Monday morning. Boyfriends always stayed over, drinking her liquor, stealing whatever they could put into their pockets. She let them do it—take advantage of her until she got bored or angry. Then, she'd tell them to get the hell out of her house." Zoe's forehead furrowed as if she were in pain. "Between lovers, I felt sad for her. I tried to tell her that I loved and needed her." Zoe's jaw tightened. "She always picked the biggest losers on the planet, mostly young, unemployed actors. The only man I loved and hoped would be my father was a man she walked over like a rug. She never understood or trusted anyone who had pure motives."

"Not even you?"

Zoe smiled weakly. "I had a good teacher."

A short, burly man smoking a cigar jumped down from the cab of the snowplow. Zoe lowered the window.

"You ladies okay?"

"We're fine. Can you see what's holding up traffic?"

The man pulled the cigar from his mouth, pinching it between two fingers and pointing with it. "Accident up ahead. Most likely we'll be here thirty, maybe forty minutes until the wrecker gets the car out of the ditch. You know how it goes, a little snow on the road and some idiot thinks he can drive like it's a sunny day in May. Hey, you two got plenty of gas?"

Zoe glanced at the gauge. "Three-quarters."

The man gave her a nod, clamped the cigar back between his teeth and went on to the car behind them. "What a nice man," Georgia said, getting into her purse and finding a pack of peanuts left over from her flight back home. She offered some to Zoe, but she waved her hand and refused. "I love them." Georgia popped a few into her mouth.

"I hate them. They remind me of the circus." Zoe unwound the red wool scarf draped around her neck. "I hate waiting like this. When I was a kid, Mama sometimes took me to the studio for her photo shoots. I had to sit very still, sometimes for hours at a time."

"No fun, huh?" Georgia slipped off her gloves and unbuttoned her coat. She flicked the heater fan to low. After all these months, Georgia had wanted to know what exactly had caused Zoe to be so standoffish and mistrusting. But now, Georgia wasn't so sure she wanted to hear any more of the lies and deceptions Zoe had gone through in her young lifetime. It was all too awful to think about.

Zoe's expression soured. "Remember the magazine article, my twelfth birthday?"

"Yes," Georgia said, glancing out the window and watching the snow come down harder. "Susan carried the ripped cover photo until it fell to pieces."

Zoe pulled off her leather gloves and folded them into her purse. "Mama hired a small circus, anything to make us look good to the press and hopefully help her career." She tugged at the red scarf around her neck, pulling it off and throwing it into the backseat. "Georgia, I don't know why I'm telling you this. God knows, I haven't told a soul, well, except Florry, who knew everything that went on in that house. And, of course, I've told Jake just enough to be truthful with him."

Tears welled up in Zoe's eyes. Georgia said, "We don't have to talk about this right now. It's the holidays, you know, all that emotional stuff coming to the surface and making everyone sad."

"No, Georgia. Right now, being here and talking to you feels right. Jake deserves better than the likes of me. I'm not strong enough to let him go. More than anything, I want to be with him."

Georgia's ears perked at the mention of Jake's name. "If you truly love Jake, there shouldn't be any question about your marrying him. Everything else can be worked out."

Zoe held up an objecting hand. "Please, just listen, okay?"

Georgia was irritated that Zoe kept cutting her off. "I think you're mixing up your past and future. Past regrets are moldy containers in the back of the refrigerator. You've got to clean them out." This last comment brought a faint smile to Zoe's lips.

"You're too funny, Georgia. It's so like you to think of metaphors about food. Okay, I give up." From the side pocket on the driver's door, Zoe pulled the tabloid purchased at the store. "Tell me what you think of this." Zoe tossed the paper in Georgia's lap, exposing a grainy photograph that took up most of the front page. Georgia gasped as she read the headline: *Greedy Daughter Secludes Movie Legend in Desert.*

"Oh my God." Georgia said, recognizing Zoe behind her mother's wheelchair in the courtyard of the nursing home. No doubt, the photographer must have been perched on the roof of another building, or perhaps had paid one of the employees.

Georgia leafed through until she found the article. As she read, her eyes blurred with tears. "This is obscene. How can they do this?"

"The tabloids make us public property. You know that firsthand, getting your picture on the front page with Jake. I try not to get too upset. Putting my mother's picture on the front page only tells me the gossip was slow for the week. Next week, it'll all be forgotten."

"It isn't right, Zoe. This article is nothing but lies." Georgia's heart went out to Zoe, wishing she could do something to make the publishers of this smut sheet own up to the truth.

Zoe heaved a deep sigh, "You don't realize who I really am, Georgia. I'm not a nice person. I've done things in my life I'm not proud of."

"We're all guilty of that."

Zoe slowly shook her head.

Georgia shrugged. "I'm listening."

"At that birthday party, Mama invited a bunch of kids who didn't want to be there anymore than I wanted them there. After the circus performance, I went off by myself to be alone because some boy whose father starred on some stupid cop series called me ugly as mud. He made me cry." Zoe's jaw tightened. "For the rest of the party, I stayed in Mama's bedroom, playing with the pretty bottles on her dressing table, looking in the mirror and trying to convince myself I wasn't as ugly as that boy said I was."

"You were never ugly, Zoe."

"Try telling that to a gangly twelve-year old girl."

"Kids can be so mean," Georgia said, realizing the pain and ridicule Zoe must have suffered at the hands of her peers.

Zoe coughed, clearing her throat. "I heard Mama coming down the hallway. I didn't want her to find me messing around in her bedroom, so I hid under her dressing table, behind the curtain. She wasn't alone. A man, I didn't recognize his voice, but I knew they were kissing. I felt trapped. If she found me hiding in her room, she'd accuse me of spying on her."

"Oh, Zoe," Georgia said, leaning forward in the seat, suppressing the urge to hug her.

"I had no choice but to stay hidden. At that age, my legs were two times longer than the rest of me, and the space under the dressing table was so cramped."

Georgia nodded, understanding. She had felt the same way the time she'd hidden under Zoe's balcony, listening in on her private conversation with Jake.

Zoe laughed. "Mother had an endless line of boyfriends she brought to the house, but I never spied on her. I knew better. But, still, I was curious, trying to figure out where she'd found a man during my party? Most likely one of the kid's dads, maybe even the cop show dad. Mama loved screwing television heroes. She called them two-season wonders, meaning their fame lasted about as long as their short-lived series."

"What happened?" Georgia held her breath, as Zoe stared out the windshield as if the cold exhaust spewing from the back of the snowplow could somehow provide an answer. Georgia persisted. "Were you afraid of your mother?"

"You're kidding, right?"

"No."

Zoe wiped at her face with the tissue Georgia had pulled from her purse and given to her. Her voice quivered. "I was terrified of her. Mama's criticism could slice through you like a razor blade." Zoe paused and choked back what Georgia thought to be tears. "When she drank too much, she was dangerous. I used to think I'd done something to make her that way, but after the birthday party, hiding under her dressing table, I knew for sure she purely hated me and didn't have to have a reason, she just did." Tears welled up in her eyes.

"What happened? Did your mother find you?"

Zoe's mouth relaxed into a soft smile. "No. The clown did."

"Clown?" Georgia asked, confused. "What clown?"

"Under the dressing table, I heard someone opening and closing drawers in the bedroom. And when I peeked from behind the curtain, I saw Mama passed out on the bed—the clown from the circus was going through her things, looking for money, I suppose."

"No?"

Zoe sunk further down in the seat, closing her eyes, as if suddenly exhausted. "It goes without saying that my birthday party was memorable from that point on. That's why I hate anything that has to do with the circus, peanuts included."

"Did he find you?"

Turning the rearview mirror in her direction, Zoe fussed with an unruly curl poking out from beneath her knit cap. She flipped the mirror back and gave her attention back to Georgia. "Oh, yeah. The pervert smiled at me, a big toothy grin from inside that painted-on grin."

"And your mother?"

Again, Zoe's jaw tensed. "She wasn't feeling any pain. I only remember the clown jerking me out from under the table, but I kicked him and got away."

Horrified, Georgia could only imagine what might have happened if the man had managed to keep hold of her. But was Zoe telling her the whole truth? "Zoe?"

Zoe shook her head. "No. He didn't hurt me."

Georgia swallowed the sour liquid burning inside her throat. "Thank God for that. "

"The man ran out of the house. The next morning, Florry packed our bags and took me to New Orleans to live with Mary and Gabe. Mama checked into a clinic in Colorado to dry out. Five months she stayed there. When she finally came home, I begged Mama to let me stay with Gabe and Mary. I was happy in New Orleans. For the first time in my life, I felt loved."

Georgia took one of Zoe's trembling hands. "You did the right thing, asking to stay with Florry's relatives. What your mother did was inexcusable, getting drunk and leaving you at the mercy of a strange man in the house." Georgia crushed the empty peanut package in her hands.

Zoe struggled to speak. "I feel so much hatred toward her, but I love her, too. The last five years, she's been so appreciative most of the time. I know she has regrets about the way she treated me but won't apologize." Zoe clenched her hands into two tight fists. "Why can't that stubborn old woman tell me she loves me?"

Georgia gently patted Zoe's shoulder. "I wish I could help you, but think of it this way. Maybe your mother has given everything she's capable of giving."

Zoe wiped at her nose with a fresh tissue. She gave Georgia a grateful look and said, "Thank you, Georgia."

"For what?"

"Listening."

The snowplow moved slowly at first, emitting a puffy cloud of exhaust. The wrecker passed them going in the opposite direction headed for Flagstaff with an SUV hooked on back, its left front side smashed, looking as if the owner had hit a tree.

The snowfall had all but stopped by the time they drove into Sedona. Trish had gone on an errand. Zoe offered to help unload the groceries. Mary Jo had already finished putting away the last of the dishes and finished sweeping the dining room before going home for the night.

Zoe told them a quick goodbye and returned to the Moon Tide to help close the shop for the night. Georgia had hoped Gloria's presence at her Thanksgiving dinner might be healing for Zoe, but now, after having heard Zoe's sad story, she began to question the sanity of bringing everyone together for a traditional holiday meal. This could be a disaster of major proportion, one she was incapable of stopping—the doomsday clock was now officially ticking.

Georgia went upstairs to take a shower and get ready for bed. She needed all the rest she could get before getting up early and starting the food preparation. She would call Trish after her shower and remind her that she had promised to get up early and help with the pies.

Georgia dried off from her shower and reached for the phone, knocking over a box holding business cards she had collected since arriving in Sedona. She gathered them up to put back into the box when she found the pink card from the Cutesy Curl in Oklahoma City. Lou Ann, the tiny pregnant girl with the upbeat personality who had cut her hair and given her a makeover. Georgia took this to be a good omen, especially after running into Luke in Flagstaff that afternoon.

Georgia dialed the number on the card, glancing at her watch and thinking more than likely the shop would be closed for the day. She really didn't expect anyone to answer.

"Cutesy Curl. Can I help you?" There was no mistaking Lou Ann's energetic voice.

"Lou Ann?"

"Speaking."

Suddenly, Georgia couldn't think of a thing to say. Lou Ann probably wouldn't even remember her. How silly to have called. The thought occurred to Georgia that she could simply hang up the phone, but the conversation had already passed *hello*. "Lou Ann," she repeated. "This is Georgia Mae Brown. You did my hair and makeup back in April. You..."

"Ohmygod!"

"You remember me?"

"Are you kidding? How many fifty dollar tips does a girl get in a lifetime? Like zero." She laughed at the other end of the line.

"I called because I wanted to know how your pregnancy turned out. Boy? Girl?"

"Girl. Eight pounds three ounces. I named her Molly, after my grandmother."

"Are you married?"

Silence at the other end. "No. I gave Molly my last name since Joey kind of ran away before the wedding and all. Good riddance, though. Thank God I tucked that money you gave me inside a sock in my dresser drawer. He took everything else, including my jar of pennies. Can you believe that?"

"I'm sorry, Lou Ann. You're fine now?"

"Totally."

"I'm happy for you."

"Georgia, you won't believe this, but I was thinking about you today, you know, giving me that money and all. I kept that fifty dollar bill until I absolutely had to spend it on baby food, but I kept one dollar for myself and bought a lottery ticket. Guess what?"

"You won?" Georgia said, excited.

"Nope, well, not exactly. You see, I bought one of those instant winner cards you need a penny or quarter to scratch off the numbers with. Well, I didn't have any coins, duh, since Joey took my penny jar, so I borrowed a quarter from this guy pumping gas next to me." She sighed. "I didn't win anything, but the guy who gave me the quarter asked me out! He owns his own construction company, and he's real nice to me. We're in love!"

"Really? Lou Ann—" Georgia said, doubtfully. This scenario sounded as if it might go the way of Joey and the penny jar—gone without a trace.

"Noooo," Lou Ann gushed. "We're engaged! The ring's on my finger right this minute. Sure, the diamond's no bigger than a pin head, but it's mine. And we're getting married next week. That's a fact."

"Married?"

"He's a good man, Georgia. A good father for my baby."

"Well, then, I'm happy for you."

"Fate. Don't you see? If you'd never given me that money I'd never have taken that dollar and bought a lottery ticket. Sometimes, Georgia, you just got to take a chance."

Georgia hung up the phone, happy that Lou Ann had found a nice man to love her and be a good father to her daughter. Happy ending? She hoped so.

Georgia's thoughts shifted back to tomorrow's dinner with her family and new friends gathered around the long table decorated with pumpkins, ornamental leaves and soft candlelight. In the waning light of the afternoon, Georgia said out loud, "You're absolutely right, Lou Ann. Sometimes, you just have to take a chance."

# CHAPTER NINETEEN

From a kitchen drawer, Georgia pulled out a ruffled apron she had purchased on sale in Flagstaff. Nervous about her family's impending arrival, she asked Trish to help tie the bow in back. "I'm all fingers."

Trish laughed. "This apron would make a better lampshade."

"Don't make fun. It's festive."

Trish finished with the bow. "What do you think, Doc?"

Doc looked up from arranging the last of the carrot sticks and celery on the vegetable tray, giving Georgia an appreciative smile. "Georgia looks stunning, as usual."

Trish raised both eyebrows. "Well, you're just too prejudice about Georgia, Doc. Everyone in Sedona knows you're secretly in love with her. Anything she says or does is okay with you." She gave Georgia a sly wink.

"Stop it, Trish." She felt her face color with embarrassment and glanced over at Doc, but he appeared to not hear Trish's teasing. She slapped Trish playfully on the hand. "Go help Mary Jo. Make sure she has everything she needs to finish setting the table. They should be here any minute now."

Trish leaned close to Georgia. "Don't worry. Everything's perfect."

Georgia hardly had time to catch her next breath when she heard the café door open, and then the high-pitched voices of her grandchildren filled the dining room, excitedly talking over each other. Georgia squeezed both of Trish's hands. "They're here."

"Knock 'em dead, Georgia."

Just then Mary Jo rushed in from the dining room. "Georgia, they're here!"

Georgia followed Mary Jo into the dining room, and her family stood before her. Susan was unbuttoning her coat, looking around, her eyes taking in the café, followed by Louie who carried a neatly wrapped present tied with a red bow. When Ben and Samantha saw Georgia, they lunged for her, almost throwing her off balance. The children were talking so fast she couldn't make out a word they were saying.

Susan nervously smoothed the front of her black dress slacks and straightened the collar of her silk blouse. Georgia mentally crossed her fingers, hoping Susan had flown far enough from home not to have a crisis brewing, none that would overtake dinner conversation. Susan, when nervous, tended to chatter like a magpie, but at the moment, she seemed quite content to wander around the café and take in her mother's new surroundings.

Georgia pulled out a chair from the table and sat down, giving all her attention to the children. Ben cupped both hands over her ear. "It's a secret, Grandma."

Samantha scowled at Ben. "Mom, he's going to tell. Don't let him, pleeease."

Susan didn't hear, because Trish, who had followed Georgia into the dining room, was introducing both herself and Doc to Susan and Louie. So far, so good. Susan complimented Trish on how nice the table looked and how wonderful it must be to own such a wonderful café.

Georgia's eyes for the first time took in the dining room set for the holiday dinner, the long table set with white linen, complete with china and crystal, on loan from Zoe, gleamed in the reflected firelight from the creek stone hearth at the far corner of the dining room. The café felt like home. Her gaze drifted back to Susan who now looked at her with tears brimming in the lower rims of her eyes. "Oh, Mom, this is all so beautiful. I'm so glad to be here." The room grew quiet. Everyone watched with open hearts, knowing how important this family gathering was for Georgia. Mary Jo clasped both hands together, saying, "Oh, this is so sweet."

Soft dinner music played in the background making the dinner with her friends and family a perfect dream, a dream from which Georgia did not want to wake. She quickly reminded herself, this was for real and she should savor every moment. Then, it occurred to her that someone was missing. She pulled back from Susan. "Where's David?"

"He's with Zoe. They drove on to the motel to get us checked in. The children wanted to see you first."

Trish said, "Well, everything's ready." She handed Susan and Louie glasses of wine. "Your mother has created quite the feast."

The door suddenly opened with a sweep of chilly air, and Zoe came in with David behind her. Georgia's first thought about her son was that his face seemed drawn into a tense smile, most likely feeling uncomfortable about his first Thanksgiving without Lori. She went to him, reaching up and taking his face in her hands. He leaned over and kissed her on the cheek.

"Hello, Mother."

"David." She gave his arm an affectionate squeeze. "You look real good, Mom. Sedona suits you fine." His eyes took in the café, and then he sighed. "So this is it, huh?"

Suddenly, Georgia remembered she wanted to introduce him to Trish, but when she turned around Trish had disappeared into the kitchen. She grabbed Mary Jo and Doc, instead. "David, these are my good friends, Mary Jo and her grandfather, Doctor Ezekiel Stevens."

"Whoa, there, Georgia, don't start me out so formal." Doc took David's hand and gave it a vigorous shake. "Call me Doc or Zeke, none of that Ezekiel stuff, okay?"

"Okay." David took Mary Jo's hand and it didn't escape

Georgia's eye that David seemed instantly smitten with the young woman's blonde, willowy beauty.

Georgia closed her eyes and begged, oh no, God, please not Mary Jo. Sure, Mary Jo was a nice girl, but way too young for David. A natural flirt, Mary Jo collected boyfriends like warm, dry air collects static electricity.

Trish came through the swinging door from the kitchen carrying a platter of sliced ham. "Come on now, let's sit down and get settled before all the food gets cold."

Georgia turned to Zoe. "Where's Jake and your mother?"

"I tried Jake's cell, but the call wouldn't go through. Let's start without them."

Georgia started to object, but Zoe cut her off. "Don't worry, they'll be here. No sense ruining dinner."

Reluctantly, Georgia took a seat at the head of the table with Ben and Samantha on either side of her, while Doc sat at the other end of the table. Georgia couldn't believe how much the children had grown since she had seen them in September. Another turn of the age-wheel and they'd be grown and on their own. Georgia took comfort in thinking that in another year or so, they could fly out here and spend a few summer weeks in Sedona, that is, if they wanted to.

"Grandma?" Ben said, tugging at the sleeve of her sweater. "I dropped my fork. I need another one." Samantha, not to be outdone for attention, said, "Grandma, last week I had an ear infection. I had to go to the doctor." Georgia got up to go into the kitchen to get Ben a clean fork. When she returned to the dining room, Jake and Gloria had arrived. Jake's arm was securely wrapped around Gloria's frail frame to support her unsteady, wobbly steps. Even with the stroke-ravished left side of her face, Gloria looked stunning, dressed to the nines, makeup flawless, a beautiful red silk scarf draped around her neck.

Oh dear, Georgia had fully intended to tell her family about Zoe's mother but in all the confusion had forgotten and now there was no time. Susan's jaw dropped open and for the first time in her life was speechless. Susan's eyes shifted back and forth from Zoe to Gloria. Susan managed to point at Gloria and say, "You're... oh, my God!" Her eyes then shot to Zoe.

Zoe gave Susan a sympathetic look as she helped her mother out of her coat. "And I'm the greedy daughter you've read about in the tabloids."

Susan's eyes brightened. "Yes, I read that in the grocery store yesterday. Not that I believe anything they say, of course, but it's entertaining while standing in those long lines. I didn't mean to sound—"

"Don't worry. No offense taken." Zoe pulled out a chair next to her mother.

Gloria had slumped forward in the chair, her head almost hitting the table. "Mama?" Zoe leaned over and touched the back of her mother's neck. At that precise moment, Gloria straightened up, hitting Zoe square on the jaw.

"I have a bad pain in my breast," Gloria said loud enough so everyone in the room stopped talking. Although her words were a bit slurred, what she said was well understood. The old woman smiled, as if pleased to have captured everyone's attention.

Zoe rubbed at her jaw, moving it up and down as if checking to see if she still had all her teeth. She patted her mother on the back and smiled at Georgia. "Okay, Mama. Let me know if you get another pain."

"I only get two a day."

Georgia hurried to Gloria's side. "I'm glad you could come today, Gloria. Do you like turkey?"

"Turkey?" she said with disgust. "I hate turkey. I'm a strict vegetarian."

Zoe's eyes went to the ceiling. "Mama, you are not a vegetarian."

"I'm not?" Gloria's left eye drooped from the paralysis in such a way that whenever she cocked her head and looked around the long table of assembled guests, she appeared almost sinister. "Who are all these people? I don't know any of them."

Georgia was quick to answer. "Gloria, this is my family from Ohio. They've come for Thanksgiving dinner, too. Remember, I told you that last week when Zoe and I came to visit you?"

"Is that so," Gloria said, giving the silk scarf around her neck a dignified pat. "Well, tell them to stop staring at me."

Susan could barely contain her excitement. She smiled across the table at Gloria. "Miss Atwater, I'm so honored to meet you. When I was a little girl, my mother and I used to watch all your old movies on television."

"Is that so," Gloria shot back.

"You were so beautiful." Susan's face clouded with instant regret, and her hands covered her mouth as if she'd give anything to be able to pull those words back inside her. "Of, course, I didn't mean—"

"But, of course you did, my dear. I *am* old." Gloria glanced up at Zoe. "Where's Florry. She disappears every chance she gets." Tapping manicured fingers impatiently against the rim of the china plate, she said, "I do have an important appointment after this engagement," she said to Susan. "I hope this won't take long, because I have a meeting with my director. He's a brute about punctuality. But I can handle him." She again fussed with the ends of the red silk scarf, her eyes nervously darting to Zoe who looked as jumpy as a rabbit about to dart across the road in front of a car.

Trish came through the swinging door from the kitchen carrying the turkey platter and placed it in the middle of the table. She gave the carving utensils to David. "You do the honors. My brother may be a famous space hero, but I've seen him carve meat and it *ain't* pretty." She smiled at David, but not in a flirty way, more like he was a customer who came into the café for a bite to eat. Again, Georgia felt a pinch of disappointment that the two of them didn't seem to be hitting it off as well as she had hoped. They spoke to each other with all the cordialness of two unaffected strangers, no flicker of promise whatsoever.

It seemed that David was more fascinated with his boyhood astronaut hero, Jake Rizzo. The idea of a romance happening between David and Trish now seemed rather silly, especially so soon after his divorce from Lori.

All things considered, the dinner surpassed Georgia's expectations, the meal next to perfect, no lull in conversation, only lots of laughter and good stories. Even Gloria, who periodically slipped in and out of her own world during the meal, seemed to enjoy herself.

Jake and Zoe were sitting together and having a nice conversation with everyone seated at the table, still unclear as to where their lives would go from here. Certainly, after the first of the year, Jake would be moving to Washington, leaving Zoe with the choice of either going with him or staying behind.

And what was up with Trish? Unusually quiet and withdrawn, watching Georgia's grandchildren with an almost strange, perplexing interest. No eye contact at all between Trish and David.

Gloria finished her last bite of turkey and said, "What holiday is this?" Everyone at the table stopped talking and in unison said, "Thanksgiving!" They all laughed, and the old woman appeared pleased as punch to have gotten the attention of everyone at the table. She put down her fork. "You know, my breast still hurts. It's hurt me all day. I keep telling those doctors but they keep giving me petroleum and it keeps me up all hours of the night."

"Mother, you mean they give you pills that give you gas. Your head hurts, not your breast."

Susan, who sat directly across from Gloria, said, "That's all right, we all have moments when we get mixed up."

Gloria's mouth bunched up indignantly. "You're so smart, huh?"

Surprised by Gloria's sharp reply, Susan let out a deflated, "Ohhh."

Zoe gave Susan a sympathetic look. "Now, Mama, Susan's trying to be nice. Oh, look. Trish is bringing out dessert. You love dessert, Mama. Pumpkin pie with real whipped cream. Mmmm. I bet Trish will give you the first slice." Zoe took one of the plates and set it down in front of her mother. "This is a nice party, isn't it?"

Everyone at the table slipped back into conversation, but Georgia noticed Zoe's hands had begun to tremble. Jake noticed, too, because he excused himself, got up and went to the spot between Zoe and her mother. Something had happened, but what?

Gloria's stroke-ravaged face turned pale and her chin tucked into her chest. "I'm so sorry. I didn't mean to. My head hurts."

Zoe sniffed back tears. "That's okay, Mama. You can't help it. We'll make it better." Zoe gave Georgia a look that said, Come help me. Not until Georgia came around to that side of the table did she realize what had happened.

Gloria's expression was that of child who had done something naughty. Looking plaintively at Zoe, she said, "I took off my diaper when the nurse wasn't looking."

The undeniable odor hit Georgia's nostrils about the same time it did everyone else at the table.

David saved the day by scooping up the pumpkin pie. "Let's all go into the kitchen. We'll make more coffee. Mom said something about a fat cheesecake tucked away in the refrigerator." It didn't take much coaxing to get everyone to move out of their seats and into the kitchen. Doc told Zoe and Georgia to stand back, ordering Mary Jo to run and fetch his medical bag from his car. Jake helped Doc move Gloria to the floor and covered her with a tablecloth pulled from the linen closet to use as a makeshift blanket until Trish brought one of Georgia's blankets from upstairs.

Gloria patted Jake's hand. "What a gentleman you are. I wish my daughter would find someone nice like you to marry."

Jake smiled down at her. "Me, too."

"Oh?" Gloria stared up at him with focused interest. "Do you know my daughter?"

"Yes, I do."

"She helps me, you know. I'm sick. But she helps me." Gloria took Jake's hands and put her tiny, shriveled hand inside his.

Tears filled her eyes. "It's been a long time since anyone loved me."

Jake gently said, "Your daughter loves you."

Gloria's head turned in search of Zoe. "She does? Too bad I have nothing to leave her when I die."

From a distance, Georgia tearfully took in Zoe's hopeful expression as she rushed forward and knelt beside her mother.

"I do love you, Mama. And it doesn't matter about the money. I don't care."

"Oh?"

Zoe nodded, expectantly. "You adopted me when no one else wanted me. I love you."

Gloria sniffed back the tears and coughed. "Zoe, I..."

"Yes, Mama? What is it you want to say?"

"Zoe..." She sniffed again and made an awful face. "What's that awful smell?"

Later that evening, Georgia snuggled deep in the brass bed with her grandchildren tucked beneath the down comforter. Although Oscar had taken to sleeping with Georgia, tonight he kept his distance, sleeping instead on the needlepoint rug by the register in the bathroom.

As holidays go, this one hadn't turned out so badly, all considered. Gloria's dinner accident had somehow drawn Zoe closer to her mother, and Jake could not have been kinder. Zoe would be a damn fool to let that man go.

Doc had examined Gloria and told Zoe the only damage done seemed to be her clothing. Georgia had quickly gone up to the apartment and brought down one of her nightgowns for Gloria to put on until she got back to the nursing home. After getting Gloria cleaned up, Jake and Zoe drove her to Phoenix, and no one mentioned another word about the incident.

Doc had been a dear to stay behind and help clear the dishes. And before he'd left, Doc had given Georgia a kiss on the cheek, which surprised her so much she dropped the butter dish on the tiled floor where it broke into a thousand pieces.

"Grandma?"

"Yes, Samantha." She pulled her granddaughter close to her in the bed.

"What happened to that old woman?"

Georgia sighed and pushed back stray curls from Samantha's earnest face.

"Honey, she's sick. She's not responsible for what she does."

Ben spoke up. "What does she have, Grandma? A cold or somethin'?"

"She's old, Ben. Her mind's gone kind of haywire."

"Haywire?" Ben giggled. "Hay-wire," he repeated over and over in a fit of giggles.

Then Samantha suffered a case of the giggles. Before long, all three of them were laughing and ruffling the covers, playing hide and seek in the bed. The children squirmed and poked their elbows and bony feet into Georgia's ribs and she couldn't stop laughing. She thought, yes, perhaps Norman Rockwell did live here, after all.

# CHAPTER TWENTY

Two days after Thanksgiving, Georgia spread out the café bills on the kitchen table along with the checkbook. She poured a fresh cup of coffee, catching sight of Trish through the open pantry door, standing on the last rung of a stepladder and attempting to slide mixing bowls onto the top shelf. David stood at the foot of the ladder. When the ladder wobbled and started to tip, David quickly steadied it. "Whoa," he said, lightly touching Trish's waist. Her cheeks then turned the prettiest shade of fuchsia as she placed the last bowl on the shelf.

Georgia added a bit of cream to her coffee, smiling, watching as Trish placed a hand over her heart, feigning distress, saying with a great deal of dramatics, "Oh, thank you, kind sir. I might've broken my stupid neck." She laughed as she stepped down from the ladder. She gave him a flirtatious look as she pushed a curl back into her braid. "I must look a fright."

"Don't think so," David said, putting both hands around her waist to assist her.

"They make a nice looking couple," Doc observed from across the table as Georgia sat back down. This morning, instead of ordering bacon and eggs in the dining room, Doc had followed Georgia into the kitchen and asked if he might eat there instead. Georgia had replied matter-of-factly, "Suit yourself." Secretly, she was delighted to have his company.

After Doc had helped with Gloria's embarrassing episode the day before, Georgia somehow felt closer to him, as if she knew him better now. He had coolly ordered Mary Jo to fetch his medical bag from his car to check Gloria over more thoroughly to make sure she hadn't suffered another stroke and needed transport to the hospital. Gloria was fine. By the time Georgia and Zoe dressed her in fresh clothing, the old woman had completely forgotten all about the incident.

Georgia stamped the last of the envelopes, thinking if she hurried she'd make the post office before it closed. Yesterday morning, Louie, Susan and the children all drove up to the Grand Canyon and stayed overnight, but David stayed behind, making up some lame excuse about not feeling well, saying he might get chilled. Chilled? Ridiculous, considering David had never seen the Grand Canyon and normally would have jumped at the chance to go with the others, even if he were running a temperature of one hundred and two degrees.

David said from the pantry, "I like rescuing damsels in distress."

Trish sauntered out of the pantry, coyly brushing past David, tucking a wisp of hair behind one ear, saying, "Oh, prince of my dreams. Where have you been all my life?" She said this teasingly, but David, like a fish caught on a hook, followed her into the kitchen.

Doc grabbed up the envelopes and handed them to Trish on her way past the table. "Why don't the two of you take a walk to the post office and mail these for Georgia, huh?"

David's eyes lit up at this suggestion, but Trish, at first, looked immeasurably uncomfortable, but only for a second. Her mouth suddenly broke into a charming smile. "Sure, why not?"

Trish had barely discarded her apron when David appeared behind her, holding her coat.

When she gave him a questioning look, he said, "This *is* your coat, isn't it?"

"Yes." Trish slipped into the coat and pulled on a red knit cap and matching mittens. Her smile turned solemn, as if David's gentlemanly gesture of holding out her coat had somehow ruined their flirtatious game and put new boundaries into place. "Thank you."

David shrugged into his heavy wool coat meant for subzero Boston winters. He gave his mother a wink, and then they were gone.

"Well, what do you make of that?" Georgia said, as she gathered up the checkbook and receipts to file away. She was thoroughly dumbfounded. Yesterday, David and Trish had barely spoken to each other. For sure, something had transpired between these two in the last twenty-four hours to make them so cutesy and flirty with each other this morning. Georgia had barely opened the back door of the café before David arrived, asking for coffee and wanting to know what time Trish came into work.

"More coffee?"

"No," Doc said, amused.

"What?" Georgia could see the teasing behind his eyes.

"You know exactly *what*," Doc replied, adding more cream to his coffee. "You've had this planned out in your mind for weeks."

Georgia fluttered her eyelashes and said in her best southern accent, "Sir, I haven't the faintest idea what ya'll are talkin' about."

"Mary Jo tells me everything that goes on in this place."

"Your granddaughter's a horrible gossip," Georgia teased.

"Runs in the family, I suppose."

"Well, you can't blame me, can you? Trish and David have had a hard time of it. They deserve to find a little happiness. If they become good friends, I'll call that a blessing."

Georgia was startled when Doc gently placed a hand against her cheek. So warm and firm, his touch made Georgia's stomach do a quick somersault. Her head instinctively leaned into his hand. He said, "I hope it works out fine for them."

Suddenly, it felt as if the room had heated up another twenty degrees. Her entire body tingled with an exhilaration she hadn't known in years. Lord, don't let it stop. "Who knows?" She stammered like a giddy schoolgirl talking to her first beaux.

He removed his hand. Georgia fought the urge to grab it back and press it to her cheek again. When she spoke, she tried to keep her voice from quivering. "Well, love's fickle, and I'm not going to make any more of it than what it is."

"And what is that?"

Georgia nonchalantly filed the paid bills in an expandable folder in the bottom desk drawer, aware that Doc was no longer speaking about Trish and David. She replied innocently, "Nothing at the moment."

"But maybe, perhaps, there is something there."

"Well, I don't know. We'll have to wait and see, won't we?"

Doc slid the empty mug to one side and leaned back in his chair, appearing a bit uncomfortable. "I want to discuss something with you, Georgia. You may not like it."

Seeing his face turn serious, she sat down again at the table. "Doc, what is it?" Her thoughts circled around to yesterday, thinking perhaps Susan had read more into their relationship and took it upon herself to confront Doc. Oh, good Lord, she hoped not.

"It's you, Georgia."

"Me?" Flabbergasted, she frantically thought back to what she had said to him that might have upset him. Unable to think clearly, she stumbled, "I don't understand."

"When you first came to Sedona, do you remember what you were looking for?"

Georgia felt her eyes shift aimlessly around the room. April seemed so far away now, and her life had changed so much. How could she possibly explain how she felt to anyone? And what did it really matter, anyway? She was here now, and the past no longer mattered. Turning to Doc, she gave him what she thought to be the safest answer. "I wanted more time for myself."

"Ah, I see." He studied her for a moment, as if trying to read her thoughts.

"Well, Doctor," Georgia said with a teasing smile, wanting to disclose a brief and more romantic version of her departure from Ohio. "I left home one morning in April to go to the grocery store, started daydreaming and accidentally drove right by the mall. Silly, don't you think?"

"And?"

She shrugged. "I ended up in Cincinnati, pulled into a gas station with every intention of turning around. But then I met a woman from Arizona who told me if I ever went west, I simply had to visit Sedona."

"And?"

Georgia shook her head, now getting a little annoyed by his therapist-like persistence. She sighed, exasperated. "Then, it started to rain, and somehow I couldn't turn around, not after I'd run over the daffodils." Oops, she hadn't meant to mention the flowers.

"Daffodils?" Doc looked confused.

She bit into her lower lip, incapable of explaining about the daffodils being the reason she couldn't go back because then she would've had to have seen them flat on the ground and dead like the rest of her life.

She stammered, finally saying, "I turned in the opposite direction and ended up in Nashville."

Doc came closer. "Perfectly understandable. You were dealing with the grief of losing your husband."

Georgia almost laughed, remembering how that morning it had been her postmortem anger at Ed that actually made her miss the turn into the grocery store and flee down the interstate. She studied Doc for moment, wishing she could fully confide in him. "Grieving? Not really, Doc. I was lost in mediocrity. I wanted more than what I had, but it didn't involve possessing anything tangible. Most of all, I wanted away from myself."

"You were hurting—"

"No," she objected. "Not hurting. The minute I turned onto the interstate, I stopped hurting."

"What happened that first night, Georgia. Did you call Susan?"

"Yes." Tears prickled at the backs of her eyes. "I stayed at some broken-down motel and had to use a pay phone inside the lobby. Of course, Susan didn't understand what had happened to me. Looking back now, I suppose she had every right to think I'd flipped my lid." Georgia laughed, a bit nervous about exposing too much of herself to Doc. She kept expecting Mary Jo to come through the door with an order to prepare, but everything remained quiet, so quiet she could plainly hear the drip-drip-drip of the faucet in the kitchen sink.

Doc said soothingly, "I understand."

He made what she had done sound so normal, not crazy at all, but something any woman would have done under the same circumstances. The early memories of her journey flickered behind her eyes, and there was Edith sitting in the worn recliner with the bag of potato chips, eavesdropping on Georgia's conversation with Susan. Georgia said to Doc, "The owner of the motel told me she'd sold it to a developer. Edith chain-smoked. She was moving to Seattle to live with her daughter, but the daughter told her she had to quit smoking." Georgia paused. "Not that I approve of smoking. It's just the idea of family members suddenly telling you what you can and can't do. Like, you're incapable of running your life anymore. Right then, I decided I couldn't go back to what I was before. You know what Edith told me, Doc?"

"What?"

"Edith said she always wanted to take a bus trip to Alaska, but when I asked why she wouldn't go after she sold the motel, she told me, 'Maybe sometime.' Well, I knew right then she'd never see Alaska. For her, Alaska would never be any more than a dream.

I didn't want to end up like Edith, wishing my life away when I had every opportunity to do what I wanted to do." Georgia gulped in a new breath. "Can you see what I mean?"

Doc's kind eyes never left hers. "Yes, dear sweet, Georgia. I see what you mean."

Tears streamed down Georgia's cheeks. She hadn't felt them until Doc pulled a handkerchief from his pocket and gently dabbed at her face. "This is so silly." She brushed at the front of her apron. "There's nothing wrong. I don't understand why I'm crying."

"You need to talk this out."

Georgia went on with her story, telling Doc about the Virgin Mary in the ceiling of the old motel room outside of Nashville, and then about a pregnant Lou Ann giving her the makeover. Then, she went on about how in Texas she had given Luke a ride to Flagstaff. She laughed. "And would you believe it? Zoe and I ran into Luke and his girlfriend at the supermarket in Flagstaff the day before Thanksgiving. They're engaged!" She told him about getting back to her apartment and calling Lou Ann and asking what she had, a boy or girl, and how her life had turned out since. "And if I knew how to get in touch with Edith, I'd do that, too. I'd like to know if she'd changed her mind and bought a bus ticket to Alaska."

Doc sighed. "You've told me a beautiful story, Georgia. You're a damn good woman. You bring life to everyone you meet. This old town hasn't been the same since you arrived here. I've never seen people so enamored of anyone, what with your hospitality at the Soft Rock and the amount of love you put into your cooking. What I'm trying to say is, you've found your calling, so to speak."

Georgia squirmed in her chair. She had never felt comfortable receiving compliments, but coming from Doc, she gratefully accepted every word, reverently tucking them inside a lonely part of her heart. "Thank you, Doc."

"I'm not finished yet," he said, looking as if he were about to deliver a bit of bad news. "Looks to me, considering all the work you've done matching up David with Trish and all but ordering

Zoe to marry Jake, well it's like you're asking for the same trouble all over again."

Ouch. That hurt. Especially coming from Doc. Fresh tears nettled behind her eyes. In defense, she said, "I haven't pushed anyone to get married. I..." she faltered. "I just want the people I love to be happy, that's all."

"You can't make people happy. People have to learn to work out their own problems. No matter how much you love them. Georgia, don't spend the rest of your life trying to make other people comfortable with themselves, when it's you that's uncomfortable with yourself."

"I've never pushed Zoe," she added defensively. "As for David and Trish, you said yourself they make a nice looking couple."

Doc patted her hand. "Now, Georgia, take it easy. I'm not saying you're wrong. I'd like Zoe and Jake to get married and see Trish fall in love. Even my granddaughter, Mary Jo, could use a little advice now and then, but I kick myself every time I step up on the soapbox with her. It's her life, not mine. What I'm trying to say Georgia is stop being a martyr to your family. Last year, you lost your husband. You were vulnerable, losing everything familiar."

Vulnerable? Georgia almost laughed. She had never talked about Ed and what really happened when he died to anyone since she had come here. Not once. In her mind, she had buried her past when she had returned to Ohio and sold the house and the business.

"Georgia? Is something wrong?"

She opened her mouth to speak, wanting to let everything out at once and be done with it. If she could tell anyone about her marriage, she could tell Doc. "Doc, I..."

As if on cue, Mary Jo shoved through from the dining room with a food order, followed by Susan, Louie and the children, laughing and talking about what fun they'd all had at the Grand Canyon. Upon seeing her mother, Susan said, "Mom, it was so amazing!" The excitement in Susan's eyes made Georgia's day, reaffirming that she had made the right decision leaving home and heading for a place she had never seen before.

Ben rushed forward, eyes shining, wearing a ball cap with Grand Canyon across the front. "Grandma, it was a great big hole in the ground!"

Mary Jo flagged the order in front of Georgia's face. With Trish gone to the post office with David, Georgia would have to take over the rest of the breakfast shift and start rinsing the vegetables for the lunch menu. Much to Georgia's surprise, Susan took the order from Mary Jo and laid it on the counter. "Don't worry about a thing, Mom. I'll wash up and tie on an apron and give you a hand."

"We'll talk later," Doc said, scooting back the chair and getting up. Georgia gave him the kind of look that apologized, but, really she felt grateful for the interruption. What she might have told Doc, she would have undoubtedly regretted later.

The rest of the week seemed to fly by. Louie and Susan flew home with the children on Sunday, but not without Susan begging her mother to at least commit to coming back to Ohio for Christmas. "You can stay with us, Mom, and have Christmas with Ben and Samantha." Georgia didn't think twice before saying, "No. I'll miss all of you, but I want to stay here for Christmas." Georgia had no good explanation except that this was her first holiday without Ed, and she wanted the time and space to make this her own special time. "Maybe next year," she told Susan, giving her a quick kiss on the cheek. Surprisingly, Susan accepted Georgia's decision and gave her mother another hug before getting into the rental car with Louie and the children.

David flew back to Boston early that same morning. Trish seemed not to be missing him all that much, going about her life as if they had never met. Only once did Georgia ask Trish if she and David planned on seeing each other again.

Trish had merely shrugged. "Maybe. Don't know, for sure."

And that was that. Nothing more said. Georgia, after her talk with Doc, decided to back off and leave all the romancing and matchmaking to cupid.

# CHAPTER TWENTY-ONE

"**T**wo days before Christmas. Can you believe it, Zoe?" Georgia finished stapling the day's receipts, and then added quite innocently, "I know about Trish's secret. She's going to Boston to see David."

They were alone at the Moon Tide after closing. For the last few days, Georgia had been helping Zoe with the Christmas rush. Everyone in Sedona seemed to be caught up in the holiday spirit. Bright, festive lights decorated the streets. All the lamp posts were tied up with wreaths with dangling red bows that greeted the shoppers along the sidewalks.

"What?" Zoe stopped rearranging the earrings on the glass counter and turned to stare at Georgia.

"She's not fooling anyone," Georgia said, tapping the top of the receipt box.

Zoe let out an exaggerated sigh. "Oh, I know. I would've told you except Trish swore me to secrecy. And honestly, if this whole David thing doesn't work out, I thought it would be better if you didn't know what was going on behind your back. Trish is quite a mess, you know. She's fallen hard for David. She didn't really make up her mind about Boston until yesterday. I told her to either go to David or stay home. But, beware Georgia. David's not the first guy Trish has fallen hard for, and then dumped three dates later."

Georgia wandered over to a Comfort Zone and started picking

up discarded books and returning them to the bookshelves. "Maybe both of them have to take that chance."

"Oh, please, Georgia, don't get all *Oprah and Dr. Phil* on me. I know you. If Trish comes back and nothing popped between the two of them, you'll be disappointed. Don't even pretend you won't be."

Georgia shrugged. "Probably, but at least then, I'll stop fussing about it."

Zoe pulled down the shade on the door. "Well, don't start crying and getting all emotional on me, if Boston doesn't kick-start some great romance. Promise?"

Georgia held up two fingers, "Scout's honor."

Zoe pointed a finger at her. "And don't tell Trish you know she's not really going to Tucson for Christmas. It's better that way."

Georgia pulled out a bottle of glass cleaner and paper towels from the cleaning cupboard and started wiping fingerprints from the glass countertop. "I won't."

Zoe raised one eyebrow. "Are you seeing Doc over the holidays?"

"No." Georgia rubbed in earnest at the smudges on the glass. She didn't want to talk about Doc, especially not to Trish or Zoe. They already teased her constantly about his coming into the café every morning and eating his breakfast in the kitchen with her. The girls made too much of it. She and Doc talked about nothing in particular; they were good friends, absolutely nothing more than that.

Zoe fussed at a row of Navajo dolls, straightening them so that they now stared straight ahead with shiny, black button eyes. "He's a good man, Georgia. I think—"

"Don't start, Zoe," Georgia snapped, throwing down the paper towel and coming around the counter. "If you do, I'll start asking my own questions about you."

"Me?" Zoe said, straightening the red silk belt tied around her waist. Georgia often wondered how any one woman could possibly own so many gorgeous clothes. Today, Zoe wore a black silk jumpsuit accented with the red silk tie belt, very simple but oh-so-chic. On Zoe, the outfit looked nothing less than spectacular.

"I know about the ring Jake gave you."

Zoe's face hardened. "Trish. That girl can't keep a secret if her front teeth depended on it."

Someone tapped on the front window and Zoe lifted the shade. She turned to Georgia and quipped, "Speak of the devil." Zoe unlatched the door and opened it, letting in a bundled up Trish holding a plate of sandwiches. She moved into the shop, stomping her feet on the mat, and bringing with her a cold blast of air and swirling snow.

Trish pulled off her knit cap, saying, "You've been so busy, I thought you'd like something to eat." She handed the plate to Zoe as she shrugged out of her coat and threw it over a nearby chair. "*Brrr*, it's cold." She gave Zoe a quizzical look. "Say, why the sour look?" She didn't wait for an answer but took the plate back from Zoe and went directly to the kitchen to set the kettle on the stove.

Zoe followed. "You told Georgia about the ring, didn't you?"

"So? I didn't think it was a big secret."

Zoe sank into the cushioned chair outside the kitchen door, letting her head fall into her hands. "I didn't *tell* you, Trish. You *found* the ring when you ransacked my dresser drawers."

"Well," she faltered. "I needed to borrow that sweater I gave you last Christmas."

"You were snooping."

Georgia backed away from the two women, shaking her head, not wanting to get involved in yet another one of their spats. They could go on for hours about nothing. Her curiosity about Jake would have to wait until later.

Trish, hands on hips, suddenly turned on Georgia. "Jake gave her an ultimatum."

"What?" Georgia bumped into the chair where Trish had thrown her coat and hat. She thought even if Jake did give Zoe an ultimatum, he would never follow through with whatever he had threatened. He loved Zoe too much. If he ever did make good on any threat to leave Zoe, it would certainly devastate him.

The teakettle whistled and Georgia rushed into the kitchen to turn down the heat. Her hands trembled. She wanted to tell Zoe not to waste this wonderful opportunity for happiness with Jake, but mindful of Doc's words a few weeks ago, she tried to keep her opinions to herself. She bit into her lower lip, determined not to stick her nose into Zoe's business.

Both women trailed after Georgia into the kitchen. They'd had enough of these late afternoon gab sessions in the past months to know the routine. Zoe lifted mugs from the rack while Trish opened the box of tea and arranged sandwiches on a platter. Zoe, still fuming over Trish's snooping, said under her breath. "You're a blabbermouth, Trish."

Georgia couldn't stand it any longer. She repeated, "What ultimatum?" It suddenly seemed as if her friends couldn't get through two days in a row without some crisis nipping at their heels, and then would spend hours debating whether or not it was worth debating.

Trish sat down and took a bite of sandwich and chewed, her eyes darting to Zoe. "Jake proposed and gave Zoe a ring the size of a marble."

"Oh my. Where is it?"

"In the dresser drawer." Zoe narrowed her eyes at Trish. "Under a sweater that *used* to be there."

Georgia exclaimed, "Let's see it."

"No."

"Ah, come on, Zoe, show Georgia the ring."

"Why should I? If I see it again, I might just give it back."

Georgia pushed back the sandwiches, not hungry anymore. Insistent, she asked, "What's Jake's ultimatum?"

Zoe shrugged. "He's leaving New Years Eve for Washington to look for a house."

"Whew, sounds nice," Georgia said, hoping she sounded upbeat.

"He wants me to go with him."

"So, what's the problem?"

Trish interrupted. "She's going to hem and haw around until Jake gives up and leaves. He's not coming back. I know my brother."

"Ah, Zoe," Georgia said, exasperated. "I thought after the election all that had been settled about marrying Jake?"

"Well, I don't know. I can't up and leave now, not with Mama having had that stroke and getting worse by the day."

Trish waved her hand. "Geez, Zoe. Gloria wouldn't know if you visited today or three weeks from today."

"She's right, you know," Georgia encouraged. "You could fly back every two weeks or so and check on your mother. Trish and I could take turns every week checking in on her. Won't we Trish?"

Trish looked hesitant, but said, "Sure. Georgia and I will take care of everything. Even the Moon Tide. It's not as if we're rookies."

Zoe pushed back her hair, her beautiful face showing faint worry lines in her forehead. "I know the two of you mean well, but don't push me, okay? Maybe I'm not ready to live in a fishbowl in Washington. Here, I feel safe. Jake can always come back whenever he wants."

"So, what's that make you?" Trish said venomously, crossing her arms against her chest. "His mistress?"

Zoe's face turned stone-cold. "That's enough. I'm through talking about Jake. It's my decision and no one else's." She tore crust from her bread and threw it on the wax paper. For the next few minutes they all ate in silence.

Trish spoke first. "Georgia, I'm going to Boston to visit David." Then, she quickly added, "We're just friends." She moistened a finger with her tongue and dabbed at the crumbs left on her napkin. "I'm leaving tomorrow."

Georgia finished the last of her tea and nonchalantly said, "You'd better dress in something warmer than that tiny skirt you're wearing."

Trish blushed. "Oh, Georgia, please tell me you're okay with me going there. David's a great guy, but I can't promise things will work out between us. And I don't want to go to Boston if it might jeopardize our friendship."

Georgia took her cup and saucer to the sink. "You and David are adults. You'll find out for yourselves if you're meant to be together, or not. I don't figure into the equation at all."

As Trish slipped into her coat, Georgia smiled and reached for her *Made in Scotland* wool scarf hanging over her own coat on the hook by the door. She wrapped it snug around Trish's neck and small shoulders. Georgia cupped Trish's face in her hands and kissed her on the cheek. "Have a wonderful time and give David a kiss for me."

"I..." Trish's fingers lovingly ran the length of the scarf. "Thank you."

Georgia put the empty plate in Trish's hands. "Don't worry about the café. I'll take care of everything." Whatever happened in Boston was out of Georgia's hands, but at the same time, she couldn't help but consider Trish's commitment record with men, that being exactly zero. The thought of her son's heart being broken by Trish brought on a pain in her own heart. Doc had been right. She never should have meddled in David's and Trish's lives, but, of course, she hadn't, not really. They had done it all on their own. She gave Trish one more hug before letting go of her.

"Goodnight," Trish said, pausing in the open doorway, the snow swirling crazy-like around her head and shoulders. The yarn tassel on Trish's knit cap twirled spasmodically in the wind, as if it couldn't decide which way to go. Trish's eyes filled with tears. "Georgia?"

"Yes."

"Oh, never mind." Trish lowered her head, securing the knit cap down around her ears before running her fingers along the length of *Made in Scotland* scarf around her neck. For one moment, Georgia thought Trish might give back the gift, but she didn't. Trish only waved as she turned and walked away, disappearing into the falling snow.

# CHAPTER TWENTY-TWO

A steady rain poured over Sedona, dissolving what remained of the pretty Christmas snow. The second day of January was bleak and chilly, the café empty of patrons, except for Doc who sat at the long table drinking coffee with another rancher from Cottonwood. In the kitchen, Georgia cracked eggs into a bowl, adding milk for Doc's late breakfast order of scrambled eggs and whole wheat toast, no butter. Through the service window, she listened as the two men talked about cattle prices, water rights, and the good old days when their grandfathers had lived hard lives, losing children and wives in childbirth, and finally spending their final years sitting in cafés or feed stores drinking coffee and talking cattle prices, water rights, and the good old days. Nothing ever really changes.

Georgia closed her eyes. If she didn't know any better, she'd swear she was back in her kitchen on Stilson Avenue fixing Ed's breakfast.

She hadn't thought about Ed much in the past few weeks, but when she did, she honestly missed him. Not a heartache kind of missing, but more like soap—missing it only after you've gotten wet in the shower and finding no soap in the little ceramic tray. Just a passing moment's worth of missing. She added milk to the eggs, smiling as she whisked everything together, feeling good about her single life and running the café in Trish's absence. And, thinking about Ed, she reminded herself, she wasn't cooking for free anymore. This breakfast would cost Doc $6.95.

Only to herself did Georgia have the nerve to admit that she more than liked Doc, and she knew, for sure, he more than liked her, too. She wished Trish and Zoe would let it be and not tease her so much about the man. She looked forward to Doc's daily visits to the café, pouring his coffee, serving his meals, and when she wasn't busy, sitting across the table from him and talking about nothing in particular. At the end of the day, though, she looked forward to retreating into the privacy of her cozy apartment over the café where she would read a book or watch an old movie, crying at the sad parts.

Today, the streets were mostly deserted, the holidays over for another year. Many of the businesses were closed until Monday. Georgia had spent the last week dividing her time between watching over both the café and the Moon Tide. Trish would be getting back from Boston tonight. Zoe had driven to Phoenix to visit her mother for a few days. Jake had left for Washington on New Year's Eve and Zoe stayed behind. She had refused to disclose the details and made it clear she had made the right decision. Georgia's sympathies were more on Jake's side, knowing the risk he had taken by giving Zoe a now-or-never ultimatum. He had lost the bet, at least for now. What other choice did he have but to get on the plane and leave Zoe behind? None. Georgia couldn't help but wonder if Zoe fully understood the consequences of her decision? She supposed only God knew the truth about that.

Georgia watered the Christmas cactus in the window over the desk and then dried her hands on the towel draped over one shoulder. Doc came through the swinging door with a tray of dirty dishes, taking them to the washroom where he rinsed and put everything in the wash racks. Georgia tried to recall if Ed had ever in his entire life taken dishes to the sink and rinsed them off. Nope, she couldn't recall one instance. She laughed out loud.

"What's so funny," Doc said, turning to face her. He smiled

at her so endearingly that a hot blush pressed against Georgia's cheeks. For the past week, she had more than enjoyed being alone with Doc in the café.

"It's funny you helping with the dishes."

"Funny?"

"Compared to other men I've known, yes."

He gave her such an endearing look, and the space in the kitchen suddenly seemed too close. Flustered by the more intimate nature of their words, she sat at the desk and slipped on her glasses, pretending to go over a list to be called in to the supplier before noon tomorrow.

Doc leaned against the sink, arms crossed, looking quite handsome in faded jeans, western belt and a laundry-pressed denim work shirt. As usual, his cowboy hat was hanging on a peg beside the dining room door. He said to her, "My dear, sweet mama, God rest her soul, taught me to be respectful of anyone who feeds me."

Georgia put the list aside and adjusted her half-glasses, giving him all her attention. "Oh, really? Well, it's not as if you don't pay for your meals." *God, she was flirting, too.* She stood up and handed him the bill for his breakfast.

Doc lowered his head and scuffed one toe of his cowboy boot over the other. Georgia noticed a line of pink scalp in the part of his silver hair and caught the clean scent of his cologne. She wanted more than anything to reach out and touch his face. He suddenly looked up and caught her staring. "Georgia, I was wondering if you'd go to dinner with me sometime."

She worked at the front pocket of her apron to keep her hands from trembling. "I'd like that."

"You would? What I mean is, how about next Saturday?"

Georgia untied her apron and gave it a toss into the laundry hamper. "Yes, that would be nice." She hesitated. "But I want to be up-front with you, Doc. I'm not looking for a relationship. I like who I am right now."

"Oh, now, Georgia," Doc sputtered. "I'm asking you to dinner, not for a life's commitment, okay?" Sliding his hands into the front pockets of his jeans, he looked wounded.

"I'm sorry," Georgia said quickly. "That sounded rude, didn't it? Yes, Doc. I'd love to go to dinner with you."

\* \* \*

Trish arrived home later that afternoon. Georgia didn't see her come into the café. Standing on a stepstool, Georgia was busy dusting the top of the corner cabinet in the dining room, singing along with a country song playing on the radio. The day had been slow, mostly locals. Georgia had spent most of her time cleaning shelves and scraping gum from the underside of tables. When she got down from the stool, she turned and saw Trish watching her from the doorway. "Trish," she gasped. "You startled me."

Trish pulled off her gloves and helped herself to a cup of coffee. She didn't take off her coat so Georgia understood she had only dropped in to check on the café before going home. Trish said oh-so-calmly, "Everything run smoothly while I was gone?"

"Great. Slow today, but I guess that's normal in January."

"Yep," she said, lifting the mug and taking a cautious sip.

"How was Boston?"

Trish grimaced. Georgia didn't know, for sure, if the coffee was too hot or if the question had bothered her.

Trish plopped down in a nearby chair and unbuttoned her coat. "We did everything but throw tea into Boston harbor."

"Oh?"

Trish responded with a lopsided grin. "Georgia, this is all too weird talking to you about spending the week with David."

"I suppose so. Well tell me you had a good time and I'll drop it."

"I had a good time."

"Okay." True to her word, she let the subject drop even though she was dying to know how the week had played out for them.

Trish's secret little smile only made her all the more curious, but being David's mother, she fully understood why Trish wasn't anxious to elaborate.

Trish stuffed her gloves into her pocket and slid into a booth with her coffee. "Where's Zoe?"

"Phoenix. She's coming back in the morning."

"Oh? I guess that means she's not going to marry Jake."

Georgia threw the dust rag over her shoulder and sat beside Trish. "I think Jake's gone for good this time."

"Zoe's such an idiot. If she's not careful some bloodsucking vamp is going to sink her hooks into my brother's heart, and I'll be forced to like her."

"I know. I feel the same way."

Silence.

Trish said, "Rain all day?"

"All day."

"Business slow?"

"You already asked that."

Trish got up and slipped the gloves back on her hands. "Well, I suppose I'd better get home and let the cat out."

Georgia grinned and shook her head. "You don't have a cat."

Trish feigned surprise. "I don't? Oh, yeah, you have a cat. How is Oscar, anyway?"

"Oscar's fine. He's upstairs napping on my silk blouse I forgot to hang up yesterday."

"Ahhh, he has good taste in clothes. Well, maybe I'll get a cat, too." At the door, she pointed to the hooks along the wall. "I see Doc's left his cowboy hat again. That man's getting mighty forgetful, don't you think?"

Georgia locked the door behind Trish and started upstairs when the phone rang. "Soft Rock," she said, sliding the receiver under her chin, at the same time turning out the dining room lights.

"Georgia?"

"Zoe? What's wrong?"

"My mother, she's dead, Georgia. Last night. A stroke. She died a few minutes ago."

"Oh, Zoe. I'm so sorry." Georgia pressed the receiver tight to her ear.

Zoe said, "She's being cremated tonight. I'm driving back to Sedona in the morning."

"You're going to spread her ashes here?"

"No." There was a long pause on the other end of the line. "Georgia, I've got a favor to ask. I want you and Trish to drive to Los Angeles with me."

Georgia wasn't certain she'd heard her right. "Do what?"

"Please, Georgia."

Georgia slumped down on the stool beside the chopping block, pulling her sweater around her shoulders. "What about Jake. You should wait until you hear from him. I know he'll want to be with you." A small sigh came from the other end.

"I left a message but he hasn't called back."

"He will." By God she'd call Jake herself after hanging up.

"I don't know. I don't think he'll ever forgive me for not marrying him. Georgia, please say you'll go with me to Los Angeles."

"I'll call Trish. We'll be ready to leave as soon as you get here tomorrow."

"Thank you."

"Zoe, will you be all right tonight by yourself?"

"I'm afraid."

"Afraid? Where are you now?"

"A motel."

"Where?"

"Not far from the nursing home. I wanted to be alone, but now that I'm alone, I needed to hear your voice. All I can think about is how I'm glad she's dead."

"Zoe, don't do this to yourself."

Zoe sniffled into the receiver. Her next words were difficult to understand. "I begged her to tell me if Florry was my real mother."

"You did?"

"She told me no, that it wasn't that simple."

"Zoe, your mother wasn't right in the head. You know that."

"Before she died, I told her I loved her. She looked me straight in the eye and told me I was too damn emotional. Can you believe that?"

"It doesn't matter now. For your own sake, Zoe, don't try to figure her out. Let it go."

"God knows I want to. What do you suppose she meant by that?"

"Zoe, go to sleep. We'll talk tomorrow."

"Georgia?"

"Yes."

"I'm going to hell for hating her."

"I don't think so."

Zoe sighed. "No good ever comes from hating anyone."

"No good at all." Georgia agreed.

Georgia hung up the phone, worried about Zoe being alone and depressed in a motel room. She dialed Jake's cell phone number in Washington. No answer. Not wanting to leave a message, she dialed Trish's number. She answered on the second ring. When she told Trish about Gloria's death, Trish said, "Ohmygod." When she told Trish about Zoe wanting them to go with her to Los Angeles, Trish responded, "Ohmygod!"

Upstairs in her apartment Georgia called Susan and got the voice mail. She left a message about Zoe's mother's death and how they were driving to LA early the next morning. "I'll call when we get there." Then, as an afterthought she added, "Call David and let him know what's happened."

Turning out the light, Georgia crawled into bed, thankful for the warmth of the down comforter. She drew up her knees, hugging them to her chest, listening to her own frayed breath in the darkness. A part of her wished she could think of a plausible excuse not to go with Zoe. She hated funerals.

After Ed died, Georgia had gone to the funeral home, wanting to be alone with him before friends and family arrived for the viewing. She had tiptoed across the thick carpet to Ed's casket with every intention of having the last word with him about how he died on his damn boat during an afternoon tryst with another woman. Stepping up to the edge of the coffin and seeing Ed's body dressed in his favorite suit, she forgot all about being angry. His face didn't look quite right, and then she realized he wasn't wearing his glasses. Ed just didn't look like Ed without them. His eyeglasses were at home on the kitchen counter with his wallet, car keys and loose change collected in a plastic zip-lock bag and given to her by the emergency room nurse.

Numb with grief, Georgia stared at Ed's face, thinking he looked more asleep than dead in the three thousand dollar oak casket with the ivory satin lining. It seemed at any moment Ed might open his eyes and say, *For God's sake, Georgia, get me out of this damn thing.*

Smoothing the lapels of his suit, she lightly touched his folded hands, her fingers stroking the gold wedding band on his finger. A tear slid down her cheek and dropped onto Ed's forehead. He didn't flinch. Georgia dabbed at the tear with her pinky finger and smudged his makeup. Horrified, she first looked around to see if anyone had seen what she had done, before digging into the pocket of her coat for a tissue. Moistening an end with her tongue, she dabbed at Ed's forehead until everything blended in again.

Now, wide awake, Georgia rolled over in bed. The memory of Ed's funeral thankfully faded into the darkness. Stretching her legs into the cold parts of the bed, she wriggled her toes to make everything around them warm. She closed her eyes. The more she concentrated on sleep, the more restless she felt. Sitting up, she plumped the pillows and let her head fall into them. Eyes open, she tried to recollect the last time she and Ed had made love. She bit hard into her lower lip. No memory. In the last years of their marriage, their lovemaking had become almost nonexistent and as boring as the same book read two thousand times over. You know all the words, paragraphs and chapters by heart, the ending always turning out the same way.

Georgia rolled over onto her side, her thoughts shifting to Doc. She feared falling in love with him and having to face the possibility of giving up the part of herself that she had worked so hard to find. And the last question, the one she did not want to think about: Could she even remember how to make love?

A rapid knocking at the door brought Georgia out of the deep sleep she had worked so hard to get into. Thinking at first she had overslept, she glanced at the clock and saw it was only two in the morning. Throwing off the covers, she ran to the door, shouting, "Who's there?"

A quavering voice answered, "Georgia, it's me."

Georgia opened the door and found Trish shivering inside a wool blanket, a suitcase at her feet. "What on earth?" She pulled her inside and out of the cold and quickly closed the door. Trish dropped the suitcase and gave it a kick out of her way. Georgia took her by the shoulders, seeing Trish's swollen eyes from crying. "Trish what happened?"

"I'm scared. Can I sleep on your sofa tonight? I promise I won't be any trouble."

"Of course you can." Georgia lifted the blanket from around her shoulders, and underneath, Trish wore a nightgown and untied sneakers.

"I'm sorry I woke you up."

"Don't apologize." Georgia set the teakettle on the stove and turned up the flame.

Trish followed close behind. "If you don't mind, Georgia, do you have any whiskey. I sure could use a shot."

Georgia turned off the teakettle and opened the cabinet by the sink, pulling out an unopened bottle of good whiskey. She poured a generous amount into two tumblers and handed one to Trish. "Here. I think we could both use some bolstering tonight."

Trish sank into the cushions of the sofa and took a sip, making a sour face. "God, that burns."

Georgia sat in the rocker and pulled her terry housecoat snug around her legs. "Give it time."

"I'm in love with David."

Georgia's ears perked with this news. She laughed. "You came over here in the middle of the night all shaky and crying to tell me you love my son? That's a strange reaction to falling in love."

The tears started up again. Trish covered her face with her hands. "Georgia, I can't love David. I've done something so bad I can't ever tell him. And I can't tell you or even Zoe."

Trish's jaw quivered. Georgia knew she would not get another wink of sleep tonight what with having to pull Trish together before Zoe's early morning arrival with Gloria's ashes. What in heaven's name could be so wrong that Trish felt so unworthy of being loved? On the other hand, David had a beautiful heart, and she didn't want it broken by a young, flighty woman who always seemed on the verge of some self-induced crisis. "Let's get some sleep. We'll talk in the morning."

"I'm not going with you."

"Of course you are. This is for Zoe, not for us. We're both going because she's our friend and needs us there for support. Do you hear me?"

Trish retrieved her blanket and wrapped up in it again. "I know you're right. I'll go."

Georgia's eyes felt gritty from lack of sleep. "Trish?"

"Yeah?"

"Nothing's unforgivable."

A groggy voice came from beneath the blanket. "Did you forgive Ed?" When Georgia failed to answer, Trish said, "Exactly."

# CHAPTER TWENTY-THREE

In the kitchen, Georgia gave Mary Jo last minute instructions about managing the café in their absence. Mary Jo looked stunned, her mouth visibly trembling at the thought of being left alone in the café for the next three days.

Trish called out from the dining room. "She's here, Georgia! God, you're not going to believe this."

"I'm coming." Turning back to Mary Jo, Georgia said in one quick breath, "Now, don't worry, you'll be fine." She picked up her suitcase and started for the door, already regretting her decision to leave Mary Jo in charge of the café. The girl had practically hyperventilated when she first told her about going to LA with Trish and Zoe. On the way out Georgia grabbed a paper carryout bag and slapped it into Mary Jo's hand. "Here, breathe into this. You'll be fine."

Bursting into tears, Mary Jo wailed, "But Georgia, I've never been in charge of anything in my life."

Exasperated, Georgia told her again, "Business is slow, mostly locals. If something comes up you can't handle, call Doc. Your grandfather assured me he'd check in on you every day to make sure you're all right. We'll be back by the end of the week. Promise."

The Fleetwood was parked in front, trunk open. Trish reached down for Georgia's bag and rolled her eyes in Zoe's direction, saying, "I'm afraid we're way underdressed."

Georgia coughed to keep herself from laughing when Zoe came around the side of the car. "Zoe?"

"It's me," Zoe verified from behind huge sunglasses, her body wrapped head to foot in a silver fox coat, movie star gorgeous and ready for her close-up, Mr. Director.

Trish slammed the trunk shut. "I told her she's too early for the academy awards ceremony."

"It's Mother's," Zoe said casually, as if the coat needed an explanation. "She left it in the vault at the nursing home." She shrugged off Trish's comment. "Besides, it was chilly this morning." She looked pointedly at Trish. "Don't make it a big deal, okay?"

Trish shot back, "Tell that to the innocent foxes who sacrificed their lives for that coat."

Zoe sniffed as she folded the driver seat back and pointedly told Trish to get in.

Trish balked. "Oh sure. Put me in the back seat and, yeah, guess what? Gloria's back here, too, in a tin box. Geez, can't you put her in the trunk?"

"No. Mama rides in the car with us. That's being respectful."

"You're kidding, right?"

Zoe took off the dark glasses, her eyes all puffy and red as if she'd done some serious crying on the way to Sedona.

"Do you want me to drive," Georgia asked, concerned. She squeezed one of Zoe's gloved hands and noticed a diamond bracelet around her wrist.

"No, thank you. I'd rather drive."

"Don't mind Trish's teasing. It's only her way of dealing with her own problems." Georgia's misgivings about Zoe's driving evaporated as soon as they moved into the outskirts of town. Zoe relaxed behind the wheel and except for Trish's incessant griping about having to ride with Gloria's ashes in the backseat, the trip to LA started out fine.

In Flagstaff, they caught Route 40 and headed west. The trip would take about eight hours, driving first across the desert, into California, and then on to the LA basin. Georgia only hoped that the three of them would make it to LA without killing each other.

A few miles outside of Flagstaff, Georgia asked. "Are you sure you want us to stay at your mother's house? I mean, Trish and I can register at a nearby motel so you can be alone."

"You'll stay with me," Zoe said. "No arguments."

Georgia shifted in the seat, dreading the memorial service, imagining Zoe reciting the eulogy, dressed in her mother's clothing. Georgia anxiously wished she had been successful in getting hold of Jake. He would have known what to do with Zoe.

After traveling a few hours, Trish announced she had to pee. Zoe pulled into the next gas station and filled up the car. Georgia stretched her legs. She asked Zoe, "Do you want me to drive awhile?"

"Thanks, but no. It keeps my mind busy." The temperature stretched in the mid-eighties. Zoe unlocked the trunk, slipped off the coat, and then threw it over the suitcases as if it were nothing more than an old blanket.

Georgia remarked, "Beautiful coat."

Zoe sniffed. "I suppose it is."

"Zoe?"

"Yes."

"I know you're hurting. Talk to me, tell me what you need from us, okay?"

Zoe sighed and tilted her chin up to the cloudless blue sky. "Okay, I confess. I can't do this alone. I can't deal with my mother's house, the furniture, her clothing, her stupid Oscars—what the hell am I going to do with three Oscars?"

"I don't know. Keep them? You wouldn't sell them, would you?"

Zoe let out a sharp laugh. "More than likely, everything's mortgaged to the hilt. I never handled Mama's finances. Milton Thayer, her attorney, did all that, making sure I had enough to pay her bills in Arizona. I've always suspected that Milton paid some of the bills himself the last few years. He loved her, you know."

Georgia leaned against the side of the car. "I'm sorry your mother didn't say what you wanted her to say before she died. I know she hurt you terribly."

"Florry wasn't my mother, if that's what you're referring to." Zoe crossed her arms and leaned against the car, too.

"She told you that?" Georgia asked.

"Yeah, I asked her straight out. She denied it."

"You believed her?"

Zoe nodded as she stood up and stretched. "I believed her."

At that moment, Trish came out of the service station, cradling bottles of water and snacks in her arms.

Zoe mumbled, "I shouldn't have asked Trish to come with us."

Feeling obliged to defend Trish, Georgia said, "The only reason you don't want Trish around is she's Jake's sister. It's not her fault you pushed Jake away. And if you don't let go of all the venom about your childhood, it's going to eat you up. You'll end up as bitter and sarcastic as your mother."

"Okay. Okay. Okay. You're right, I'm wrong."

At that moment, the water bottles slipped from Trish's arms, dropped to the pavement and rolled in every direction. Trish fought to keep a tight hold on the snacks as she ran after the bottles.

Zoe's lips trembled as if she might break out laughing, but instead said, "Something's really bothering Trish. I can tell. When Trish gets upset, she gets really klutzy." Zoe opened the car door. She then said to Georgia very matter-of-factly, "Mama knew she was going to die. Can people really do that?"

"You're asking me? You're the one who claims to talk to the dead." Georgia watched Trish come toward them armed with bottled water and snacks. It suddenly occurred to her how much she cared for these two women who both seemed to have trouble letting the people in their lives love them.

"Here." Trish handed a bottle to each of them. "Hey, Georgia, can we put the top down?"

Georgia shrugged. "If you can figure it out."

"It's easy." Within a few minutes, Trish had the top folded back. The three of them climbed back inside the car. From the glove compartment, Zoe pulled out a long silk scarf and draped it over her hair, tying back the ends. With the sunglasses and silk scarf, she looked Paramount gorgeous behind the wheel of the Fleetwood.

\* \* \*

Out in the middle of nowhere, the car whizzed by an exit for some small desert town in California. Georgia wondered who in their right mind would choose to live in a place so utterly devoid of life. A billboard for a motel zipped past the window. Georgia didn't dare look at the speedometer. Using her folded sweater as a pillow, she rested her head against the window. The sun warmed her face; the wind whipped through the open car. Georgia finally let her eyelids drift shut.

She heard music, *Norwegian Wood*. Georgia and Ed were slow dancing at their senior prom. The gymnasium had been transformed into a magical nightclub scene, the usual dirty sock smell, basketballs and athletic equipment gone. In their place, hundreds of white and purple streamers, a huge sparkling silver ball hanging in the center of the gym. Cafeteria tables looked elegant, covered in white linen tablecloths the senior class had rented from Sue's Perfect Weddings.

With Ed's arms encircling her waist, Georgia rested her head on his shoulder, unaware that her life was about to take a serious turn into the unknown. Not until six weeks later would she know about the baby growing inside her, the baby conceived the night of her senior prom.

She breathed in Ed's smell, an adolescent mix of peppermint, Zest, High Karate and...lusty hormones. When he blew softly into her ear, Georgia's stomach dipped and swelled like the tide pulling her out to sea. She let her hand linger at the back of his neck. He tenderly kissed the top of her head as if she belonged to him. Suddenly, nothing else mattered to Georgia, except for this one beautiful night.

Tonight, every nerve in Georgia's body seemed poised and ready to jump out of her skin. The night was perfect, and she was with Ed, the most popular guy in her class. Life was good.

*Norwegian Wood* floated inside her head, sad, lonely words accompanied by a single guitar. She sighed heavily for all the grief in the world. Ed must have taken her sigh to mean that she wanted to leave the prom and be alone with him.

As he pulled her toward the exit door, she tried to straighten the beautiful orchid corsage that got crushed from their dancing so close. She wiped tiny beads of perspiration from her forehead. The silver ball twirled above her head, making her dizzy as they wormed their way through the maze of couples. She kept her head down, eyes focused on the foul lines on the gymnasium floor, almost surprised to see that it was only the gym, after all. Tomorrow, everything would go back to normal, the streamers pulled down, the tables returned to the cafeteria.

Ed rested his hand on the small of her back as he guided her out the side exit and into a parking lot bathed in bluish white light. Inside some of the parked cars, kids were necking, for the first time ignoring all the stupid rules about not being allowed to loiter in the parking lot, all because they were seniors.

Instead of staying and necking on school property, Ed drove the narrow road to Moody's Orchard, where they sat for the longest time gazing up at the stars. Georgia felt beautiful, and, for the first time, free of her childhood. Giddy and full of herself, she kicked off her dyed-to-match heels and propped her bare feet on the open car window, deciding her life would only get better from this moment on.

"Wanna smoke?"

Head resting in Ed's lap, she looked up lazily and considered the underside of his chin that appeared too thin and boyish from this angle. "No." She didn't like cigarettes even though she had smoked occasionally at parties to look cool. "Go ahead, if you want." Georgia knew that Ed smoked more than occasionally, and it wouldn't matter a twit if she objected or not. He'd still smoke.

He leaned over and from under the seat pulled out a small paper bag. "I got something special for tonight, Georgia. I thought maybe you could, you know, try it."

Georgia immediately sat up straight, the full skirt of her enchanting prom dress rustling as she crossed her legs on the seat. "You mean you've got..." My God, she couldn't even say the word. Ed smiled in a way that made him look irresistibly cute and sexy like Robert Redford in Butch Cassidy. She'd already seen that movie five times. "Sure," he said, pleased as punch she didn't say no.

He hopped out of the car and released the trunk of the '67 Mustang, bringing back two beers. "I stole these from my old man's fridge in the garage." Digging into the glove compartment he found an opener and popped the caps, handing Georgia one of the bottles. She took a sip and leaned back in her fluff of dress with a neckline low enough to be a tad daring for a prom dress, and let the first sip foam up in her mouth until it got warm before letting it tickle down her throat. At first, she didn't much care for the taste, but after the second and third sips, the beer went down much smoother. Her head went into a delightful spin, and she thought how wonderful to let go of all her inhibitions. She was tired of being a *good* girl.

Ed pulled a joint from the paper bag. She watched him light it with a fancy gold lighter. The flame appeared mystically serene in the darkness, and she never thought to object when he handed it to her. She giggled and thought, Why not?

The inside of the car smelled of burnt rope and beer, nasty but oh-so-tempting. Her resolve to keep Ed's hand from sliding down the front of her prom dress and cupping one breast, dissolved into a yearning she had never known before. "Sweet," he said from somewhere faraway. A soft moan escaped her throat when he reached behind and unzipped her dress. She didn't stop him. The straps fell around her shoulders, and he carefully flattened the bodice down around her waist and helped her wiggle out of it. The last of her childhood took flight, loving the freedom of sitting in Ed's car and wearing nothing but her strapless bra and black bikini underwear.

He offered her another hit and she fell back against the seat. He leaned over and kissed her, soft and sweet-like, then his lips moved down her neck and shoulder. Every place he touched, her skin tingled with delight, his fingers played with the flatness of her stomach, sliding down into the moistness between her legs. Again, she moaned when Ed asked, "Does it feel good?" His voice sounded raspy and breathless, and she thought how kind that he would ask.

She loved Ed, and tonight whatever he wanted was all that mattered. "Yes," she murmured. "Yes, it feels good. I love you so much." She closed her eyes, thinking her life would never get any better than this.

Georgia opened her eyes, the dream still fresh in her mind, fresh enough that she still smelled the marijuana they had shared in Ed's Mustang in Moody's Orchard. She sniffed again, sitting up straight in the seat and looking over at Zoe. The smell was real. Zoe lifted her sunglasses, directing Georgia's attention to the back seat. Georgia turned, seeing Trish lounging the full length of the seat, her eyes closed, a joint pinched between two fingers. Trish opened her eyes. Seeing Georgia, she quickly sat up, coughing and fanning the air around her. She tossed what remained of the joint out the side of the car. Trish gasped for breath. "God, Georgia, I'm sorry. You were asleep and I figured—"

"Well, you figured wrong!" Georgia yelled above the air rushing around inside the car, angry at Trish for smoking that stuff in her car. "You bought more than snacks at that gas station back there, didn't you?" Georgia's throat hurt from yelling.

Trish looked confused. "I found your stash right here. See." Trish pulled down the center armrest and sure enough there was a plastic bag filled with what looked like dried oregano. Georgia blinked. "*My* stash?"

"Hey," Trish said throwing up both hands. "I pulled down the armrest and there it was. I thought it was yours."

Georgia sputtered, "Mine?"

"Sure, you grew up in the sixties, didn't you?"

Georgia's throat really hurt now, but she managed to scream at Trish, "Not everyone who grew up in the sixties smoked dope."

"Never?"

"Once," Georgia said, motioning for Trish to hand over the bag.

"Oh yeah, I get it. Like Clinton never inhaled. Sure. I understand." Trish handed it to Georgia who ripped open the bag and held it outside the car and let the wind scatter the weed. Georgia seethed inside. One more of Ed's little surprises. One more thing she hadn't known about her husband. Her head pounded with frustration, thinking about how she had driven the Fleetwood for almost a year without knowing about what he'd hidden in the armrest of the back seat.

Trish collapsed into a fit of giggles, standing up and throwing her arms out wide as if she were about to fly off the side of a cliff. "I feel soooo mellow!"

"Stop laughing." Georgia nudged Trish back into the seat. "Get your seatbelt on. Right now!"

Trish covered her mouth with her hands. "I'm so sorry," she said, a silly smile pasted across her face.

Zoe said, "Come on, Georgia. Lighten up a little. It is funny. Here I am driving along with little Miss-straight-as-an-arrow, who all along had a stash hidden in her car. Can't you see the humor in it?"

"I told you before. I didn't know it was there," Georgia snapped, glancing back at Trish who still hadn't put on her seatbelt, laughing so hard that tears streaked down both her cheeks. Then, it happened. So quickly no one could have ever stopped it from happening. Trish doubled up with laughter, accidentally kicking Gloria's can of ashes at her feet.

"She's high as a kite," Zoe said, keeping her eyes on the road. "Georgia, make her put on her seatbelt."

"You heard Zoe, Trish. Fasten that seatbelt right now!"

Exasperated, Zoe said, "Georgia, get the ashes and bring them up here with us before she kicks open the lid."

"Hand me the ashes, Trish," Georgia ordered, leaning back over the seat and holding out her hand.

Trish held the can a few inches out of Georgia's reach, teasing, "You mean this?"

"Yes," Georgia yelled over the wind blowing through the car. "Stop fooling around."

Trish leaned forward, still joking, holding the can away from Georgia. "Gloria, it's been nice—Whoops!"

"Trish!" Georgia screamed, watching the can slip through Trish's fingers and fly out the back of the car, landing in the middle of the road with a thump and roll. Miraculously, the can seemed to be intact. Georgia breathed a sigh of relief, that is, until an eighteen wheeler speeding up behind them hit the can and sent it spinning to the side of the road.

Georgia couldn't believe it. Thirty seconds ago, everything had been fine. Now, in the blink of an eye, they had a serious, full-blown disaster on their hands. "Oh God, Zoe, stop the car. Quick!"

Zoe slammed on the brakes, causing the semi to swerve into the passing lane, air horn blaring, to avoid rear-ending them. Zoe pulled to the side of road and threw the car into park. All three of them clamored out of the car and started running back toward a patch of silver shining in the sun like a lost hubcap.

Zoe couldn't keep up in her three inch heels. She yelled, "Damn it, Trish. I could kill you."

Trish called out, "I'm sorry, Zoe. I'm so sorry."

Georgia and Trish reached the can at the same time and froze in place, the dented lid laying about fifteen feet away from them. Hesitant to stoop down and check if anything of Gloria, by some small miracle, remained inside, they waited until Zoe caught up. It was Georgia who finally knelt down and peeked inside.

Zoe roughly pushed Trish aside before crouching beside Georgia. "Is it..."

She grabbed the can from Georgia and peeked inside, Zoe shrieked, "Oh, God!" She turned her stricken face to Georgia. "What the hell am I supposed to do now?"

Trish wailed, "I didn't do it on purpose. Please forgive me."

Zoe pulled off one of her high heels and threw it at Trish, screaming, "When hell freezes over."

Georgia got up and retrieved the lid, pleased that it at least still fit, securing the remaining ashes.

Zoe whispered under her breath, "Fuck. Fuck. Fuck." Georgia thought the obscenity was quite appropriate for the occasion.

Georgia said, "What'll we do now?"

Throwing up both hands, Zoe said, "Oh, I don't know. Let's ask Trish. She's the smart one in this group. Okay, Trish, now what?"

"Well," Trish offered, "maybe we don't have to do anything."

Zoe's eyes narrowed with suspicion. "Do nothing?" Zoe growled, holding up two fingers inches from Trish's face. "Two days from now there's going to be a memorial service for my mother." She pointed inside the can. "How am I going to explain what happened to her ashes?" Zoe dissolved into tears, sobbing convulsively into her open hands. "God, all I ever wanted was for my mother to love me. It's all so hopeless."

Cautiously patting the distraught woman on the back, Trish said, "I feel awful. But the can doesn't have to be empty at the service."

"Trish," Georgia warned, "don't—"

"No, really. This'll work." Trish then pulled and stretched at the front of her T-shirt and dumped the rest of the ashes into it. Zoe grabbed for the tin can, but Trish pushed her arm away. "Wait! You'll make me lose what's left of her."

Zoe clenched her teeth and came to within inches of Trish's face. She yelled, "Are you crazy?"

Trish gathered the ashes in a tight knot as if to protect them. "Look," she said scooping up sand around her feet and filling the can. A few inches from the top, she slid what remained of Gloria's ashes from the knot in her shirt, enough to cover the sand. "See, no one will ever know. And anyhow, what's the difference if she's spread out over the desert or locked away in some crypt for all eternity?"

Zoe stopped crying and watched as Trish secured the lid. Work or not, at least for the moment Zoe was calm.

"Okay?" Trish said, dusting off her hands on the front of her shirt and handing the can to Georgia for safekeeping.

Zoe sniffed. "There's an urn I'm suppose to put the ashes in before the service." Zoe swiped the back of one hand under her nose and sniffed again. "I'll seal the urn myself. I suppose no one has to know what's really inside." Zoe gave Trish a feeble smile before turning back to Georgia. "What do you think?"

Georgia shrugged. "Not a bad idea. Unless you want to explain what happened."

Trish and Zoe shouted in unison, "No!"

They had started back to the car when Zoe pulled back. "Wait a minute. We have to promise not to tell anyone about what really happened to Mama's ashes. My God, if one of those damn tabloids finds out Gloria Atwater is blowing up and down Route 40, they'll hang me out to dry."

Trish rested her hand on top of the lid. "I swear on your mother's ashes I won't tell a soul about what happened."

Georgia followed suit, placing her hand on top of Trish's saying, "I swear I won't tell, either."

Then, finally, Zoe placed her hand on top of Georgia's, saying, "As far as I'm concerned, this whole thing never happened."

Back at the car, Zoe opened the trunk. Georgia said, "Do you think we ought to say something, you know, like a prayer or something?"

Zoe took the can from Georgia's hands and wrapped it inside Gloria's silver fox coat. "Yeah, sure. Rest in peace, Mama." That said, Zoe shut the trunk and dusted off her hands. "Let's get this show on the road."

They had only traveled a few more miles before Georgia noticed Zoe's hands were shaking on the steering wheel. Deep inside, Georgia knew Zoe really loved her mother, no matter how badly she sometimes talked about her. Now, with Gloria dead, Georgia wondered if Zoe could ever find peace within herself.

Georgia covered one of Zoe's trembling hands with her own. "Why don't you let me drive, okay?" And for once, Zoe didn't object.

# CHAPTER TWENTY-FOUR

An immense earthen bowl filled with a sparkling, wanderlust city, sprawled the coastline for as far as the eye could see. With a steady hand, Georgia moved the car into the heavy traffic of Los Angeles, overwhelmed not only by the fickleness of sixteen lanes of highway, but also the enormity of the city that lay before her.

"Impressive, isn't it," Zoe said.

"It's huge!" Georgia marveled. "I've never seen so many cars." She drove only a few more miles, before pulling to the side of the road. "This traffic's making me too nervous. Zoe. Take over. Please."

"Georgia, I'm disappointed," Trish quipped from the back seat. "I thought you could handle anything."

"Not quite." Georgia got out and hurried around to the passenger side, letting Zoe slide behind the wheel. Georgia adjusted her sunglasses and fastened her seat belt, feeling more relaxed as a passenger, letting Zoe do the driving.

Trish leaned forward in the seat, "You gave up too soon, Georgia. Just claim your lane. If someone slows down, get nose-to-ass with their bumper or jump another lane. Be aggressive."

Georgia sniffed, ignoring her. Already she wished she were back in Sedona with nothing more stressful than preparing ten pounds of chicken salad for tomorrow's lunch crowd.

Not until mid-afternoon did they finally arrive at Gloria's residence, a house hidden behind high, thick hedges with an ornate front gate. Zoe stopped at the entrance and punched in a security code. When the gate opened, they traveled up the curved driveway to a stately stone mansion with green shutters. Georgia stared in drop-jawed awe at the imposing front steps with twin urns overflowing with a profusion of wandering vines and lush flowers. Georgia had never in her life seen urns this size outside of a cemetery. Leaded glass side panels framed a massive door with a brass doorknocker that could have once hung on the door of a medieval castle.

A low-slung sports car sat parked further up the driveway. As Zoe pulled up behind, a suave older gentleman got out and waved at them. "Zoe, darling!" he said, rushing to the car and helping her out. He gave her a familial hug. "I'm devastated about your mother. Of course..." His voice lowered to a whisper, pulling her close, his eyes shifting with mild discomfort to look at Georgia and Trish.

Georgia took the hint and politely excused herself, following Trish along a worn stone path to the back of the house. She nearly gasped at her first view of the wide manicured lawn, with tennis courts and Olympic-size swimming pool, complete with a cabana. Georgia whispered, "It's gorgeous." The house and grounds must have taken in no less than five acres, everything immaculate, maintained as if someone actually lived there. As far as Georgia knew, Zoe had never once returned to the house since moving to Arizona with her mother.

Trish let out a low whistle. "I bet Lucy used to live on the next street."

"Actually, she did." Zoe said, coming up behind them. "Sorry for being rude. I should've introduced you to Milton Thayer, Mama's attorney. He wanted to tell me everything's been arranged for the service, day after tomorrow. He gave me this." Zoe unfolded a newspaper clipping of Gloria's obituary and photograph taken perhaps twenty years ago. Gloria looked stunning in a simple black sweater, her only accessory, a single strand of pearls around her famous neck.

"How nice," Georgia said, genuinely meaning what she had said.

"Listen to this," Zoe said, her voice taking on a clipped, snobby tone. "Ms. Atwater, a true humanitarian, gave graciously to a number of charities and individuals in need." Zoe folded the clipping and stuffed it into her pocket. "My mother never gave a cent to anyone unless she got three cents back for her trouble."

"Who wrote it?" Trish asked.

"Why, Mama, of course. A few years ago, she planned everything right down to the caterers and menu for the after-funeral party." She laughed. "Even in death, the woman still calls the shots."

They gathered their luggage and dropped everything inside the marbled entrance hall. On either side were identical rooms filled with heavily draped furniture. It seemed to Georgia as if the house were merely sleeping, patiently awaiting the gallant return of its famous mistress.

Zoe wandered into the formal living room. She lightly touched the draped arm of the couch as she came around to the enormous glass coffee table. A brief smile came to her lips as she lifted a leather-bound book from the table and leafed through its pages. She then returned the book to the table exactly where she had found it. From a side table she picked up a photograph and studied it for a moment before slamming it face-down on the recently polished wood surface. Both Georgia and Trish jumped at the sound. They watched helplessly as Zoe then made her way to the fireplace where three antique vases were safely tucked on the mantle. One by one, she tipped the vases over the edge and watched them smash against the marble hearth, the pieces scattering around Zoe's feet like confetti. She then brushed her hands together and turned to Georgia and Trish, lips upturned in a smile, saying, "I always wanted to do that."

\* \* \*

The refrigerator in the gourmet kitchen had been recently stuffed with every imaginable delicacy: smoked turkey, fruits, a variety of exotic cheeses and a vegetable platter. Zoe said, "Milton said he'd had someone stock the kitchen with food." She shut the refrigerator door. "Good job."

"I'd say so," Trish said reaching into the freezer and pulling out a quart of expensive ice cream. "God, I'm hungry. I could eat ten gallons of this stuff."

"You'd better watch it," Zoe teased. "Someday you won't be able to take off the pounds so easily."

Trish shrugged, planting a big spoon in the center of the ice cream and digging out a big scoop. "Guess I might as well enjoy it now. Trish turned to close the freezer door. "Say, what's this?" She reached into the back part of the freezer. "Ohmygod, look at this!" She pulled out something wrapped in a terry hand towel and laid it on the counter. When she unfolded it, she took a step back and gasped. "A gun!" Her head jerked to Zoe. "Is this real?"

Zoe nudged Trish away from the counter and folded the towel around the gun. "Get out of the way before you shoot someone."

Georgia started in on the carton of ice cream with her own spoon. Gun or no gun, she hadn't eaten all day, and right now she felt hungry enough to eat the tiny yellow flowers right off the designer kitchen wallpaper.

Zoe reopened the freezer. "She kept it for protection."

"Your mother knew how to shoot a gun?" Georgia said, stuffing her mouth with ice cream.

Shoving the gun behind a butcher's pack of T-bones, Zoe said, "I'll take it to Milton tomorrow. He'll know how to dispose of it. She kept it in the house for protection." She pulled a spoon from the drawer and attacked the ice cream. "Mama could shoot the eyelashes off a fruit fly. She was quite the skeet competitor. Or, should I say, predator?"

Later that evening, they ate a dinner of smoked turkey on rye, fresh vegetables and fruit on the back patio, the pool illuminated by soft underwater lights. In all her life Georgia could never have imagined a more romantic setting than this house with its gorgeous stone terraces and well-tended gardens. For Georgia, being here with Zoe and Trish was nothing less than a miracle. Less than a year ago, her only contact with a celebrity had been standing in line at the grocery store and reading tabloid headlines.

Zoe said, "I'm meeting Milton at his office at eight in the morning to sign papers and pick up some things she left in his safe. I shouldn't be more than a couple of hours."

Georgia started clearing the dishes. "Is there anything we can do here?"

"Nothing. But if you decide to drive somewhere, don't get lost."

Georgia said, "Don't you need the car to drive to the attorney's office?"

Zoe put plastic wrap over the bowl of fruit. "There are two cars in the garage."

Georgia looked up, surprised. "Cars? You have cars?"

"Yes, I have cars. Why the strange look?"

Trish said, "I think Georgia's wondering why you've been driving her car for the last six months when you have cars of your own, like a Jag and Mercedes."

"Someone stole my car," Zoe explained to Georgia, "In Phoenix not long before you came to Sedona. At first, I thought the police might find it." She shrugged. "They didn't. More than likely, it's somewhere in Mexico by now. I intended to get another one, but you were always so good about lending the car to me."

Later that evening, Zoe disappeared inside her mother's office and closed the door. Georgia said goodnight to Trish, thankful to escape upstairs and get ready for bed. The next two days would be draining for all of them, most of all for Zoe.

Too exhausted to give the guestroom more than an admiring glance, Georgia shrugged out of her clothing and stepped into the shower. She fought sleep long enough to brush her teeth and fall into bed with damp hair. Then, she couldn't sleep.

Her mind played over the events of the afternoon, a first-class trip into the *Twilight Zone*. Hollywood Boulevard was definitely not the glamorous strip she had imagined it to be with its seedy strip joints and tacky tourist shops, T-shirts hanging from awnings and flapping in the breeze like cheap kites. Scantily clad girls loitered on street corners, some not looking any older than thirteen or fourteen. Zoe told her they were prostitutes, most likely runaways, arriving in Hollywood with pie-in-the-sky dreams of being *discovered*, but ultimately ending up in the hands of vultures cruising Hollywood Boulevard and waiting until the girls grew hungry and desperate enough to do their bidding. Zoe said the lucky ones called relatives, asking for bus fare home. The not-so-lucky ended up as street prostitutes, becoming drug addicts, and looking worn out before they reached twenty.

In the blink of an eye, their journey along Hollywood Boulevard had magically morphed into Beverly Hills, the landscape changing from cheap and superficial to swank and super rich within a few short blocks. Designer stores and trendy restaurants lined the well-tended streets, and glimpses of mansions could be seen from behind stone walls or hedges guarded by high security gates to keep ordinary folks outside.

Georgia reached over and switched off the light, kicking her legs into the cooler parts of the bed. Rolling onto her side, she stared out the open floor-length window and into Gloria's backyard. Her eyes finally adjusted to the pale outside light, surprised to see Zoe walking across the lawn in a white nightgown, surreal and ghost-like in the moonlight. Reaching the lower terrace, she sat down in the grass and wrapped her arms around her knees, her face turned up to night sky.

Just then, the bedroom door cracked open. Georgia jumped at the sound. Trish stuck her head inside. "Georgia? Are you sleeping?"

"No," Georgia answered, wondering what would it matter if she were? She reached for the light on the nightstand. "What's wrong?"

"Don't!" Trish whispered. "Let's talk in the dark, okay?"

"Okay."

Trish blindly searched for the chair by the window where she curled up in it, tucking her legs beneath her. Georgia scooted up in the bed with one of the soft pillows behind her. She took a quick glance out the window, still mindful of Zoe sitting outside, alone.

"Georgia, last night when I came to your apartment, I wanted to tell you something."

"Hmmm." Only half-listening to Trish, her eyes were still fixed on Zoe, thinking how the entire day had been exhausting, what with tiptoeing around Zoe's grief, and then Trish smoking a joint in the backseat of her car and stupidly letting Gloria's ashes fly all over creation. "Trish, I—"

"I'm falling in love with David."

Hearing her son's name, she forgot about Zoe, "You told me that last night. Does David feel the same?"

"Yes."

"That's good. I think." Georgia didn't want to say too much. Not yet. Trish often said one thing and the next day something else. Her version of commitment was whichever way the wind was blowing at the moment. The more she thought about it, the more Georgia had serious doubts about Trish being the best choice for her son.

Trish lowered her head. "Last night," she whispered, "I started to tell you something."

"Maybe you shouldn't—" She turned back to the window, wanting Trish to hush and go back to her room.

"I'm scared, Georgia."

"Scared?" Georgia inwardly sighed, a little aggravated, not wanting to be drawn into Trish's insecurities, at least not tonight. She thought that she should go outside and make sure Zoe was all right.

"I lied."

Georgia bit into her lower lip, hesitating, not wanting to ask, but knew she had no choice. "About what?"

"About Boston. I've been there before."

In the dim light, Georgia could just make out Trish's eyes, soft and liquid with tears. "Why would you lie about that?"

Trish sank deeper into the chair. "I got pregnant at fifteen, a boy I thought I was in love with. My mother took me to Boston to live with my aunt and her husband while she flew to Italy to meet one of her lovers."

Georgia sat up straight in the bed. "You had a baby?"

Trish's voice quivered with the fear of a small child. "Yes, but I..."

"Your mother left you?"

"Yes."

"She abandoned you?" Georgia said, now angry at the thought of a mother leaving a child in trouble. She pulled at the second pillow on the bed and gave it a good punch before adding to the other behind her. "My God, Trish. You were only a child."

Trish deserted the chair, climbing up on the foot of the bed. She sat there with knees drawn up to her chest, chin resting on her knees. Georgia could see her small frame trembling beneath her nightgown. Georgia thought about getting up and shutting the window but didn't want to chance making any noise with Zoe out in the yard.

"I don't know what to say," Georgia whispered. "I can't imagine a mother dumping a troubled child on relatives, and then running off on holiday."

Trish woefully tugged at the sides of her face, tears sprouting from the corners of her eyes. "I'm so awful. I gave my baby up for adoption. My mother made me sign the documents."

"You were only fifteen, Trish. Not old enough to be awful. Maybe your mother had good intentions." Georgia felt her heart thump against her breastbone.

"I was carrying twins."

"Twins?" Could the story get any more bizarre?

"One died."

"At birth? What are you saying, Trish?" Georgia could barely breathe.

"I went into labor six weeks early. The cord got wrapped around the neck of one of the babies." Silvery streaks of tears flowed down Trish's cheeks. "I was alone at my aunt's house when my water broke. I wanted to die. I thought if I died that would take care of the problem."

"Where was your aunt?" Georgia could not believe what Trish was telling her, a mere child, pregnant, going into labor with no one there to help, unbelievable.

Trish sniffled. "She had to help some sick lady in her church. I was okay when she left. By the time she got home and took me to the hospital, the first baby died. The other one, a girl, lived." Trish looked plaintively at Georgia. "I could've called my aunt for help. I didn't. I was just so scared and hurting."

"My God! Surely, your mother came back after you had the baby?"

Trish wiped at her nose with the back of her hand. "Not right away. She stayed in Italy a few weeks longer. By then, I wanted to keep the baby. My mother wouldn't hear of it. She told me to give her up for adoption."

"So, you gave her up?"

"Not exactly. My aunt convinced my mother to let her adopt the baby. You see, she couldn't have children of her own."

"Does your daughter know about you?"

Trish stopped crying. "I wasn't sure, not until I went to Boston. I hadn't seen my aunt since I left with my mother after having my daughter. It was fate, you see, David living in Boston. When I went there at Christmas to see him, I had to see Claire. She's beautiful, Georgia. She knows who I am and wants to come here, to Arizona, and go to college. I know this is crazy, but I want to move back to

Tucson and buy a house. I'm hoping Claire will come live with me, at least for a while."

Georgia shook her head in disbelief. "Trish, you did nothing wrong. You were just a kid. Your mother abandoned you, left you with an aunt you barely knew. Even though your aunt and uncle adopted your baby, they must've realized that someday you'd come back looking for her."

"That's the amazing part of the story. I showed up at my aunt's house, unannounced. Do you know what she did?"

"What?"

"She hugged me and told me she knew I'd come back some day. Claire has always known about me."

"Who else knows about Claire?"

Trish wiped her eyes with the edge of the sheet. "No one except Jake."

"You've never told Zoe?"

"No. Although, I'm sure Jake's told her." She hesitated. "I'm not sure."

"David?"

"Definitely not David. That's the whole problem. I'm afraid if I tell him I have a daughter about to graduate from high school, he'll never speak to me again." She paused to take in a breath, "Whew, that sounds unbelievable, doesn't it?"

"You need to tell David the truth."

"Georgia, I wanted to tell him at Christmas. I couldn't. We had a fantastic, romantic week together falling in love. I didn't want to ruin it. I know I was wrong, maybe selfish. I even tried to convince myself I didn't really love David, but I do. I have to tell him, especially now." Trish stopped and looked at Georgia. "It's you, Georgia. You changed my life. The second I laid eyes on Claire, I knew then I couldn't walk out of her life for a second time."

"Claire really wants to come to Arizona?"

"Oh, yes."

Georgia sighed. "Well, it won't be easy, suddenly having a

grown daughter going off to college. Don't expect too much in the beginning. Claire might have resentments she doesn't even know she has about you. Give yourselves time to get acquainted."

"Oh, we know that. Claire's made it clear from the beginning she considers Aunt Louise and Uncle Bert to be her real parents. But she wants me in her life." Trish pressed her fingertips to her mouth. "Can you believe that?"

"That's wonderful, Trish, but be careful, okay? No matter how easy it seems now, it won't be."

Trish took hold of Georgia's hands and squeezed hard. Georgia's wedding band cut into her fingers. Trish said, "I love my daughter and want to be a part of her life. I love your son and want to marry him. David's a good man. If you ask me how I know, it's because I know what a fantastic lady his mother is. Oh, Georgia, do you think David will accept Claire?"

Georgia patted the empty side of the bed, and Trish gratefully crawled up beside her. Georgia tucked her under an arm as she had done so many times with Susan, because, in more ways than one, Trish had become like a daughter to her. She smoothed back Trish's hair and kissed her forehead. "Tell me what frightens you most."

"I think about the other baby. I'm afraid God won't ever forgive me for not getting help right away."

Georgia kissed the top of her head. "God doesn't work that way, Trish."

"What about Claire? Do you think it's possible she'll forgive me for all the years I could've made contact and didn't?"

"That's the chance you'll have to take."

"I love David and if I'm ever going to have a life with him, I've got to start facing my past."

"That's a good girl. David will respect you for doing that."

"Georgia?"

"Hmmm?"

"I'm serious about moving back to Tucson. I want to sell the café to you. Are you interested?"

Georgia's ears perked at this offer. "Are you serious? Of course, I'm interested."

"Good. After we get back to Sedona, we'll sit down and hash out the details. I know a good attorney in Boston who'll give us free advice."

"Oh yeah? What a coincidence. I happen to know someone there, too."

They laughed.

Trish suddenly sat up in the bed and looked out the window. "Hey, Zoe's out there sitting on the ground."

"I know. She's been there for the last twenty minutes or so."

"Do you think we should go check on her?" Trish hiccoughed from crying.

"Good idea." Georgia shoved back the covers and grabbed the lap blanket from the chair, throwing it around her shoulders. "Come on."

Georgia padded down the back stairway with Trish close on her heels. When they reached the bottom step, Trish pulled back on Georgia's arm. "Hey, wait a minute. I need to know something before we go out there. Zoe told you about the clown, didn't she?"

"Clown?" Georgia drew back in surprise. She had never considered the possibility that Zoe had told Trish, too. Or maybe Jake had told Trish. Hesitating, she said, "At her twelfth birthday party, right?" Trish took in a gulp of air. Georgia knew right then that there was much more to the story than what Zoe had disclosed that day before Thanksgiving, stuck behind that snowplow. "What?"

"Georgia, that man raped Zoe."

Georgia gasped, covering her mouth with both hands. "My God, she was only twelve."

"Georgia, it was bad. That man tore up Zoe's insides. She can't have children." Trish wiped at her face with the skirt of her nightgown. "I wanted you to know the truth. What with Gloria's death and all, there's no telling what's going on inside Zoe's head. I'm worried."

Georgia fell back against the banister of the stairway. "What happened? Did they arrest that monster?"

Trish sank down on the first step. "They never called the police. I'm guessing Gloria didn't want the bad publicity, especially since she's the one who invited the pervert inside the house in the first place."

Georgia glanced around the beautiful tiled kitchen with its huge refrigerator and stainless steel appliances, everything anyone could ever desire in a home. Yet, to Zoe, this house represented nothing except pain, rejection, and a whole lot of bad memories. Georgia pulled Trish up from the step. "Now, I understand why Zoe didn't want to come back here by herself. If only I could've reached Jake before we left Sedona. I'm sure he's heard about Gloria's death by now. Hopefully, he'll get here in time for the memorial service."

Trish's face suddenly brightened. "He's coming."

"Jake?"

"Yes! He swore me to secrecy, but he's coming, for sure."

"Oh, Trish, you should've told me?"

"Jake didn't want Zoe to know, because she'd only tell him to stay in Washington. Georgia, he's taking Zoe back with him, he said, even if he has to hog-tie her and put her on the plane."

Georgia held a conspiratorial finger to her lips. "The secret's safe with me."

\* \* \*

Barefooted, they carefully made their way down the stone steps to the garden. Almost to the bottom step, Trish whispered, "You go on without me. I'll be back in a minute." Without further explanation, Trish turned and hurriedly retraced her steps back to the house.

Georgia reached the expanse of lawn below the terraces, keeping her eyes on Zoe, half-expecting her to turn around when Trish had slammed the door after going back inside. Instead, Zoe sat very still, arms hugging her knees, her beautiful face upturned to the moon. Georgia secured the blanket around her shoulders as she lowered herself to the ground to sit beside Zoe.

"Well," Georgia mused. "You told me we'd see plenty of stars, but this—" She pointed at the explosion of stars in the night sky. "This isn't exactly what I had in mind."

Silence.

Georgia tried again. "What are you doing out here by yourself?"

Zoe responded with a yawn and stretched out her legs, wriggling her toes, the mauve polish on her toenails glistening like tiny seed pearls in the moonlight. "When I was a little girl this was my most favorite place in the world. Out here, in the night, I could be whoever I wanted to be, separate and all-knowing. Sometimes, I could almost make myself believe that I had a real mother and father living inside the house. There was this really small voice inside my head that told me that all I had to do was to get up and walk back to the house and everything I dreamed would be true."

They both turned to look at Trish, coming across the lawn carrying a bottle of wine and three long-stemmed glasses clinking between her fingers. Trish chortled, "I've never been to a lawn party, but I've got something here to make it the real thing."

Sitting cross-legged in the grass, Trish uncorked the bottle and poured the wine. Together, they toasted their friendship and the memory of Gloria Atwater. Trish raised her glass to the heavens, "God bless Gloria. Wherever the hell she is."

"Amen to that," Zoe said, taking a sip.

After second glasses, the mood lightened, Zoe giggling as Trish recollected how her friendship with Georgia began with her arrival in Sedona. "I remember you were wearing a long skirt and a hippy blouse and, *ohmygod*, espadrilles on your feet. You were feeling ill and had a real hard time accepting any help."

Zoe leaned back on her hands. "I remember Trish calling and saying some sick woman was going to come into the shop and to keep an eye on you." Sighing, she said, "Don't you ever wonder why the three of us ever became good friends? Do you believe in fate?"

Trish hugged her knees to her chest. "I do."

"Me, too," Georgia agreed.

Trish winked at Georgia. "Or, maybe the three of us were attracted by, you know, the total chaos in our lives—like intuitively attracted to one another because all three of us were like, dysfunctional, and all that stuff."

Zoe doubled over in laughter. "My goodness, Trish, *intuitively*? I didn't know you knew any words with more than two syllables."

"Shut up, Zoe."

Georgia ignored their bickering and sipped the last of her wine. She stared up at the full moon, thinking if only she could somehow capture this surreal moment and all the magnificence of being in Hollywood. Funeral aside, this was very exciting, sitting on Gloria Atwater's lawn, sipping wine.

Zoe asked with a yawn. "What do you think life really is, Georgia?"

The grass prickled at the backs of Georgia's legs. No doubt, they would all have chiggers from sitting on the damp lawn. She sighed, feeling a smile form on her lips. "I guess life's kind of like the moon up there. If we ever had the chance to get really close to it, all the mystery—everything that made us love it in the first place—would be gone."

# CHAPTER TWENTY-FIVE

Georgia sliced a lemon for her iced tea, nearly jumping out of her skin when Zoe shouted "*NO!*" from somewhere in another part of the house. The knife cut into her thumb. Not deep, but just enough to bleed into the lemon wedge.

Heart pumping with adrenalin, she slapped a paper towel around her finger and rushed down the hallway. Reaching the foyer, she found Milton Thayer standing just inside the open door, holding out a large brown envelope to Zoe. He said sternly, "Take it Zoe. This belongs to you."

Zoe knocked the envelope out of his hand. It hit the marble floor with a heavy thud. "I told you, go to hell." Seeing Georgia, she burst into tears and ran up the stairs.

Milton shook his head at Georgia, as if thoroughly exhausted. He said, "Zoe's had quite a shock." He scratched helplessly at the back of his neck. "I followed her home from the office to make sure she didn't get into an accident." He cleared his throat. "I'll call later." He then picked up the envelope and handed it to Georgia. "Give this to her after she's calmed down. She knows what's inside." He shook his head and walked out, softly closing the door behind him.

The envelope felt heavy, no doubt filled with whatever grief that had been heaped on Zoe by her dead mother during the appointment at the law office that morning. The hallway closed in around Georgia, making it hard to breathe. She suddenly had a wild impulse to run away. In two seconds flat, she could be in the car and headed back to Sedona where the familiar routine of the café would soothe her frazzled nerves. She visualized Doc sitting at the kitchen table drinking coffee and talking about nothing in particular while Georgia baked pies. She wished Doc were here now. For sure, he would know exactly what to say to Zoe to calm her down.

Trish sashayed in from the direction of the kitchen, sipping Georgia's iced tea, oblivious to the drama that had just transpired in the front hallway. A door slammed somewhere upstairs, and both Georgia and Trish started at the sound. Georgia's stomach felt ill over the prospect of calming Zoe down enough to get ready for the memorial service the next day. Damn that Milton Thayer for leaving her here like this.

"Zoe?" Trish asked, jerking her head in the direction of the stairway. "What's wrong now?"

Georgia hurriedly took the glass from Trish and hooked her elbow, tucking the envelope under her other arm. She gently guided Trish upstairs. "Something terrible has happened. I've never seen Zoe so upset."

"What?" Trish pulled back, but Georgia kept her moving on up the stairway.

"I don't know, but it has something to do with her appointment with Milton Thayer this morning." She held up the envelope, keeping her voice low. "He told me to make sure Zoe got this."

"Gloria," Trish whispered, her eyes narrowing. "I bet that old witch didn't leave Zoe a dime."

As much as Georgia hated to admit it, she, too, had that same thought. "I don't like intruding, but we don't have a choice, not with Gloria's service tomorrow." She held the envelope firmly in her hand and gave Trish's shoulder a nudge. On the upstairs landing, they tiptoed down the hallway, hearing Zoe, in a full rage, yelling obscenities at the top of her lungs, slamming drawers and throwing things against the wall of the bedroom.

Reaching the doorway, Georgia gently turned the knob, cracking the door open to see inside. What she saw there made her knees grow weak, gasping at the sight of Zoe ransacking Gloria's beautiful bedroom of pale green satin and deep white carpeting. All the drawers in her mother's high top dresser had been opened, the contents scattered across the carpet. Now, Zoe was rattling through the delicate bottles and ivory boxes on her mother's dressing table, looking dangerously out of control, capable of anything, perhaps even burning down the house, if she had a mind to do it.

"Zoe?" Trish said, pushing past Georgia and throwing open the door. "What the hell are you doing?"

Georgia caught Trish by the hand. "Wait," she ordered.

"Are you kidding?" Trish said, breaking free of Georgia's grip. "She's going nuts in there." Again, Trish started into the room. Just then, Zoe let out a bloodcurdling scream, and Trish jumped back to the safety of the hallway. A cold shiver spilled down Georgia's back. Lord, she didn't know what to do or who to call. Zoe didn't seem to notice they were standing in the doorway, watching her.

"Damn you, Mama. Why?" Zoe snatched the cushions off the white sofa in the alcove, throwing them helter-skelter. Thoroughly frustrated, she ripped off the wide-brimmed black hat she had worn to the appointment that morning and viciously tossed it across the room. The brim hit Georgia square on the bridge of her nose.

"Ow!" Georgia drew back, rubbing her nose. Something had to be done before someone got hurt. She knelt down and picked up the hat and boldly walked into the room. Trish followed behind, her fingernails digging into Georgia's shoulder.

Zoe continued to ransack the room, shoving an elegant damask stool over to an antique highboy where she opened drawers and pulled out the contents. Everything tumbled to the floor: silk nightgowns, lace stockings, fancy bras Georgia could never imagine an eighty-year-old woman wearing.

Georgia ventured to within an arm's length of Zoe. "What are you looking for, Zoe? Let us help you."

Zoe shoved the last highboy drawer shut, and then brushed past Georgia, almost losing her balance. She stumbled into a huge walk-in closet where she ripped into a zippered storage bag filled with sweaters and accessories. Silk scarves of every imaginable color swished through the air like vibrant brush strokes before landing in a soft heap around Zoe's bare feet. She then attacked dressing room drawers filled with nothing but gloves of every style and color. Zoe discarded these over her shoulder, a colorful mid-air flurry of hands and fingers, before landing lifelessly on the carpet around her.

Georgia's chest suddenly constricted with a new fear. What if Zoe didn't stop? What if Zoe's anger escalated into a violent, psychotic rage with only herself and Trish to handle the situation? Damn Milton Thayer. *Damn. Damn. Damn.*

"Trish, go get Zoe a glass of water." When Trish didn't react, she shouted, "Now!" Without further ado, Trish skedaddled posthaste out of the room. Then, as an afterthought, Georgia yelled after her, "Bring ice!" If Zoe ended up fainting from exhaustion, they'd need it.

Georgia kept her distance from Zoe, expecting the worst. Then, like a balloon losing air, Zoe slumped to the floor, whimpering and talking to herself, saying over and over again, "It's got to be here somewhere." She looked up at Georgia with pleading eyes, her face soaked with tears, "Mama never threw anything away."

Georgia's head throbbed with exhaustion, careful not to say anything that might trigger another tirade. "Zoe, honey, let us help find whatever you're looking for."

Zoe fumbled with an empty clothing bag on the floor beside her, pulling at the cardboard liner at the bottom. Nothing there, she tore at the plastic until it ripped apart.

"Zoe," Georgia cooed. She stretched out her hand, wanting to coax Zoe downstairs, away from Gloria's bedroom. In the kitchen she could fix Zoe a calming cup of hot tea, and then they could talk rationally about what had happened at the lawyer's office this morning.

"Georgia?"

"Yes. I'm here."

At that same moment, Trish reappeared with a pitcher of water, a glass, and a pile of ice cubes scattered like confetti on the silver tray. Trish set the tray on a small table in the dressing room. She leaned close to Georgia's ear and whispered, "I tried to get hold of Jake. He didn't answer."

"No!" Zoe cried out. She pushed away from Georgia's outstretched hand. "Not Jake. I don't want him to see me like this. Not now. Not ever." Zoe glared at Trish. "Dammit! Why don't you mind your own business?"

"Tell us what's wrong, Zoe," Georgia pleaded, careful to keep her hands at her side. "Please."

Zoe shook her head. "The two of you just won't stop, will you?" She gave them a sardonic smile. "Milton told me about Gabe."

"Gabe?" Georgia said, confused.

Zoe lowered her head so that her features were hidden behind a tangle of wild curls. Georgia struggled to keep her talking. "I remember you talking about Gabe, honey. Florry's brother, right?"

Zoe raised her head, her face and eyes swollen from crying. She kicked at the scarves with her bare foot. "Milton told me the truth." She then picked up a blue cashmere sweater and attempted to fold it, but gave up and tossed it aside. "Milton loved her."

"He loved Gloria?" Trish asked, shocked.

"Yes, he would've done anything for her. Even hide the body."

"Body? What body?" Georgia shook her head, now really confused.

Zoe whispered, "The clown."

Trish let out a small gasp. Georgia quickly shushed her, fearing any sudden movement or sound might send Zoe spinning out of control again, and this time she might not come back to her senses. In the back of her mind, Georgia kept asking herself what Dr. Phil would say in this situation. Totally idiotic, but nonetheless, TV psychology was all Georgia knew and prayed to God she wouldn't make things worse than they already were.

"Mama killed him," Zoe whispered. "Milton helped dump the body along the Pacific Coast highway. All these years, I suspected she'd killed him, but I never knew for sure. I gave Milton the gun this morning, the one Trish found in the freezer."

Georgia shivered, wondering if Zoe was telling the truth, or perhaps had lost her mind and was talking pure nonsense. "I'm sorry," she offered, unsure how to react to what Zoe had just told her.

"For what? I'm glad Mama killed him. I'll probably rot in hell for thinking that, but I am." Her eyes softened. "At least I can love Mama for that."

"It must've been painful for Milton, loving a woman who never loved him back," Georgia ventured. "Even to the point of covering up a murder."

Zoe's eyes darkened. "It wasn't murder, Georgia. She saved me. I'm only angry about all the damn secrets they kept from me."

"Secrets? Surely, you don't mean there's more?"

"This morning, I insisted Milton tell the truth about my birth. He agreed, but warned me I wouldn't like it."

"About your real mother?" Georgia asked, cautiously.

"Yes."

"Milton told you?" Trish wiggled out of Georgia's grip and leaned close to Zoe.

"Yes."

"Florry?" Trish blurted out.

"No."

"Who?" Georgia rubbed at her throbbing temples, hoping Zoe

might now be able to face the truth about her real mother. And if she could do that, maybe then Zoe could finally feel worthy of being loved. "Zoe, honey, don't keep all this inside. Save yourself."

Zoe snorted. "Save myself? I don't think so."

"You mentioned Gabe. What about him?" Trish pulled a green cashmere sweater out from under her and folded it into her lap.

"Gabe was my father."

Georgia gasped.

Trish's eyes widened. "Ohmygod!"

"Father?" Georgia said, shocked. "Are you sure?"

"Milton gave me my real birth certificate this morning. It's in that envelope."

"Your mother?" Georgia whispered. "Who was she?"

Zoe's bottom lip trembled. "Gloria was my real mother."

Trish let out a gasp. "What?"

Stunned, Georgia whispered, "Why in God's name did she lie about you?"

Zoe's whole body stiffened when Georgia made a move to comfort her. "Don't touch me. I can't bear your pity, Georgia." A handful of scarves still clutched in both fists, Zoe scrambled up from the floor and escaped into the bedroom, curling up at the end of Gloria's enormous silk-covered bed. She tucked her head between her arms, ears securely covered, as if wanting to shut out the whole world. Georgia and Trish stood over her, arms helplessly at their sides, unsure what to do next.

"Don't leave me," Zoe whimpered. "I need you. I trust both of you with my life."

Trish hurried to offer Zoe a glass of water, but she pushed it away, saying, "I can't swallow anything." She sniffed, raising her head to look at them. "Milton wrote the obituary in the paper, not Mama. It's true about the charities. Mama gave anonymously, mostly to orphanages in third-world countries. No one ever knew, except Milton." Her eyes grew wide. "Oh, what I said before, about the body, promise you won't tell anyone. We have to protect

Milton. He's the only one left now. No one must ever know about what he did for my mother."

"That's nothing I want to repeat," Trish said with a caustic laugh.

For once Georgia had to agree with Trish. "Me, too."

Zoe looked around the room as if noticing for the first time the mess she had created in her mother's bedroom. "I apologize for acting the way I did."

"What were you looking for?" Georgia edged close to the bed.

Zoe shrugged. "It's nothing. Mama probably destroyed it years ago." Zoe held out her hand to Trish, now wanting the glass of water. She took a long drink before handing it back to her. "I really scared Milton this morning. I kind of lost it when I found out Mama grew up with Florry and Gabe in Arkansas."

"You're kidding," Trish said, taking a sip of Zoe's water.

"They were dirt poor, close friends. All three of them made a pact that one day they'd leave together, make a better life for themselves. Mama and Gabe were in love, the kind of love that got a black man tortured and hung from a tree in 1945."

"What happened?" Trish said, visibly intrigued.

"Mama's daddy caught them together one night. He sent Mama home. He beat Gabe with a tire iron, leaving him for dead. But for the grace of God, he survived. Some kind soul found him in a ditch, patched him up, and then put him on the next bus out of town. He ended up in New Orleans. Mama's daddy didn't waste any time telling her he'd killed Gabe. The next morning, Mama stole some money and left with only the clothes on her back. She bought train tickets to California for her and Florry to make a fresh start. Of course, the rest is history. Mama found work at a five and dime making sodas. A director walked in from the summer heat, ordered a cool drink, saw Mama, and offered her a screen test."

"How romantic, star-crossed lovers," Trish gushed.

"What happened to Gabe?" Georgia asked. "He was only a boy, alone in New Orleans." She could not conceive the cruelty of a father who would go so far as to murder his daughter's lover, and then have the nerve to brag about it.

"Gabe found work as a janitor at jazz clubs along Bourbon Street. A blind musician took him in, fed him and nurtured his talent on the horn. A few years later, Gabe didn't need any help getting a job. By the time I moved in with Gabe and Mary, people from all over the world came to New Orleans just to hear him perform."

"But how—" Trish asked, bolting ahead of the story to how Zoe had been conceived. "When did they get back together again?"

"Yes, how?" Georgia asked, unable to suppress her own curiosity.

"Gabe was determined to forget about my mother, thinking it would do more harm than good to go back for her. He fell in love with Mary and married her. It wasn't until a few years later, he recognized Mama in one of those movie magazine photographs. He couldn't resist. He called to let Mama know he was still alive and to ask about Florry. The next day, both Mama and Florry flew to New Orleans to see him. Mama and Gabe fell in love all over again, but this time Mama got pregnant—with me."

Georgia struggled to piece together the tragic romance of Gloria and Gabe. "How did she ever hide her pregnancy?"

"Oh, this is so sad." Trish wiped at the tears running down her cheeks.

"Milton arranged for Mama to move to Jamaica. She refused to have an abortion. Her publicist gave out a story about Mama growing weary of public life and had taken an extended vacation. In Jamaica, Milton rented a house where she lived until delivering me. The arrangements with the orphanage were all very secret. A few weeks after giving me up, she went back to complete the adoption. Then, she went back to Hollywood where she was quite the heroine for adopting an underprivileged, minority orphan."

"What about Gabe?" Trish pressed. "Didn't he object?"

"Gabe loved my mother, no doubt about that, but he had

no intention of leaving Mary. Gabe agreed to keep everything a secret. If they went public about their love affair, Mama's film career would've been over."

Georgia's head throbbed from the intake of information. "I can't believe Milton knew all along and didn't tell you, even after your mother fell ill."

"Milton would never have betrayed my mother."

"Abominable."

"Milton would've done anything to protect her. *Anything.*"

"They should've told you—"

Trish piped in, "Yes, they should've."

"I don't blame Milton. Sure, I gave him a hard time this morning, but he knows I'll eventually get over it. This isn't the first time he's handed bad news to me about my mother. Milton's a good man. I used to dream he would marry my mother and be my father. I wanted a father so desperately. Now, I wish Gabe would've told me the truth."

"If he had, what would you have done?" Georgia asked.

Zoe shrugged. "I don't know about then, but now I understand he couldn't, because it would've destroyed Mary. She didn't know about Mama and Gabe being in love, or about me. Gabe loved my mother, but he also loved Mary. I watched them together when I lived with them in New Orleans."

Trish stretched out on the bed, elbow supporting her head. "But why did Gloria treat you so mean?"

"Milton said that if Mama hadn't let the booze take over her life, she might've been a better mother. He said Mama had a big fear of being dirt poor again. He said she really loved me, but couldn't show it, because she was so scared all the time of losing her money, losing me, losing everything."

Zoe slid off the bed and started picking up clothing she had earlier thrown from the dresser. She said over one shoulder, "Milton's going to take charge of getting rid of the contents of the house. Everything will be sold. When I leave here tomorrow, I won't be coming back." She added nonchalantly, "Trish, did you reach Jake yet?"

Trish's surprised eyes darted to Georgia. "Uh, no. Maybe someone stole his cell."

"Hmmm." Zoe closed a drawer and started on another. "It's probably just as well he never answered."

Georgia helped fold clothing back into the armoire. She sighed, feeling weary of all the drama and emotion they had all gone through today. She glanced over at Trish who was busy picking shards of glass from a photo frame out of the carpet. "Trish, be careful. The last thing we need is rushing you to the emergency room for stitches."

"Oh!" Trish yipped.

Georgia groaned, thinking Trish had cut herself. She rushed over expecting blood, but instead found Trish on her knees, ripping apart the broken frame to get at something beneath an old glamour shot of Gloria.

Georgia moved in close. "What is it?"

"I think it's another picture. I've almost got it out."

Hearing this, Zoe let out a yelp and leapt across the bed for Trish. "You found it!" She snatched the photo from Trish's hands and examined it. She laughed. "It was here all the time." Zoe then hopped up and did a little dance around the room. "Can you believe it?"

Zoe's wild, high-pitched squeal sounded like music to Georgia's ears. "That's what you were looking for? A photograph?"

"Yes," she said, holding it out in front of her so they all could see.

"Who are they," Trish asked, angling for a better look.

The photo showed a black boy and girl, standing on either side of a pretty blonde girl, arms interlocked, smiling into the camera. The three of them were probably no older than fifteen or sixteen at the time it was taken.

"I found this when I was a kid. Of course, I didn't know who they were back then." Zoe touched each image with her fingertips. "They look so young, don't they?"

"When did you first find it?"

"Playing in Mama's room, opening drawers I wasn't supposed to be in. When I found it, I took it to Mama and asked who they were. She slapped me and grabbed it out of my hands. Then, after Milton told me the truth, I remembered the photograph and understood who those people were—my real family."

Georgia studied the photograph in Zoe's hand, a testimony of truth, all the lies and deceit finally revealed, now leaving Zoe to blindly interpret the good and bad parts of the people who had, together, both loved and betrayed her.

"It's so strange, Georgia. I don't feel angry anymore."

"That's a good start."

Trish put her arm around Zoe and squeezed hard. "I love you."

"I love you, too, Trish. You've been a good friend, the best. You, too, Georgia."

Zoe pushed back her hair, and then clapped her hands like a teacher demanding order in her classroom. "Now, the sad part of the day is over. Dry your eyes and let's get dressed up. I promised you Rodeo Drive."

Relieved to see Zoe attempting to get back to her old self, Georgia joined in on the enthusiasm. "That would be nice. I want to find something decent to wear to Gloria's service tomorrow. I'm depending on both of you to help me." Although Georgia had packed a dark skirt and blouse for the funeral, she thought the outing might be good for all of them. Too much sadness lived inside this beautiful house, too many bad memories for Zoe.

Zoe looked down at the photo. "Sounds good." She wiped her face with the back of her hand. "First, we'll have lunch at some pricey restaurant. After that, we'll shop Rodeo Drive for three gorgeous dresses, complete with accessories."

Trish's eyes widened. "OHMYGOD! Georgia, she must've inherited, like, a zillion dollars!"

"Almost," Zoe said, carefully sliding the photograph into the brown envelope Georgia had brought upstairs with her. She winked conspiratorially at Trish. "What do you think for Georgia? Chanel? Versace?"

Trish raised an eyebrow. "Georgia's a bit demure for Versace, don't you think?"

Georgia blushed, knowing they were making fun of her fashion ignorance, but she didn't care. With Zoe feeling better, nothing mattered. She willingly played into their hands, saying "What's a Ver-sace?"

Trish and Zoe gleefully took Georgia's arms and led her out of the bedroom. Zoe said lightheartedly, "Georgia, by the end of the day, you'll know them all: Chanel, Gucci, Prada, Versace. Right Trish?"

Trish nodded affirmatively, "Uh-huh."

Georgia suddenly pulled back. "Wait just a minute, Zoe. I refuse to have you pay for anything. A simple black dress is all I need. I have my own money."

Zoe gave Trish a sugary smile, saying, "Now isn't Georgia the sweetest thing, ever? She has her own money. Well, in that case, lunch is on you, Trish."

Trish feigned surprise. "Me?"

Zoe laughed and gave Trish a hearty smack on the back. "Yes, you're paying. That's for letting Mama's ashes fly out the back of the car. Don't you think that's fair, Georgia?"

"I do," Georgia agreed, giving them her brightest smile. Lordy! Versace? Prada? Chanel? One thing for sure, Georgia was in for one unforgettable day on Rodeo Drive.

# CHAPTER TWENTY-SIX

"Stop, Trish. You're pinching me!" Georgia yelped, squirming out of her reach.

"Well, straighten up, then. Stop fidgeting, and for heaven's sake don't slouch." Trish pulled her back, and this time, Georgia stood up straight and tucked in her stomach. Trish then easily zipped the dress and helped Georgia into a matching jacket. Finally, Georgia slipped into her new Manolo Blahniks, the prettiest shoes she had ever seen.

Trish said, "Now turn around and take a look."

Georgia took in a surprised breath when she saw her reflection. She whispered, "Goodness gracious." She'd never owned anything so elegant as this black dress and jacket. And the shoes! They were beautiful, even though she'd argued with Zoe about not needing them, but Zoe had insisted on buying them, anyway. Imagine spending four hundred fifty dollars on a single pair of shoes? Unbelievable.

"Here, let me help you with the pearls." Trish gathered the strand from a velvet case and told her to turn around. "You've got great legs, Georgia. You always keep them hidden under jeans and those dreadful long skirts."

Yesterday, when Georgia had first emerged from a dressing room in an elegant shop along Rodeo Drive, Trish and Zoe had both exclaimed, "Georgia!" Even the well-dressed sales assistants with the icy smiles took in breaths of amazement as Georgia took a fashion turn in front of Trish and Zoe.

Trish's choice, a Versace, size 4, with sleek lines, except for the sassy ruffle at the bottom of the dress. The assistant had exclaimed, "Sophisticated enough for a funeral, yet spicy enough without the short jacket for a night out dancing."

Zoe had insisted on paying for everything, right down to the gorgeous strand of pearls at Georgia's throat. Now, only an hour before the funeral service, Georgia said to Trish, "I don't feel right about all this stuff."

"What stuff?" Trish said, playing dumb.

Georgia sucked in a breath and ran her fingers down the ornate buttons of her jacket. "This dress, the jacket—it's all too beautiful." She lifted one foot. "And the shoes." She threaded her fingers along the strand of pearls and whispered, "It's all too much. I'm not used to putting on clothes that cost more than the furniture in my house."

Trish took an admiring glance in the mirror at her own dress. "There you go again, Georgia. Stop thinking and just accept the gifts. Do you really think we should deprive Zoe of the joy in giving us these clothes? Not me, girlfriend. Really, Georgia, you're being totally selfish."

Georgia made the bed, fluffing the pillows and tucking them neatly under the spread. "Not selfish," she said, smoothing out the last wrinkle. "Uncomfortable."

Trish swept her hair into a ponytail that fell down her back in a dark, silky stream. "I refuse to listen to your play of conscience."

Georgia nervously picked a piece of lint from the sleeve of her jacket. "Have you seen Zoe this morning?"

"About an hour ago, down in the kitchen, drinking a glass of orange juice and talking to Milton Thayer. He came by to pick up the urn to take to the church." Trish yanked out the hair wrap and repeated the routine of brushing and drawing her hair back from her face and securing it again. "The limo's coming at ten. Zoe said to be ready."

"Limo?"

Trish struck a model's pose and with a mock air of sophistica-tion said, "Well, of course, dah-ling. Do you think *one* goes to a Hollywood funeral in *one's* own car?" Trish laughed, leaning into the mirror above the dresser to check her lipstick.

"You look beautiful," Georgia said, glancing nervously out the window to the lawn where the night before last all three of them had sat in a circle drinking expensive wine on the damp grass. "You're really leaving for Tucson when we get back?"

"Yes. And I meant what I said about selling the café. You're still interested, I hope?"

"More than."

Trish moved to Georgia's side. "I think after today, nothing will be the same. I called David this morning. He's coming to Sedona on Friday."

Georgia let the curtains fall back into place. "He's going to Tucson with you?"

"Yes. He's helping me find a house. And I hope you don't mind that I mentioned that you're taking over the Soft Rock."

Georgia eyed Trish with suspicion. "Does he know about—"

"Claire? Not yet. It's on my list."

"It's all for the best, the truth I mean." Georgia gathered her new black gloves from the dresser.

Trish suddenly looked stricken. "Oh, Georgia, I hope you're right about him understanding about Claire."

She patted Trish's cheek. "I know my son."

"He worries about you, you know."

"David?"

"He wants you to be happy."

"I am happy."

"Georgia, can I ask you something personal?"

"If I said no, would that stop you?" Georgia teased. She stuffed two clean handkerchiefs inside the sweet black clutch Zoe had picked out for her at Gucci.

"Did you love Ed? I mean, did you always love him?"

Georgia hesitated. Even with the funeral service, she hadn't thought about Ed all day. She anxiously checked her watch. "We'd better get downstairs. And the answer's yes. I loved Ed. If I wasn't exactly happy all the time, I was content. That's more than most people can say about their lives."

Zoe called out from the downstairs hallway, "Limo's here, girls!" Trish went to the door and yelled down, "We're coming."

Georgia straightened her shoulders. "Well, are we ready?"

"Any regrets?" Trish asked, gathering up her jacket.

"About what?"

"Your life."

Georgia checked the last button on the front of her jacket. "I have one."

"One?"

"The biggest one."

At that moment Zoe rushed into the room, interrupting their conversation. Dressed in a black Valentino with a delicate lace shawl draping one shoulder and clipped at her waist with an antique broach, she looked amazing. On her head, Zoe wore a stunning black picture hat banded in black satin, complete with a short chenille-dotted veiling bow. "Here," Zoe said, holding out two more hats. "Today, we look the part of daughter and friends of a movie legend. Mama would be proud." She handed a black cloche with a silk flower trim to Trish and a chic flat crown hat with mixed feather accents and wide brim to Georgia. She then helped them properly set the hats in place. "You both look gorgeous. Now, let's go."

The inside of the limo easily accommodated their elegant hats. Outside the front gate of Gloria's estate, the car moved slowly past a small gathering of people standing on the sidewalk, many of them holding flowers. Scattered petals covered the stone entrance and even with the windows closed, Georgia could smell their sweetness. Safe behind the smoke-glassed windows of the limo, Georgia watched in stunned silence as a woman fell to her knees and sobbed as if she had lost her own mother instead of someone she had never known outside of a movie theatre. Georgia whispered, "They really loved her, didn't they?"

"I don't think Mama really knew how much."

Georgia nervously worked a lace handkerchief through her gloved hands. She hoped Jake's flight was on time and he'd be waiting at the church when they arrived. A small thought nagged at her that maybe they should have forewarned Zoe about Jake being at the service. It did cross her mind that Zoe might not be too pleased with yet another deception by someone close to her. She sighed, putting that thought to rest, knowing it was too late to worry about Jake's surprise arrival at the church. Her eyes slid to Zoe, who had slipped on her mother's enormous dark glasses after entering the limo, her chin held high, her mouth set in a mysterious half-smile. She looked every inch a movie star's daughter.

They had only been in the car for a few minutes before Zoe cracked her veneer of fortitude and panicked. "Ohmygod, we've got to turn around. I forgot the urn!"

"Don't you remember?" Georgia said. "Milton came by this morning and picked it up. Relax."

"That's right," Trish added. "I gave the urn to Milton myself."

Zoe breathed a sigh of relief and settled back in the seat. "Thank God. My insides are rattling like glass beads down a drainpipe."

Georgia glanced at Trish, and they both broke into a fit of giggles. "Glass beads down a drainpipe?" Trish repeated with a snort. "Zoe, you've definitely lost your grip."

Zoe opened her purse. "I forgot my handkerchief."

"Here." Trish offered hers.

"Thank you." She pressed it to her nose and blew. "When we get to the church, stay close to me, okay? I feel sick." Georgia linked an arm through hers. "We won't leave you."

"I really did love her, you know," Zoe said, her voice trembling.

The limo pulled up to the front entrance of the church. The

chauffeur opened the door and assisted all three of them out of the car. Velvet ropes separated the crowd of onlookers from invited mourners who waited to enter the church. Cameras pressed close to the boundary ropes along the sidewalk, shouting "Zoe, look over here! How do you feel about your mother's death?" While special duty police officers worked feverishly along the ropes in an effort to press the crowd back from Zoe, another officer guided the three women to the front steps of the church.

Georgia felt her jaw drop when she recognized several movie stars entering the church ahead of them. One famous bejeweled woman moved slowly up the steps with the assistance of a young gentleman. The silver-haired screen legend stopped inside the church and waited for Zoe, and then wrapped her in warm embrace, saying, "I am so sorry, dear. We'll all miss your mother."

Walking into the church, Georgia couldn't believe the gathering of celebrities who filled the pews. Sitting with Zoe in a front pew, Trish leaned close to Georgia and whispered, "I'm worried. Jake should be here by now."

"Maybe his plane's late," Georgia whispered back.

"No, I checked before we left the house. It landed on time. So, where *is* he?"

"I-don't-know." Georgia held a finger to her lips, shushing her. "Nothing can be done about it now." It was then that Georgia turned and glanced down the aisle and saw Jake entering the church. Zoe saw him, too, and her entire body seemed to instantly relax. Neither spoke a word, as Zoe scooted to make room in the pew for Jake. When he took her hand in his and kissed it, Georgia breathed a sigh of relief.

Jake's appearance at the funeral service sent a shock wave of whisperings throughout the pews, no doubt an eruption of inquiries regarding the handsome, newly-elected senator from Arizona and the beautiful daughter of Gloria Atwater.

Gloria's urn had been placed on the pedestal at the front. The minister extended the invitation to anyone to come forward who wanted to speak a few words. Eulogy after eulogy followed. All three women in the front pew bowed their heads, each one knowing exactly what the urn really held. Trish tightened her hand around Georgia's, her pretty mouth turned up at the corners. No doubt, they were all thinking about Gloria's ashes being swept across the desert terrain along Route 40.

By the end of the service, there wasn't a dry eye in the house. At the final prayer, Georgia took note that Jake's arm had curled around Zoe's shoulder, gently caressing the back of her neck. Anyone sitting behind them would have no doubt that Jake was more than just an acquaintance.

Outside the church, Jake eased Zoe through the crush of people to his waiting limo. Within moments, they were gone. Milton came up behind Georgia. "Come on ladies, let's go." He rushed them to their waiting limo, dodging curious onlookers as if they were in a Hollywood movie scene.

Once settled inside the limo, Trish said excitedly, "Did you see the look on Zoe's face when she saw Jake? I wish I'd brought my camera."

For no reason at all, tears streaked down Georgia's face, her delicate hanky, already damp, of no use. Trish pulled a wad of tissues from a box on the console and stuffed them into her hand. "Georgia, what's wrong?"

"Nothing," Georgia wailed. "It's, you know, like you said. Everything's going to change now." Her tears gained momentum. "Zoe's going to Washington with Jake. You're moving to Tucson."

"Georgia, it's not that bad. Maybe, if things work out, David will move to Tucson, too."

Georgia sniffed, "I hadn't thought about that possibility." She smiled and sniffed again. "I'd like that very much. But if you and David are truly in love, I don't care where you live."

Trish adjusted her hat. "This morning, you said something about the one thing you regretted about Ed. What was it?"

"Oh, that." Georgia shook her head. "It was nothing."

"No, I want to know."

Georgia heaved a sigh. "Okay. My biggest regret about Ed is the day he brought home the Fleetwood. I was angry at him for buying such an expensive car. Imagine, a red convertible with white leather seats and me toting around two small children. I wanted a van, something I could put kids and groceries in. Anyway, he came home with the car and announced that he wanted to travel, see new places. He said we should learn to enjoy ourselves."

"Oh, Georgia, that's so sweet. What did you say?"

"I told him he was nuts. We had responsibilities. I called him irresponsible and selfish to think we could just up and go as we pleased."

"Oh," Trish said, throwing crumpled tissues into a small trash container under the console. "You should've gone, at least for a while. After a few days, he probably would've been ready to go back home."

"I know." Georgia said, seeing the disappointment on Trish's face. "Later, it occurred to me that he was trying to tell me something about us, but I wouldn't listen. Then, after Ed died, I realized he'd kept the car all these years because of what it represented, a way to hang onto his youth. I regret the way I treated him about the car."

Trish grabbed more tissues for her own eyes. "Oh, that's sad. And now look at you, riding around in the Fleetwood like Ed wanted." Trish shook her head. "Georgia, he should've flat-out told you he was getting an *itch*. Men can be such idiots."

Georgia crushed her purse to her stomach and sighed. "My biggest regret was I didn't give Ed more of myself."

At these words, Trish's eyes brightened. "But that's exactly what you've done. Don't you see? You've taken the car on an incredible journey, and it's not only changed your life, but everyone else's, too. Look, if you hadn't come to Sedona, I would've never met David, never had the courage to contact my aunt and meet Claire. Zoe wouldn't be back with Jake." Trish paused, considering further. She then said, "Most of all, you wouldn't be having dinner Saturday night with Doc."

Georgia's head jerked around. "How did you know about that? Mary Jo, I bet. That girl can't keep a secret if her life depended on it."

Smiling triumphantly, Trish said, "I think ol' Ed's up there right now smiling down on you and saying, 'That's my Georgia.'"

Georgia folded the last unused tissue and opened her purse, but Trish took it from her and delicately dabbed at the mascara around Georgia's eyes. "You feel better now?  Oh look, we're at Forest Lawn. Isn't it gorgeous? Did you know people actually get married here?"

"Here? In a cemetery?" She gazed out over the beautiful gardens and decided, yes, it was easy to understand why couples chose this place, a cemetery, to begin a new life. She then thought of a song she had once heard on the radio, the words saying something about the end of one story being the beginning of another.

# CHAPTER TWENTY-SEVEN

Cooler desert night air washed over Georgia through the open window of the car. Another hour of driving, and they would be home. She turned down the volume on the radio but not so low she couldn't hear *Old Devil Moon*. Curled up on the passenger seat, head turned toward the door, Trish slept like a baby. She had fallen asleep not long after they'd passed the place in the road where the accident with Gloria's ashes had occurred. Both Georgia and Trish had waved, said a small prayer and moved right on down the road at seventy-five miles an hour.

Georgia didn't mind the night drive to Sedona, especially after the chaotic events of the last few days in L.A. The hushed quiet after Trish had nodded off was a pleasant respite with the night air massaging every nerve in her body. She felt at peace.

The last song faded into the background, and then the deep drowsy voice of the announcer poured from the radio giving his listening audience a few reflective words of wisdom before the next song, *Unforgettable*.

Already, she missed Zoe, and good ol' Nat brought that loneliness home. Although excited to see her son tomorrow, she dreaded him leaving with Trish to search for her new home in Tucson. After all her wishing, was it really a good thing for Trish and David to become romantically involved so soon after David's divorce? Georgia tossed that thought out the window, refusing to think about the consequences. Her head already throbbed with enough regrets to last two lifetimes.

Her thoughts rolled back to the huge gathering at Gloria's mansion after the memorial service and how inside of a few hours she had been introduced and shaken hands with more Hollywood stars than she would have ever thought possible in a thousand lifetimes, let alone one. Everyone had been so friendly, not at all like the twisted, gossipy stories she always read in those tabloids.

Upon their return to Gloria's estate after the service, she was amazed at how the house had been magically transformed from cold and vacant to open and inviting. All the white coverings had been removed from the furniture in the downstairs rooms. At least a dozen caterers busily bussed drinks and food throughout the spacious rooms filled with glamorous people. By two in the afternoon the crowd had thinned to less than a dozen, and Georgia and Trish were packed and ready for the drive back to Sedona. Zoe and Jake were leaving for the airport. After a few quick hugs and kisses, Zoe and Jake were gone. Seeing the limo disappear down the driveway, Georgia felt as if something vital and necessary had been ripped from her insides. The catered crabmeat salad she had eaten earlier gurgled in protest inside her stomach

"She'll be back in a few weeks," Trish had offered when they got into the car to leave. "She'll have to come back once she figures out what she's going to do with the Moon Tide." Trish's eyes suddenly brightened. "Say, Georgia, why don't you take over Zoe's shop, too?"

"I don't know," Georgia said, leaning over the seat to carefully smooth out the garment bags hanging on a hook in the back. "That's too much to think about right now. Anyway," she said, settling into the driver's seat, "The last thing Zoe's thinking about right now is the Moon Tide."

Now, six hours later, traveling back to Sedona, Trish moaned softly and stirred in her sleep before slowly sitting up. She stretched and yawned. Georgia adjusted the volume on the radio, turning it up a little, hoping Trish wouldn't be so talkative the rest of the way home.

"I've got a kink in my neck," Trish said, rubbing at the base of her skull and glancing at the clock on the dash. "My God, I can't believe I've slept so long."

"Like a baby."

"How far?" Trish asked, still groggy from sleep. She looked out into the black of night as if searching for some clue as to where they were.

"Maybe forty-five minutes."

Trish yawned and settled back into the seat. "Can you believe the past few days? Even though it was a funeral, it was more like a beautiful dream, wasn't it?"

"Hmmm." Georgia kept her eyes fixed on the road, not really wanting to get into a deep, reflective conversation with Trish so close to home. Right now she wanted nothing more than to fall into bed and get a few hours of sleep before having to get up at five and start the dough for the breakfast rolls. "Yes," she agreed, "A beautiful dream. But tomorrow it's back to work for this Cinderella."

Trish closed her eyes. "Like a fairytale. Jake coming in at the eleventh hour to save the princess, swooping her up and taking her to his kingdom in Washington."

"A fairytale, for sure." Georgia chuckled. "The kind of fairytale the press will eat up. I only pray everything works out for them in Camelot, D.C."

Trish turned in the seat. "Do you think they'll really get married?"

Georgia shrugged. "I suppose so. Zoe seems to have worked out the reasons she had for not marrying Jake. In NASA language, thumb's up—it's a go."

"Did she tell you something I don't know?"

"I overheard her tell Milton they were getting married but didn't say when."

"She did? Well, she should've told us first, you know."

"She really didn't have much time with so many people at the house. Besides, I was eavesdropping when she told Milton. Zoe will tell us when she's ready to tell us."

Trish persisted. "It was so romantic, wasn't it?"

"Yes, very."

"Georgia?"

"Hmmm."

"What you told me about Ed and the car, you know, when he first brought it home and asked you to go away with him. I—"

"Oh Trish, let's don't go into that right now, okay? It's late. I'm tired. The last thing I want to think about tonight is Ed."

"I was only going to say that maybe things turned out for the best, I mean you not going with him when he first bought the Fleetwood. I know it's selfish, but, like I said before, if you had gone with Ed, everything might not have happened the way it did. It's fate. What do you think?"

Georgia moved into the city limits of Flagstaff, not giving Trish an answer, hoping her silence indicated she was in no mood to talk about fate, philosophy or anything else at this early hour of the morning. It didn't work.

"Don't you see?" Trish persisted. "Since you came to Sedona, everything's changed for the better."

"Trish, we've been all through this before. I'm tired. All I want is to go to bed and sleep." They were twenty minutes from Trish's stone cottage. "And about my having dinner with Doc tomorrow night—don't make more of it than what it is."

"Real-ly."

"We're friends, nothing more."

"You-don't-say," Trish teased. "As older men go, Doc's gorgeous. Like Ralph Lauren in that television commercial wearing a cowboy hat."

Georgia lowered the window for a full dose of fresh air. "We're only friends," she repeated. "I don't need a matchmaker, okay?"

"He's definitely right for you, Georgia."

"Stop."

"You're attracted to him. Who wouldn't be?"

"I'm not."

"You're lying, Georgia."

"Well, he did feed Oscar the past few days and kept an eye on Mary Jo. Even so, that doesn't mean I'm ready to get serious about anyone."

"You gave him a key to your apartment?"

"To feed the cat."

Trish gave her a sly wink and said, "Uh huh, I hear you girlfriend."

# CHAPTER TWENTY-EIGHT

"Oh my," Georgia said, genuinely impressed. Doc stood on the porch outside her door looking every bit as comfortable in a dark tailored suit, white shirt and conservative blue tie, as he did in everyday faded, ranch-worn jeans, blue denim shirt and cowboy boots. He held out a bouquet of white daisies. Georgia felt her face go numb with surprise. She couldn't remember the last time anyone had thought to give her flowers.

"I once heard you say you liked daisies," he said, giving her a shy smile and taking a step back to admire her. "You look real pretty, Georgia."

"Thank you." Her face grew hot again. She escaped to the cramped kitchenette in search of something to put the flowers in, rummaging under the sink until finding a quart Mason jar. She then discarded the cellophane wrapped around the stems and plunked the daisies into the water. Oscar jumped up on the counter, sniffing at the flowers, and Georgia shooed him to the floor. God, even her fingers were tingling with excitement. "They're lovely, Doc."

Earlier, she had carefully removed her designer dress and matching jacket from the clothing bag and dressed. She fastened the pearls around her neck, dabbing Chanel No. 5 behind each ear and at the base of her throat, and then—*what the heck*—gently applied a bit behind each knee. By the time Doc was supposed to arrive, she had worked herself into a girlish tizzy. Before answering the knock at the door, she had leaned close to her reflection in the mirror, telling herself to calm down. After all, the evening was nothing more than two friends getting together for dinner, nothing serious.

But from the moment she saw him standing on the threshold, the rules had somehow changed with the flowers and the courtly way in which Doc attended her elbow as he led her to his car, and then opened the door for her. They drove to Flagstaff and ate dinner in an Italian restaurant where they shared a bottle of wine. To cut through the awkward silence, they critiqued the food, Georgia commenting on the oversized portions of lasagna needing more sauce and less cheese, and Doc totally agreeing with her. The more they talked, the more they relaxed into the familiarity they were used to back at the café.

"You're a beautiful woman, Georgia," Doc said, finishing his dessert and taking a leisurely sip of his coffee. The waiter removed the dessert dishes while Doc nervously folded and refolded his napkin.

Georgia's cheeks burned like dry grass struck with the flame of a wood match. "Thank you, Doc." She made a gesture with her hand to take in the beautiful atmosphere of the restaurant and accidentally hit the waiter in the face. "Oh, excuse me." Sickness filled her stomach as she apologized to the waiter who mumbled something like *No problem* and continued to clear the table.

When they were alone again, Georgia said, "This was all so nice, the flowers, the dinner, your good company." She cleared her throat. "You're a good friend."

Doc's eyebrows furrowed as if he were genuinely hurt. "Georgia, I want to be more than your friend."

Gazing across the candlelit table, her head still light from the last of the wine, she let herself imagine becoming romantically involved with Doc. The idea wasn't exactly unappealing. He was a handsome man, kind and gentle. What more could she ask? When he scooted his chair closer to hers, she didn't object.

"Please tell me how you feel." He took her hand giving it a determined squeeze.

Georgia closed her eyes to keep the room from spinning, as if she were on a merry-go-round. His hand over hers was warm and strong, thickly callused from ranch work and *City Slicker* trail drives. She liked that. "I need time, Doc. My last date was over thirty years ago."

He squeezed her hand tighter. "No rush."

Georgia raised both eyebrows. "Persistent, aren't you."

"I am. But only if you think there might be some feelings for me, too. I hope so."

A nervous giggle erupted from the back of her throat. "You sure know how to put a girl on the spot, don't you?"

"Georgia, I've loved you since the first day you came into the café, all scared and lonely, and looking for somewhere to call home."

"I had a home in Ohio."

Doc shook his head. "You belong here, now. This is your home."

Tears burned behind Georgia's eyes. She silently willed herself not to start blubbering about how she really felt about Sedona and the café, how everything around her was more than a home to her now. In her heart, she could never imagine living anywhere else but here, in Arizona. The events of the past year flickered behind her eyes, light against dark, as if the inside of her were sitting in an old movie theatre. Her heart ached at the memories of Trish and Zoe taking her into their lives and becoming her friends. They both admired her because she had taken a risk, the same risk Georgia had seen as being purely impulsive and the act of a coward. Now, she was about to become the owner and proprietor of the Soft Rock Café and a permanent resident in Sedona.

Earlier that afternoon, before her date with Doc, and at Trish's insistence, David had contacted an attorney he knew in Flagstaff, setting into motion the paperwork needed to officially close on the café. "Mom, you're sure this is what you want?" David asked, no doubt concerned she was making a hasty decision. Georgia quickly replied, "More than sure." David had smiled and replied, "Okay, that's all I need to know."

Trish and David then left for Tucson, promising to be back in a few days. Watching them get into Trish's Jeep, Georgia waved tiredly, and said a prayer that the more time the two of them spent together, the deeper they would fall in love.

In a good mood, Georgia left Mary Jo in charge of the café for the remainder of the afternoon while she hurried upstairs to take a leisurely bath and get ready for her dinner with Doc.

Now, sitting alone with him in a romantic restaurant, her insides twitched as if she'd swallowed a bag of Mexican jumping beans. Keeping Doc at arm's-length proved to be more difficult than she had anticipated. She enjoyed Doc's company, and even if she wasn't ready to admit it, she knew, without a doubt, she wanted more than a friendship.

"So, the café's all yours now?" he asked.

Georgia crossed her legs, accidentally kicking Doc under the table. "Oh, I'm so sorry." She sat up straight in the chair, embarrassed. "I'm such a klutz tonight."

Doc shook his head. "You're anything but a klutz, Georgia. I've never met a woman quite like you."

A pleasing tingling sensation started at the base of her neck, and then skipped down each bumpy vertebra to the small of her back. She swallowed the last of her wine, hoping it might help quiet her nerves. "Oh, I doubt that." She shrugged off his compliment. "Twelve months ago my idea of wild abandonment was buying an expensive brand of ice cream and hiding it at the bottom of the freezer. I'd keep it all for myself." She laughed. "How pathetic was that?"

Doc's eyes softened. He leaned in close, practically nose-to-nose with her. "Georgia, you have a right to be happy. It's okay to keep something back for yourself to enjoy."

Within kissing distance of Doc, she fought to keep her voice even. "I really hadn't thought about it that way."

She could smell the scent of his cologne, clean and seductive, and she liked how his Adam's apple gently rubbed against the stiff collar of his dress shirt whenever he spoke.

She cleared her throat. "Yes," she said, referring back to his question about the café. "The café's mine, or will be as soon as we set a closing date. I'll miss Trish and Zoe. I'm grateful Mary Jo's staying on for another month. I'll hate losing her, but I'm glad she's going back to college." She sighed. "Life goes on, doesn't it?"

"Sure does," he said.

"What about you Doc? After your wife died, you raised a daughter only to have her move to New York. You must've missed her terribly. How is it you've never remarried?"

He shrugged. "No reason. Just never found anyone who really mattered enough to ask."

Georgia felt herself blush. "I see, and if you did, uh, find someone, would you?" She was flirting with him. She hadn't flirted since she was eighteen years old. It felt so natural, much like getting on a bicycle after twenty years and being pleasantly surprised the sense of balance was still there.

A slow, easy smile warmed Doc's face. "If I did, I'd marry her in an instant."

Georgia, painfully self-conscious, lowered her head. "You make me feel like a schoolgirl."

"That's good, huh?" He gazed adoringly at Georgia.

She raised her head and looked into eyes the same exact color as a mountain lake on a blue-sky morning. Her body shivered with a sort of giddy, adolescent anticipation. "Yes, it's good." She gave his hand an affectionate squeeze. The endearing smile that came over his face was pure sunshine to Georgia, something she could easily enjoy every day for the rest of her life.

Leaving the restaurant, Doc lifted his coat over their heads to shield them against the sleet and rain that had begun to fall. They made a run for the car where he opened the door, and then held the coat over her while she got inside. Sleet pelted against the roof of the car. Georgia worried that they might have a difficult time driving back to Sedona.

Georgia shivered as Doc quickly slid inside and started the car. He flipped on the heater fan and turned to her, saying, "We'll wait until it lets up." And much to Georgia's surprise, he leaned over and gave her a brief kiss on the lips. When Georgia made no objection, he pulled her into his arms and kissed her again.

His lips felt warm and smooth, nice. Georgia leaned into his embrace, surprised at how eagerly her body responded to his touch. She felt a hunger she hadn't known in years, and for the first time since Ed's death, she knew that falling in love again was a very real possibility.

He whispered into her ear, "Georgia, I love you. I've known it for a long time." Again, he kissed her, more urgently this time.

She couldn't breathe. The silliness of making out in a car at their age drifted into her thoughts. She pulled away. "I don't know what to say." She sat up, trying to catch her breath. She nervously fussed with the buttons on her coat. The windows had fogged over, and her lips felt bruised from all the kissing. A slow liquid heat burned in her lower abdomen, feeling both pleasing and frightening. What in heaven's name had she gotten herself into by going to dinner with a man who professed love on a first date? That kind of romance only happened in the movies.

He collected her hands in his, pressing her fingers to his lips. "You don't have to say anything right now. Tomorrow I'm leaving for Montana. I'll be gone for a month. When I get back, we'll talk more about where we're going with this, okay?"

"A month?" Georgia's mind raced in circles, trying to make sense of all that had happened within a few hours. She couldn't think about Doc going away now, not after he had just professed his love for her.

"When I get back, we'll talk about marriage." He held up a

hand when she started to speak. "Don't answer now. Think about it, okay?"

Georgia sat with hands folded in her lap, trying to make sense of the last few hours and her whirlwind romance. She stared at the sleet that splattered against the windshield. "Oh dear, I thought this was only dinner."

He chuckled, "I took you by surprise?"

"You certainly did."

"I took your breath away?"

"Definitely."

"Does that mean you'll see me again?"

"Of course, I'll see you again. You come into the café every morning."

Doc leveled his gaze at her. "You know what I mean, Georgia."

"Yes."

"Is that a yes?"

"I think so," she said, teasing. Secretly, she hoped he would kiss her again, but he didn't. Instead, he backed out of the parking space and pulled into the street, headlights from oncoming vehicles reflecting on the wet pavement.

"You'll say yes, Georgia Mae. You can't live without me now."

Treacherous weather followed them back to Sedona. Georgia insisted Doc stay with her to avoid the extra twenty miles to his ranch in Cottonwood. In her apartment, she made up a makeshift bed for him on the couch. She slept alone in the brass bed, taking comfort in knowing Doc was only a few steps away in the next room. She liked that. Snuggling into the warmth of the bed, she shivered in secret delight at the thought of what else the night might bring?

\* \* \*

The next morning, Doc followed her down into the kitchen and sat at the table drinking his first cup of coffee, his eyes lovingly taking in Georgia's every move. Leaving the dough to work in a warm corner of the kitchen, she went to Doc and smoothed back his hair. "Ezekiel, I have only one thing to say before this goes any further."

"What's that," he said with a sleepy smile.

"Don't try to change me. I like who I am right now."

He pulled her into his lap and gazed into her eyes. "Lord, Georgia, that's one thing I would never try to do. I love you just the way you are."

*Six months later...*

# CHAPTER TWENTY-NINE

Georgia stood over the stove in the café kitchen spooning hot custard into a bowl of egg yolks. She then mixed the smaller batch into the rest of the hot liquid, letting it thicken and bubble over medium heat, occasionally lifting the pan to prevent scorching. She said over her shoulder, "The trick to making lemon meringue pie is to keep a good watch over it. If you cook the custard too long, it's rubbery—not enough, it's gooey and runny."

She glanced over her shoulder at Doc who had disappeared behind the Sunday paper. Georgia turned back to her work, smiling. "Seems to me after a man asks a woman to marry him, he should pay closer attention to what she says at least until after the wedding."

"Huh?"

"I said—"

He folded back a section of the paper and held out the society section with the wedding photo of Zoe and Jake. "I didn't miss a word you said. You were talking about pies and how they shouldn't be left alone on the stove, right?"

"Hmmm," she said, coming over and reading over Doc's shoulder. She had slid the custard off the stove to cool before pouring it into the baked pie shells. "It was a nice wedding. I've never seen Zoe so happy."

Doc squeezed Georgia's waist. "Jake's a good man, and I have no doubt they'll charm Washington."

Georgia sighed. "Zoe was a beautiful bride." She went to the desk to get the scissors to cut the photo from the newspaper to later place inside her new album. "I still wish she would've given more thought to the price of the Moon Tide. She practically gave it away."

"I don't think Zoe cares about the money." He took the scissors from her and cut out the photo for her. "Anyway, she can't take it back now, even if she wanted to—not with that big, gaping hole you put in the wall."

Georgia laughed as she scraped the last of the cooled custard from the pan and into the shells, and then spread each pie with a heaping mound of meringue. "I suppose she wouldn't, but it'll be worth all the effort after finishing the remodeling and opening up to the public again. I'm anxious to serve breakfast and lunch to more than the locals and get back into a regular routine." She looked through the serving window at the far side of the dining room where she had broken through the brick wall and into the interior of the Moon Tide. She said to Doc, "Opening the wall was Trish's idea, but you should've seen her face when she came into the café one morning and found a sledgehammer in my hands."

Doc chuckled. "When you bought that sledgehammer and started hacking away at the wall, I did, too. I was afraid you'd break either an arm or your stubborn head battering away at that brick wall. Thank God, you finally let me call a contractor to finish the job."

She slid the pies into the oven and set the timer, and then sat down at the table beside Doc. "That was a good day for me, more like therapy—closing the past and opening something new and exciting." She took his hand and held it to her lips. "The last six months have been the best of my life. I sincerely mean that."

Doc's eyes narrowed. "Does that mean you're ready to set a date?"

"I was thinking maybe around Thanksgiving. What do you think?"

"Hmmm, I'll have to check my schedule," he teased, glancing over one shoulder, just to make sure the kitchen was empty. He then leaned into Georgia and kissed her on the lips. As if on cue, Mary Jo bustled through the door from the dining room. "Oh, for heaven's sake, why don't the two of you get a room."

"You should knock first," Doc said, joking.

"Oh, yeah, sure. This is a fine way to treat your granddaughter on her last day of work." Next week Mary Jo was moving to Phoenix to begin culinary school, deciding a few months ago that food preparation was her life's ambition. Both Georgia and Doc could not have been more surprised.

Doc gave his granddaughter an affectionate kiss on the cheek. "We'll miss you. Just don't forget us, okay?"

"You're kidding? Who do you think I have in mind as a silent partner in my new restaurant?"

He shook his head, "You have to graduate first and then get a few years' experience under your belt."

"You mean that? About helping me?"

Doc smiled at Mary Jo. "I'd be honored to invest in any venture you stake out for your own." He took hold of Georgia's hand. "Georgia's been a fine teacher for you."

Next, David and Trish pushed through the door from the dining room. Trish saying, "Hey, what's going on here? A party? And we weren't invited."

David gave his mother a quick hug. "Hey, something smells good." At that same moment, the timer went off. Georgia jumped to her feet, but Trish told her to sit back and relax. "I'll take care of the pies." She gave David a wink. "About time I learned my way around the kitchen, don't you think? When I marry this man, I don't want him expecting something I can't deliver."

Georgia put a hand to her throat. "What?"

Trish leaned back and held out her hand to display one of the most beautiful diamonds Georgia had ever seen, of course, next to her own. Georgia promptly held out her own hand next to Trish's, and the two diamonds sparkled in the late morning sun that shone through the kitchen window.

"Congratulations," Doc said, hurrying to his feet to give Trish a hearty hug.

The oven had shut with a flat swoosh of the door. Suddenly remembering the pies, all three raised their heads. "Don't worry," David said. "I saved them." With thick potholders in hand, he carried the pies to the counter to cool.

"See, I raised that boy right," Georgia said, smiling.

"Sure did, Mom. But I have to confess, my motives aren't entirely pure. Lemon meringue pie is my favorite." He threw the potholders on the counter and turned to Trish, "Well, are you going to tell them or should I?"

"We already did," she said with a smug, secretive grin. "Oh, yeah, I forgot to tell them the other part of the good news." Trish came up beside David and hugged him around the waist. She looked at Georgia and Doc. "Well, we've bought a house in Tucson, together. David's decided to take the Arizona bar and go into private practice in Tucson!"

Georgia jumped up and gleefully clapped her hands, "You're staying in Tucson!"

"And," Trish said, pausing to take in a quick breath. "When David and I were in Boston last week, we visited my aunt and Claire. They're both coming to Tucson for a visit after we get settled in our new house. Claire's going to tour colleges while she's here."

Georgia's heart overflowed with happiness. She said to Trish, "Claire will grow into loving you. I know she will."

"I hope so. But I won't worry about that now." She squeezed David's arm, and he leaned over and kissed the top of her head. They were in love, and this time Georgia was certain her son would find a lifetime of happiness with Trish.

Later, they ate lunch in the café kitchen finishing off the meal with thick slices of lemon meringue pie and coffee. Georgia couldn't be happier, having her family gathered at her table and enjoying a home cooked meal. Doc poured a second round of coffee as Georgia and Trish cleared away the dishes.

Georgia informed David and Trish that Susan had called that morning and she and the children were planning a visit after she reopened the cafe. There seemed so much to celebrate this day, and Georgia felt truly blessed.

* * *

After dessert, David and Trish left to drive back to Tucson. Georgia finished the cleanup. Doc was taking her to a movie later in the afternoon. When she heard someone knock on the locked front door, Georgia paused, listening as Doc opened the front door of the café. She heard voices. Assuming Trish had returned to collect something she had forgotten, Georgia pulled the broom from the closet and attacked the floor.

A few seconds later, she heard the low creak of the swinging door between the kitchen and dining room. Without looking up, Georgia said, "What did Trish forget this time?" No one answered. She then glanced up from her sweeping and let out a small gasp. A little girl, somewhere around the age of two, dark curls and dressed in yellow pajamas and red sneakers, stood just inside the doorway with her thumb tucked neatly into her mouth. Seeing Georgia, the child removed her thumb and said, "Cook-ie?"

"I'll be darned. Where on earth did you come from?" The child boldly toddled over to Georgia and said more assertively, "Cook-ie." Georgia called out for Doc. When he didn't answer, she yelled, "Doc!"

He came through the swinging door, followed by a young woman dressed in jeans and a darling white blouse embroidered with tiny red and yellow flowers. Georgia didn't recognize her at first glance, but when the young woman's face broke into a wide smile, she dropped the broom.

"Georgia? It's me! Lou Ann. You know, from the beauty shop in Oklahoma City."

"Oh-my-Lord. Lou Ann?" Georgia hardly recognized her. Lou

Ann had cut her punk hair into a pixie that brought out her heart-shaped face, minus the sparkly eye shadow and dark lipstick.

They hugged each other, both talking at once. Georgia pulled back to get a good look at Lou Ann, and then nodded at the toddler who had followed Doc to the cookie jar. "That's Molly?"

Lou Ann eagerly nodded. "Isn't she a cutie?"

"She's adorable. What on earth are you doing here?" Georgia then noticed and ugly purplish bruise on one side of her face. She gently tilted her chin into the light. "What happened?"

Tears sprung from Lou Ann's eyes. "I was wrong about that guy I told you about. Remember?" She wiped the tears from her face with the sleeve of her blouse. "I was so stupid to believe him."

Georgia grabbed up a handful of tissues from the counter. "Here, wipe your face, dear."

Doc packed up several cookies to go and led Molly into the dining room saying, "How about if I take Molly for a walk down the street to meet my granddaughter? Mary Jo's finished packing. I'm sure she'd love to meet our little friend here." Lou Ann sniffed and looked at Georgia for reassurance that the man she'd met five minutes ago was trustworthy. Georgia nodded and Lou Ann relaxed, telling Doc, "Thank you."

Georgia brewed a pot of tea, and they sat at the kitchen table. Lou Ann told her about how she had up and left Oklahoma City with no particular destination in mind. "I remembered when you called me at the beauty shop at Thanksgiving how you said you were working at the Soft Rock Café in Sedona." Lou Ann shrugged, squeezing a wedge of lemon into her tea. "I swear, Georgia, when I made up my mind to leave, that's all I could think about was you talking about this place." Lou Ann's smile quivered. "You were so nice to me, you know, leaving me that fifty dollar tip." She quickly added, "Now don't get all nervous on me. I'm not asking for a handout. I'm going to get a job, first thing. I've waited on tables before, lots of times while going to hairdressing school." She swallowed hard and then bulldozed forward. "Do you think your boss would at least give me a try?" Pure determination filled Lou Ann's eyes, and yet around the edges there lurked a fear of rejection. Georgia suspected what now held Lou Ann together on the inside was nothing more than the resilient glue of youth.

Georgia studied Lou Ann, seeing in her a good bit of herself the day she'd left Ohio, bound for a journey that had changed her life. Yes, Lou Ann deserved a second-chance. "Can you cook?"

A wide grin spread across Lou Ann's face. "Georgia, I make the best meatloaf in the whole world. Not to mention a real tasty apple pie."

"You bake, too?"

"Sure do." Lou Ann picked out a nice apple from the bowl in the center of the table and inspected it. "I could make you one right now."

"You would do that?"

"Watch me." She got up from the table and grabbed an apron from the hook by the pantry door and tied it on, quickly collecting eight apples and tucking them in the gathered skirt of the apron. "Say, this is all right, isn't it? I sure don't want to get you in trouble with the boss or anything like that."

Georgia took another sip of tea. "No trouble. No trouble at all." Watching Lou Ann search through cupboards and drawers, Georgia got up and helped her find what she needed to make the pie. Lou Ann expertly arranged the utensils and ingredients on the counter. Georgia said, "Well, you certainly seem to know what you're doing."

"Well I should. When I was a kid, my mama baked pies for half the tables in Oklahoma City."

"Is your mother still living?"

Lou Ann stopped cutting the shortening into the flour. "She died when I was fifteen, brain tumor."

"Oh."

"She was a real nice lady, raised me alone. My daddy took off not long after Mama had me."

"I'm sorry, Lou Ann, growing up without a father."

Lou Ann shrugged. "Can't miss what I never had."

"I suppose—"

"Don't feel sorry for me," Lou Ann said as she rolled out the dough. "I can't stand pity."

Georgia picked up a paring knife and started peeling apples, slicing and cutting out the cores and seeds not saying a word. They worked in a comfortable silence, Georgia marveled at how quickly Lou Ann seemed to feel at home in her kitchen. She smiled as she focused on her peeling. "What do you plan on doing now?"

Lou Ann gingerly patted the bottom crust into the pie plate. "Don't know for sure. Like I said before, I was hoping you'd put in a good word with your boss about me. I like this place. Hey, what's he doing out there in the dining room, anyway? Remodeling? If he's making the place bigger, he'll need extra help, right?" Lou Ann poured sugar and cinnamon over the apple slices. "Hey, that man who took Molly for a walk? He's your boss, isn't he? She stopped for a moment, hands on hips. "Are the two of you an item?"

Georgia burst out laughing at the thought of Lou Ann thinking Doc was the owner of the Soft Rock. "Item? If you mean a couple, yep, you're right."

"You're blushing, Georgia."

"I've been blushing ever since he asked me to marry him."

Lou Ann slapped the flour off her hands. "You're getting married? Now aren't you the smart one, marrying the owner of this fine café here."

"Are you serious about staying?"

Lou Ann spooned the sugared apples into the pie shell. "I won't kid you. I need a job, and I'm sure as hell not going back to Oklahoma." She touched the side of her bruised face, which left an endearing print of flour on her cheek. "No one deserves to be hit, right?"

"Right. You made a smart choice not hanging around for more. But wouldn't you rather be a hairdresser? We have them in Sedona, you know."

Lou Ann wrinkled her nose. "Nope. I never felt as comfortable with hair like I do with food." She looked at Georgia, almost pleading. "Do you think he'd hire me?"

"I'd say there's a good possibility," she said, watching Lou Ann dab the apple slices with pats of butter. Lou Ann then rolled out the top crust, arranged it over the apples and finished off a perfect fluted edge. She was good, no doubt about it.

"Your boss won't regret hiring me. I'm a hard worker. All I need is a place to stay until I get settled in."

Georgia thought of Trish's now vacant stone house at the edge of town, thinking it would be perfect for Lou Ann and Molly. Lou Ann's sudden appearance might just be the blessing she needed with both Trish and Mary Jo leaving Sedona. She cautioned herself not to commit to anything too quickly, not without giving it more thought.

Lou Ann slid the pie into the oven and turned to Georgia. "Maybe you could convince him to take a chance on me?"

A chance? It was as if Lou Ann had read her mind. Where would her own life be, if she had not taken that one unexpected turn in the road. Over a year ago, she had traveled to a place she had never been before and her life had changed for the better. Trish and Zoe had both taken a chance on her, taking her in and then becoming her friends. Now, looking at Lou Ann, she thought perhaps it was her turn to help someone. Seeing the bruise on Lou Ann's face again sealed the deal. "Yes," she said. "You deserve the chance."

"You mean it! You'll talk to the owner?"

"You're talking to the owner."

There was a long pause as Lou Ann's jaw dropped in surprise. She then slapped her knee as if finally getting the meaning of a complicated joke. "Geezy-peezy, why didn't you say so in the first place?"

The aroma of baked apples and cinnamon filled the kitchen. Even before Lou Ann had slipped the pie into the oven, Georgia knew it would taste delicious. "You're hired. Tomorrow we'll work out the details. As soon as Doc and Molly get back, we'll find you a room for the night, okay?"

Lou Ann wrapped her floury hands around Georgia in a grateful hug. "Oh, Georgia, you won't regret this."

Georgia sighed and looked at Lou Ann, seeing a young woman with a child who had no idea how much hard work and determination it would take to build a new life from scratch. She said to Lou Ann, "It won't be easy, you know, leaving everything behind, even the parts that weren't good. You think at first you won't miss anything, but you will."

"I won't."

"You will, because it's part of you."

"Well, maybe so, but right now, Georgia, I'm feeling on top of the world."

"You're willing to take the risk? Staying here and uprooting yourself from your past?"

"For Molly, I'd walk through the fires of hell and ask the devil himself for a glass of water."

Georgia chuckled. "Well, I hope it won't be that difficult."

Through the kitchen window Georgia watched Doc holding Molly's hand as they crossed the street on their way back to the cafe. Doc walked at a slower pace to accommodate Molly's short, determined steps, her face shining up at Doc.

"Lou Ann, honey, come here," Georgia said, not having a second thought about getting involved with Lou Ann and Molly. She would do what came naturally. She took Lou Ann by the shoulders and said, "Welcome to Sedona!"

"Thank you, Georgia," Lou Ann said, turning to scoop up Molly as she came through the door with Doc. "Hey, Molly Bee, we have a new home!"

Doc's eyes brightened. "Smells good, apple pie?"

"Lou Ann made it. She's coming to work for me," Georgia gave him a wink as she tied on a fresh apron. Although they had just finished eating lemon meringue with Trish and David, they would certainly not hurt Lou Ann's feelings by refusing to taste her apple pie. "I'll put on a pot of coffee."

"Wonderful," Doc said, patting his stomach and giving Georgia a quick kiss on the back of her neck. He then helped Molly climb on a chair at the table with paper and crayons collected from a drawer in Georgia's desk.

"Everyone sit down," Lou Ann politely ordered. "I'll serve the pie. Do you have ice cream, Georgia?"

"Sure do," Doc said, pulling the carton from the freezer. "Lou Ann, I hope you learn your job fast. Georgia needs time off for our honeymoon." Doc sent a smile in Georgia's direction.

Georgia blushed, leaving the coffee to drip when Doc came over and took her into his arms. She rested her head on his shoulder, watching Molly scribble bright colors on a sheet of brown wrapping paper. The colors reminded Georgia of a gorgeous Sedona sunset.

Oscar appeared in the open doorway, fresh from his nap from somewhere in the renovation work inside the Moon Tide. Nose sniffing the air, the cat arrogantly took in the strange woman and child in his mistress's kitchen, and then sauntered over to Molly, rubbing against her legs.

"Kitty!" Molly said, bubbling with new excitement. She slid down from the chair and sat on the floor where she petted Oscar from his head to the tip of his tail.

Georgia sighed as her heart expanded with the joyful prospect of having Lou Ann work with her in the café. *Oh, whatever.* Who was she kidding? She didn't know anything about Lou Ann, except for the one time they had met in the beauty shop, and then the impromptu phone call made to her the day before Thanksgiving. Truth was, Georgia had no idea what she was getting herself into by taking in this young woman and her child, but she believed Lou Ann could make a better life for herself and Molly here in Sedona. After all, if a woman is willing to risk everything for what she believes, the rest of the journey is pure faith.

THE END

# GEORGIA'S SOFT ROCK CAFÉ SWEET ROLLS

Warm the following ingredients in pan:

| | |
|---|---|
| 1 cup evaporated milk | 1 cup water |
| ½ stick butter | 1/3 cup sugar |
| 1 teaspoon salt | |

1 Tablespoon yeast and 1 teaspoon sugar—dissolve in ¼ cup warm water

Pour milk mixture into mixing bowl and add two cups sifted bread flour

Add working yeast mixture to milk mixture, stir

Start dough hook and set timer for six minutes

Slowly add 3 more cups of sifted bread flour and mix for approx. 6 minutes—at the end of 6 minutes the dough should be sticky and elastic

Roll dough out and knead, adding more flour as needed (approx. 3 minutes) until dough turns silky

Spray oil lightly in big bowl. Place plastic wrap (sprayed lightly with oil) over the top of the bowl and then a damp cloth over the bowl, and put in a warm place to work.

Let dough rise approximately 1-½ hours, or until double

Roll out dough on floured surface into a rectangle and slather the top with the other ½ stick of soft butter, and then sprinkle top with a mixture of one (1) Tablespoon of cinnamon and one-half (½) cup sugar

Roll up and seal the edge by dabbing water on the edge

Cut rolls approximately 1-½ inches and place on parchment paper

Raise again for 1-1/2 hours, or until double

Bake at 375 deg. for approximately 15 minutes, or until a golden brown

Frosting

2 cups of confectioner's sugar

1 tsp. of vanilla and ½ tsp. butter flavoring

Slowly add equal parts evaporated milk and water and slowly add to confectioner's sugar until the frosting is creamy, but not too thin. Brush on sweet rolls. These are BEST while still warm from the oven!